ABOUT THE AUTHOR

STEPHEN KING. Photograph © Shane Leonard

There is a reason why Stephen King is one of the bestselling writers in the world, *ever*. He writes stories that draw you in and are *impossible to put down*.

During the years 1966-1973, just before he published the seminal masterpiece *Carrie*, Stephen King wrote under two names.

Under his pseudonym Richard Bachman, King wrote horror stories for magazines, followed by a series of novels, first published in the early 80s in the collection *The Bachman Books*.

It was on publication of his next Bachman novel *Thinner* that people realised the author was in fact Stephen King.

Bachman died of cancer of the pseudonym but in 1995 *The Regulators* surfaced and was published simultaneously with Stephen King's *Desperation*.

Blaze, 'an essential missing piece in King's oeuvre' (*Independent on Sunday*) was the last novel written during Bachman's early period, and was rediscovered and published in 2007.

Two of Bachman's novels, *Thinner* and *The Running Man*, were also made into motion pictures.

THE BACHMAN BOOKS

A one-volume collection comprising three spellbinding stories of
future shock and suspense: *The Long Walk*, *Roadwork* and
The Running Man.

THE RUNNING MAN

Welcome to America in 2025 where the best men don't run for
President. They run for their lives . . . 'Love *The Hunger Games*?
Don't miss *The Running Man*. This prescient novel is a fast-paced
and fun read – a harbinger of reality TV – and you'll root for Ben
to outwit the Games Network in this grim fight to the death' –
Today Books, NBC News

By Stephen King and published by
Hodder & Stoughton

NOVELS:
Carrie
'Salem's Lot
The Shining
The Stand
The Dead Zone
Firestarter
Cujo
Cycle of the Werewolf
Christine
Pet Sematary
IT
The Eyes of the Dragon
Misery
The Tommyknockers
The Dark Half
Needful Things
Gerald's Game
Dolores Claiborne
Insomnia
Rose Madder
Desperation
Bag of Bones
The Girl Who Loved Tom Gordon
Dreamcatcher
From a Buick 8
Cell
Lisey's Story
Duma Key
Under the Dome
Blockade Billy
11.22.63

The Dark Tower I: The Gunslinger
The Dark Tower II: The Drawing
of the Three
The Dark Tower III: The Waste Lands
The Dark Tower IV: Wizard and Glass
The Dark Tower V: Wolves of the Calla
The Dark Tower VI: Song of Susannah
The Dark Tower VII: The Dark Tower
The Wind through the Keyhole: A Dark
Tower Novel

As Richard Bachman
Thinner
The Running Man
The Bachman Books
The Regulators
Blaze

STORY COLLECTIONS:
Night Shift
Different Seasons
Skeleton Crew
Four Past Midnight
Nightmares and Dreamscapes
Hearts in Atlantis
Everything's Eventual
Just After Sunset
Stephen King Goes to the Movies
Full Dark, No Stars

NON-FICTION:
Danse Macabre
On Writing (A Memoir of the Craft)

STEPHEN KING

WRITING AS
RICHARD BACHMAN

THINNER

HODDER

To my wife,
Claudia Inez Bachman

Quotation from 'Mr Bojangles' by Jerry Jeff Walker
Copyright © 1968 by Cotillion Music Inc. – Daniel Music, Inc.
Used by permission. All rights reserved.

First published in Great Britain in 1985 by New English Library
a division of Hodder & Stoughton
An Hachette UK company

This paperback edition published in 2012

A Hodder paperback

1

A CIP catalogue record for this title is available from the British Library

ISBN 978 1 444 72355 7

Printed and bound by Clays Ltd, St Ives plc

Hodder & Stoughton policy is to use papers that are natural,
renewable and recyclable products and made from wood grown in
sustainable forests. The logging and manufacturing processes are expected
to conform to the environmental regulations of the country of origin.

Hodder & Stoughton
338 Euston Road
London NW1 3BH

www.hodder.co.uk

THINNER

CHAPTER ONE
246

'Thinner,' the old Gypsy man with the rotting nose whispers to William Halleck as Halleck and his wife, Heidi, come out of the courthouse. Just that one word, sent on the wafting, cloying sweetness of his breath. 'Thinner.' And before Halleck can jerk away, the old Gypsy reaches out and caresses his cheek with one twisted finger. His lips spread open like a wound, showing a few tombstone stumps poking out of his gums. They are black and green. His tongue squirms between them and then slides out to slick his grinning, bitter lips.

Thinner.

This memory came back to Billy Halleck, fittingly enough, as he stood on the scales at seven in the morning with a towel wrapped around his middle. The good smells of bacon and eggs came up from downstairs. He had to crane forward slightly to read the numbers on the scale. Well . . . actually, he had to crane forward more than slightly. Actually he had to crane forward quite a lot. He was a big man. Too big, as Dr Houston delighted in telling him. *In case no one ever told you, let me pass you the information,* Houston had told him after his last checkup. *A man of your age, income, and habits enters heart-attack country at roughly age thirty-eight, Billy. You ought to take off some weight.*

But this morning there was good news. He was down three pounds, from 249 to 246.

Well . . . the scale had actually read 251 the last time he'd had the courage to stand on it and take a good look, but he'd had his pants on, and there had been some change in his pockets, not to mention his keyring and his Swiss army knife. And the upstairs bathroom scale weighed heavy. He was morally sure of it.

As a kid growing up in New York he'd heard Gypsies had the gift of prophecy. Maybe this was the proof. He tried to laugh and could only raise a small and not very successful smile; it was still too early to laugh about Gypsies. Time would pass and things would come into perspective; he was old enough to know that. But for now he still felt sick to his too-large stomach at the thought of Gypsies, and hoped heartily he would never see another in his life. From now on he would pass on the palm-reading at parties and stick to the Ouija board. If that.

'Billy?' From downstairs.

'Coming!'

He dressed, noting with an almost subliminal distress that in spite of the three-pound drop the waist of his pants was getting tight again. His waist size was forty-two now. He had quit smoking at exactly 12:01 on New Year's Day, but he had paid. Oh, boy, had he paid. He went downstairs with his collar open and his tie lying around his neck. Linda, his fourteen-year-old daughter, was just going out the door in a flirt of skirt and a flip of her pony-tail, tied this morning with a sexy velvet ribbon. Her books were under one arm. Two gaudy cheerleader's pom-poms, purple and white, rustled busily in her other hand.

' 'Bye, Dad!'

'Have a good day, Lin.'

He sat down at the table, grabbed *The Wall Street Journal*.

'Lover,' Heidi said.

THINNER

'My dear,' he said grandly, and turned the *Journal* facedown beside the lazy Susan.

She put breakfast in front of him: a steaming mound of scrambled eggs, an English muffin with raisins, five strips of crisp country-style bacon. Good eats. She slipped into the seat opposite him in the breakfast nook and lit a Vantage 100. January and February had been tense – too many 'discussions' that were only disguised arguments, too many nights they had finished sleeping back to back. But they had reached a *modus vivendi*: she had stopped dunning him about his weight and he had stopped yapping at her about her pack-and-a-half-a-day butt habit. It had made for a decent-enough spring. And beyond their own private balance, other good things had happened. Halleck had been promoted, for one. Greely, Penschley, and Kinder was now Greely, Penschley, Kinder and Halleck. Heidi's mother had finally made good on her long-standing threat to move back to Virginia. Linda had at last made J.V. cheerleaders and to Billy this was a great blessing; there had been times when he had been sure Lin's histrionics would drive him into a nervous breakdown. Everything had been going just great.

Then the Gypsies had come to town.

'Thinner,' the old gypsy man had said, and what the hell was it with his nose? Syphilis? Cancer? Or something even more terrible, like leprosy? And by the way, why can't you just quit it? Why can't you just let it alone?

'You can't get it off your mind, can you?' Heidi said suddenly – so suddenly that Halleck started in his seat. *'Billy, it was not your fault.* The judge said so.'

'I wasn't thinking about that.'

'Then what *were* you thinking about?'

'The *Journal*,' he said. 'It says housing starts are down again this quarter.'

3

Not his fault, right; the judge had said so. Judge Rossington. Cary, to his friends.

Friends like me, Halleck thought. *Played many a round of golf with old Cary Rossington, Heidi, as you well know. At our New Year's Eve party two years ago, the year I thought about giving up smoking and didn't do it, who grabbed your oh-so-grabbable tit during the traditional happy-new-year kiss? Guess who? Why, my stars! It was good old Cary Rossington, as I live and breathe!*

Yes. Good old Cary Rossington, before whom Billy had argued more than a dozen municipal cases. Good old Cary Rossington with whom Billy sometimes played poker down at the club. Good old Cary Rossington who hadn't disqualified himself when his good old golfing-and-poker buddy Billy Halleck (Cary would sometimes clap him on the back and yell, 'How they hangin', Big Bill?') came before him in court, not to argue some point of municipal law, but on a charge of vehicular-manslaughter.

And when Cary Rossington did not disqualify himself, who said boo, children? Who in this whole fair town of Fairview was the boo-sayer? Why, nobody, that's who! Nobody said boo! After all, what were they? Nothing but a bunch of filthy Gypsies. The sooner they were out of Fairview and headed up the road in their old station wagons with the NRA stickers on the back bumpers, the sooner we saw the rear ends of their home-carpentered trailers and camper caps, the better. The sooner the —

— thinner.

Heidi snuffed her cigarette and said, 'Shit on your housing starts. I know you better.'

Billy supposed so. And he supposed she had been thinking about it, too. Her face was too pale. She looked her age — thirty-five — and that was rare. They had married very, very young, and he still remembered the traveling salesman who had come to the door selling vacuum cleaners one day after they had been married three years. He had looked at the

4

twenty-two-year-old Heidi Halleck and had asked politely, 'Is your mother home, hon?'

'Not hurting my appetite any,' he said, and that was certainly true. Angst or no angst, he had lain waste to the scrambled eggs, and of the bacon there was now no sign. He drank half his orange juice and gave her a big old Billy Halleck grin. She tried to smile back and it didn't quite happen. He imagined her wearing a sign: MY SMILER IS TEMPORARILY OUT OF ORDER.

He reached across the table and took her hand. 'Heidi, it's all right. And even if it's not, it's all over.'

'I know it is. I know.'

'Is Linda –?'

'No. Not anymore. She says . . . she says her girlfriends are being very supportive.'

For about a week after it had happened, their daughter had had a bad time of it. She had come home from school either in tears or close to them. She had stopped eating. Her complexion had flared up. Halleck, determined not to overreact, had gone in to see her homeroom teacher, the assistant principal, and Linda's beloved Miss Nearing, who taught phys ed and cheerleading. He ascertained (ah, there was a good lawyerly word) that it was teasing, mostly – as rough and unfunny as most junior-high-school teasing is apt to be, and tasteless to be sure, considering the circumstances, but what could you expect of an age group that thought dead-baby jokes were the height of wit?

He had gotten Linda to take a walk with him up the street. Lantern Drive was lined with tasteful set-back-from-the-road homes, homes which began at roughly $75,000 and worked up into the $200,000 indoor-pool-and-sauna range by the time you got to the country-club end of the street.

Linda had been wearing her old madras shorts, which were now torn along one seam . . . and, Halleck observed, her legs had now grown so long and coltish that the leg bands of her yellow cotton panties showed. He felt a pang of mingled regret and terror. She was growing up. He supposed she knew the old madras shorts were too small, worn out in the bargain, but he guessed she had put them on because they made a link with a more comforting childhood, a childhood where daddies did not have to go to court and stand trial (no matter how cut-and-dried that trial might be, with your old golf buddy and that drunken grabber of your wife's tit, Cary Rossington, driving the gavel), a childhood where kids did not rush up to you on the soccer field during period four while you were eating your lunch to ask you how many points your dad had gotten for bagging the old lady.

You understand it was an accident, don't you, Linda?

She nods, not looking at him. Yes, Daddy.

She came out between two cars without looking either way. There was no time for me to stop. Absolutely no time.

Daddy, I don't want to hear about it.

I know you don't. And I don't want to talk about it. But you are hearing about it. At school.

She looks at him fearfully. Daddy! You didn't –

Go to your school? Yeah. I did. But not until three-thirty yesterday afternoon. There were no kids there at all, at least that I could see. No one's going to know.

She relaxes. A little.

I heard you've been getting some pretty rough handling from the other kids. I'm sorry about that.

It hasn't been so bad, she says, taking his hand. Her face – the fresh scatter of angry-looking pimples on her forehead – tells a different story. The pimples say the handling has been rough indeed.

Having a parent arrested is not a situation even Judy Blume covers (although someday she probably will).

I also hear you've been handling it pretty well, Billy Halleck says. *Not making a big thing out of it. Because if they ever see they're getting under your skin . . .*

Yeah, I know, she says glumly.

Miss Nearing said she was especially proud of you, he says. It's a small lie. Miss Nearing hadn't said precisely that, but she had certainly spoken well of Linda, and that meant almost as much to Halleck as it did to his daughter. And it does the job. Her eyes brighten and she looks at Halleck for the first time.

She did?

She did, Halleck confirms. The lie comes easily and convincingly. Why not? He has told a lot of lies just lately.

She squeezes his hand and smiles at him gratefully.

They'll let it go pretty soon, Lin. They'll find some other bone to chew. Some girl will get pregnant or a teacher will have a nervous breakdown or some boy will get busted for selling pot or cocaine. And you'll be off the hook. Get it?

She throws her arms around him suddenly and hugs him tight. He decides she isn't growing up so fast after all, and that not all lies are bad. *I love you, Daddy,* she says.

I love you too, Lin.

He hugs her back and suddenly someone turns on a big stereo amplifier in the front of his brain and he hears the double-thud again: the first as the Ninety-Eight's front bumper strikes the old Gypsy woman with the bright red cloth kerchief over her scraggly hair, the second as the big front wheels pass over her body.

Heidi screams.

And her hand leaves Halleck's lap.

Halleck hugs his daughter tighter, feeling goose flesh break all over his body.

★

7

'More eggs?' Heidi asked, breaking into his reverie.

'No. No, thanks.' He looked at his clean plate with some guilt: no matter how bad things got, they had never gotten bad enough to cause him to lose either sleep or his appetite.

'Are you sure you're . . . ?'

'Okay?' He smiled. 'I'm okay, you're okay, Linda's okay. As they say on the soap operas, the nightmare is over – can we please get back to our lives?'

'That's a lovely idea.' This time she returned his smile with a real one of her own – she was suddenly under thirty again, and radiant. 'Want the rest of the bacon? There's two slices left.'

'No,' he said, thinking of the way his pants nipped at his soft waist (*what waist, ha-ha? a small and unfunny Don Rickles spoke up in his mind – the last time you had a waist was around 1978, you hockey puck*), the way he had to suck in his gut to hook the catch. Then he thought of the scale and said, 'I'll have one of them. I've lost three pounds.'

She had gone to the stove in spite of his original no – *sometimes she knows me so well it gets to be depressing*, he thought. Now she glanced back. 'You *are* still thinking about it, then.'

'I'm *not*,' he said, exasperated. 'Can't a man lose three pounds in peace? You keep saying you'd like me a little . . .'
thinner

'. . . a little less beefy.' Now she had gotten him thinking about the Gypsy again. *Dammit!* The Gypsy's eaten nose and the scaly feel of that one finger sliding along his cheek in the moment before he had reacted and jerked away – the way you would jerk away from a spider or from a clittering bundle of beetles fuming in a knot under a rotted log.

She brought him the bacon and kissed his temple. 'I'm sorry. You go right ahead and lose some weight. But if you don't, remember what Mr Rogers says –'

'– I like you just the way you are,' they finished in unison.

He prodded at the overturned *Journal* by the lazy Susan, but that was just too depressing. He got up, went outside, and found the New York *Times* in the flowerbed. The kid always threw it in the flowerbed, never had his numbers right at the end of the week, could never remember Bill's last name. Billy had wondered on more than one occasion if it was possible for a twelve-year-old kid to become a victim of Alzheimer's disease.

He took the paper back inside, opened it to the sports, and ate the bacon. He was deep in the box scores when Heidi brought him another half of English muffin, golden with melting butter.

Halleck ate it almost without being aware he was doing so.

CHAPTER TWO
245

In the city, a damage suit that had dragged on for over three years – a suit he had expected to drag on in one shape or another for the *next* three or four years – came to an unexpected and gratifying end at midmorning, with the plaintiff agreeing during a court recess to settle for an amount that was nothing short of stupefying. Halleck lost no time getting said plaintiff, a paint manufacturer from Schenectady, and his client to sign a letter of good intent in the judge's chambers. The plaintiff's lawyer had looked on with palpable dismay and disbelief while his client, president of the Good Luck Paint Company, scratched his name on six copies of the letter and as the court clerk notarized copy after copy, his bald head gleaming mellowly. Billy sat quietly, hands folded in his lap, feeling as if he had won the New York lottery. By lunch hour it was all over but the shouting.

Billy took himself and the client to O'Lunney's, ordered Chivas in a water glass for the client and a martini for himself, and then called Heidi at home.

'Mohonk,' he said when she picked up the phone. It was a rambling upstate New York resort where they had spent their honeymoon – a gift from Heidi's parents – a long, long time ago. Both of them had fallen in love with the place, and they had spent two vacations there since.

'What?'

'Mohonk,' he repeated. 'If you don't want to go, I'll ask Jillian from the office.'

'No, you *won't*! Billy, what *is* this?'

'Do you want to go or not?'

'Of *course* I do! This weekend?'

'Tomorrow, if you can get Mrs Bean to come in and check on Linda and make sure the wash gets done and that there aren't any orgies going on in front of the TV in the family room. And if –'

But Heidi's squeal temporarily drowned him out. 'Your case, Billy! The paint fumes and the nervous breakdown and the psychotic episode and –'

'Canley is going to settle. In fact, Canley *has* settled. After about fourteen years of boardroom bullshit and long legal opinions meaning exactly nothing, your husband has finally won one for the good guys. Clearly, decisively, and without a doubt. Canley's settled, and I'm on top of the world.'

'Billy! God!' She squealed again, this time so loud the phone distorted. Billy held it away from his ear, grinning. 'How much is your guy getting?'

Billy named the figure and this time he had to hold the phone away from his ear for almost five seconds.

'Will Linda mind us taking five days off, do you think?'

'When she can stay up until one watching HBO late-night and have Georgia Deever over and both of them can talk about boys while they gorge themselves on my chocolates? Are you kidding? Will it be cold up there this time of year, Billy? Do you want me to pack your green cardigan? Do you want your parka or your denim jacket? Or both? Do you –?'

He told her to use her judgment and went back to his client. The client was already halfway through his huge glass of Chivas and wanted to tell Polish jokes. The client looked as if he had been hit with a hammer. Halleck drank his martini and listened to standard witticisms about Polish carpenters and Polish restaurants with half an ear, his mind clicking cheerily away on other matters. The case could have far-reaching implications; it was too soon to say it was going to change the course of his career, but it might. It very well might. Not bad for the sort of case big firms take on as charity work. It could mean that –

– *the first thud jolts Heidi forward and for a moment she squeezes him; he is faintly aware of pain in his groin. The jolt is hard enough to make her seat belt lock. Blood flies up – three dime size drops – and splatters on the windshield like red rain. She hasn't even had time to begin to scream; she will scream later. He hasn't had time to even begin to realize. The beginning of realization comes with the second thud. And he –*

– swallowed the rest of his martini in a gulp. Tears came to his eyes.

'You okay?' the client, David Duganfield by name, asked.

'I'm so okay you wouldn't believe it,' Billy said, and reached across the table to his client. 'Congratulations, David.' He would not think about the accident, he would not think about the Gypsy with the rotting nose. He was one of the good guys; that fact was apparent in Duganfield's strong grip and his tired, slightly sappy smile.

'Thank you, man,' Duganfield said. 'Thank you so much.' He suddenly leaned over the table and clumsily embraced Billy Halleck. Billy hugged him back. But as David Duganfield's arms went around his neck, one palm slipped up the angle of his cheek and he thought again of the old Gypsy man's weird caress.

He touched me, Halleck thought, and even as he hugged his client, he shivered.

He tried to think about David Duganfield on the way home – Duganfield was a good thing to think about – but instead of Duganfield he found himself thinking about Ginelli by the time he was on the Triborough Bridge.

He and Duganfield had spent most of the afternoon in O'Lunney's, but Billy's first impulse had been to take his client to Three Brothers, the restaurant in which Richard Ginelli held an informal silent partnership. It had been years now since he had actually been in the Brothers – with Ginelli's reputation it would not have been wise – but it was the Brothers he always thought of first, still. Billy had had some good meals and good times there, although Heidi had never cared much for the place or for Ginelli. Ginelli frightened her, Billy thought.

He was passing the Gun Hill Road exit on the New York Thruway when his thoughts led back to the old Gypsy man as predictably as a horse going back into its barn.

It was Ginelli you thought of first. When you got home that day and Heidi was sitting out in the kitchen, crying, it was Ginelli you thought of first. 'Hey, Rich, I killed an old lady today. Can I come into town and talk to you?'

But Heidi was in the next room, and Heidi would not have understood. Billy's hand hovered over the telephone and then fell away. It occurred to him with sudden clarity that he was a well-to-do lawyer from Connecticut who, when things got hairy, could think of only one person to call: a New York hoodlum who had apparently developed the habit of shooting the competition over the years.

Ginelli was tall, not terribly good-looking, but a natural clothes horse. His voice was strong and kind – not the sort of voice one would associate with dope, vice, and murder. He was associated with all three, if you believed his rap sheet. But it had been Ginelli's voice Billy wanted to hear on that terrible afternoon after Duncan Hopley, the Fairview chief of police, had let him go.

'– or just sit there all day?'

'Huh!' Billy said, startled. He realized he was sitting in one of the few booths at the Rye toll plaza actually staffed by a human being.

'I said, are you going to pay or just –?'

'Okay,' Billy said, and gave the toll-taker a dollar. He got his change and drove on. Almost to Connecticut; nineteen exits to go to Heidi. Then off to Mohonk. Duganfield wasn't working as a diversion; so try Mohonk. Just let's forget the old Gypsy woman and the old Gypsy man for a while, what say?

But it was Ginelli his thoughts drifted back to.

Billy had met him through the firm, which had done some legal work for Ginelli seven years ago – incorporation work. Billy, then a very junior lawyer with the firm, had been given the assignment. None of the senior partners would have touched it. Even then Rich Ginelli's reputation had been very bad. Billy had never asked Kirk Penschley why the firm had taken Ginelli on as a client at all; he would have been told to go peddle his papers and leave questions of policy to his elders. He supposed Ginelli had known about a skeleton in someone's closet; he was a man who kept his ear to the ground.

Billy had begun his three months' work on behalf of Three Brothers Associations, Inc., expecting to dislike and perhaps fear the man he was working for. Instead, he found himself drawn to him. Ginelli was charismatic, fun to be around. More, he treated Billy himself with a dignity and respect which Billy would not find in his own firm for another four years.

Billy slowed for the Norwalk tolls, tossed in thirty-five cents, and pulled back into traffic. Without even thinking about it, he leaned over and opened the glove-compartment. Under the maps and the owner's manual were two packages of Twinkies. He opened one and began to eat rapidly, a few crumbs spilling down onto his vest.

All of his work for Ginelli had been completed long before a New York grand jury had indicted the man for ordering a wave of gangland-style executions in the wake of a drug war. The indictments had come down from New York Superior Court in the fall of 1980. They were buried in the spring of 1981, due mostly to a fifty-percent mortality rate among the state's witnesses. One had been blown up in his car along with two of the three police detectives who had been assigned to protect him. Another had been stabbed through the throat with the broken-off handle of an umbrella as he sat in a Grand Central Station shoeshine chair. The two other keys decided, not so surprisingly, that they could no longer be sure it was Richie 'The Hammer' Ginelli they had overheard giving the orders to kill a Brooklyn dope baron named Richovsky.

Westport. Southport. Almost home. He was leaning over again, feeling around in the glove compartment . . . Aha! Here was an only partially consumed packet of airline peanuts. Stale, but edible. Billy Halleck began to munch them, tasting them no more than he had tasted the Twinkies.

He and Ginelli had exchanged Christmas cards over the years and had gotten together for the occasional meal, usually at Three Brothers. Following what Ginelli stolidly referred to as 'my legal problems,' the meals ceased. Part of that was Heidi's doing – she had developed into a world-class nag when it came to Ginelli – but part of it had also been Ginelli's.

'You better stop coming around for a while,' he had told Billy.

'What? Why?' Billy had asked innocently, just as if he and Heidi had not argued over this very thing the night before.

'Because as far as the world is concerned, I am a gangster,' Ginelli had replied. 'Young lawyers who associate with gangsters do not get ahead, William, and that's what it's really all about – keeping your nose clean and getting ahead.'

'That's what it's all about, huh?'

Ginelli had smiled strangely. 'Well . . . there *are* a few other things.'

'Such as?'

'William, I hope you never have to find out. And come around for *espresso* once in a while. We'll have some talk and some laughs. Keep in touch, is what I'm saying.'

And so he had kept in touch, and had dropped in from time to time (although, he admitted to himself as he swung up the Fairview exit ramp, the intervals had grown longer and longer), and when he had found himself faced with what might be a charge of negligent vehicular manslaughter, it had been Ginelli he thought of first.

But good old tit-grabbing Cary Rossington took care of that, his mind whispered. *So why are you thinking about Ginelli now? Mohonk — that's what you ought to be thinking of. And David Duganfield, who proves that nice guys don't always finish last. And taking off a few more pounds.*

But as he turned into the driveway, what he found himself thinking about was something Ginelli had said: *William, I hope you never have to find out.*

Find out what? Billy wondered, and then Heidi was flying out the front door to kiss him, and Billy forgot everything for a while.

CHAPTER THREE
Mohonk

It was their third night at Mohonk and they had just finished making love. It was the sixth time in three days, a giddy change from their usual sedate twice-a-week pace. Billy lay beside her, liking the feel of her heat, liking the smell of her perfume – Anaïs Anaïs – mixed with her clean sweat and the smell of their sex. For a moment the thought made a hideous cross-connection and he was seeing the Gypsy woman in the moment before the Olds struck her. For a moment he heard a bottle of Perrier shattering. Then the vision was gone.

He rolled toward his wife and hugged her tight.

She hugged him back one-armed and slipped her free hand up his thigh. 'You know,' she said, 'if I come my brains out one more time, I'm not going to have any brains left.'

'It's a myth,' Billy said, grinning.

'That you can come your brains out?'

'Nah. That's the truth. The myth is that you *lose* those brain cells forever. The ones you come out always grow back.'

'Yeah, you *say*, you *say*.'

She snuggled more comfortably against him. Her hand wandered up from his thigh, touched his penis lightly and lovingly, toyed with the thatch of his pubic hair (last year he'd been sadly astounded to see the first threads of gray down there in what his father had called Adam's thicket), and then slid up the foothill of his lower belly.

She sat up suddenly on her elbows, startling him a little. He hadn't been asleep, but he had been drifting toward it.

'You really *have* lost weight!'

'Huh!'

'Billy Halleck, you're *skinnier!*'

He slapped his belly, which he sometimes called the House That Budweiser Built, and laughed. 'Not much. I still look like the world's only seven-months-pregnant man.'

'You're still big, but not as big as you were. I *know*. I can tell. When did you weigh yourself last?'

He cast his mind back. It had been the morning Canley had settled. He had been down to 246. 'I told you I'd lost three pounds, remember?'

'Well, you weigh yourself again first thing in the morning,' she said.

'No scales in the bathroom,' Halleck said comfortably.

'You're kidding.'

'Nope. Mohonk's a *civilized* place.'

'We'll find one.'

He was beginning to drift again. 'If you want, sure.'

'I want.'

She had been a good wife, he thought. At odd times over the last five years, since the steady weight gain had really started to show, he had announced diets and/or physical-fitness programs. The diets had been marked by a lot of cheating. A hot dog or two in the early afternoon to supplement the yogurt lunch, or maybe a hastily gobbled hamburger or two on a Saturday afternoon, while Heidi was out at an auction or a yard sale. Once or twice he had even stooped to the hideous hot sandwiches available at the little convenience store a mile down the road – the meat in these sandwiches usually looked like toasted skin grafts once the microwave had had its way with them, and yet he could never remember throwing away a portion uneaten. He liked his beer, all right, that was a given, but even more than that, he liked to eat. Dover sole in one of New York's finer restaurants was great, but if he was sitting up and watching the Mets on TV, a bag of Doritos with some clam dip on the side would do.

The physical-fitness programs would last maybe a week, and then his work schedule would interfere, or he would simply lose interest. In the basement a set of weights sat brooding in a corner, gathering cobwebs and rust. They seemed to reproach him every time he went down. He tried not to look at them.

So he would suck in his gut even more than usual and announce boldly to Heidi that he had lost twelve pounds and was down to 236. And she would nod and tell him that she was very glad, of *course* she could see the difference, and all the time she would know, because she saw the empty Doritos bag (or bags) in the trash. And since Connecticut had adopted a returnable bottle-and-can law, the empties in the pantry had become a source of guilt almost as great as the unused weights.

She saw him when he was sleeping; even worse, she saw him when he was peeing. You couldn't suck in your gut when you were taking a piss. He had tried and it just wasn't possible. She knew he had lost three pounds, four at most. You could fool your wife about another woman – at least for a while – but not about your weight. A woman who bore that weight from time to time in the night knew what you weighed. But she smiled and said *Of course you look better, dear*. Part of it was maybe not so admirable – it kept him quiet about her cigarettes – but he was not fooled into believing that was all of it, or even most of it. It was a way of letting him keep his self-respect.

'Billy?'

'What?' Jerked back from sleep a second time, he glanced over at her, a little amused, a little irritated.

'Do you feel quite well?'

'I feel fine. What's this "do-you-feel-quite-well" stuff?'

'Well ... sometimes ... they say an unplanned weight loss can be a sign of something.'

'I feel *great*. And if you don't let me go to sleep, I'll prove it by jumping your bones again.'

'Go ahead.'

He groaned. She laughed. Soon enough they slept. And in his dream, he and Heidi were coming back from the Shop 'n Save, only he *knew* it was a dream this time, he *knew* what was going to happen and he wanted to tell her to stop what she was doing, that he had to concentrate all his attention on his driving because pretty soon an old Gypsy woman was going to dart out from between two parked cars – from between a yellow Subaru and a dark green Firebird, to be exact – and this old woman was going to have a child's five-and-dime plastic barrettes in her graying grizzled hair and she was not going to be looking anywhere but straight ahead. He wanted to tell Heidi that this was his chance to take it all back, to change it, to make it right.

But he couldn't speak. The pleasure woke again at the touch of her fingers, playful at first, then more serious (his penis stiffened as he slept and he turned his head slightly at the metallic clicking sound of his zipper going down notch by notch); the pleasure mixed uneasily with a feeling of terrible inevitability. Now he saw the yellow Subaru ahead, parked behind the green Firebird with the white racing stripe. And from between them a flash of pagan color brighter and more vital than any paint job sprayed on in Detroit or the Toyota Village. He tried to scream *Quit it, Heidi! It's her! I'm going to kill her again if you don't quit it! Please, God, no! Please, good Christ, no!*

But the figure stepped out between the two cars. Halleck was trying to get his foot off the gas pedal and put it on the brake, but it seemed to be stuck right where it was, held down with a dreadful, irrevocable firmness. *The Krazy Glue of inevitability*, he thought wildly, trying to turn the wheel, but the wheel wouldn't turn, either. The wheel was locked and blocked. So he tried to brace himself for the crash and then the Gypsy's head turned and it wasn't the old woman, oh no, huh-uh, it was the Gypsy man with the rotted nose. Only now his eyes were gone. In the instant before the Olds struck him and bore him under, Halleck saw the empty, staring sockets. The old Gypsy man's lips spread in an obscene grin – an ancient crescent below the rotted horror of his nose.

Then: *Thud/thud.*

One hand flailing limply up above the Olds's hood, heavily wrinkled, dressed in pagan rings of beaten metal. Three drops of blood splattered the windshield. Halleck was vaguely aware that Heidi's hand had clenched agonizingly on his erection, retaining the orgasm that shock had brought on, creating a sudden dreadful pleasure-pain . . .

And he heard the Gypsy's whisper from somewhere underneath him, drifting up through the carpeted floor of the expensive car, muffled but clear enough: '*Thinner.*'

He came awake with a jerk, turned toward the window, and almost screamed. The moon was a brilliant crescent above the Adirondacks, and for a moment he thought it was the old Gypsy man, his head cocked slightly to the side, peering into their window, his eyes two brilliant stars in the blackness of the sky over upstate New York, his grin lit somehow from within, the light spilling out cold like the light from a mason jar filled with August fireflies, cold like the swamp-fellas he had sometimes seen as a boy in North

Carolina – old, cold light, a moon in the shape of an ancient grin, one which contemplates revenge.

Billy drew in a shaky breath, closed his eyes tight, then opened them again. The moon was just the moon again. He lay down and was asleep three minutes later.

The new day was bright and clear, and Halleck finally gave in and agreed to climb the Labyrinth Trail with his wife. Mohonk's grounds were laced with hiking trails, rated from easy to extremely difficult. Labyrinth was rated 'moderate,' and on their honeymoon he and Heidi had climbed it twice. He remembered how much pleasure that had given him – working his way up the steep defiles with Heidi right behind him, laughing and telling him to hurry up, slowpoke. He remembered worming through one of the narrow, cavelike passages in the rock, and whispering ominously to his new wife, 'Do you feel the ground shaking?' when they were in the narrowest part. It had been narrow, but she had still managed to give his butt a pretty good swat.

Halleck would admit to himself (but never, never to Heidi) that it was those narrow passages through the rock that worried him now. On their honeymoon he had been slim and trim, only a kid, still in good shape from summers spent in a logging crew in western Massachusetts. Now he was sixteen years older and a *lot* heavier. And, as jolly old Dr Houston had so kindly informed him, he was entering heart-attack country. The idea of having a heart attack half-way up the mountain was uncomfortable but still fairly remote; what seemed more possible to him was getting stuck in one of those narrow stone throats through which the trail snaked on its way to the top. He could remember that they'd had to crawl in at least four places.

He didn't want to get stuck in one of those places.

Or . . . how's this, gang? Ole Billy Halleck gets stuck in one of those dark crawly places and *then* has a heart attack! Heyyyy! Two for the price of one!

But he finally agreed to give it a try, if *she* would agree to go on by herself if he was simply not in good enough shape to make it to the top. And if they could go down to New Paltz first so he could buy some sneakers. Heidi agreed willingly to both stipulations.

In town, Halleck found that 'sneakers' had become *declassé*. No one would even admit to remembering the word. He bought a pair of dandy green-and-silver Nike walking-and-climbing shoes and was quietly delighted at how good they felt on his feet. That led to the realization that he hadn't owned a pair of canvas shoes in . . . Five years? Six? It seemed impossible, but there it was.

Heidi admired them and told him again that he certainly *did* look as if he had lost weight. Outside the shoe store was a penny weighing machine, one of those that advertises 'YOUR WATE AND FATE.' Halleck hadn't seen one since he was a kid.

'Hop up, hero,' Heidi said. 'I've got a penny.'

Halleck held back for a moment, obscurely nervous.

'Come on, hurry up. I want to see how much you've lost.'

'Heidi, those things don't weigh true, you know that.'

'A ballpark figure's all I want. Come *on*, Billy – don't be a poop.'

He reluctantly gave her the package containing his new shoes and stepped up on the scale. She put a penny in. There was a clunk and then two curved silvery metal panels drew back. Behind the top one was his wate; behind the lower one, the machine's idea of fate. Halleck drew in a harsh, surprised breath.

'I *knew* it!' Heidi was saying beside him. There was a kind of doubtful wonder in her voice, as if she was not sure if she should feel happiness or fear or wonder. 'I *knew* you were thinner!'

If she had heard his own harsh gasp, Halleck thought later, she no doubt thought it was because of the number at which the scale had red-lined – even with all his clothes on, and his Swiss army knife in the pocket of his corduroy pants, even with a hearty Mohonk breakfast in his belly, that line was centered neatly at 232. He had lost fourteen pounds since the day Canley had settled out of court.

But it wasn't his wate that had made him gasp; it was his fate. The lower panel had not slid aside to reveal FINANCIAL MATTERS WILL SOON IMPROVE or OLD FRIENDS WILL VISIT or DO NOT MAKE IMPORTANT DECISION HASTILY.

It had revealed a single black word: 'THINNER.'

CHAPTER FOUR
227

They rode back to Fairview mostly in silence, Heidi driving until they were within fifteen miles of New York City and the traffic got heavy. Then she pulled into a service plaza and let Billy take them the rest of the way home. No reason why he should not be driving; the old woman had been killed, true enough, one arm almost torn from her body, her pelvis pulverized, her skull shattered like a Ming vase hurled onto a marble floor, but Billy Halleck had not lost a single point from his Connecticut driver's license. Good old tit-grabbing Cary Rossington had seen to that.

'Did you hear me, Billy?'

He glanced at her for only a second, then returned his eyes to the road. He was driving better these days, and although he didn't use his horn any more than he used to, or shout and wave his arms any more than he used to, he was more aware of other drivers' errors and his own than he ever had been before, and was less forgiving of both. Killing an old woman did wonders for your concentration. It didn't do shit for your self-respect, and it produced some really hideous dreams, but it certainly did juice up the old concentration levels.

'I was woolgathering. Sorry.'

'I just said thank you for a wonderful time.'

She smiled at him and touched his arm briefly. It *had* been a wonderful time – for Heidi, at least. Heidi had indubitably Put It Behind Her – the Gypsy woman, the preliminary hearing at which the state's case had been dismissed, the old

Gypsy man with the rotted nose. For Heidi it was now just an unpleasantness in the past, like Billy's friendship with that wop hoodlum from New York. But something else was on her mind; a second quick side glance confirmed it. The smile had faded and she was looking at him and tiny wrinkles around her eyes showed.

'You're welcome,' he said. 'You're *always* welcome, babe.'

'And when we get home –'

'I'll jump your bones again!' he cried with bogus enthusiasm, and manufactured a leer. Actually, he didn't think he could get it up if the Dallas Cowgirls paraded past him in lingerie designed by Frederick's of Hollywood. It had nothing to do with how often they had made it up at Mohonk; it was that damned fortune. THINNER. Surely it had said no such thing – it had been his imagination. But it hadn't *seemed* like his imagination, dammit; it had seemed as real as a New York *Times* headline. And that very reality was the terrible part of it, because THINNER wasn't *anybody's* idea of a fortune. Even YOUR FATE IS TO SOON LOSE WATE didn't really make it. Fortune writers were into things like long journeys and meeting old friends.

Ergo, he had hallucinated it.

Yep, that's right.

Ergo, he was probably losing his marbles.

Oh, come on, now, is that fair?

Fair enough. When your imagination got out of control, it wasn't good news.

'You can jump me if you want to,' Heidi said, 'but what I really want is for you to jump on *our* bathroom scales –'

'Come on, Heidi! I lost some weight, no big deal!'

'I'm very proud of you for losing some weight, Billy, but we've been together almost constantly for the last five days, and I'll be darned if I know *how* you're losing it.'

He gave her a longer look this time, but she wouldn't look back at him; she only stared through the windshield, her arms folded across her bosom.

'Heidi . . .'

'You're eating as much as you ever did. Maybe more. The mountain air must have really gotten your motor revving.'

'Why gild the lily?' he asked, slowing down to slam forty cents into the basket of the Rye tollbooth. His lips were pressed together into a thin white line, his heart was beating too fast, and he was suddenly furious with her. 'What you mean is, I'm a great big hog. Say it right out if you want, Heidi. What the hell. I can take it.'

'I didn't mean anything *like* that!' she cried. 'Why do you want to hurt me, Billy? Why do you want to do that after we had such a good time?'

He didn't have to glance over this time to know she was near tears. Her wavering voice told him that. He was sorry, but being sorry didn't kill the anger. And the fear that was just under it.

'I don't want to hurt you,' he said, gripping the Olds's steering wheel so hard his knuckles showed white. 'I never do. But losing weight is a *good* thing, Heidi, so why do you want to keep hitting on me about it?'

'*It is not always a good thing!*' she shouted, startling him, making the car swerve slightly. '*It is not always a good thing and you know it!*'

Now she *was* crying, crying and rooting through her purse in search of a Kleenex in that half-annoying, half-endearing way she had. He handed her his handkerchief and she used it to wipe her eyes.

'You can say what you want, you can be mean, you can cross-examine me if you want, Billy, you can even spoil the time we just had. But I love you and I'm going to say what I have to say. When people start to lose weight even though they're not on a diet, it can mean they're sick. It's one of the seven warning signs of cancer.' She thrust his handkerchief back at him. His fingers touched hers as he took it. Her hand was very cold.

Well, the word was out. Cancer. Rhymes with *dancer* and *You just shit your pants, sir.* God knew the word had bobbed up in his own mind more than once since getting on the penny scale in front of the shoe store. It had bobbed up like some evil clown's dirty balloon and he had turned away from it. He had turned away from it the way you turned away from the bag ladies who sat rocking back and forth in their strange, sooty little nooks outside the Grand Central Station . . . or the way you turned away from the capering Gypsy children who had come with the rest of the Gypsy band. The Gypsy children sang in voices that somehow managed to be both monotonous and strangely sweet at the same time. The Gypsy children walked on their hands with tambourines outstretched, held somehow by their bare dirty toes. The Gypsy children juggled. The Gypsy children put the local Frisbee jocks to shame by spinning two, sometimes three of the plastic disks at the same time – on fingers, on thumbs, sometimes on noses. They laughed while they did all those things, and they all seemed to have skin diseases or crossed eyes or harelips. When you suddenly found such a weird combination of agility and ugliness thrust in front of you, what else was there to do but turn away? Bag ladies, Gypsy children, and cancer. Even the skittery run of his thoughts frightened him.

Still, it was maybe better to have the word out.

'I've felt fine,' he repeated, for maybe the sixth time since the night Heidi had asked him if he felt quite well. And, dammit, it was true! 'Also, I've been exercising.'

That was also true . . . of the last five days, anyway. They had made it up the Labyrinth Trail together, and although he'd had to exhale all the way and suck in his gut to get through a couple of the tightest places, he'd never come even close to getting stuck. In fact, it had been Heidi, puffing and out of breath, who'd needed to ask for a rest twice. Billy had diplomatically not mentioned her cigarette jones.

'I'm sure you've felt fine,' she said, 'and that's great. But a checkup would be great, too. You haven't had one in over eighteen months, and I bet Dr Houston misses you –'

'I think he's a little dope freak,' Halleck muttered.

'A little what?'

'Nothing.'

'But I'm telling you, Billy, you can't lose almost twenty pounds in two weeks just by exercising.'

'I am not sick!'

'Then just humor me.'

They rode the rest of the way to Fairview in silence. Halleck wanted to pull her to him and tell her sure, okay, he would do what she wanted. Except a thought had come to him. An utterly absurd thought. Absurd but nevertheless chilling.

Maybe there's a new style in old Gypsy curses, friends and neighbors – how about that possibility? They used to change you into a werewolf or send a demon to pull off your head in the middle of the night, something like that, but everything changes, doesn't it? What if that old man touched me and gave me cancer? She's right, it's one of the tattletales – losing twenty pounds just like that is like when the miners' canary drops dead in his cage. Lung cancer . . . leukemia . . . melanoma . . .

It was crazy, but the craziness didn't keep the thought away: *What if he touched me and gave me cancer?*

Linda greeted them with extravagant kisses and, to their mutual amazement, produced a very creditable lasagna from the oven and served it on paper plates bearing the face of that lasagna-lover *extraordinaire*, Garfield the cat. She asked them how their second honeymoon had been ('A phrase that belongs right up there with second childhood,' Halleck observed dryly to Heidi that evening, after the dishes had been done and Linda had gone flying off with two of her girlfriends to continue a Dungeons and Dragons game that had been going on for nearly a year), and before they could do more than begin to tell her about the trip, she had cried, 'Oh, that reminds me!' and spent the rest of the meal regaling them with Tales of Wonder and Horror from Fairview Junior High – a continuing story which held more fascination for her than it did for either Halleck or his wife, although both tried to listen with attention. They had been gone for almost a week, after all.

As she rushed out, she kissed Halleck's cheek loudly and cried, ''Bye, skinny!'

Halleck watched her mount her bike and pedal down the front walk, ponytail flying, and then turned to Heidi. He was dumbfounded.

'Now,' she said, 'will you please listen to me?'

'You told her. You called ahead and told her to say that. Female conspiracy.'

'No.'

He scanned her face and then nodded tiredly. 'No, I guess not.'

Heidi nagged him upstairs, where he finally ended up in the bathroom, naked except for the towel around his waist. He was struck by a strong sense of *déjà vu* – the temporal dislocation was so complete that he felt a mild physical nausea. It was an almost exact replay of the day he had stood on this same scale with a towel from this same powder-blue set wrapped around his waist. All that was lacking was the good smell of frying bacon coming up from downstairs. Everything else was exactly the same.

No. No, it wasn't. One thing was remarkably different.

That other day he had craned over in order to read the bad news on the dial. He had to do that because his bay window was in the way.

The bay window was there, but it was smaller. There could be no question about it, because now he could look straight down and still read the numbers.

The digital readout said 229.

'That settles it,' Heidi said flatly. 'I'm making you an appointment with Dr Houston.'

'This scale weighs light,' Halleck said weakly. 'It always has. That's why I like it.'

She looked at him coldly. 'Enough bullshit is enough bullshit, my friend. You've spent the last five years bitching about how it weighs heavy, and we both know it.' In the harsh white bathroom light he could see how honestly anxious she was. The skin was drawn shinily tight across her cheekbones.

'Stay right there,' she said at last, and left the bathroom. 'Heidi?'

'Don't move!' she called back as she went downstairs.

She returned a minute later with an unopened bag of sugar. 'Net wt., 10 lbs.,' the bag announced. She plonked it on the scale. The scale considered for a moment and then printed a big red digital readout: 012.

'That's what I thought,' Heidi said grimly. 'I weigh myself, too, Billy. It doesn't weigh light, and it never has. It weighs heavy, just like you always said. It wasn't just bitching, and we both knew it. Someone who's overweight *likes* an inaccurate scale. It makes the actual facts easier to dismiss. If –'

'Heidi –'

'If this scale says you weigh two-twenty-nine, that means you're really down to two-twenty-seven. Now, let me —'

'Heidi —'

'Let me make you an appointment.'

He paused, looking down at his bare feet, and then shook his head.

'Billy!'

'I'll make it myself,' he said.

'When?'

'Wednesday. I'll make it Wednesday. Houston goes out to the country club every Wednesday afternoon and plays nine holes.' *Sometimes he plays with the inimitable tit-grabbing, wife-kissing Cary Rossington.* 'I'll speak to him in person.'

'Why don't you call him tonight? Right now?'

'Heidi,' he said, 'no more.' And something in his face must have convinced her not to push it any further, because she didn't mention it again that night.

CHAPTER FIVE
221

Sunday, Monday, Tuesday.

Billy purposely kept off the scale upstairs. He ate heartily at meals even though, for one of the few times in his adult life, he was not terribly hungry. He stopped hiding his munchies behind the packages of Lipton Cup o' Soup in the pantry. He ate pepperoni slices and Muenster cheese on Ritz crackers during the Yankees-Red Sox doubleheader on Sunday. A bag of caramel corn at work Monday morning, and a bag of Cheez-Doodles on Monday afternoon – one of them or possibly the combination brought on a rather embarrassing farting spell that lasted from four o'clock until about nine that night. Linda marched out of the TV room halfway through the news, announcing that she would be back if someone passed out gas masks. Billy grinned guiltily, but didn't move. His experience with farts had taught him that leaving the room to pass that sort of gas did very little good. It was as if the rotten things were attached to you with invisible rubber bands. They followed you around.

But later, watching *And Justice for All* on Home Box Office, he and Heidi ate up most of a Sara Lee cheesecake.

During his commute home on Tuesday, he pulled off the Connecticut Turnpike at Norwalk and picked up a couple of Whoppers with cheese at the Burger King there. He began eating them the way he always ate when he was driving, just working his way through them, mashing them up, swallowing them down bite by bite . . .

He came to his senses outside of Westport.

For a moment his mind seemed to separate from his physical self − it was not *thinking*, not *reflection*; it was *separation*. He was reminded of the physical sense of nausea he had felt on the bathroom scale the night he and Heidi had returned from Mohonk, and it occurred to him that he had entered a completely new realm of mentation. He felt almost as if he had gained a kind of astral presence − a cognitive hitchhiker who was studying him closely. And what was that hitchhiker seeing? Something more ludicrous than horrible, most likely. Here was a man of almost thirty-seven with Bally shoes on his feet and Bausch & Lomb soft contact lenses on his eyes, a man in a three-piece suit that had cost six hundred dollars. A thirty-six-year-old overweight American male, Caucasian, sitting behind the wheel of a 1981 Oldsmobile Ninety-Eight, scarfing a huge hamburger while mayonnaise and shredded bits of lettuce dripped onto his charcoal-gray vest. You could laugh until you cried. Or screamed.

He threw the remains of the second Whopper out the window and then looked at the mixed slime of juices and sauce on his hand with a desperate kind of horror. And then he did the only sane thing possible under the circumstances: he laughed. And promised himself: No more. The binge would end.

That night, as he sat in front of the fireplace reading *The Wall Street Journal*, Linda came in to bestow a good-night kiss on him, drew back a little, and said: 'You're starting to look like Sylvester Stallone, Daddy.'

'Oh, Christ,' Halleck said, rolling his eyes, and then they both laughed.

★

Billy Halleck discovered that a crude sort of ritual had attached itself to his procedure for weighing himself. When had it happened? He didn't know. As a kid he had simply jumped on once in a while, taken a cursory glance at his weight, and then jumped off again. But at some point during the period when he had drifted up from 190 to a weight that was, as impossible as it seemed, an eighth of a ton, that ritual had begun.

Ritual, hell, he told himself. *Habit. That's all it is, just a habit.*

Ritual, his deeper mind whispered inarguably back. He was an agnostic and he hadn't been through the doors of any church since age nineteen, but he recognized a ritual when he saw it, and this weigh-in procedure was almost a genuflection. *See, God, I do it the same every time, so keep this here white, upwardly mobile lawyer safe from the heart attack or stroke that every actuarial table in the world says I can expect right around the age of forty-seven. In the name of cholesterol and saturated fats we pray. Amen.*

The ritual begins in the bedroom. Take off the clothes. Put on the dark green velour robe. Chuck all the dirty clothes down the laundry chute. If this is the first or second wearing of the suit, and if there are no egregious stains on it, hang it neatly in the closet.

Move down the hall to the bathroom. Enter with reverence, awe, reluctance. Here is the confessional where one must face one's wate, and, consequently, one's fate. Doff the robe. Hang it on the hook by the tub. Void the bladder. If a bowel movement seems a possibility – even a *remote* possibility – go for it. He had absolutely no idea how much the average bowel movement might weigh, but the principle was logical, unshakable: throw all the ballast overboard that you could.

Heidi had observed this ritual, and she had once sarcastically asked him if he wouldn't like an ostrich feather for his birthday. Then, she said, he could stick it down his throat and vomit once or twice before weighing himself. Billy told her not to be a wise-ass . . . and later that night had found himself musing that the idea actually had its attractions.

One Wednesday morning, Halleck threw this ritual overboard for the first time in years. On Wednesday morning Halleck became a heretic. He had perhaps become something even blacker, because, like a devil-worshipper who deliberately perverts a religious ceremony by hanging crosses upside down and reciting the Lord's Prayer backward, Halleck entirely reversed his field.

He dressed, filled his pockets with all the change he could find (plus his Swiss army knife, of course), put on his clunkiest, heaviest shoes, and then ate a gigantic breakfast, grimly ignoring his throbbing bladder. He downed two fried eggs, four strips of bacon, toast, and hash browns. He drank orange juice and a cup of coffee (three sugars).

With all that sloshing around inside of him, Halleck grimly made his way up the stairs to the bathroom. He paused for a moment, looking at the scale. Looking at it had been no treat before, but it was even less pleasant now.

He steeled himself and got on.

221.

That can't be right! His heart, speeding up in his chest. *Hell, no! Something's out of whack! Something –*

'Stop it,' Halleck whispered in a low, husky voice. He backed away from the scale as a man might back away from a dog he knew meant to bite. He put the back of his hand up to his mouth and rubbed it slowly back and forth.

'Billy?' Heidi called up the stairs.

Halleck looked to the left and saw his own white face staring back at him from the mirror. There were purple pouches under his eyes that had never been there before, and the ladder of lines in his forehead seemed deeper.

Cancer, he thought again, and mixing with the word, he heard the Gypsy whispering again.

'Billy? Are you upstairs?'

Cancer, sure, you bet, that's it. He cursed me somehow. The old woman was his wife . . . or maybe his sister . . . and he cursed me. Is that possible? Could such a thing be? Could cancer be eating into my guts right now, eating me inside, the way his nose . . . ?

A small, terrified sound escaped his throat. The face of the man in the mirror was sickly horrified, the hag-face of a long-term invalid. In that moment Halleck almost believed it: that he had cancer, that he was riddled with it.

'Bil-lee!'

'Yeah, I'm here.' His voice was steady. Almost.

'God, I've been yelling *forever!*'

'Sorry.' *Just don't come up here, Heidi, don't see me looking like this or you'll have me in the fucking Mayo Clinic before the noon whistle blows. Just stay down there where you belong. Please.*

'You won't forget to make an appointment with Michael Houston, will you?'

'No,' he said. 'I'll make one.'

'Thank you, dear,' Heidi called up softly, and mercifully retreated.

Halleck urinated, then washed his hands and face. When he thought he had begun to look like himself again – more or less – he went downstairs, trying to whistle.

He had never been so afraid in his life.

CHAPTER SIX
217

'*How* much weight?' Dr Houston asked. Halleck, determined to be honest now that he was actually facing the man, told him he had lost about thirty pounds in three weeks. '*Wow!*' Houston said.

'Heidi's a little worried. You know how wives can –'

'She's right to be worried,' Houston said.

Michael Houston was a Fairview archetype: the Handsome Doctor with White Hair and a Malibu Tan. When you glimpsed him sitting at one of the parasol-equipped tables which surrounded the country club's outdoor bar, he looked like a younger version of Marcus Welby, MD. The poolside bar, which was called the Watering Hole, was where he and Halleck were now. Houston was wearing red golfing pants held up with a shiny white belt. His feet were dressed in white golfing shoes. His shirt was Lacoste, his watch a Rolex. He was drinking a piña colada. One of his standard witticisms was referring to them as 'penis coladas.' He and his wife had two eerily beautiful children and lived in one of the larger houses on Lantern Drive – they were in walking distance of the country club, a fact of which Jenny Houston boasted when she was drunk. It meant that their house had cost well over a hundred and fifty K. Houston drove a brown Mercedes four-door. She drove a Cadillac Cimarron that looked like a Rolls-Royce with hemorrhoids. Their kids went to a private school in Westport. Fairview gossip – which was true more often than not – suggested that Michael and Jenny Houston had reached a *modus vivendi*: he was an obsessive philanderer and she started in on the whiskey sours around three in the afternoon. *Just a typical Fairview family*, Halleck thought, and suddenly felt tired as well as scared. He either knew these people too well or thought he did, and either way it came to the same.

He looked down at his own shiny white shoes and thought: *Who are you kidding? You wear the tribal feather.*

'I want to see you in my office tomorrow,' Houston said.

'I've got a case —'

'Never mind your case. This is more important. In the meantime, tell me this. Have you had any bleeding? Rectal? Mouth?'

'No.'

'Notice any bleeding from the scalp when you comb your hair?'

'No.'

'How about sores that don't want to heal? Or scabs that fall off and just reform?'

'No.'

'Great,' Houston said. 'By the way, I carded an eighty-four today. What do you think?'

'I think it'll still be a couple of years before you make the Masters,' Billy said.

Houston laughed. The waiter came. Houston ordered another penis colada. Halleck ordered a Miller. *Miller Lite*, he almost told the waiter — force of habit — and then held his tongue. He needed a light beer like he needed . . . well, like he needed some rectal bleeding.

Michael Houston leaned forward. His eyes were grave and Halleck felt that fear again, like a smooth steel needle, very thin, probing at the lining of his stomach. He realized miserably that something had changed in his life, and not for the better. Not for the better at all. He was scared a lot now. Gypsy's revenge.

Houston's grave eyes were fixed on Billy's and Billy heard him say: *The chances that you have cancer are five in six, Billy. I don't even need an X ray to tell you that. Is your will up-to-date? Are Heidi and Linda provided for adequately? When you're a relatively young man you don't think it can happen to you, but it can. It can.*

In the quiet tone of a man imparting great information, Houston asked: 'How many pallbearers does it take to bury a nigger from Harlem?'

Billy shook his head, smiling a counterfeit smile.

'Six,' Houston said. 'Four to carry the coffin and two to carry the radio.'

He laughed, and Billy Halleck went through the motions. In his mind, clearly, he saw the Gypsy man who had been waiting for him outside the Fairview courthouse. Behind the Gypsy, at the curb, in a no-parking zone, stood a huge old pickup truck with a homemade camper cap. The cap was covered with strange designs around a central painting – a not-very-good rendering of a unicorn on its knees, head bowed, before a Gypsy woman with a garland of flowers in her hands. The Gypsy man had been wearing a green twill vest, with buttons made out of silver coins. Now, watching Houston laugh at his own joke, the alligator on his shirt riding the swells of his mirth, Billy thought: *You remember much more about that guy than you thought. You thought you only remembered his nose, but that's not true at all. You remember damn near everything.*

Children. There had been children in the cab of the old van, looking at him with depthless brown eyes, eyes that were almost black. 'Thinner,' the old man had said, and in spite of his callused flesh, his caress had been the caress of a lover.

Delaware plates, Billy thought suddenly. *His rig had Delaware plates. And a bumper sticker, something . . .*

Billy's arms dimpled out in goose flesh and for one moment he thought he might scream, as he had once heard a woman scream right here when she thought her child was drowning in the pool.

Billy Halleck remembered how they had seen the Gypsies for the first time; the day they had come to Fairview.

They had parked along one side of the Fairview town common, and a flock of their kids had run out onto the greensward to play. The Gypsy women stood gossiping and watching them. They were brightly dressed, but not in the peasant garb an older person might have associated with the Hollywood version of Gypsies in the thirties and forties. There were women in colorful sundresses, women in calf-length clamdigger pants, younger women in Jordache or Calvin Klein jeans. They looked bright, alive, somehow dangerous.

A young man jumped out of a VW microbus and began to juggle oversized bowling pins. EVERYONE NEEDS SOME-THING TO BELIEVE IN, the young man's T-shirt read, AND RIGHT NOW I BELIEVE I'LL HAVE ANOTHER BEER. Fairview children ran toward him as if drawn by a magnet, yelling excitedly. Muscles rippled under the young man's shirt, and a giant crucifix bounded up and down on his chest. Fairview mothers gathered some of the kids up and bore them away. Other mothers were not as fast. Older town children approached the Gypsy children, who stopped their play to watch them come. *Townies,* their dark eyes said. *We see townie children everywhere the roads go. We know your eyes, and your haircuts; we know how the braces on your teeth will flash in the sun. We don't know where we'll be tomorrow, but we know where*

you will be. Don't these same places and these same faces bore you?
We think they do. We think that's why you always come to hate
us.

Billy, Heidi, and Linda Halleck had been there that day,
two days before Halleck would strike and kill the old Gypsy
woman less than a quarter of a mile from here. They had
been having a picnic lunch and waiting for the first band
concert of the spring to begin. Most of the others abroad on
the common that day had been there for the same reason, a
fact the Gypsies undoubtedly knew.

Linda had gotten up, brushing at the seat of her Levi's as
if in a dream, and started toward the young man juggling
the bowling pins.

'Linda, stay here!' Heidi said sharply. Her hand had gone
to the collar of her sweater and was fiddling there, as it often
did when she was upset. Halleck didn't think she was even
aware of it.

'Why, Mom? It's a carnival . . . at least, I *think* it is.'

'They're Gypsies,' Heidi said. 'Keep your distance.
They're all crooks.'

Linda looked at her mother, then at her dad. Billy
shrugged. She stood there looking, as unaware of her wistful
expression, Billy thought, as Heidi was of her hand at her
collar fiddling it uneasily up against her throat and then back
down again.

The young man tossed his bowling pins back into the
open side door of the microbus one by one, and a smiling
dark-haired girl whose beauty was almost ethereal tossed him
five Indian clubs, one after another. The young man now
began to juggle these, grinning, sometimes tossing one up
under his arm and yelling '*Hoy!*' each time he did it.

An elderly man wearing Oshkosh bib overalls and a
checked shirt began handing out fliers. The lovely young
woman who had caught the bowling pins and tossed out the

Indian clubs now jumped lightly down from the van's doorway with an easel. She set it up and Halleck thought: *She is going to exhibit bad seascapes and perhaps some pictures of President Kennedy*. But instead of a painting, she propped a bull's eye target on the easel. Someone from inside the van tossed her a slingshot.

'Gina!' the boy juggling the Indian clubs yelled. He grinned broadly, revealing the absence of several front teeth. Linda sat down abruptly. Her concept of masculine beauty had been formed by a lifetime of network TV, and the young man's handsomeness had been spoiled for her. Heidi stopped fiddling with the collar of her cardigan.

The girl flipped the slingshot to the boy. He dropped one of the clubs and began to juggle the slingshot in its place. Halleck remembered thinking *That must be almost impossible*. The boy did it two or three times, then flipped the slingshot back to her and somehow managed to pick up the club he had dropped while keeping the others in the air. There was scattered applause. Some of the locals were smiling – Billy himself was – but most of them looked wary.

The girl stepped away from the target on the easel, produced some ball bearings from her breast pocket, and shot three quick bull's-eyes – *plop, plop, plop*. Soon she was surrounded by boys (and a few girls) clamoring for a turn. She lined them up, organizing them as quickly and efficiently as a nursery-school teacher prepares pupils for the 10:15 bathroom break. Two teenage Gypsy boys of approximately Linda's age popped out of an old LTD station wagon and began to scruff the spent ammunition out of the grass. They were alike as two peas in a pod, obviously identical twins. One wore a gold hoop in his left ear; his brother wore the mate in his right. *Is that how their mother tells them apart?* Billy thought.

No one was selling anything. Quite carefully, quite obviously, no one was selling anything. There was no Madame Azonka telling the tarot.

Nevertheless, a Fairview police car arrived soon enough, and two cops stepped out. One was Hopley, the chief of police, a roughly handsome man of about forty. Some of the action stopped, and more mothers took the opportunity the lull afforded to recapture their fascinated children and bear them away. Some of the older ones protested, and Halleck observed that some of the younger ones were in tears.

Hopley began discussing the facts of life with the Gypsy who had been doing the juggling act (his Indian clubs, painted in jaunty red and blue stripes, were now scattered around his feet) and the older Gypsy in the Oshkosh biballs. Oshkosh said something. Hopley shook his head. Then the juggler said something and began to gesticulate. As the juggler spoke, he moved closer to the patrolman who had accompanied Hopley. Now the tableau began to remind Halleck of something, and after a moment it came. It was like watching baseball players argue with the umps over a close call in a game.

Oshkosh put a hand on Juggler's arm, pulling him back a step or two, and that enhanced the impression – the manager trying to keep the young hothead from getting the boot. The young man said something more. Hopley shook his head again. The young man began to shout, but the wind was wrong and Billy got only sounds, no words.

'What's happening, Mom?' Linda asked, frankly fascinated.

'Nothing, dear,' Heidi said. Suddenly she was busy wrapping things. 'Are you done eating?'

'Yes, please. Daddy, what's going on?'

For a moment it was on the tip of his tongue to say, *You're watching a classic scene, Linda. It's right up there with the Rape of the Sabine Women. This one is called the Rousting of the*

Undesirables. But Heidi's eyes were on his face, her mouth was tight, and she obviously felt this was not a time for misplaced levity. 'Not much,' he said. 'A little difference of opinion.'

In truth, *not much* was the truth – no dogs were unleashed, there were no swinging billy clubs, no Black Maria pulled up to the edge of the common. In an almost theatrical act of defiance, Juggler shook off Oshkosh's grip, picked up his Indian clubs, and began to juggle them again. Anger had screwed up his reflexes, however, and now it was a poor show. Two of them fell to the ground almost at once. One struck his foot and some kid laughed.

Hopley's partner moved forward impatiently. Hopley, not put out of countenance at all, restrained him much as Oshkosh had restrained Juggler. Hopley leaned back against an elm tree with his thumbs hooked into his wide belt, looking at nothing in particular. He said something to the other cop, and the patrolman produced a notebook from his hip pocket. He wet the ball of his thumb, opened the book, and strolled to the nearest car, a converted Cadillac hearse of early-sixties vintage. He began writing it up. He did this with great ostentation. When he had finished, he moved on to the VW microbus.

Oshkosh approached Hopley and began to speak urgently. Hopley shrugged and looked away. The patrolman moved on to an old Ford sedan. Oshkosh left Hopley and went to the young man. He spoke earnestly, his hands moving in the warm spring air. For Billy Halleck the scene was losing whatever small interest it had held for him. He was beginning not to see the Gypsies, who had made the mistake of stopping in Fairview on their way from Hoot to Holler.

Juggler abruptly turned and went back to the microbus, simply allowing his remaining Indian clubs to drop onto the grass (the microbus had been parked behind the pickup with the woman and the unicorn painted on the homemade camper cap). Oshkosh bent to retrieve them, speaking anxiously to Hopley as he did so. Hopley shrugged again, and although Billy Halleck was in no way telepathic, he knew Hopley was enjoying this as well as he knew that he and Heidi and Linda would be having leftovers for supper.

The young woman who had been shooting ball bearings at the target tried to speak to Juggler, but he brushed by her angrily and stepped into the microbus. She stood for a moment looking at Oshkosh, whose arms were full of Indian clubs, and then she also went into the bus. Halleck could erase the others from his field of perception, but for a moment she was impossible not to see. Her hair was long and naturally wavy, not bound in any way. It fell to below her shoulder blades in a black, almost barbarous flood. Her print blouse and modestly kick-pleated skirt might have come from Sears or J. C. Penney's, but her body was exotic as that of some rare cat – a panther, a cheetah, a snow leopard. As she stepped into the van the pleat at the back of her skirt shifted for a moment and he saw the lovely line of her inner thigh. In that moment he wanted her utterly, and he saw himself on top of her in the blackest hour of the night. And that want felt very old. He looked back at Heidi and now her lips were pressed together so tightly they were white. Her eyes like dull coins. She had not seen his look, but she had seen the shift in the kick pleat, what it revealed, and understood it perfectly.

The cop with the notebook stood watching until the girl was gone. Then he closed his notebook, put it back in his pocket, and rejoined Hopley. The Gypsy women were shooing their children back to the caravan. Oshkosh, his arms full of Indian clubs, approached Hopley again and said something. Hopley shook his head with finality.

And that was it.

A second Fairview police cruiser pulled up, its flashers turning lazily. Oshkosh glanced at it, then glanced around at the Fairview town common with its expensive safety-tested playground equipment and its band shell. Streamers of crepe still fluttered gaily from some of the budding trees; leftovers from the Easter-egg hunt the Sunday before.

Oshkosh went back to his own car, which was at the head of the line. As its motor roared into life, all the other motors did likewise. Most were loud and choppy; Halleck heard a lot of missing pistons and saw a lot of blue exhaust. Oshkosh's station wagon pulled out, bellowing and farting. The others fell into line, heedless of the local traffic bound past the common and toward downtown.

'They've all got their lights on!' Linda exclaimed. 'Gorry, it's like a funeral!'

'There's two Ring-Dings left,' Heidi said briskly. 'Have one.'

'I don't want one. I'm full. Daddy, are those people –?'

'You'll never have a thirty-eight-inch bust if you don't eat,' Heidi told her.

'I've decided I don't want a thirty-eight-inch bust,' Linda said, doing one of her Great Lady bits. They always knocked Halleck out. 'Asses are in these days.'

'Linda Joan *Halleck*!'

'I'll have a Ring-Ding,' Halleck said.

Heidi looked at him briefly, coolly – *Oh . . . is that what you'll have?* – and then tossed it to him. She lit a Vantage 100. Billy ended up eating both of the Ring-Dings. Heidi smoked half a pack of cigarettes before the band concert was over, and ignored Billy's clumsy efforts to cheer her up. But she warmed up on the way home and the Gypsies were forgotten. At least, until that night.

★

When he went into Linda's room to kiss her good night, she asked him: 'Were the police running those guys out of town, Dad?'

Billy remembered looking at her carefully, feeling both annoyed and absurdly flattered by her question. She went to Heidi when she wanted to know how many calories were in a piece of German chocolate cake; she came to Billy for harder truths, and he sometimes felt this was not fair.

He sat on her bed, thinking that she was still very young and very sure she was on that side of the line where the good guys unquestionably stood. She could be hurt. A lie could avoid that hurt. But lies about the sort of thing that had happened that day on the Fairview common had a way of coming back to haunt the parents – Billy could very clearly remember his father telling him that masturbation would make him stutter. His father had been a good man in almost all ways, but Billy had never forgiven him that lie. Yet Linda had already run him a hard course – they had been through gays, oral sex, venereal disease, and the possibility that there was no God. It had taken having a child to teach him just how tiring honesty could be.

Suddenly he thought of Ginelli. What would Ginelli tell his daughter if he was here now? *You got to keep the undesirables out of town, sweetness. Because that is really what it's all about – just keeping the undesirables out of town.*

But that was more truth than he could muster.

'Yes, I suppose they were. They were Gypsies, hon. Vagabonds.'

'Mom said they were crooks.'

'A lot of them run crooked games and tell fake fortunes. When they come to a town like Fairview, the police ask them to move on. Usually they put up a show of being mad, but they really don't mind.'

Bang! A little flag went up inside his head. Lie #1.

'They hand out posters or fliers saying where they'll be – usually they make a cash deal with a farmer or with someone who owns a field outside of town. After a few days they leave.'

'Why do they come at all? What do they do?'

'Well . . . there are always people who want their fortunes read. And there are games of chance. Gambling. Usually they *are* crooked.'

Or maybe a fast, exotic lay, Halleck thought. He saw the kick pleat of the girl's skirt shift again as she stepped into the van. *How would she move?* His mind answered: *Like the ocean getting ready to storm, that's how.*

'Do people buy drugs from them?'

These days you don't need to buy drugs from Gypsies, dear; you can buy those in the schoolyard.

'Hashish, maybe,' he said, 'or opium.'

He had come to this part of Connecticut as a teenager, and had been here ever since – in Fairview and neighboring Northport. He hadn't seen any Gypsies in almost twenty-five years . . . not since he had been a kid growing up in North Carolina, when he had lost five dollars – an allowance saved up carefully over almost three months to buy his mother a birthday present – playing the wheel of fortune. They weren't supposed to allow anyone under sixteen to play, but of course if you had the coin or the long green, you could step up and put it down. Some things never changed, he reckoned, and chief among them was the old adage that when money talks, *nobody* walks. If asked before today, he would have shrugged and guessed that there were no more traveling Gypsy caravans. But of course the wandering breed never died out. They came in rootless and left the same way, human tumbleweeds who cut whatever deals they could and then blew out of town with dollars in their greasy wallets that had been earned on the time clocks they themselves spurned.

They survived. Hitler had tried to exterminate them along with the Jews and the homosexuals, but they would outlive a thousand Hitlers, he supposed.

'I thought the common was public property,' Linda said. 'That's what we learned in school.'

'Well, in a way it is,' Halleck said. ' "Common" means commonly owned by the townspeople. The taxpayers.'

Bong! Lie #2. Taxation had nothing at all to do with common land in New England, ownership of or use of. See *Richards vs. Jerram, New Hampshire*, or *Baker vs. Olins* (that one went back to 1835), or . . .

'The taxpayers,' she said in a musing voice.

'You need a permit to use the common.'

Clang! Lie #3. That idea had been overturned in 1931, when a bunch of poor potato farmers set up a Hooverville in the heart of Lewiston, Maine. The city had appealed to Roosevelt's Supreme Court and hadn't even gotten a hearing. That was because the Hooverites had picked Pettingill Park to camp in, and Pettingill Park happened to be common land.

'Like when the Shrine Circus comes,' he amplified.

'Why didn't the Gypsies get a permit, Dad?' She sounded sleepy now. Thank God.

'Well, maybe they forgot.'

Not a snowball's chance in hell, Lin. Not in Fairview. Not when you see the common from Lantern Drive and the country club, not when that view is part of what you paid for, along with the private schools which teach computer programming on banks of brand-new Apples and TRS-80's, and the relatively clean air, and the quiet at night. The Shrine Circus is okay. The Easter-egg hunt is even better. But Gypsies? Here's your hat, what's your hurry. We know dirt when we see it. Not that we touch it, Christ, no! We have maids and housekeepers to get rid of dirt in our houses. When it shows up on the town common, we've got Hopley.

But those truths are not for a girl in junior high, Halleck

thought. Those are truths that you learn in high school and in college. Maybe you get it from your sorority sisters, or maybe it just comes, like a shortwave transmission from outer space. *Not our kind, dear. Stay away.*

'Good night, Daddy.'

'Good night, Lin.'

He had kissed her again, and left.

Rain, driven by a sudden strong gust of wind, slatted against his study window, and Halleck awoke as if from a doze. *Not our kind, dear,* he thought again, and actually laughed in the silence. The sound made him afraid, because only loonies laughed in an empty room. Loonies did that all the time; it was what made them loony.

Not our kind.

If he had never believed it before, he believed it now.

Now that he was thinner.

Halleck watched as Houston's nurse drew one-two-three ampoules of blood from his left arm and put them into a carrier like eggs in a carton. Earlier, Houston had given him three stool cards and told him to mail them in. Halleck pocketed them glumly and then bent over for the proctological, dreading the humiliation of it, as always, more than the minor discomfort. That feeling of being invaded. Fullness.

'Relax,' Houston said, snapping on the thin rubber glove. 'As long as you can't feel *both* of my hands on your shoulders, you're all right.'

He laughed heartily.

Halleck closed his eyes.

★

Houston saw him two days later – he had, he said, seen to it that his bloodwork was given priority. Halleck sat down in the denlike room (pictures of clipper ships on the walls, deep leather chairs, deep-pile gray rug) where Houston did his consulting. His heart was hammering hard, and he felt droplets of cold sweat nestled at each temple. *I'm not going to cry in front of a man that tells nigger jokes*, he told himself with fierce grimness, and not for the first time. *If I have to cry, I'll drive out of town and park the car and do it.*

'Everything looks fine,' Houston said mildly.

Halleck blinked. The fear had by now rooted deep enough so that he was positive he had misheard Houston. 'What?'

'Everything looks fine,' Houston repeated. 'We can do some more tests if you want, Billy, but I don't see the point right now. Your blood looks better than it has at your last two physicals, as a matter of fact. Cholesterol is down, same with the triglycerides. You've lost some more weight – the nurse got you at two-seventeen this morning – but what can I say? You're still almost thirty pounds over your optimum weight, and I don't want you to lose sight of that, but . . .' He grinned. 'I'd sure like to know your secret.'

'I don't have one,' Halleck said. He felt both confused and tremendously relieved – the way he had felt on a couple of occasions in college when he had passed tests for which he was unprepared.

'We'll hold judgment in abeyance until we get the results on your Hayman-Reichling Series.'

'My what?'

'The shit cards,' Houston said, and then laughed heartily. 'Something might show up there, but really, Billy, the lab ran twenty-three different tests on your blood, and they all look good. That's persuasive.'

Halleck let out a long, shaky sigh. 'I was scared,' he said.

'It's the people who aren't who die young,' Houston

replied. He opened his desk drawer and took out a bottle with a small spoon dangling from the cap by a chain. The spoon's handle, Halleck saw, was in the shape of the Statue of Liberty. 'Tootsweet?'

Halleck shook his head. He was content, however, to sit where he was, with his hands laced together on his belly – on his *diminished* belly – and watch as Fairview's most success-ful family practitioner snorted coke first up one nostril and then up the other. He put the little bottle back in his desk and took out another bottle and package of Q-tips. He dipped a Q-tip in the bottle and then rammed it up his nose.

'Distilled water,' he said. 'Got to protect the sinuses.' And he tipped Halleck a wink.

He's probably treated babies for pneumonia with that shit running around in his head, Halleck thought, but the thought had no real power. Right now he couldn't help liking Houston a little, because Houston had given him good news. Right now all he wanted in the world was to sit here with his hands laced across his diminished belly and explore the depth of his shaky relief, to try it out like a new bicycle, or test-drive it like a new car. It occurred to him that when he walked out of Houston's office he was probably going to feel almost newborn. A director filming the scene might well want to put *Thus Spake Zarathustra* on the soundtrack. This thought made Halleck first grin, then laugh aloud.

'Share the funny,' Houston said. 'In this sad world we need all the funnies we can get, Billy-boy.' He sniffed loudly and then lubricated his nostrils with a fresh Q-tip.

'Nothing,' Halleck said. 'It's just . . . I was scared, you know. I was already dealing with the big C. Trying to.'

'Well, you may have to,' Houston said, 'but not this year. I don't need to see the lab results on the Hayman-Reichling cards to tell you that. Cancer's got a look. At least when it's already gobbled up thirty pounds, it does.'

'But I've been eating as much as ever. I told Heidi I'd been exercising more, and I have, a little, but she said you couldn't lose thirty pounds just by beefing up your exercise regimen. She said you'd just make hard fat.'

'That's not true at all. The most recent tests have showed exercise is much more important than diet. But for a guy who is – who *was* – as overweight as you were, she's got a point. You take a fatty who radically increases his level of exercise, and what the guy usually gets is the booby prize – a good solid class-two thrombosis. Not enough to kill you, just enough to make sure you're never going to walk around all eighteen holes again or ride the big roller coaster at Seven Flags Over Georgia.'

Billy thought the cocaine was making Houston talkative.

'*You* don't understand it,' he said. '*I* don't understand it, either. But in this business I see a lot of things I don't understand. A friend of mine who's a neurosurgeon in the city called me in to look at some extraordinary cranial X rays about three years ago. A male student at George Washington University came in to see him because he was having blinding headaches. They sounded like typical migraines to my colleagues – the kid fit the personality type to a tee – but you don't want to screw around with that sort of thing because headaches like that are symptomatic of cranial brain tumors even if the patient isn't having phantom olfactory referents – smells like shit, or rotten fruit, or old popcorn, or whatever. So my buddy took a full X-ray series, gave the kid an EEG, sent him to the hospital to have a cerebral axial tomography. Know what they found out?'

Halleck shook his head.

'They found out that the kid, who had stood third in his highschool class and who had been on the dean's list every semester at George Washington University, had almost no brain at all. There was a single twist of cortical tissue running up through the center of his skull – on the X rays my colleague showed me, it looked for all the world like a macrame drape-pull – and that was all. That drape-pull was probably running all of his involuntary functions, everything from breathing and heart rate to orgasm. Just that one rope of brain tissue. The rest of the kid's head was filled with nothing but cerebrospinal fluid. In some way we don't understand, that fluid was doing his thinking. Anyway, he's still excelling in school, still having migraines, and still fitting the migraine personality type. If he doesn't have a heart attack in his twenties or thirties that kills him, they'll start to taper off in his forties.'

Houston pulled the drawer open, took out the cocaine, and took some. He offered it to Halleck. Halleck shook his head.

'Then,' Houston resumed, 'about five years ago I had an old lady come into the office with a lot of pain in her gums. She's died since. If I mentioned the old bitch's name, you'd know it. I took a look in there and Christ Almighty, I couldn't believe it. She'd lost the last of her adult teeth almost ten years before – I mean, this babe was pushing ninety – and here was a bunch of new ones coming up . . . five of them in all. No wonder she was having gum pain, Billy! She was growing a third set of teeth. She was teething at eighty-eight years of age.'

'What did you do?' Halleck asked. He was hearing all of this with only a very limited part of his mind – it flowed over him, soothing, like white noise, like Muzak floating down from the ceiling in a discount department store. Most of his mind was still dealing with relief – surely Houston's cocaine must be a poor drug indeed compared to the relief he was feeling. Halleck thought briefly of the old Gypsy with the rotten nose, but the image had lost its darkish, oblique power.

'What did I do?' Houston was asking. 'Christ, what *could*

I do? I wrote her a prescription for a drug that's really nothing more than a high-powered form of Num-Zit, that stuff you put on a baby's gums when it starts to teethe. Before she died, she got three more in – two molars and a canine.

'I've seen other stuff, too, a lot of it. Every doctor sees weird shit he can't explain. But enough of Ripley's *Believe It Or Not*. The fact is, we don't understand very goddamn much about the human metabolism. There are guys like Duncan Hopley . . . You know Dunc?'

Halleck nodded. Fairview's chief of police, rouster of Gypsies, who looked like a bush-league Clint Eastwood.

'He eats like every meal was his last one,' Houston said. 'Holy Moses, I never seen such a bear for chow. But his weight sticks right around one-seventy, and because he's six feet tall, that makes him just about right. He's got a souped-up metabolism; he's burning the calories off at twice the pace of, let's say, Yard Stevens.'

Halleck nodded. Yard Stevens owned and operated Heads Up, Fairview's only barber shop. He went maybe three hundred pounds. You looked at him and wondered if his wife tied his shoelaces.

'Yard is roughly the same height as Duncan Hopley,' Houston said, 'but the times I've seen him at lunch, he's just picking at his food. Maybe he's a big closet eater. Could be. But I'd guess not. He's got a hungry *face*, you know what I mean?'

Billy smiled a little and nodded. He knew. Yard Stevens looked, in his mother's phrase, 'like his food wasn't doing him any good.'

'I'll tell you something else, too – although I s'pose it's tales out of school. Both of those men smoke. Yard Stevens claims a pack of Marlboro Lights a day, which means he probably smokes a pack and a half, maybe two. Duncan claims he smokes two packs of Camels a day, which could mean he's doing three, three and a half. I mean, did you ever see Duncan Hopley without a cigarette in his mouth or in his hand?'

Billy thought about it and shook his head. Meanwhile, Houston had helped himself to another blast. 'Gah, that's enough of that,' he said, and slammed the drawer shut with authority.

'Anyway, there's Yard doing a pack and a half of low-tar cigarettes a day, and there's Duncan doing three packs of black lungers every day – maybe more. But the one who's really inviting lung cancer to come in and eat him up is Yard Stevens. Why? Because his metabolism sucks, and metabolic rate is somehow linked to cancer.

'You have doctors who claim that we can cure cancer when we crack the genetic code. Some kinds of cancer, maybe. But it's never going to be cured completely until we understand metabolism. Which brings us back to Billy Halleck, the Incredible Shrinking Man. Or maybe the Incredible Mass-Reducing Man would be better. Not Mass-*Producing*; Mass-*Reducing*.' Houston laughed a strange and rather stupid whinnying laugh, and Billy thought: *If that's what coke does to you, maybe I'll stick to Ring-Dings.*

'You don't know why I'm losing weight.'

'Nope.' Houston seemed pleased by the fact. 'But my guess is that you may actually be thinking yourself thin. It *can* be done, you know. We see it fairly often. Someone comes in who really wants to lose weight. Usually they've had some kind of scare – heart palpitations, a fainting spell while playing tennis or badminton or volleyball, something like that. So I give them a nice, soothing diet that should enable them to lose two to five pounds a week for a couple of months. You can lose sixteen to forty pounds with no pain or strain that way. Fine. Except most people lose a lot more than that. They follow the diet, but they lose more weight than the diet alone can explain. It's as if some mental sentry who's been fast asleep for years wakes up and starts hollering the equivalent of "Fire!" The metabolism itself speeds up ... because the sentry *told* it to evacuate a few pounds before the whole house burned down.'

'Okay,' Halleck said. He was willing to be convinced. He had taken the day off from work, and suddenly what he wanted to do more than anything else was go home and tell Heidi he was okay and take her upstairs and make love to her while the afternoon sunlight shafted through the windows of their bedroom, 'I'll buy that.'

Houston got up to see him out: Halleck noticed with quiet amusement that there was a dusting of white powder under Houston's nose.

'If you continue to lose weight, we'll run an entire metabolic series on you,' Houston said. 'I may have given you the idea that tests like that aren't very good, but sometimes they can show us a lot. Anyway, I doubt if you'll have to go to that. My guess is your weight loss will start to taper off – five pounds this week, three next week, one the week after that. Then you're going to get on the scales and see that you've put on a pound or two.'

'You've eased my mind a lot,' Halleck said, and gripped Houston's hand hard.

Houston smiled complacently, although he had really done no more than present Halleck with negatives – no, he didn't know what was wrong with Halleck, but no, it wasn't cancer. Whew. 'That's what we're here for, Billy-boy.'

Billy-boy went home to his wife.

'He said you're *okay*?'

Halleck nodded.

She put her arms around him and hugged him hard. He

could feel the tempting swell of her breasts against his chest.

'Want to go upstairs?'

She looked at him, her eyes dancing. 'My, you *are* okay, aren't you?'

'You bet.'

They went upstairs and had magnificent sex. For one of the last times.

Afterward, Halleck fell asleep. And dreamed.

CHAPTER SEVEN
Bird Dream

The Gypsy had turned into a huge bird. A vulture with a rotting beak. It was cruising over Fairview and casting down a gritty, cindery dust like chimney soot that seemed to come from beneath its dusky pinions . . . its wingpits?

'Thinner.' *The Gypsy-vulture croaked, passing over the common, over the Village Pub, the Waldenbooks on the corner of Main and Devon, over Esta-Esta, Fairview's moderately good Italian restaurant, over the post office, over the Amoco station, the modern glass-walled Fairview Public Library, and finally over the salt marshes and out into the bay.*

Thinner, *just that one word, but it was a malediction enough,* Halleck saw, *because everyone in this affluent upper-class-commute-to-the-city-and-have-a-few-drinks-in-the-club-car-on-the-way-home suburb, everyone in this pretty little New England town set squarely in the heart of John Cheever country, everyone in Fairview was starving to death.*

He walked faster and faster up Main Street, apparently invisible – the logic of dreams, after all, is only whatever the dream demands – and horrified by the results of the Gypsy's curse. Fairview had become a town filled with concentration-camp survivors. Big-headed babies with wasted bodies screamed from expensive prams. Two women in expensive designer dresses staggered and lurched out of Cherry on Top, Fairview's version of the old ice-cream shoppe. Their faces were all cheekbones and bulging brows stretching parchment-shiny skin; the necklines of their dresses slipped from jutting

63

skin-wrapped collarbones and deep shoulder hollows in a hideous parody of seduction.

Here came Michael Houston, staggering along on scarecrow-thin legs, his Savile Row suit flapping around his unbelievably gaunt frame, holding out a vial of cocaine in one skeletal hand. 'Toot-sweet?' he screamed at Halleck — it was the voice of a rat caught in a trap and squealing out the last of its miserable life. 'Toot-sweet? It helps speed up your metabolism, Billy-boy! Toot-sweet? Toot — '

With deepening horror Halleck realised the hand holding the vial was not a hand at all but only clattering bones. The man was a walking, talking skeleton.

He turned to run, but in the way of nightmares, he could seem to pick up no speed. Although he was on the Main Street sidewalk, he felt as if he was running in thick, sticky mud. At any moment the skeleton that had been Michael Houston would reach out and he — it — would touch his shoulder. Or perhaps that bony hand would begin to scrabble at his throat.

'Toot-sweet, toot-sweet, toot-sweet!' Houston's squalling, ratlike voice screamed. The voice was drawing closer and closer; Halleck knew that if he turned his head, the apparition would be close to him, so very close — sparkling eyes bulging from sockets of naked bone, the uncovered jawbone jerking and snapping.

He saw Yard Stevens shamble out of Heads Up, his beige barber's smock flapping over a chest and a belly that were now nonexistent. Yard was screeching in a horrid, crowlike voice, and when he turned toward Halleck, he saw it was not Yard at all, but Ronald Reagan. 'Where's the rest of me?' he screamed. 'Where's the rest of me? WHERE'S THE REST OF ME?'

'Thinner,' Michael Houston was now whispering into Halleck's ear, and now what Halleck had feared happened: those finger bones touched him, twiddling and twitching at his sleeve, and Halleck thought he would go mad at the feeling. 'Thinner, so much thinner, toot-de-sweet, and thin-de-thin, it was his wife, Billy-boy, his wife, and you're in trouble, oh-baby, sooo much trouble . . .'

CHAPTER EIGHT
Billy's Pants

Billy jerked awake, breathing hard, his hand clapped across his mouth. Heidi slept peacefully beside him, deeply buried in a quilt. A mid-spring wind was running around the eaves outside.

Halleck took one quick, fearful look around the bedroom, assuring himself that Michael Houston – or a scarecrow version of him – was not in attendance. It was just his bedroom, every corner of it known. The nightmare began to drain away . . . but there was still enough of it left so that he scooted over next to Heidi. He did not touch her – she woke easily – but he got into the zone of her warmth and stole part of her quilt.

Just a dream.

Thinner, a voice in his mind answered implacably.

Sleep came again. Eventually.

The morning followed the nightmare, the bathroom scales showed him at 215, and Halleck felt hopeful. Only two pounds. Houston had been right, coke or not. The process was slowing down. He went downstairs whistling and ate three fried eggs and half a dozen link sausages.

On his ride to the train station, the nightmare recurred to him in vague fashion, more as a feeling of *déjà vu* than actual memory. He looked out the window as he passed Heads Up (which was flanked by Frank's Fine Meats and

Toys Are Joys) and for just a moment he expected to see a half-score of lurching, shambling skeletons, as if comfortable, plushy Fairview had somehow been changed into Biafra. But the people on the streets looked okay; better than okay. Yard Stevens, as physically substantial as ever, waved. Halleck waved back and thought: *Your metabolism is warning you to quit smoking, Yard.* The thought made him smile a little, and by the time his train pulled into Grand Central, the last vestiges of the dream were forgotten.

His mind at rest on the matter of his weight loss, Halleck neither weighed himself nor thought much about the matter for another four days ... and then an embarrassing thing very nearly happened to him, in court and in front of Judge Hilmer Boynton, who had no more sense of humor than your average land turtle. It was stupid; the kind of thing you have bad dreams about when you're a grade-school kid.

Halleck stood to make an objection and his pants started to fall down.

He got halfway up, felt them sliding relentlessly down his hips and buttocks, bagging at the knees, and he sat down very quickly. In one of those moments of almost total objectivity – the ones which come unbidden and which you would often just as soon have forgotten – Halleck realized that his movement must have looked like some sort of bizarre hop. William Halleck, attorney-at-law, does his Peter Rabbit riff. He felt a blush mount into his cheeks.

'Is it an objection, Mr Halleck, or a gas attack?'

The spectators – mercifully few of them – tittered.

'Nothing, your Honor,' Halleck muttered. 'I ... I changed my mind.'

Boynton grunted. The proceedings droned on and

Halleck sat sweating, wondering just how he was going to get up.

The judge called a recess ten minutes later. Halleck sat at the defense table pretending to pore over a sheaf of papers. When the hearing room was mostly empty, he rose, hands stuffed into his suit coat pockets in a gesture he hoped looked casual. He was actually holding his trousers up through his pockets.

He took off the suit in the privacy of a men's room stall, looked at his pants, and then took off his belt. His pants, still buttoned and zipped, slithered down to his ankles; his change made a muffled jingle as his pockets struck the tile. He sat down on the toilet, held the belt up like a scroll, and looked at it. He could read a story there which was more than unsettling. The belt had been a Father's Day present two years ago from Linda. He held the belt up, reading it, and felt his heart speeding up to a frightened run.

The deepest indentation in the Niques belt was just beyond the first hole. His daughter had bought it a little small, and Halleck remembered thinking at the time – ruefully – that it was perhaps forgivable optimism on her part. It had, nevertheless, been quite comfortable for a long while. It was only since he'd quit smoking that it got to be a bit hard to buckle the belt, even using the first hole.

After he'd quit smoking . . . but before he'd hit the Gypsy woman.

Now there were other indents in the belt: beyond the second hole . . . and the fourth . . . and the fifth . . . finally the sixth and last.

Halleck saw with growing horror that each of the indents was lighter than the last. His belt told a truer, briefer story than Michael Houston had done. The weight loss was still going on, and it wasn't slowing down; it was speeding up. He had gotten to the last hole in the Niques belt he'd believed only two months ago he would have to quietly retire as too small. Now he needed a seventh hole, which he didn't have.

He looked at his watch and saw he'd have to get back soon. But some things were more important than whether or not Judge Boynton decided to enter a will into probate.

Halleck listened. The men's room was quiet. He held up his pants with one hand and stepped out of the stall. He let his pants drop again and looked at himself in one of the mirrors over the row of sinks. He raised the tails of his shirt in order to get a better look at the belly which until just lately had been his bane.

A small sound escaped his throat. That was all, but that was enough. The selective perception couldn't hold up; it shattered all at once. He saw that the modest potbelly which had replaced his bay window was now gone. Although his pants were down and his shirt was pulled up over his unbuttoned vest, the facts were clear enough in spite of the ludicrous pose. Actual facts, as always, were negotiable – you learned that quickly in the lawyer business – but the metaphor which came was more than persuasive; it was undeniable. He looked like a kid dressed up in his father's clothes. Halleck stood in disarray before the short row of sinks, thinking hysterically: *Who's got the Shinola? I've got to daub on a fake mustache!*

A gagging, rancid laughter rose in his throat at the sight of his pants bundled around his shoes and his black nylon socks climbing three-quarters of the way up his hairy calves. In that moment he suddenly, simply, believed . . . everything. The Gypsy had cursed him, yes, but it wasn't cancer; cancer would have been too kind and too quick. It was something else, and the unfolding had only begun.

A conductor's voice shouted in his mind, *Next stop, Anorexia Nervosa! All out for Anorexia Nervosa!*

The sounds rose in his throat, laughter that sounded like

screams, or perhaps screams that sounded like laughter, and what did it really matter?

Who can I tell! Can I tell Heidi? She'll think I'm crazy.

But Halleck had never felt saner in his life.

The outer door of the men's room banged open.

Halleck retreated quickly into the stall and latched it, frightened.

'Billy?' John Parker, his assistant.

'In here.'

'Boynton's coming back soon. You okay?'

'Fine,' he said. His eyes were shut.

'Do you have gas? Is it your stomach?'

Yeah, it's my stomach, all right.

'I just got to mail a package. I'll be out in a minute or so.'

'Okay.'

Parker left. Halleck's mind fixed on his belt. He couldn't go back into Judge Boynton's court holding up his pants through the pockets of his suit coat. What the hell was he going to do?

He suddenly remembered his Swiss army knife – good old army knife, which he had always taken out of his pocket before weighing himself. Back in the old days, before the Gypsies had come to Fairview.

No one asked you assholes to come – why couldn't you have gone to Westport or Stratford instead?

He took the knife out and quickly cored a seventh hole in the belt. It was ragged and unlovely, but it worked. Halleck buckled the belt, put on his coat, and exited the stall. For the first time he was aware of just how much his pants were swishing around his legs – his thin legs. *Have other people been seeing it?* he thought with fresh and stinging embarrassment. *Seeing how poorly my clothes fit? Seeing and pretending not to? Talking . . .*

He splashed water on his face and left the men's room.

As he came back into the courtroom, Boynton was just entering in a swish of black robes. He looked forbiddingly at Billy, who made a wan gesture of apology. Boynton's face remained fixed; apology definitely *not* accepted. The droning began again. Somehow, Billy got through the day.

He stood on the scales that night after Heidi and Linda were both asleep, looking down, not believing. He looked for a long, long time.

195.

CHAPTER NINE
188

The next day he went out and bought clothes; he bought them feverishly, as if new clothes, clothes that fit him well, would solve everything. He bought a new, smaller Niques belt as well. He became aware that people had stopped complimenting him on his weight loss; when had *that* started? He didn't know.

He put on the new clothes. He went to work and came home. He drank too much, ate second helpings that he didn't want and which sat heavily in his stomach. A week passed, and the new clothes did not look trim and neat anymore; they had begun to bag.

He approached the bathroom scales, his heart thudding so heavily that it made his eyes throb and his head ache. He would discover later that he had bitten his lower lip hard enough to make it bleed. The image of the scale had taken on childish overtones of terror in his mind – the scale had become the goblin of his life. He stood before it for perhaps as long as three minutes, biting down hard on his lower lip, unaware of either the pain or the salty taste of blood in his mouth. It was evening. Downstairs, Linda was watching *Three's Company* on TV, and Heidi was running the weekly household accounts on the Commodore in Halleck's study.

With a kind of lunge, he got onto the scale.

188.

He felt his stomach roll over in a single giddy tumble, and for one desperate moment it seemed impossible that he would not vomit. He struggled grimly to keep his supper down – he needed that nourishment, those warm healthy calories.

At last the nausea passed. He looked down at the calibrated dial, dully remembering what Heidi had said – *It doesn't weigh heavy, it weighs light*. He remembered Michael Houston saying that at 217 he was still thirty pounds over his optimum weight. *Not now, Mikey, he thought tiredly. Now I'm . . . I'm thinner*.

He got off the scales, aware that he now felt a certain measure of relief – the relief a Death Row prisoner might feel, seeing the warden and the priest appear at two minutes of twelve, knowing that the end had come and there was going to be no call from the governor. There were certain formalities to be gone through, of course, yes, but that was all. It was real. If he talked about it to people, they would think he was either joking or crazy – no one believed in Gypsy curses anymore, or maybe never had – they were definitely *declassé* in a world that had watched hundreds of marines come home from Lebanon in coffins, in a world that had watched five IRA prisoners starve themselves to death, among other dubious wonders – but it was true, all the same. He had killed the wife of the old Gypsy with the rotting nose, and his sometime golf partner, good old tit-grabbing Judge Cary Rossington, had let him off without even so much as a tap on the wrist, and so the old Gypsy had decided to impose his own sort of justice on one fat Fairview lawyer whose wife had picked the wrong day to give him his first and only handjob in a moving car. The sort of justice a man like his sometime friend Ginelli might appreciate.

Halleck turned off the bathroom light and went downstairs, thinking of Death Row convicts walking down the last mile. *No blindfold, Faddah . . . but who's got a cigarette?* He smiled wanly.

Heidi was sitting at his desk, the bills on her left, the glowing screen in front of her, the Marine Midlands checkbook propped on the keyboard like sheet music. A common enough sight on at least one night during the first week of the new month. But she wasn't writing checks or running figures. She was only sitting there, a cigarette between her fingers, and when she turned to him, Billy saw such woe in her eyes that he was almost physically staggered.

He thought of selective perception again, the funny way your mind had of not seeing what it didn't want to see . . . like the way you kept pulling your belt smaller and smaller to hold your oversized pants up around your shrinking waistline, or the brown circles under your wife's eyes . . . or the desperate question in those eyes.

'Yeah, I'm still losing weight,' he said.

'Oh, Billy,' she said, and exhaled in a long, trembling sigh. But she looked a little better, and Halleck supposed she was glad it was out in the open. She hadn't dared mention it, just as no one at the office had dared to say: *Your clothes are starting to look like they came from Omar the Tentmaker, Billy-boy . . . Say, you haven't got a growth or anything, do you? Somebody hit you with the old cancer-stick, did they, Billy? You got yourself a great big old tumor inside you someplace, all black and juicy, sort of a rotted human toadstool down there in your guts, sucking you dry?* Oh, no, nobody says that shit; they let you find it out for yourself. One day you're in court and you start to lose your pants when you stand up to say, 'Your Honor, I object!' in the best Perry Mason tradition, and nobody has to say a motherfucking word.

'Yeah,' he said, and then actually laughed a little, as if to cover same.

'How much?'

'The scale upstairs says I'm down to one-eighty-eight.'

'Oh, *Christ!*'

He nodded toward her cigarettes. 'Can I have one of those?'

'Yes, if you want one. Billy, you're not to say a word to Linda about this – not one!'

'Don't have to,' he said, lighting up. The first drag made him feel dizzy. That was okay; the dizziness was kind of nice. It was better than the numb horror that had accompanied the end of the selective perception. 'She knows I'm still losing weight. I've seen it on her face. I just didn't know what I was seeing until tonight.'

'You've got to go back to see Houston,' she said. She looked badly frightened, but that confused expression of doubt and sorrow was gone from her eyes now. 'The metabolic series –'

'Heidi, listen to me,' he said . . . and then stopped.

'What?' she asked. 'What, Billy?'

For a moment he almost told her, told her everything. Something stopped him, and he was never sure later what it was . . . except that, for one moment, sitting there on the edge of his desk and facing her with their daughter watching TV in the other room and one of her cigarettes in his hand, he felt a sudden savage moment of hate for her.

The memory of what had happened – what had *been* happening – in the minute or so before the old Gypsy woman darted out into the traffic returned to him in a flash of total recall. Heidi had scooted over next to him and had put her left arm around his shoulders . . . and then, almost before he was aware it had happened, she had unzipped his fly. He felt her fingers, light and oh so educated, slip through the gap, and then through the opening in his shorts.

In his teens, Billy Halleck had occasionally perused (with sweaty hands and slightly bulging eyes) what were referred to by his peers as 'stroke books.' And sometimes in these 'stroke books,' a 'hot bimbo' would wrap her 'educated fingers' around some fellow's 'stiffening member.' All nothing but wet dreams set in type, of course . . . except here was Heidi, here was his wife gripping his own stiffening member. And, by damn, she was beginning to jerk him off. He had glanced at her, astonished, and had seen the roguish smile on her lips.

'Heidi, what are you –?'

'Shhh. Don't say a word.'

What had possessed her? She had never done such a thing before, and Halleck would have sworn that such a thing had never crossed her mind. But she had done it, and the old Gypsy woman had darted –

Oh, tell the truth! As long as the scales are dropping from your eyes, you might as well drop all of them, don't you think? You got no business lying to yourself; the hour's gotten too late for that. Just the facts, ma'am.

All right, the facts. The *fact* was that Heidi's unexpected move had excited him tremendously, probably because it *had* been unexpected. He had reached for her with his right hand and she had pulled her skirt up, exposing a perfectly ordinary pair of yellow nylon panties. Those panties had never excited him before, but they did now . . . or perhaps it was the way she had pulled up her skirt that had excited him; she had never done that before, either. The *fact* was that about eighty-five percent of his attention had been diverted from his driving, although in nine out of ten parallel worlds, things probably *still* would have turned out perfectly okay; during the business week, Fairview's streets were not just quiet, they were downright somnolent. But never mind that, the *fact* was that he hadn't been in nine out of ten parallel worlds; he had been in this one. The *fact* was that the old Gypsy woman hadn't *darted* out from between the Subaru and the Firebird with the racing stripe; the *fact* was that she simply *walked* from between the two cars, holding a net bag full of purchases in one gnarled and liver-spotted hand, the sort of net bag Englishwomen often take with them when they go shopping along the village high street. There had been a box of Duz laundry powder in the Gypsy woman's net bag; Halleck remembered that. She had not looked; that was true enough. But the final *fact* was just that Halleck had been doing no more than thirty-five miles an hour and he must have been almost a hundred and fifty feet from the Gypsy woman when she stepped out in front of his Olds. Plenty of time to stop if he had been on top of the situation. But the *fact* was that he was on the verge of an explosive orgasm, all but the tiniest fraction of his consciousness fixed below his waist as Heidi's hand squeezed and relaxed, slipped up and down with slow and delicious friction, paused, squeezed, and relaxed again. His reaction had been hopelessly slow, hopelessly too late, and Heidi's hand had clamped on him, stifling the orgasm that shock had brought on for one endless second of pain and a pleasure that was inevitable but still gruesome.

Those were the *facts*. But hold it a second, folks! Hang on a bit, friends and neighbors! There were two more *facts*, weren't there? The first *fact* was that if Heidi hadn't picked that particular day to try out a little autoeroticism, Halleck would have been on top of his job and his responsibility as the operator of a motor vehicle, and the Olds would have stopped at least five feet short of the old Gypsy woman, stopped with a screech of brakes that would have caused the mothers wheeling their babies across the common to look up quickly. He might have shouted, 'Why don't you look where you're going?' at the old woman while she looked at him with a species of stupid fright and incomprehension. He and Heidi would have watched her scurry across the street, their hearts thudding too hard in their chests. Perhaps Heidi would have wept over the fallen grocery bags and the mess on the carpet in the back.

But things would have been all right. There would have been no hearing, and no old rotten-nosed Gypsy waiting outside to caress Halleck's cheek and whisper his dreadful one-word curse. That was the first ancillary *fact*. The second ancillary *fact*, which proceeded from the first, was that all this could be traced directly back to Heidi. It had been her fault, all of it. He had not asked her to do what she had done; he had not said, 'Say! How about you jack me off while we drive home, Heidi? It's three miles, you got time.' No. She had just done it . . . and, should you wonder, her timing had been ghastly.

Yes, it had been her fault, but the old Gypsy hadn't known that, and so Halleck had received the curse and Halleck had now lost a grand total of sixty-one pounds, and there she sat, and there were brown circles under her eyes and her skin looked too sallow, but those brown circles weren't going to *kill* her, were they? No. Ditto the sallow skin. The old Gypsy hadn't touched *her*.

So the moment when he might have confessed his fears to her, when he might have said simply: *I believe I'm losing weight because I have been cursed* – that moment passed. The moment of crude and unalloyed hate, an emotional boulder shot out of his subconscious by some crude and primitive catapult, passed with it.

Listen to me, he said, and like a good wife she had responded: *What, Billy?*

'I'll go back and see Mike Houston again,' he said, which was not what he had originally intended to say at all. 'Tell him to go ahead and book the metabolic series. As Albert Einstein was wont to say, "What the fuck."'

'Oh, Billy,' she said, and held her arms out to him. He went into them, and because there was comfort there, he felt shame for his bright hate of only moments ago . . . but in the days which followed, as Fairview spring proceeded at its usual understated and slightly preppy pace into Fairview summer, the hate recurred more and more often, in spite of all he could do to stop it or hold it back.

CHAPTER TEN
179

He made the appointment for the metabolic series through Houston, who sounded less optimistic after hearing that Halleck's steady weight-loss had continued and that he was, in fact, down twenty-nine pounds since his physical the month before.

'There still may be a perfectly normal explanation for all this,' Houston said, calling back with the appointment and the information three hours later, and that told Halleck all he needed to know. The perfectly normal explanation, once the odds-on favorite in Houston's mind, had now become the dark horse.

'Uh-huh,' Halleck said, looking down at where his belly had been. He never would have believed you could miss the gut that jutted out in front of you, the gut that had eventually gotten big enough to hide even the tips of your shoes – he'd had to lean and peer to find out if he needed a shine or not – especially he never would have believed it if you'd told him such a thing was possible while he was climbing a flight of stairs after too many drinks the night before, clutching his briefcase grimly, feeling a dew of sweat on his forehead, wondering if this was the day the heart attack was going to come, a paralysing pain on the left side of his chest which suddenly broke free and ripped down his left arm. But it was true; he *missed* his damn gut. In some weird way he couldn't understand even now, that gut had been a *friend*.

'If there's still a normal explanation,' he said to Houston, 'what is it?'

'This is what those guys are going to tell you,' Houston said. 'We hope.'

The appointment was at the Henry Glassman Clinic, a small private facility in New Jersey. They would want him there for three days. The estimated cost of his stay and the menu of tests they expected to run on him made Halleck very glad he had complete medical coverage.

'Send me a get-well card,' Halleck said bleakly, and hung up.

His appointment was for May 12 – a week away. During the days between, he watched himself continue to erode, and he strove to contain the panic that nibbled slowly away at his resolve to play the man.

'Daddy, you're losing too much weight,' Linda said uneasily at dinner one night – Halleck, sticking grimly by his guns, had downed three thick pork chops with applesauce. He'd also had two helpings of mashed potatoes. With gravy. 'If it's a diet, I think it's time you quit it.'

'Does it look like I'm dieting?' Halleck said, pointing at his plate with his fork, which dripped gravy.

He spoke mildly enough, but Linda's face began to work and a moment later she fled from the table, sobbing, her napkin pressed to her face.

Halleck looked bleakly at his wife, who looked bleakly back at him.

This is the way the world ends, Halleck thought inanely. *Not with a bang but a thinner.*

'I'll talk to her,' he said, starting to get up.

'If you go to see her looking like you do right now, you'll

scare her to death,' Heidi said, and he felt that surge of bright metallic hate again.

186. 183. 181. 180. It was as if someone – the old Gypsy with the rotting nose, for instance – was using some crazy supernatural eraser on him, rubbing him out, pound by pound. When had he last weighed 180? College? No . . . probably not since he had been a senior in high school.

On one of his sleepless nights between the fifth of May and the twelfth, he found himself remembering an explanation of voodoo he had once read – it works because the victim *thinks* it works. No big supernatural deal; simply the power of suggestion.

Perhaps, he thought, *Houston was right and I'm thinking myself thin . . . because that old Gypsy wanted me to. Only now I can't stop. I could make a million bucks writing a response to that Norman Vincent Peale book . . . call it* The Power of Negative Thinking.

But his mind suggested the old power-of-suggestion idea was, in this case at least, a pile of crap. *All that Gypsy said was 'Thinner.' He didn't say 'By the power vested in me I curse you to lose six to nine pounds a week until you die.' He didn't say 'Eenie-meenie-chili-beanie, soon you will need a new Niques belt or you will be filing objections in your Jockey shorts.' Hell, Billy, you didn't even remember what he said until* after *you'd started to lose weight.*

Maybe that's just when I became consciously *aware of what he said,* Halleck argued back. *But . . .*

And so the argument raged.

If it *was* psychological, though, if it *was* the power of suggestion, the question of what he was going to do about it remained. How was he supposed to combat it? Was there a way he could think himself fat again? Suppose he went to a hypnotist – hell, a psychiatrist! – and explained the problem. The shrink could hypnotize him and plant a deep suggestion that the old Gypsy man's curse was invalid. That might work.

Or, of course, it might not.

Two nights before he was scheduled to check into Glassman Clinic, Billy stood on the scales looking dismally down at the dial – 179 tonight. And as he stood looking down at the dial, it occurred to him in a perfectly natural way – the way things so often occur to the conscious mind after the subconscious has mulled them over for days and weeks – that the person he really ought to talk to about these crazy fears was Judge Cary Rossington.

Rossington was a tit-grabber when he was drunk, but he was a fairly sympathetic and understanding guy when he was sober . . . up to a point, at least. Also, he was relatively close-mouthed. Halleck supposed it was possible that at some drunken party or other (and as with all the other constants of the physical universe – sunrise in the east, sunset in the west, the return of Halley's Comet – you could be certain that *somewhere* in town after nine P.M., people were guzzling manhattans, fishing green olives out of martinis, and, quite possibly, grabbing the tits of other mens' wives), he might be indiscreet about ole Billy Halleck's paranoid-schizo ideas regarding Gypsies and curses, but he suspected that Rossington might think twice about spilling the tale even while in his cups. It was not that anything illegal had been done at the hearing; it had been a textbook case of municipal hardball, sure, but no witnesses had been suborned, no evidence had been eighty-sixed. It was a sleeping dog just the same, though, and old shrewdies like Cary Rossington did not go around kicking such animals. It was always possible – not likely, but fairly possible – that a question concerning Rossington's failure to disqualify himself might come up. Or the fact that the investigating officer hadn't bothered to give

Halleck a breathalyzer test after he'd seen who the driver was (and who the victim was). Nor had Rossington inquired from the bench as to why this fundamental bit of procedure had been neglected. There were other inquiries he could have made and had not.

No, Halleck believed his story would be safe enough with Cary Rossington, at least until the matter of the Gypsies dwindled away a bit in time . . . five years, say, or seven. Meantime, it was this year Halleck was concerned about. At the rate he was going, he would look like a fugitive from a concentration camp before the summer was over.

He dressed quickly, went downstairs, and pulled a light jacket out of the closet.

'Where are you going?' Heidi asked, coming out of the kitchen.

'Out,' Halleck said. 'I'll be back early.'

Leda Rossington opened the door and looked at Halleck as if she had never seen him before – the overhead light in the hall behind her caught her gaunt but aristocratic cheekbones, the black hair which was severely pulled back and showing just the first traces of white (*No*, Halleck thought, *not white, silver . . . Leda's never going to have anything as plebeian as white hair*), the lawn-green Dior dress, a simple little thing that had probably cost no more than fifteen hundred dollars.

Her gaze made him acutely uncomfortable. *Have I lost so much weight she doesn't even know who I am?* he thought, but even with his new paranoia about his personal appearance he found that hard to believe. His face was gaunter, there were a few new worry lines around his mouth, and there were discolored pouches under his eyes from lack of sleep, but otherwise his face was the same old Billy Halleck face. The ornamental lamp at the other end of the Rossington dooryard (a wrought-iron facsimile of an 1880's New Year streetlamp, Horchow Collection, $687 plus mailing) cast only a dim wash of light up this far, and he was wearing his jacket. Surely she couldn't see how much weight he'd lost . . . or could she?

'Leda? It's Bill. Bill Halleck.'

'Of course it is. Hello, Billy.' Still her hand hovered below her chin, half-fisted, touching the skin of her upper throat in a quizzical, pondering gesture. Although her features were incredibly smooth for her fifty-nine years, the face lifts hadn't been able to do much for her neck; the flesh there was loose, not quite wattled.

She's drunk, maybe. Or . . . He thought of Houston, tidily tucking little Bolivian snowdrifts up his nose. *Drugs? Leda Rossington? Hard to believe of anyone who can bid a two no-trump with a strictly ho-hum hand . . . and then make it good.* And on the heels of that: *She's scared. Desperate. What's this? And does it tie in somehow with what's happening to me?*

That was crazy, of course . . . and yet he felt an almost frenzied need to know why Leda Rossington's lips were pressed so tight, why, even in the dim light and despite the best cosmetics money could buy, the flesh under her eyes looked almost as baggy and discolored as the flesh under his own, why the hand that was now fiddling at the neckline of her Dior dress was quivering slightly.

Billy and Leda Rossington considered each other in utter silence for perhaps fifteen seconds . . . and then spoke at exactly the same time.

'Leda, is Cary —' 'Cary's not here, Billy. He's —'

She stopped. He made a gesture for her to go on.

'He's been called back to Minnesota. His sister is very ill.'

'That's interesting,' Halleck said, 'since Cary doesn't have any sisters.'

She smiled. It was an attempt at the well-bred, pained

sort of smile polite people save for those who have been unintentionally rude. It didn't work; it was merely a pulling of the lips, more grimace than smile.

'Sister, did I say? All of this has been very trying for me – for *us*. His brother, I mean. His –'

'Leda, Cary's an only child,' Halleck said gently. 'We went over our sibs one drunk afternoon in the Hastur Lounge. Must have been . . . oh, four years ago. The Hastur burned down not long after. That head shop, the King in Yellow, is there now. My daughter buys her jeans there.'

He didn't know why he was going on; in some vague way he supposed it might set her at ease if he did. But now, in the light from the hall and the dimmer light from the wrought-iron yard lamp, he saw the bright track of a single tear running from her right eye almost to the corner of her mouth. And the arc below her left eye glimmered. As he watched, his words tangling in each other and coming to a confused stop, she blinked twice, rapidly, and the tear overflowed. A second bright track appeared on her left cheek.

'Go away,' she said. 'Just go away, Billy, all right? Don't ask questions. I don't want to answer them.'

Halleck looked at her, and saw a certain implacability in her eyes, just below the swimming tears. She had no intention of telling him where Cary was. And on an impulse he didn't understand either then or later, with absolutely no fore-thought or idea of gain, he pulled down the zipper of his jacket and held it open, as if flashing her. He heard her gasp of surprise.

'Look at me, Leda,' he said. 'I've lost seventy pounds. Do you hear me? *Seventy pounds!*'

'That doesn't have anything to do with me!' she cried in a low, harsh voice. Her complexion had gone a sick clay color; spots of rouge stood out on her face like the spots of color on a clown's cheeks. Her eyes looked raw. Her lips had drawn back from her perfectly capped teeth in a terrorized snarl.

'No, but I need to talk to Cary,' Halleck persisted. He came up the first step of the porch, still holding his jacket open. *And I do*, he thought. *I wasn't sure before, but I am now.* 'Please tell me where he is, Leda. Is he here?'

Her reply was a question, and for a moment he couldn't breathe at all. He groped for the porch rail with one numb hand.

'Was it the Gypsies, Billy?'

At last he was able to pull breath into his locked lungs. It came in a soft whoop.

'Where is he, Leda?'

'Answer my question first. Was it the Gypsies?'

Now that it was here – a chance to actually say it out loud – he found he had to struggle to do so. He swallowed – swallowed hard – and nodded. 'Yes. I think so. A curse. Something like a curse.' He paused. 'No, not *something like*. That's bullshit equivocation. I think I've had a Gypsy curse laid on me.'

He waited for her to shriek derisive laughter – he had heard that reaction so often in his dreams and in his conjectures – but her shoulders only slumped and her head bowed. She was such a picture of dejection and sorrow that in spite of his fresh terror, Halleck felt poignant, almost painful empathy for her – her confusion and her terror. He climbed the second and third porch steps, touched her arm gently . . . and was shocked by the bright hate on her face when she raised her head. He stepped back suddenly, blinking . . . and then had to grab for the porch railing to keep from tumbling off the steps and landing on his pratt. Her expression was a perfect reflection of the way he had momentarily felt about Heidi the other night. That such an expression should be directed against him he found both inexplicable and frightening.

'It's your fault!' she hissed at him. 'All your fault! Why did you have to hit that stupid Gypsy cunt with your car? *It's all your fault!*'

He looked at her, incapable of speaking. *Cunt?* He thought confusedly. *Did I hear Leda Rossington say 'cunt'? Who would have believed she even knew such a word?* His second thought was: *You've got it all wrong, Leda, it was Heidi, not me . . . and she's just great. In the pink. Feeling her oats. Hitting on all cylinders. Kicking up dickens. Taking . . .*

Then Leda's face changed: she looked at Halleck with a calmly polite expressionlessness.

'Come in,' she said.

She brought him the martini he'd asked for in an oversize glass – two olives and two tiny onions were impaled on the swizzle stick, which was a tiny gold-plated sword. Or maybe it was solid gold. The martini was very strong, which Halleck did not mind at all . . . although he knew from the drinking he'd done over the last three weeks that he'd be on his ass unless he went slow; his capacity for booze had shrunk along with his weight.

Still, he took a big gulp to start with and closed his eyes with gratitude as the booze exploded warmth out from his stomach. *Gin, wonderful high-calorie gin*, he thought.

'He *is* in Minnesota,' she said dully, sitting down with her own martini. It was, if anything, bigger than the one she had given to Billy. 'But not visiting relatives. He's at the Mayo Clinic.'

'The Mayo –'

'He's convinced it's cancer,' she went on. 'Mike Houston couldn't find anything wrong, and neither could the derma-tologists he went to in the city, but he's still convinced it's cancer. Do you know that he thought it was herpes at first? He thought I'd caught herpes from someone.'

Billy looked down, embarrassed, but he needn't have done so. Leda was looking over his right shoulder, as if reciting her tale to the wall. She took frequent birdlike sips at her drink. Its level sank slowly but steadily.

'I laughed at him when he finally brought it out. I laughed and said, "Cary, if you think *that* is herpes, then you know less about venereal diseases than I do about thermodynamics." I shouldn't have laughed, but it was a way to . . . to relieve the pressure, you know. The pressure and the anxiety. Anxiety? The *terror*.

'Mike Houston gave him creams that didn't work, and the dermatologists gave him creams that didn't work, and then they gave him shots that didn't work. I was the one that remembered the old Gypsy, the one with the half-eaten nose, and the way he came out of the crowd at the flea market in Raintree the weekend after your hearing, Billy. He came out of the crowd and touched him . . . he touched Cary. He put his hand on Cary's face and said something. I asked Cary then, and I asked him later, after it had begun to spread, and he wouldn't tell me. He just shook his head.'

Halleck took a second gulp of his drink just as Leda set her glass, empty, on the table beside her.

'Skin cancer,' she said. 'He's convinced that's what it is because skin cancer can be cured ninety percent of the time. I know the way his mind works – it would be funny if I didn't, wouldn't it, after living with him for twenty-five years, watching him sit on the bench and make real-estate deals and drink and make real-estate deals and chase other men's wives and make real-estate deals and . . . Oh, shit, I sit here and wonder what I would say at his funeral if someone gave me a dose of Pentothal an hour before the services. I guess it would come out something like "He bought a lot of Connecticut land which is now shopping centers and snapped a lot of bras and drank a lot of Wild Turkey and left me a rich widow and I lived with him through the best years of my life and I've had more fucking Blackglama mink coats than I ever had orgasms, so let's all get out of here and go to a roadhouse somewhere and dance and after a while maybe somebody will get drunk enough to forget I've had my fucking chin tied up behind my fucking ears three fucking times, twice in fucking Mexico City and once in fucking Germany and snap *my* fucking bra." Oh, fuck it. Why am I telling you all this? The only things men like you understand are humping, plea-bargaining, and how to bet on pro-football games.'

She was crying again. Billy Halleck, who now understood the drink she had now almost finished was far from her first of the evening, shifted uncomfortably in his chair and took a big gulp of his own drink. It banged into his stomach with untrustworthy warmth.

'He's convinced it's skin cancer because he can't let himself believe in anything as ridiculously old-world, as superstitious, as penny-dreadful-novel as Gypsy curses. But I saw something deep down in his eyes, Billy. I saw it a lot over the last month or so. Especially at night. A little more clearly every night. I think that's one of the reasons he left, you know. Because he saw me seeing it.

'Refill?'

Billy shook his head numbly and watched her go to the bar and mix herself a fresh martini. She had extremely simple martinis, he saw; you simply filled a glass with gin and tumbled in a couple of olives. They left twin trails of bubbles as they sank to the bottom. Even from where he was sitting, all the way across the room, he could smell the gin.

What was it with Cary Rossington? What had happened to him? Part of Billy Halleck most definitely did not want to know. Houston had apparently made no connection between what was happening to Billy and what was happening to Rossington – why should he have? Houston didn't know about the Gypsies. Also, Houston was bombing his brain with big white torpedoes on a regular basis.

Leda came back and sat down again.

'If he calls and says he's coming back,' she told Billy calmly, 'I'm going to our place on Captiva. It will be beastly hot this time of year, but if I have enough gin, I find I barely notice the temperature. I don't think I could stand to be alone with him anymore. I still love him – yes, in my way, I do – but I don't think I could stand it. Thinking of him in the next bed . . . thinking he might . . . might *touch* me . . .' She shivered. Some of her drink spilled. She drank the rest all at once and then made a thick blowing sound, like a thirsty horse that has just drunk its fill.

'Leda, what's wrong with him? What's happened?'

'Happened? *Happened?* Why, Billy dear, I thought I'd told you, or that you knew somehow.'

Billy shook his head. He was starting to believe he didn't know *anything*.

'He's growing scales. Cary is growing scales.'

Billy gaped at her.

Leda offered a dry, amused, horrified smile, and shook her head a little.

'No – that's not quite right. His skin is *turning into* scales. He has become a case of reverse evolution, a sideshow freak. He's turning into a fish or a reptile.'

She laughed suddenly, a harsh, cawing shriek that made Halleck's blood run cold: *She's tottering on the brink of madness,* he thought – the revelation made him colder still. *I think she'll probably go to Captiva no matter what happens. She'll have to get out of Fairview if she wants to save her sanity. Yes.*

Leda clapped both hands over her mouth and then excused

herself as if she had burped – or perhaps vomited – instead of laughed. Billy, incapable of speaking just then, only nodded and got up to make himself a fresh drink after all.

She seemed to find it easier to talk now that he wasn't looking at her, now that he was at the bar with his back turned, and Billy purposely lingered there.

CHAPTER ELEVEN
The Scales of Justice

Cary had been furious – utterly furious – at being touched by the old Gypsy. He had gone to see the Raintree chief of police, Allen Chalker, the following day. Chalker was a poker-buddy, and he had been sympathetic.

The Gypsies had come to Raintree directly from Fairview, he told Cary. Chalker said he kept expecting them to leave on their own. They had already been in Raintree for five days, and usually three days was about right – just time enough for all the town's interested teenagers to have their fortunes told and for a few desperately impotent men and a like number of desperately menopausal women to creep out to the encampment under cover of darkness and buy potions and nostrums and strange, oily creams. After three days the town's interest in the strangers always waned. Chalker had finally decided they were waiting for the flea market on Sunday. It was an annual event in Raintree, and drew crowds from all four of the surrounding towns. Rather than make an issue of their continuing presence – Gypsies, he told Cary, could be as ugly as ground wasps if you poked them too hard – he decided to let them work the departing flea-market crowds. But if they weren't gone come Monday morning, he would move them along.

But there had been no need. Come Monday morning, the farm field where the Gypsies had camped was empty except for wheel ruts, empty beer and soda cans (the Gypsies apparently had no interest in Connecticut's new bottle-and-can-deposit law), the blackened remains of several small cookfires, and three or four blankets so lousy that the deputy Chalker sent out to investigate would only poke at them with a stick – a *long* stick. Sometime between sundown and sunup, the Gypsies had left the field, left Raintree, left Patchin County . . . had, Chalker told his old poker buddy Cary Rossington, left the planet as far as he either knew or cared. And good riddance.

On Sunday afternoon the old Gypsy man had touched Cary's face; on Sunday night they had left; on Monday morning Cary had gone to Chalker to lodge a complaint (just what the legal basis of the complaint might have been, Leda Rossington didn't know); on Tuesday morning the trouble had begun. After his shower, Cary had come downstairs to the breakfast nook wearing only his bathrobe and had said: 'Look at this.'

'This' turned out to be a patch of roughened skin just a little above his solar plexus. The skin was a shade lighter than the surrounding flesh, which was an attractive coffee-with-cream shade (golf, tennis, swimming, and a UV sunlamp in the winter kept his tan unvarying). The rough patch looked yellowish to her, the way the calluses on the heels of her feet sometimes got in very dry weather. She had touched it (her voice faltered momentarily here) and then drawn her finger away quickly. The texture was rough, almost pebbly, and surprisingly hard. *Armored* – that was the word that had risen unbidden in her mind.

'You don't think that damned Gypsy gave me something, do you?' Cary asked worriedly. 'Ringworm or impetigo or some damned thing like that?'

'He touched your face, not your chest, dear,' Leda had replied. 'Now, get dressed quick as you can. We've got *brioche*. Wear the dark gray suit with the red tie and dress up Tuesday for me, will you? What a love you are.'

THINNER

Two nights later he had called her into the bathroom, his voice so like a scream that she had come on the run (*All our worst revelations come in the bathroom*, Billy thought.) Cary was standing with his shirt off, his razor humming forgotten in one hand, his wide eyes staring into the mirror.

The patch of hard, yellowish skin had spread – it had become a blotch, a vaguely treelike shape that spread upward to the area between his nipples and downward, widening, toward his belly button. This changed flesh was raised above the normal flesh of his belly and stomach by almost an eighth of an inch, and she saw there were deep cracks running through it; several of them looked deep enough to slip the edge of a dime into. For the first time she thought he was beginning to look . . . well, scaly. And felt her gorge rise.

'What *is* it?' he nearly screamed at her. 'Leda, what *is* it?'

'I don't know,' she said, forcing her voice to remain calm, 'but you've got to see Michael Houston. That much is clear. Tomorrow, Cary.'

'No, not tomorrow,' he said, still staring at himself in the mirror, staring at the raised arrowhead–shaped hump of harsh yellow flesh. 'It may be better tomorrow. Day after tomorrow if it isn't better. But not tomorrow.'

'Cary –'

'Hand me that Nivea cream, Leda.'

She did, and stood there a moment longer – but the sight of him smearing the white goo over that hard yellow flesh, listening to the pads of his fingers rasp over it – that was more than she could stand, and she fled back to her room. That was the first time, she told Halleck, that she had been consciously glad for the twin beds, consciously glad he wouldn't be able to turn over in his sleep and . . . touch her. She had lain wakeful for hours, she said, hearing the soft *rasp-rasp* of his fingers moving back and forth across that alien flesh.

He told her the following night that it was better; the night after that he claimed it was better still. She supposed she should have seen the lie in his eyes . . . and that he was lying to himself more than he was to her. Even in his extremity, Cary had remained the same selfish son of a bitch she supposed he had always been. But it hadn't all been Cary's doing, she added sharply, still not turning back from the bar where she was now fiddling aimlessly with the glasses. She had developed her own brand of highly specialized selfishness over the years. She had wanted, needed the illusion almost as much as he had.

On the third night, he had walked into their bedroom wearing only his pajama pants. His eyes were soft and hurt, stunned. She had been rereading a Dorothy Sayers mystery – they were, for always and ever, her favorites – and it dropped from her fingers as she saw him. She would have screamed, she told Billy, but it seemed to her that all her breath was gone. And Billy had time to reflect that no human feeling was truly unique, although one might like to think so: Cary Rossington had apparently gone through the same period of self-delusion followed by shattering self-awakening that Billy had gone through himself.

Leda had seen that the hard yellow skin (the *scales* – there was no longer any way to think of them as anything else) now covered most of Cary's chest and all of his belly. It was as ugly and thickly humped up as burn tissue. The cracks zigged and zagged every which way, deep and black, shading to a pinkish-red deep down where you most definitely did not want to look. And although you might at first think those cracks were as random as the cracks in a bomb crater, after a moment or two your helpless eye reported a different story. At each edge the hard yellow flesh rose a bit more. Scales. Not fish scales but great rough reptile scales, like those on a lizard or a 'gator or an iguana.

The brown arc of his left nipple still showed; the rest of it was gone, buried, under that yellow-black carapace. The right nipple was entirely gone, and a twisted ridge of this strange new flesh reached around and under his armpit toward his back like the grasping surfacing claw of some unthinkable monstrosity. His navel was gone. And . . .

'He lowered his pajama pants,' she said. She was now working on her third drink, taking those same rapid birdlike sips. Fresh tears had begun to leak from her eyes, but that was all. 'That's when I found my voice again. I screamed at him to stop, and he did . . . but not before I'd seen it was sending fingers down into his groin. It hadn't touched his penis . . . at least, it hadn't yet . . . but where it had advanced, his pubic hair was gone and there were just those yellow scales.

' "I thought you said it was getting better," I said.'

' "I honestly thought it was," he answered me.' And the next day, he made the appointment with Houston.'

Who probably told him, Halleck thought, *about the college kid with no brain and the old lady with the third set of teeth. And asked if he'd like a short snort of the old brain-squirts.*

A week later Rossington had been seeing the best team of dermatologists in New York. They knew immediately what was wrong with him, they said, and a regimen of 'hard-gamma' X rays had followed. The scaly flesh continued to creep and spread. It did not hurt, Rossington told her; there was a faint itching at the borders between his old skin and this horrible new invader, but that was all. The new flesh had absolutely no feeling at all. Smiling the ghastly, shocked smile that was coming to be his only expression, he told her that the other day he had lit a cigarette and crushed it out on his own stomach . . . slowly. There had been no pain, none at all.

She had put her hands up to her ears and screamed at him to stop.

The dermatologists told Cary they had been a bit off-course. What do you mean? Cary asked. You guys said you *knew*. You said you were *sure*. Well, they said, these things happen. Rarely, ha-ha, *very* rarely, but *now* we have it licked. All the tests, they said, bore this new conclusion out. A regimen of hipovites – high potency vitamins to those unfamiliar with high-priced doc talk – and glandular injections had followed. At the same time this new treatment was getting under way, the first scaly patches had begun to show up on Cary's neck . . . the underside of his chin . . . and finally on his face. That was when the dermatologists finally admitted they were stumped. Only for the moment, of course. No such thing is incurable. Modern medicine . . . dietary regimen . . . and mumble-mumble . . . likewise blah-de-dah . . .

Cary would no longer listen to her if she tried to talk to him about the old Gypsy, she told Halleck; once she had seen the humping and roughening of the skin in the tender webbing between the thumb and forefinger on his right hand.

'Skin cancer!' he shouted at her. 'This is *skin* cancer, *skin* cancer, *skin* cancer! Now will you for Christ's sweet sake shut up about that old wog!'

Of course he was the one who was making at least a nominal sense, she was the one who was talking in four-teenth-century absurdities . . . and yet she *knew* it had been the doing of the old Gypsy who had stepped out of the crowd at the Raintree flea market and touched Cary's face. She knew it, and in his eyes, even when he raised his hand to her that time, she saw that *he knew it too*.

He had arranged for a leave of absence with Glenn Petrie, who was shocked to hear his old friend, fellow jurist, and golf partner Cary Rossington had skin cancer.

THINNER

There had followed two weeks, Leda told Halleck, that she could barely bring herself to remember or speak of. Cary had alternately slept like the dead, sometimes upstairs in their room but just as often in the big overstuffed chair in his den or with his head in his arms at the kitchen table. He began to drink heavily every afternoon around four. He would sit in the family room, holding the neck of a J. W. Dant whiskey bottle in one roughening, scaly hand, watching first syndicated comedy shows like *Hogan's Heroes* and *The Beverly Hillbillies*, then the local and national news, then syndicated game shows like *The Joker's Wild* and *Family Feud*, then three hours of prime-time, followed by more news, followed by movies until two or three in the morning. And all the while he drank whiskey like Pepsi-Cola, straight from the bottle.

On some of these nights he would cry. She would come in and observe him weeping while Warner Anderson, imprisoned inside their Sony large-screen TV, cried, 'Let's go to the videotape!' with the enthusiasm of a man inviting all his old girlfriends to go on a cruise to Aruba with him. On still other nights – mercifully few of them – he would rave like Ahab during the last days of the *Pequod*, shambling and stumbling through the house with the whiskey bottle held in a hand that was not really a hand anymore, shouting that it was skin cancer, did she hear him, it was *fucking skin cancer* and he had gotten it from the fucking UV lamp, and he was going to sue the dirty quacks that had done this to him, *sue them right down to the motherfucking ground*, litigate the bastards until they didn't have so much as a shit-stained pair of skivvies to stand up in. Sometimes when he was in these moods, he broke things.

'I finally realized that he was having these . . . these fits . . . on the nights after Mrs Marley came in to clean,' she said dully. 'He'd go up into the attic when she was here, you see. If she'd seen him, it would have been all over town

99

in no time at all. It was the nights after she'd been in and he'd been up there in the dark that he felt most like an outcast, I think. Most like a freak.'

'So he's gone to the Mayo Clinic,' Billy said.

'Yes,' she said, and at last she looked at him. Her face was drunk and horrified. 'What's going to become of him, Billy? What *can* become of him?'

Billy shook his head. He hadn't the slightest idea. Furthermore, he found he had no more urge to contemplate the question than he'd had to contemplate that famous news photograph of the South Vietnamese general shooting the supposed Vietcong collaborator in the head. In a weird way he couldn't quite understand, this was like that.

'He chartered a private plane to fly to Minnesota, did I tell you that? Because he can't bear to have people look at him. Did I tell you that, Billy?'

Billy shook his head again.

'What's going to become of him?'

'I don't know,' Halleck said, thinking: *And just by the way, what's going to become of me, Leda?*

'At the end, before he finally gave up and went, both of his hands were claws. His eyes were two . . . two bright little sparks of blue inside these pitted, scaly hollows. His nose . . .' She stood up and wobbled towards him, hitting the corner of the coffee table hard enough with her leg to make it shift – *She doesn't feel it now*, Halleck thought, *but she's going to have one hell of a painful bruise on her calf tomorrow, and if she's lucky she'll wonder where she got it, or how.*

She grasped at his hand. Her eyes were great glittering pools of uncomprehending horror. She spoke with a gruesome, breathy confidentiality that prickled the skin of Billy's neck. Her breath was rank with undigested gin.

'He looks like an alligator now,' she said in what was almost an intimate whisper. 'Yes, that's what he looks like,

Billy. Like something that just crawled out of a swamp and put on human clothes. It's like he's turning into an alligator, and I was glad he went. *Glad.* I think if he hadn't gone, I would have gone. Yes. Just packed a bag and . . . and . . .'

She was leaning closer and closer, and Billy stood up suddenly, unable to stand any more of this. Leda Rossington rocked back on her heels and Halleck just barely managed to catch her by the shoulders . . . he had also drunk too much, it seemed. If he had missed her, she might very well have brained herself on the same glass-topped, brass-bound coffee table (Trifles, $587 plus mailing) on which she had struck her leg . . . only instead of waking up with a bruise, she could have waked up dead. Looking into her half-mad eyes, Billy wondered if she might not welcome death.

'Leda, I have to go.'

'Of course,' she said. 'Just came for the straight dope, didn't you, Billy dear?'

'I'm sorry,' he said. 'I'm sorry about everything that's happened. Please believe me.' And, insanely, he heard himself adding: 'When you talk to Cary, give him my best.'

'He's hard to talk to now,' she said remotely. 'It's happening inside his mouth, you see. It's thickening his gums, plating his tongue. I can talk to him, but everything he says to me – all of his replies – come out in grunts.'

He was backing into the hall, backing away from her, wanting to be free of her soft, relentlessly cultured tones, needing to be free of her gruesome, glittering eyes.

'He really is,' she said. 'Turning into an alligator, I mean. I expect that before long they may have to put him in a tank . . . they may have to keep his skin wet.' Tears leaked from her raw eyes, and Billy saw she was dribbling gin from her canted martini glass onto her shoes.

'Good night, Leda,' he whispered.

'Why, Billy? Why did you have to hit the old woman?

Why did you have to bring this on Cary and me? Why?'

'Leda –'

'Come back in a couple of weeks,' she said, still advancing as Billy groped madly behind him for the knob of the front door, holding on to his polite smile by a huge act of will. 'Come back and let me have a look at you when you've lost another forty or fifty pounds. I'll laugh . . . and laugh . . . and laugh.'

He found the knob. He turned it. The cool air struck his flushed and overheated skin like a benison.

'Good night, Leda. I'm sorry . . .'

'Save your sorry!' she screamed, and threw her martini glass at him. It struck the doorjamb to Billy's right and shattered. 'Why did you have to hit her, you bastard? Why did you have to bring it on all of us? Why? Why? *Why?*'

Halleck made it to the corner of Park Lane and Lantern Drive and then collapsed onto the bench inside the bus shelter, shivering as if with ague, his throat and stomach sour with acid indigestion, his head buzzing with gin.

He thought: *I hit her and killed her and now I'm losing weight and I can't stop. Cary Rossington conducted the hearing, he let me off without so much as a tap on the wrist, and Cary's in the Mayo Clinic. He's in the Mayo Clinic, and if you believe his wife, he looks like a fugitive from Maurice Sendak's* Alligators All Around. *Who else was in on it? Who else was involved in a way that the old Gypsy might have decided called for revenge?*

He thought of the two cops, rousting the Gypsies when they came into town . . . when they had presumed to start doing their Gypsy tricks on the town common. One of them had just been a spear-carrier, of course. Just a patrol-car jockey following . . .

Following orders.

Whose orders? Why, the police chief's orders, of course. Duncan Hopley's orders.

The Gypsies had been rousted because they had no permit to perform on the common. But of course they would have understood that the message was somewhat broader than that. If you wanted Gypsy folk out, there were plenty of ordinances. Vagrancy. Public nuisance. Spitting on the sidewalk. You name it.

The Gypsies had made a deal with a farmer out on the west side of town, a sour old man named Arncaster. There was always a farm, always a sour old farmer, and the Gypsies always found him. *Their noses have been trained to smell out guys like Arncaster,* Billy thought now as he sat on the bench listening to the first droplets of spring rain strike the bus shelter's roof. Simple evolution. *All it takes is two thousand years of being moved along. You talk to a few people; maybe Madame Azonka does a free reading or two. You sniff for the name of the fellow in town who owns land but owes money, the fellow who has no great love for the town or for town ordinances, the guy who posts his apple orchards during hunting season out of pure orneriness — because he'd rather let the deer have his apples than let the hunters have the deer. You sniff for the name and you always find it, because there's always at least one Arncaster in the richest towns, and sometimes there are two or three to choose among.*

They parked their cars and campers in a circle, just as their ancestors had drawn their wagons and handcarts into a circle two hundred, four hundred, eight hundred years before them. They obtained a fire permit, and at night there was talk and laughter and undoubtedly a bottle or two passed from hand to hand.

All of this, Halleck thought, would have been acceptable to Hopley. It was the way things were done. Those who wanted to buy some of whatever the gypsies were selling could drive out the West Fairview Road to the Arncaster place; at least it was out of sight, and the Arncaster place was something of an eyesore to begin with – the farms the Gypsies found always were. And soon they would move on to Raintree or Westport, and from thence out of view and thought.

Except that, after the accident, after the old Gypsy man had made a nuisance of himself by turning up on the court-house steps and touching Billy Halleck, 'the way things were done' was no longer good enough.

Hopley had given the Gypsies two days, Halleck remembered, and when they showed no signs of moving along, he had *moved* them along. First Jim Roberts had revoked their fire permit. Although there had been heavy showers every day for the previous week, Roberts told them that the fire danger had suddenly gone way, way up. Sorry. And by the way, they wanted to remember that the same regulations which controlled campfires and cook-fires also applied to propane stoves, charcoal fires, and brazier fires.

Next, of course, Hopley would have gone around to visit a number of local businesses where Lars Arncaster had a credit line – a line of credit that was usually overextended. These would have included the hardware store, the feed-and-grain store on Raintree Road, the Farmers' Co-Op in Fairview Village, and Normie's Sunoco. Hopley might also have gone to visit Zachary Marchant at the Connecticut Union Bank . . . the bank that held Arncaster's mortgage.

All part of the job. Have a cup of coffee with this one, a spot of lunch with that one – perhaps something as simple as a couple of franks and lemonades purchased at Dave's Dog Wagon – a bottle of beer with the other one. And by sun-down of the following day, everyone with a claim check on a little piece of Lars Arncaster's ass had given him a call, mentioning how really *good* it would be to have those damned

Gypsies out of town . . . how really *grateful* everyone would be.

The result was just what Duncan Hopley had known it would be. Arncaster went to the Gypsies, refunded the balance of whatever sum they had agreed upon for rent, and had undoubtedly turned a deaf ear to any protests they might have made (Halleck was thinking specifically of the young man with the bowling pins, who apparently had not as yet comprehended the immutability of his station in life). It wasn't as if the Gypsies had a signed lease that would stand up in court.

Sober, Arncaster might have told them they were just lucky he was an honest man and had refunded them the unused portion of what they had paid. Drunk – Arncaster was a three-six-packs-a-night man – he might have been slightly more expansive. There were forces in town that wanted the Gypsies gone, he might have told them. Pressure had been brought to bear, pressure that a poor dirt farmer like Lars Arncaster simply couldn't stand against. Particularly when half the so-called 'good people' in town had the knife out for him to begin with.

Not that any of the Gypsies (with the possible exception of Juggler, Billy thought) would need a chapter-and-verse rendition.

Billy got up and walked slowly back home through a cold, drifting rain. There was a light burning in the bedroom; Heidi, waiting up for him.

Not the patrol-car jockey; no need for revenge there. Not Arncaster; he had seen a chance for five hundred dollars cash money and had sent them on their way because he'd had to do so.

Duncan Hopley?

Hopley, maybe. A *strong* maybe, Billy amended. In one way Hopley was just another species of trained dog whose most urgent directives were aimed at preserving Fairview's well-oiled status quo. But Billy doubted if the old Gypsy man would be disposed to take such a bloodlessly sociological view of things, and not just because Hopley had rousted them so efficiently following the hearing. Rousting was one thing. They were used to that. Hopley's failure to investigate the accident which had taken the old woman's life . . .

Ah, that was something else, wasn't it?

Failure to investigate? Hell, Billy, don't make me laugh. Failure to investigate is a sin of omission. What Hopley did was to throw as much dirt as he could over any possible culpability. Beginning with the conspicuous lack of a breathalyzer test. It was a cover-up on general principles. You know it, and Cary Rossington knew it too.

The wind was picking up and the rain was harder now. He could see it cratering the puddles in the street. The water had a queer polished look under the amber high-security streetlamps that lined Lantern Drive. Overhead, branches moaned and creaked in the wind, and Billy Halleck looked up uneasily.

I ought to go see Duncan Hopley.

Something glimmered – something that might have been the spark of an idea. Then he thought of Leda Rossington's drugged, horrified face . . . he thought of Leda saying *He's hard to talk to now . . . it's happening inside his mouth, you see . . . everything he says to me comes out in grunts.*

Not tonight. He'd had enough for tonight.

'Where did you go, Billy?'

She was in bed, lying in a pool of light thrown by the reading lamp. Now she laid her book aside on the coverlet, looked at him, and Billy saw the dark brown hollows under her eyes. Those brown hollows did not exactly overwhelm him with pity . . . at least, not tonight.

For just a moment he thought of saying: *I went to see Cary Rossington, but since he was gone I ended up having a few drinks with his wife – the kind of drinks the Green Giant must have when he's on a toot. And you'll never guess what she told me, Heidi, dear. Cary Rossington, who grabbed your tit once at the stroke of midnight on New Year's Eve, is turning into an alligator. When he finally dies, they can turn him into a brand-new product: Here Come de Judge Pocketbooks.*

'Nowhere,' he said. 'Just out. Walking. Thinking.'

'You smell like you fell into the juniper bushes on your way home.'

'I guess I did, in a manner of speaking. Only it was Andy's Pub I actually fell into.'

'How many did you have?'

'A couple.'

'It smells more like five.'

'Heidi, are you cross-examining me?'

'No, honey. But I wish you wouldn't worry so much. Those doctors will probably find out what's wrong when they do the metabolic series.'

Halleck grunted.

She turned her earnest, scared face toward him. 'I just thank God it isn't cancer.'

He thought – and almost said – that it must be nice for her to be on the outside; it must be nice to be able to see gradations of the horror. He didn't say it, but some of what he felt must have shown on his face, because her expression of tired misery intensified.

'I'm sorry,' she said. 'It just . . . it seems hard to say anything that isn't the wrong thing.'

You know it, babe, he thought, and the hate flashed up again, hot and sour. On top of the gin, it made him feel both depressed and physically ill. It receded, leaving shame in its wake. Cary's skin was changing into God knew what, something fit only to be seen in a circus-sideshow tent. Duncan Hopley might be just fine, or something even worse might be waiting for Billy there. Hell, losing weight wasn't so bad, was it?

He undressed, careful to turn off her reading lamp first, and took Heidi in his arms. She was stiff against him at first. Then, just when he began to think it was going to be no good, she softened. He heard the sob she tried to swallow back and thought unhappily that if all the storybooks were right, that there was nobility to be found in adversity and character to be built in tribulation, then he was doing a piss-poor job of both finding and building.

'Heidi, I'm sorry,' he said.

'If I could only *do* something,' she sobbed. 'If I could only *do* something, Billy, you know?'

'You can,' he said, and touched her breast.

They made love. He began thinking, *This one is for her*, and discovered it had been for himself after all; instead of seeing Leda Rossington's haunted face and shocked, glittering eyes in the darkness, he was able to sleep.

The next morning, the scale registered 176.

CHAPTER TWELVE
Duncan Hopley

He had arranged a leave of absence from the office in order to accommodate the metabolic series – Kirk Penschley had been almost indecently willing to accommodate his request, leaving Halleck with a truth he would just as soon not have faced; they wanted to get rid of him. With two of his former three chins now gone, his cheekbones evident for the first time in years, the other bones of his face showing almost as clearly, he had turned into the office bogeyman.

'Hell *yes*!' Penschley had responded almost before Billy's request was completely out of his mouth. Penschley spoke in a too-hearty voice, the voice people adopt when everyone knows something is seriously wrong and no one wants to admit it. He dropped his eyes, staring at the place where Halleck's belly used to be. 'Take however much time you need, Bill.'

'Three days should do it,' he'd replied. Now he called Penschley back from the pay phone at Barker's Coffee Shop and told him he might have to take more than three days. More than three days, yes – but maybe not just for the metabolic series. The idea had returned, glimmering. It was not a hope yet, nothing as grand as that, but it was *something*.

'How much time?' Penschley asked him.

'I don't know for sure,' Halleck said. 'Two weeks, maybe. Possibly a month.'

There was a momentary silence at the other end, and Halleck realized Penschley was reading a subtext: *What I really*

109

mean, Kirk, is that I'll never be back. They've finally diagnosed the cancer. Now comes the cobalt, the drugs for pain, the interferon if we can get it, the laetrile if we wig out and decide to head for Mexico. The next time you see me, Kirk, I'll be in a long box with a silk pillow under my head.

And Billy, who had been afraid and not much more for the last six weeks, felt the first thin stirrings of anger. *That's not what I'm saying, goddammit. At least, not yet.*

'No problem, Bill. We'll want to turn the Hood matter over to Ron Baker, but I think everything else can hang fire for a while longer.'

The fuck you do. You'll start turning over everything else to staff this afternoon, and as for the Hood litigation, you turned it over to Ron Baker last week – he called Thursday afternoon and asked me where Sally put the fucking Con-Gas dispositions. Your idea of hanging fire, Kirk-baby, has to do solely with Sunday-afternoon chicken barbecues at your place in Vermont. So don't bullshit a bullshitter.

'I'll see he gets the file,' Billy said, and could not resist adding, 'I think he's already got the Con-Gas deps.'

A thoughtful silence at Kirk Penschley's end as he digested this. Then: 'Well . . . if there's anything I can do . . .'

'There is something,' Billy said. 'Although it sounds a little Loony Tunes.'

'What's that?' His voice was cautious now.

'You remember my trouble this early spring? The accident?'

'Ye-es.'

'The woman I struck was a Gypsy. Did you know that?'

'It was in the paper,' Penschley said reluctantly.

'She was part of a . . . a . . . What? A band, I guess you'd say. A band of Gypsies. They were camping out here in Fairview. They made a deal with a local farmer who needed cash –'

'Hang on, hang on a second,' Kirk Penschley said, his voice a trifle waspy, totally unlike his former paid mourner's tone. Billy grinned a little. He knew this second tone, and liked it infinitely better. He could visualize Penschley, who was forty-five, bald, and barely five feet tall, grabbing a yellow pad and one of his beloved Flair Fineliners. When he was in high gear, Kirk was one of the brightest, most tenacious men Halleck knew. 'Okay, go on. Who was this local farmer?'

'Arncaster. Lars Arncaster. After I hit the woman –'

'Her name?'

Halleck closed his eyes and dragged for it. It was funny . . . all of this, and he hadn't even thought of her name since the hearing.

'Lemke,' he said finally. 'Her name was Susanna Lemke.'

'L-e-m-p-k-e?'

'No P.'

'Okay.'

'After the accident, the Gypsies found that they'd worn out their welcome in Fairview. I've got reason to believe they went on to Raintree. I want to know if you can trace them from there. I want to know where they are now. I'll pay the investigative fees out of my own pocket.'

'Damned right you will,' Penschley said jovially. 'Well, if they went north into New England, we can probably track them down. But if they headed south into the city or over into Jersey, I dunno. Billy, are you worried about a civil suit?'

'No,' he said. 'But I have to talk to that woman's husband. If that's what he was.'

'Oh,' Penschley said, and once again Halleck could read the man's thoughts as clearly as if he'd spoken them aloud: *Billy Halleck is neatening up his affairs, balancing the books. Maybe he wants to give the old Gyp a check, maybe he only wants to face him and apologize and give the man a chance to pop him one in the eye.*

'Thank you, Kirk,' Halleck said.

'Don't mention it,' Penschley said. 'You just work on getting better.'

'Okay,' Billy said, and hung up. His coffee had gotten cold.

He was really not very surprised to find that Rand Foxworth, the assistant chief, was running things down at the Fairview police station. He greeted Halleck cordially enough, but he had a harried look, and to Halleck's practiced eye there seemed to be far too many papers in the In basket on Foxworth's desk and nowhere near enough in the Out basket. Foxworth's uniform was impeccable . . . but his eyes were bloodshot.

'Dunc's had a touch of the flu,' he said in answer to Billy's question – the response had the canned feel of one that has been given many times. 'He hasn't been in for the last couple of days.'

'Oh,' Billy said. 'The flu.'

'That's right,' Foxworth said, and his eyes dared Billy to make something of it.

The receptionist told Billy that Dr Houston was with a patient.

'It's urgent. Please tell him I only need a word or two with him.'

It would have been easier in person, but Halleck hadn't wanted to drive all the way across town. As a result, he was sitting in a telephone booth (an act he wouldn't have been able to manage not long ago) across the street from the police station. At last Houston came on the line.

His voice was cool, distant, more than a bit irritated. Halleck, who was either getting very good at reading subtexts or becoming very paranoid indeed, heard a clear message in that cool tone: *You're not my patient anymore, Billy. I smell some irreversible degeneration in you that makes me very, very nervous. Give me something I can diagnose and prescribe for, that's all I ask. If you can't give me that, there's really no basis for commerce between us. We played some pretty good golf together, but I don't think either of us would say we were ever friends. I've got a Sony beeper, $200,000 worth of diagnostic equipment, and a selection of drugs to call on so wide that . . . well, if my computer printed them all out, the sheet would stretch from the front doors of the country club all the way down to the intersection of Park Lane and Lantern Drive. With all that going for me, I feel smart. I feel useful. Then you come along and make me look like a seventeenth-century doctor with a bottle of leeches for high blood pressure and a trepanning chisel for headaches. And I don't like to feel that way, big Bill. Not at all. Nothing toot-sweet about that. So get lost. I wash my hands of you. I'll come and see you in your coffin . . . unless, of course, my beeper beeps and I have to leave.*

'Modern medicine,' Billy muttered.

'What, Billy? You'll have to speak up. I don't want to give you short shrift, but my P.A. called in sick and I'm going out of my skull this morning.'

'Just a single question, Mike,' Billy said. 'What's wrong with Duncan Hopley?'

Utter silence from the other end for almost ten seconds. Then: 'What makes you think anything is?'

'He's not at the station. Rand Foxworth says he has the flu, but Rand Foxworth lies like old people fuck.'

There was another long pause. 'As a lawyer, Billy, I

shouldn't have to tell you that you're asking for privileged information. I could get my ass in a sling.'

'If somebody tumbles to what's in that little bottle you keep in your desk, your ass could be in a sling, too. A sling so high it would give a trapeze artist acrophobia.'

More silence. When Houston spoke again, his voice was stiff with anger . . . and there was an undercurrent of fear. 'Is that a threat?'

'No,' Billy said wearily. 'Just don't go all prissy on me, Mike. Tell me what's wrong with Hopley and that'll be the end of it.'

'Why do you want to know?'

'Oh, for Christ's sake. You're living proof that a man can be just as dense as he wants to be, do you know that, Mike?'

'I don't have the slightest idea what –'

'You've seen three very strange illnesses in Fairview over the last month. You didn't make any connection among them. In a way, that's understandable enough; they were all different in their specifics. On the other hand, they were all similar in the very fact of their strangeness. I have to wonder if another doctor – one who hadn't discovered the pleasure of plugging fifty dollars' worth of cocaine up his pump every day, for instance – might not have made the connection in spite of the diverse symptoms.'

'Now, wait a goddamn minute!'

'No, I won't. You asked why I wanted to know, and by God, I am going to tell you. I'm losing weight steadily – I go on losing weight even if I stuff eight thousand calories a day down my throat. Cary Rossington has gotten some bizarre skin disease. His wife says he's turning into a sideshow freak. He's gone to the Mayo Clinic. Now, I want to know what's wrong with Duncan Hopley, and secondarily, I want to know if you've had any other inexplicable cases.'

'Billy, it's not like that at all. You sound like you've got some crazy idea or other. I don't know what it is –'

'No, and that's all right. But I want an answer. If I don't get it from you, I'll get it some other way.'

'Hang on one second. If we're going to talk about this, I want to go into the study. It's a little more private there.'

'Fine.'

There was a click as Houston put Billy on hold. He sat in the phone booth, sweating, wondering if this was Houston's way of ditching him. Then there was another click.

'You still there, Billy?'

'Yes.'

'Okay,' Houston said, the note of disappointment in his voice both unmistakable and somehow comic. Houston sighed. 'Duncan Hopley has got a case of runaway acne.'

Billy got to his feet and opened the door of the phone booth. Suddenly it was too hot in there. *'Acne!'*

'Pimples. Blackheads. Whiteheads. That's all. You happy?'

'Anyone else?'

'No. And, Billy, I don't exactly consider pimples off-the-wall. You were starting to sound a little like a Stephen King novel for a while there, but it's not like that. Dunc Hopley has got a temporary glandular imbalance, that's all. And it's not exactly a new thing with him, either. He has a history of skin problems going back to the seventh grade.'

'Very rational. But if you add Cary Rossington with his alligator skin and William J. Halleck with his case of involuntary anorexia nervosa into the equation, it starts to sound a little like Stephen King again, wouldn't you say?'

Patiently Houston said: 'You've got a metabolic problem, Bill. Cary . . . I don't know. I've seen some –'

'Strange things, yes, I know,' Billy said. Had this cocaine-sniffing gasbag really been his family doctor for ten years?

Dear God, was that the truth? 'Have you seen Lars Arncaster lately?'

'No,' Houston said impatiently. 'He's not my patient. I thought you said you only had *one* question.'

Of course he's not your patient, Billy thought giddily, *he doesn't pay his bills on time, does he? And a fellow like you, a fellow with expensive tastes, really can't afford to wait, can he?*

'This really *is* the last one,' Billy said. 'When did you last see Duncan Hopley?'

'Two weeks ago.'

'Thank you.'

'Make an appointment next time, Billy,' Houston said in an unfriendly voice, and hung up.

Hopley did not, of course, live on Lantern Drive, but the police chief's job paid well, and he had a trim New England saltbox on Ribbonmaker Lane.

Billy parked in the driveway at dusk, went to the door, and rang the bell. There was no answer. He rang again. No answer. He leaned on the bell. Still no answer. He went to the garage, cupped his hands around his face, and peered in. Hopley's car, a conservative cordovan-colored Volvo, was parked in there. FVW 1, the license plate read. There was no second car. Hopley was a bachelor. Billy went back to the door and began hammering on it. He hammered for nearly three minutes and his arm was getting tired when a hoarse voice yelled: 'Go away! Fuck off!'

'Let me in!' Billy shouted back. 'I have to talk to you!'

There was no answer. After a minute, Billy began to hammer again. There was no response at all this time . . . but when he stopped suddenly, he heard a whisper of movement on the other side of the door. He could suddenly picture Hopley standing there – *crouching* there – waiting for the unwelcome, insistent visitor to go away and leave him in peace. Peace, or whatever passed for it in Duncan Hopley's world these days. Billy uncurled his throbbing fist.

'Hopley, I think you're there,' he said quietly. 'You don't have to say anything; just listen to me. It's Billy Halleck. Two months ago I was involved in an accident. There was an old Gypsy woman who was jaywalking –'

Movement behind the door; definite now. A shuffle-rustle.

'I hit her and killed her. Now I'm losing weight. I'm not on a diet or anything like that; I'm just losing weight. About seventy-five pounds so far. If it doesn't stop soon, I'm going to look like the Human Skeleton in a carny sideshow.

'Cary Rossington – Judge Rossington – presided at the preliminary hearing and declared that there was no case. He's developed some weird skin disease –'

Billy thought he heard a low gasp of surprise.

'– and he's gone out to the Mayo Clinic. The doctors have told him it isn't cancer, but they don't know *what* it is. Rossington would rather believe it *is* cancer than what he knows it *really* is.'

Billy swallowed. There was a painful click in his throat.

'It's a Gypsy curse, Hopley. I know how crazy that sounds, but it's the truth. There was an old man. He touched me when I came out of the hearing. He touched Rossington when he and his wife were at a flea market in Raintree. Did he touch you, Hopley?'

There was a long, long silence . . . and then one word drifted to Billy's ears through the mail slot, like a letter full of bad news from home:

'Yes . . .'

'Where? When?'

No answer.

'Hopley, where did the Gypsies go when they left Raintree? Do you know?'

No answer.

'I have to talk to you!' Billy said desperately. 'I've got an idea, Hopley. I think –'

'You can't do anything,' Hopley whispered. 'It's gone too far. You understand, Halleck? Too . . . far.'

That sigh again – papery, dreadful.

'It's a *chance*!' Halleck said furiously. 'Are you so far gone that doesn't mean anything to you?'

No answer. Billy waited, hunting inside himself for more words, other arguments. He could find none. Hopley simply wasn't going to let him in. He had begun to turn away when the door clicked open.

Billy looked at the black crack between the door and the jamb. He heard those rustling movements again, now going away, back down the darkened front hall. He felt goose flesh scutter down his back and sides and arms, and for a moment he almost went away anyhow – *Never mind Hopley,* he thought, *if anyone can find those Gypsies, Kirk Penschley can, so never mind Hopley, you don't need him, you don't need to see what he's turned into.*

Pushing the voice back, Billy grasped the knob of the police chief's front door, opened it, and stepped inside.

He saw a dim shape at the far end of the hall. A door on the left opened; the shape went in. A dim light glowed, and for a moment a shadow stretched long and gaunt across the hall floor, bending to go halfway up the far wall, where there was a framed photograph of Hopley receiving an award from the Fairview Rotary Club. The shadow's misshapen head lay on the photograph like an omen.

Billy walked down the hall, spooked now – no use kidding

himself. He half-expected the door behind him to slam shut and lock . . . *and then the Gypsy will dart out of the shadows and grab me from behind, just like the big scare scene in a cheap horror movie. Sure. Come on, asshole, get your act together!* But his triphammering heartbeat did not slow.

He realized that Hopley's little house had an unpleasant smell – low and ripe, like slowly spoiling meat.

He stood outside the open door for a moment. It looked like a study or a den, but the light was so faint it was impossible to tell for sure.

'Hopley.'

'Come in,' the papery voice whispered.

Billy did.

It was Hopley's den, all right. There were rather more books than Billy would have expected, and a warm Turkish rug on the floor. The room was small, probably cozy and pleasant under the right circumstances.

There was a blondwood desk in the center. A Tensor lamp stood on it. Hopley had bent the lamp's neck so that the shade was less than an inch from the desk blotter. There was a small and savagely concentrated circle of light on the blotter; the rest of the room was a cold land of shadows.

Hopley himself was a manlike bulk in what might have been an Eames chair.

Billy stepped over the threshold. There was a chair in the corner. Billy sat in it, aware that he had picked the chair in the room which was farthest from Hopley. Nevertheless, he found himself straining to see Hopley clearly. It was impossible. The man was nothing but a silhouette. Billy found himself almost waiting for Hopley to flip the Tensor lamp up so that it glared into his, Billy's eyes. Then Hopley would lean forward, a cop out of a 1940's *film noir*, screaming: '*We know you did it, McGonigal! Stop trying to deny it! Confess!*

Confess and we'll let you have a cigarette! Confess and we'll give you a glassa icewadduh! Confess and we'll let you go to the batroom!'

But Hopley only sat canted back in his Eames chair. There was a soft rustle as he crossed his legs.

'Well? You wanted to come in. You're in. Tell your tale, Halleck, and get out. You're not exactly my favorite person in all the world these days.'

'I'm not Leda Rossington's favorite person, either,' Billy said, 'and frankly, I don't give much of a shit what she thinks, or what you think, either. She thinks it's my fault. Probably you do too.'

'How much did you have to drink when you hit her, Halleck? My best guess is that if Tom Rangely had given you the breathalyzer, that little balloon would have floated straight up to heaven.'

'Nothing to drink, no drugs,' Billy said. His heart was still thudding, but now it was powered by rage rather than fear. Each thud sent a sick bolt of pain through his head. 'You want to know what happened? Huh? My wife of sixteen years picked that day to give me a handjob in the car. She never did *anything* like that before. I don't have the slightest *clue* why she picked that day to do it. So while you and Leda Rossington – and probably Cary Rossington as well – have been busy laying it off on me because I was behind the wheel, I've been busy laying it off on my wife because she had a hand inside my pants. And maybe we should all just lay it off on fate or destiny or something and stop worrying about blame.'

Hopley grunted.

'Or do you want me to tell you how I begged Tom Rangely on my knees for him to give me a breath test or a blood test? How I cried on your shoulder to soft-pedal the investigation and kick those Gypsies out of town?'

This time Hopley didn't even grunt. He was only a silent slumped shape in the Eames chair.

'Isn't it just a little late for *all* these games?' Billy asked. His voice had hoarsened, and he realized with some astonishment that he was on the verge of tears. 'My wife was jerking me off, true. I hit the old woman and killed her, true. She herself was at least fifty yards from the nearest crosswalk and came out from between two cars, true. You soft-pedaled the investigation and hustled them out of town as soon as Cary Rossington slapped a quick coat of whitewash on me, also true. And none of it means *shit*. But if you *do* want to sit here in the dark and hand out the guilt, my friend, don't forget to give yourself a plateful.'

'A great closing summation, Halleck. Great. You ever seen Spencer Tracy in that movie about the Monkey Trial? You must have.'

'Fuck you,' Billy said, and got up.

Hopley sighed. 'Sit down.'

Billy Halleck stood uncertainly, realizing that part of him wanted to use his anger for its own less-than-noble purposes. That part wanted to get him out of here in a manufactured huff simply because that dark slumped shape in the Eames chair scared him shitless.

'Don't be such a sanctimonious prick,' Hopley said. 'Sit down, for Christ's sake.'

Billy sat down, aware that his mouth was dry and that there were small muscles in his thighs which were jumping and dancing uncontrollably.

'Have it the way you like it, Halleck. I'm more like you than you think. I don't give a fart in a high wind for the postmortems, either. You're right – I didn't think, I just did it. They weren't the first bunch of drifters I ever busted out of town, and I've done other little cosmetic jobs when some hot-shit townie got involved in a mess. Of course I couldn't do anything if the townie in question made the mess outside the Fairview town limits ... but you'd be surprised how many of our leading lights never learned that you don't shit where you eat.

'Or maybe you wouldn't be surprised.'

Hopley uttered a gasping, wheezy laugh that made goose bumps rise on Billy's arms.

'All part of the service. If nothing had happened, none of us – you, me, Rossington – would even remember those Gypsies ever existed by now.'

Billy opened his mouth to utter a hot denial, to tell Hopley that he would remember the sick double-thud he'd heard for the rest of his life ... and then he remembered the four days at Mohonk with Heidi, the two of them laughing together, eating like horses, hiking, making love every night and sometimes in the afternoons. How long had that been after it had happened? Two weeks?

He closed his mouth again.

'What's happened has happened. I guess the only reason I let you in at all was that it's good to know someone else believes this is happening, no matter how insane it is. Or maybe I just let you in because I'm lonely. And I'm scared, Halleck. Very scared. *Extremely* scared. Are you scared?'

'Yes,' Billy said simply.

'You know what scares me the most? I can live like this for quite a while. That scares me. Mrs Callaghee does my grocery shopping and she comes in twice a week to clean and do the washing. I've got the TV, and I like to read. My investments have done very well over the years, and if I'm moderately frugal, I could probably go on indefinitely. And just how much temptation to spend does a man in my position have, anyway? Am I going to buy a yacht, Halleck? Maybe charter a Lear and fly to Monte Carlo with my honey to watch the Grand Prix race there next month? What do you think? How many parties do you think I'd be welcome at now that my whole face is sliding off?'

Billy shook his head numbly.

'So . . . I could live here and it would just . . . just go on. Like it's going on right now, every day and every night. And that scares me, because it's wrong to go on living like this. Every day I don't commit suicide, every day I just sit here in the dark watching game shows and sitcoms, that old Gypsy fuck is laughing at me.'

'When . . . when did he . . . ?'

'Touch me? Just about five weeks ago, if it matters. I went up to Milford to see my mother and father. I took them out to lunch. I had a few beers before and a few more during the meal and decided to use the men's room before we left. The door was locked. I waited, it opened, and *he* came out. Old geezer with a rotted nose. He touched my cheek and said something.'

'What?'

'I didn't hear it,' Hopley said. 'Just then, someone in the kitchen dropped a whole stack of plates on the floor. But I didn't really have to hear it. All I've got to do is look in the mirror.'

'You probably don't know if they were camped in Milford.'

'As a matter of fact, I checked that out with the Milford P.D. the next day,' Hopley said. 'Call it professional curiosity – I recognized the old Gyp; no way you're going to forget a face like that, you know what I mean?'

'Yes,' Billy said.

'They had been camped on a farm in East Milford for four days. Same sort of deal as the one they had with that hemorrhoid Arncaster. The cop I talked to said he'd been keeping pretty close tabs on them and that they appeared to have moved on just that morning.'

'After the old man touched you.'

'Right.'

'Do you think he knew you were going to be there? In that particular restaurant?'

'I never took my folks there before,' Hopley said. 'It was an old place that had just been renovated. Usually we go to a dago place way on the other side of town. It was my mother's idea. She wanted to see what they did to the rugs or the paneling or something. You know how women are.'

'You didn't answer my question. Do you think he knew you were going to be there?'

There was a long, considering silence from the slumped shape in the Eames chair. 'Yes,' Hopley said at last. 'Yes, I do. More insanity, Halleck, right? Good thing no one's keeping score, isn't it?'

'Yes,' Billy said. 'I guess it is.' A peculiar little giggle escaped him. It sounded like a very small shriek.

'Now, what's the idea of yours, Halleck? I don't sleep much these days, but I usually start tossing and turning right around this time of night.'

Asked to bring out in words what he had only thought about in the silence of his own mind, Billy found himself feeling absurd – his idea was weak and foolish, not an idea at all, not really, but only a dream.

'The law firm I work for retains a team of investigators,' he said. 'Barton Detective Services, Inc.'

'I've heard of them.'

'They are supposed to be the best in the business. I . . . That is to say . . .'

He felt Hopley's impatience radiating off the man in waves, although Hopley did not move at all. He summoned what dignity he had left, telling himself that he surely knew as much about what was going on as Hopley, that he had every bit as much right to speak; after all, it was happening to him too.

'I want to find him,' Billy said. 'I want to confront him. I want to tell him what happened. I . . . I guess I want to come completely clean. Although I suppose if he could do these things to us, he may know anyway.'

'Yes,' Hopley said.

Marginally encouraged, Billy went on: 'But I still want to tell him my side of it. That it was my fault, yes, I should have been able to stop in time – all things being equal, I *would* have stopped in time. That it was my wife's fault, because of what she was doing to me. That it was Rossington's fault for whitewashing it, and yours for going easy on the investigation and then humping them out of town.'

Billy swallowed.

'And then I'll tell him it was *her* fault, too. Yes. She was *jaywalking*, Hopley, and so okay, it's not a crime they give you the gas chamber for, but the reason it's against the law is that it can get you killed the way *she* got killed.'

'You want to tell him that?'

'I don't *want* to, but I'm going to. She came out from between two parked cars, didn't look either way. They teach you better in the third grade.'

'Somehow I don't think that babe ever got the Officer Friendly treatment in the third grade,' Hopley said. 'Somehow I don't think she ever *went* to the third grade, you know?'

'Just the same,' Billy said stubbornly, 'simple common sense –'

'Halleck, you must be a glutton for punishment,' the shadow that was Hopley said. 'You're losing weight now – do you want to try for the grand prize? Maybe next time he'll stop up your bowels, or heat your bloodstream up to about a hundred and ten degrees, or –'

'*I'm not just going to sit in Fairview and let it happen!*' Billy said fiercely. 'Maybe he can reverse it, Hopley. Did you ever think of that?'

'I've been reading up on this stuff,' Hopley said. 'I guess I knew what was happening almost from the time the first pimple showed up over one of my eyebrows. Right where the acne attacks always started when I was in high school – and I used to have some pisser acne attacks back then, let me tell you. So I've been reading up on it. Like I said, I like to read. And I have to tell you, Halleck, that there are hundreds of books on *casting* spells and curses, but very few on reversing them.'

'Well, maybe he can't. Maybe not. *Probably* not, even. But I can still go to him, goddammit. I can stare him in the face and say, "You didn't cut enough pieces out of the pie, old man. You should have cut out a piece for my wife, and one for *your* wife, and while we're at it, old man, how about a piece for you? Where were you while she was walking into the street without looking where she was going? If she wasn't used to in-town traffic, you must have known it. So where were you? Why weren't you there to take her by the arm and lead her down to the crosswalk on the corner? Why –"'

'Enough,' Hopley said. 'If I was on a jury, you'd convince me, Halleck. But you forgot the most important factor operating here.'

'What's that?' Billy asked stiffly.

'Human nature. We may be victims of the supernatural, but what we're really dealing with is human nature. As a police officer – excuse me, *former* police officer – I couldn't agree more that there's no absolute right and absolute wrong; there's just one gray shading into the next, lighter or darker. But you don't think her *husband's* going to buy that shit, do you?'

'I don't know.'

'*I* know,' Hopley said. '*I* know, Halleck. I can read that guy so well I sometimes think he must be sending me mental radio signals. All his life he's been on the move, busted out of a place as soon as the "good folks" have got all the maryjane or hashish they want, as soon as they've lost all the dimes they want on the wheel of chance. All his life he's heard a bad deal called a dirty gyp. The "good folks" got roots; you got none. This guy, Halleck, he's seen canvas tents burned for a joke back in the thirties and forties, and maybe there were babies and old people that burned up in some of those tents. He's seen his daughters or his friends' daughters attacked, maybe raped, because all those "good folks" know that gypsies fuck like rabbits and a little more won't matter, and even if it does, who gives a fuck. To coin a phrase. He's maybe seen his sons, or his friends' sons, beaten within an inch of their lives . . . and why? Because the fathers of the kids who did the beating lost some money on the games of chance. Always the same: you come into town, the "good folks" take what they want, and then you get busted out of town. Sometimes they give you a week on the local pea farm or a month on the local road crew for good measure. And then, Halleck, on top of everything, the final crack of the whip comes. This hotshot lawyer with three chins and bull-dog jowls runs your wife down in the street. She's seventy, seventy-five, half-blind, maybe she only steps out too quick because she wants to get back to her place before she wets herself, and old bones break easy, old bones are like glass, and you hang around thinking maybe this once, *just this once*, there's going to be a little justice . . . an instant of justice to make up for a lifetime of crap –'

'Quit it,' Billy Halleck said hoarsely, 'just quit it, what do you say?' He touched his cheek distractedly, thinking he must be sweating heavily. But it wasn't sweat on his cheek; it was tears.

'No, you deserve it all,' Hopley said with savage joviality, 'and I'm going to give it to you. I'm not telling you not to go ahead, Halleck — Daniel Webster talked Satan's jury around, so hell, I guess anything's possible. But I think you're still holding on to too many illusions. This guy is *mad*, Halleck. This guy is *furious*. For all you know, he may be right off his gourd by now, in which case you'd be better off making your pitch in the Bridgewater Mental Asylum. He's out for revenge, and when you're out for revenge, you're not apt to see how everything is shades of gray. When your wife and kids get killed in a plane crash, you don't want to listen to how circuit A fucked up switch B, and traffic controller C had a touch of bug D and navigator E picked the wrong time to go to shithouse F. You just want to sue the shit out of the airline . . . or kill someone with your shotgun. You want a *goat*, Halleck. You want to hurt someone. And we're getting hurt. Bad for us. Good for him. Maybe I understand the thing a little better than you, Halleck.'

Slowly, slowly, his hand crept into the narrow circle of light thrown by the Tensor lamp and turned it so that it shone on his face. Halleck dimly heard a gasp and realized it had come from him.

He heard Hopley saying: *How many parties do you think I'd be welcome at now that my whole face is sliding off?*

Hopley's skin was a harsh alien landscape. Malignant red pimples the size of tea saucers grew out of his chin, his neck, his arms, the back of his hands. Smaller eruptions rashed his cheeks and forehead; his nose was a plague zone of blackheads. Yellowish pus oozed and flowed in weird channels between bulging dunes of proud flesh. Blood trickled here and there. Coarse black hairs, beard hairs, grew in crazy helter-skelter tufts, and Halleck's horrified overburdened mind realized that shaving would have become impossible some time ago in the face of such cataclysmic upheavals. And from the center of it all, helplessly embedded in that trickling landscape, were Hopley's staring eyes.

They looked at Billy Halleck for what seemed an endless length of time, reading his revulsion and dumbstruck horror. At last he nodded, as if satisfied, and turned the Tensor lamp off.

'Oh, Christ, Hopley, I'm sorry.'

'Don't be,' Hopley said, that weird joviality back in his voice. 'Yours is going slower, but you'll get there eventually. My service pistol is in the third drawer of this desk, and if it gets bad enough I'll use it no matter what the balance is in my bankbook. God hates a coward, my father used to say. I wanted you to see me so you'll understand. I know how he feels, that old Gyp. Because I wouldn't make any pretty legal speeches. I wouldn't bother with any sweet reason. I'd kill him for what he's done to me, Halleck.'

That dreadful shape moved and shifted. Halleck heard Hopley draw his fingers down his cheek, and then he heard the unspeakable, sickening sound of ripe pimples breaking wetly open. *Rossington is plating, Hopley's rotting, and I'm wasting away*, he thought. *Dear God, let it be a dream, even let me be crazy . . . but don't let this be happening.*

'I'd kill him very slowly,' Hopley said. 'I will spare you the details.'

Billy tried to speak. There was nothing but a dry croak.

'I understand where you're coming from, but I hold out very little hope for your mission,' Hopley said hollowly. 'Why don't you consider killing him instead, Halleck? Why don't you . . . ?'

But Halleck had reached his limit. He fled Hopley's dark-ened study, cracking his hip hard on the corner of his desk, madly sure that Hopley would reach out with one of those dreadful hands and touch him. Hopley didn't.

Halleck ran out into the night and stood there breathing great lungfuls of clean air, his head bowed, his thighs trembling.

CHAPTER THIRTEEN
172

He thought restlessly for the rest of the week of calling Ginelli at Three Brothers – Ginelli seemed like an answer of some kind – just *what* kind, he didn't know. But in the end he went ahead and checked into the Glassman Clinic and began the metabolic series. If he had been single and alone, as Hopley was (Hopley had made several guest appearances in Billy's dreams the night before), he would have canceled the whole business. But there was Heidi to think about . . . and there was Linda – Linda, who truly was an innocent bystander and who understood none of this. So he checked into the clinic, hiding his crazy knowledge like a man hiding a drug habit.

It was, after all, a place to be, and while he was there, Kirk Penschley and the Barton Detective Services would be taking care of his business. He hoped.

So he was poked and prodded. He drank a horrid chalky-tasting barium solution. He was given X rays, a CAT-scan, an EEG, an EKG, and a total metabolic survey. Visiting doctors were brought around to look at him as if he were a rare zoo exhibit. *A giant panda, or maybe the last of the dodo birds*, Billy thought, sitting in the solarium and holding an unread *National Geographic* in his hands. There were Band-Aids on the backs of both hands. They had stuck a lot of needles in him.

On his second morning at Glassman, as he submitted to yet another round of poking and prying and tapping, he noticed that he could see the double stack of his ribs for the first time since . . . since high school? No, since forever. His bones were making themselves known, casting shadows against his skin, coming triumphantly out. Not only were the love handles above his hips gone, the blades of his pelvic bones were clearly visible. Touching one of them, he thought that it felt knobby, like the gearshift of the first car he had ever owned, a 1957 Pontiac. He laughed a little, and then felt the sting of tears. All of his days were like that now. Upsy-downsy, weather unsettled, chance of showers.

I'd kill him very slowly, he heard Hopley saying. *I will spare you the details.*

Why? Billy thought, lying sleepless in his clinic bed with the raised invalid sides. *You didn't spare me anything else.*

During his three-day stay at Glassman, Halleck lost seven pounds. *Not much,* he thought with his own brand of gallows joviality. *Not much, less than the weight of a medium-sized bag of sugar. At this rate I won't fade to nothing until . . . gee! Almost October!*

172, his mind chanted. *172 now, if you were a boxer you'd be out of the heavyweight class and into the middleweight . . . would you care to try for welterweight, Billy? Lightweight? Bantamweight? How about flyweight?*

Flowers came: from Heidi, from the firm. A small nosegay came from Linda – written on the card in her flat, sprawling hand was *Please get well soon, Daddy – Love you, Lin.* Billy Halleck cried over that.

On the third day, dressed again, he met with the three doctors in charge of his case. He felt much less vulnerable in jeans and a MEET ME IN FAIRVIEW T-shirt; it was really amazing how much it meant to be out of one of the goddamn hospital johnnies. He listened to them, thought of Leda Rossington, and suppressed a grim smile.

They knew exactly what was wrong with him; they were

not mystified at all. *Au contraire*, they were so excited they were damned near making weewee in their pants. Well . . . maybe a note of caution was in order. Maybe they didn't know *exactly* what was wrong with him yet, but it was surely one of two things (or possibly three). One of them was a rare wasting disease that had never been seen outside of Micronesia. One was a rare metabolic disease that had never been completely described. The third – just a possibility, mind you! – was a psychological form of *anorexia nervosa*, this last so rare that it had long been suspected but never actually proven. Billy could see from the hot light in their eyes that they were pulling for that one; they would get their names in the medical books. But in any case, Billy Halleck was definitely a *rara avis*, and his doctors were like kids on Christmas morning.

The upshot was that they wanted him to hang in at Glassman for another week or two (or possibly three). They were going to whip what was wrong with him. They were going to whip it good. They contemplated a series of megavitamins to start with (certainly!), plus protein injections (of course!), and a great many more tests (without a doubt!).

There was the professional equivalent of dismayed howls – and they were almost *literally* howls – when Billy told them quietly that he thanked them, but he would have to leave. They remonstrated with him; they expostulated; they lectured. And to Billy, who felt more and more often lately that he must be losing his mind, the trio of doctors began to look eerily like the Three Stooges. He half-expected them to begin bopping and boinking each other, staggering around the richly appointed office with their white coats flapping, breaking things and shouting in Brooklyn accents.

'You undoubtedly feel quite well now, Mr Halleck,' one of them said. 'You were, after all, quite seriously overweight to begin with, according to your records. But I need to warn you that what you feel now may be spurious. If you continue to lose weight, you can expect to develop mouth sores, skin problems . . .'

If you want to see some real skin problems, you ought to check out Fairview's chief of police, Halleck thought. Excuse me, ex-*chief.*

He decided, on the spur of the moment and apropos of nothing, to take up smoking again.

'. . . diseases similar to scurvy or beriberi,' the doctor was continuing sternly. 'You're going to become extremely susceptible to infections – everything from colds and bronchitis to tuberculosis. *Tuberculosis*, Mr Halleck,' he said impressively. 'Now if you stay here –'

'No,' Billy said. 'Please understand that it's not even an option.'

One of the others put his fingers gently to his temples as if he had just developed a splitting headache. For all Billy knew, he had – he was the doctor who had advanced the idea of psychological *anorexia nervosa.* 'What can we say to convince you, Mr Halleck?'

'Nothing,' Billy replied. The image of the old Gypsy came unbidden into his mind – he felt again the soft, caressing touch of the man's hand on his cheek, the scrape of the hard calluses. *Yes,* he thought, *I'm going to take up smoking again. Something really devilish like Camels or Pall Malls or Chesterfoggies. Why not? When the goddamn doctors start looking like Larry, Curly, and Moe, it's time to do something.*

They asked him to wait a moment and went out together. Billy was content enough to wait – he felt that he had finally reached the *caesura* in his mad play, the eye of the storm, and he was content with that . . . that, and the thought of all the cigarettes he would soon smoke, perhaps even two at a time.

They came back, grim-faced but looking somewhat exalted – men who had decided to make the ultimate sacrifice. They would let him stay free of charge, they said: he need pay only for the lab work.

'No,' Billy said patiently. 'You don't understand. The major medical coverage pays for all of that anyway; I checked. The point is, I'm leaving. Simply leaving. Bugging out.'

They stared at him, uncomprehending, beginning to be angry. Billy thought of telling them how like the Three Stooges they looked, and decided that would be an extremely bad idea. It would complicate things. Such fellows as these were not used to being challenged, to having their *gris-gris* rejected. He did not think it past possibility that they might call Heidi and suggest that a competency hearing was in order. And Heidi might listen to them.

'We'll pay for the tests too,' one of them said finally, in a this-is-our-final-offer tone.

'I'm leaving,' Billy said. He spoke very quietly, but he saw that they finally believed him. Perhaps it was the very quietness of his tone that had finally convinced him that it was not a matter of money, that he was authentically mad.

'But *why? Why*, Mr Halleck?'

'Because,' Billy said, 'although you think you can help me . . . ah . . . gentlemen, you can't.'

And looking at their unbelieving, uncomprehending faces, Billy thought he had never felt so lonely in his life.

On his way home he stopped at a smoke shop and bought a package of Chesterfield Kings. The first three puffs made him feel so dizzy and sick that he threw them away.

'So much for that experiment,' he said aloud in the car, laughing and crying at the same time. 'Back to the old draw- ing board, kids.'

CHAPTER FOURTEEN
156

Linda was gone.

Heidi, the normally tiny lines beside her eyes and the corners of her mouth now deep with strain (*she* was smoking like a steam engine, Billy saw – one Vantage 100 after another), told Halleck she had sent Linda to her Aunt Rhoda's in Westchester County.

'I did it for a couple of reasons,' Heidi said. 'The first is that . . . that she needs a rest from you, Billy. From what's happening to you. She's half out of her mind. It's gotten so I can't convince her you don't have cancer.'

'She ought to talk to Cary Rossington,' Billy muttered as he went into the kitchen to turn on the coffee. He needed a cup badly – strong and black, no sugar. 'They sound like soulmates.'

'What? I can't hear you.'

'Never mind. Just let me turn on the coffee.'

'She's not sleeping,' Heidi said when he came back. She was twisting her hands together restlessly. 'Do you understand?'

'Yes,' Billy said, and he did . . . but it felt as if there was a thorn lodged somewhere inside him. He wondered if Heidi understood that he needed Linda too, if she really understood that his daughter was also part of his support system. But part of his support system or not, he had no right to erode Linda's confidence, her psychological equilibrium. Heidi was right about that. She was right about that no matter how much it cost.

He felt that bright hate surface in his heart again. Mommy had driven his daughter off to auntie's house as soon as Billy had called and said he was on his way. And how come? Why, because the bogey-daddy was coming home! Don't run screaming, dear, it's only the Thin Man . . .

Why that *day? Why did you have to pick* that *day?*

'Billy? Are you all right?' Heidi's voice was oddly hesitant.

Jesus! You stupid bitch! Here you are married to the Incredible Shrinking Man, and all you can think to ask is if I'm all right?

'I'm as all right as I can be, I guess. Why?'

'Because you looked . . . strange for a minute.'

Did I? Did I really? Why that *day, Heidi? Why did you pick* that *day to reach into my pants after all the prim years of doing everything in the dark?*

'Well, I suppose I feel a little strange almost all the time now,' Billy said, thinking: *You've got to stop it, my friend. This is pointless. What's done is done.*

But it was hard to stop it. Hard to stop it when she stood there smoking one cigarette after another but looking and seeming perfectly well, and . . .

But you will stop it, Billy. So help me.

Heidi turned away and stubbed her cigarette out in a crystal ashtray.

'The second thing is . . . you've been keeping something from me, Billy. Something to do with this. You talk in your sleep, sometimes. You've been out nights. Now, I want to know. I *deserve* to know.' She was beginning to cry.

'You want to know?' Halleck asked. 'You really want to know?' He felt a strange dry grin surface on his face.

'Yes! Yes!'

So Billy told her.

★

Houston called him the following day, and after a long and meaningless prologue, he got to the point. Heidi was with him. He and Heidi had had a long chat (*did you offer her a toot for the human snoot?* Halleck thought of asking, and decided that maybe he had better not). The upshot of their long chat was simply this: they thought Billy was just as crazy as a loon.

'Mike,' Billy said, 'the old Gypsy was real. He touched all three of us: me, Cary Rossington, Duncan Hopley. Now, a guy like you doesn't believe in the supernatural – I accept that. But you sure as shit believe in deductive and inductive reasoning. So you've got to see the possibilities. All three of us were touched by him, all three of us have mysterious physical ailments, Now, for Christ's sake, before you decide I've gone crazy, at least consider the logical link.'

'Billy, there *is* no link.'

'I just –'

'I've talked to Leda Rossington. She says Cary is in the Mayo being treated for skin cancer. She says it's gone pretty far, but they're reasonably sure he's going to be okay. She further says she hasn't seen you since the Gordons' Christmas party.'

'She's lying!'

Silence from Houston . . . and was that the sound of Heidi crying in the background? Billy's hand tightened on the telephone until the knuckles grew white.

'Did you talk to her in person, or just on the phone?'

'On the phone. Not that I understand the difference that makes.'

'If you saw her, you'd know. She looks like a woman who's had most of the life shocked right out of her.'

'Well, when you find out your husband has skin cancer, and it's reached the serious stage –'

'Have you talked to Cary?'

'He's in intensive care. People in intensive care are allowed telephone calls only under the most extreme circumstances.'

'I am down to a hundred and seventy,' Billy said. 'That's a net loss of eighty-three pounds, and I call that pretty extreme.'

Silence from the other end. Except for that sound that might be Heidi crying.

'*Will* you talk to him? Will you try?'

'If his doctors allow him to take a call, and if he'll talk to me, yes. But, Billy this hallucination of yours –'

'IT IS NO FUCKING HALLUCINATION!' *Don't shout, God, don't do that.*

Billy closed his eyes.

'All right, all right,' Houston soothed. 'This *idea*. Is that a better word? All I wanted to say is that this *idea* is not going to help you get better. In fact, it may be the root cause of this psycho-anorexia, if that's really what you're suffering from, as Dr Yount believes. You –'

'Hopley,' Billy said. Sweat had broken out on his face. He mopped his brow with his handkerchief. He had a flicker-flash of Hopley, that face that really wasn't a face anymore but a relief map of hell. Crazy inflammations, trickling wetness, and the sound, the unspeakable *sound* when he raked his nails down his cheek.

There was a long silence from Houston's end.

'Talk to Duncan Hopley. He'll confirm –'

'I can't, Billy. Duncan Hopley committed suicide two days ago. He did it while you were in the Glassman Clinic. Shot himself with his service pistol.'

Halleck closed his eyes tightly and swayed on his feet. He felt as he had when he tried to smoke. He pinched his cheek savagely to keep from fainting dead away.

'Then you know,' he said with his eyes still closed. 'You know, or someone knows – someone saw him.'

'Grand Lawlor saw him,' Houston said. 'I called him just a few minutes ago.'

Grand Lawlor. For a moment Billy's confused, frightened mind didn't understand – he believed that Houston had uttered a garbled version of the phrase *grand jury*. Then it clicked home. Grand Lawlor was the county coroner. And now that he thought of it, yes, Grand Lawlor had testified before a grand jury or two in his time.

This thought brought on an irrational giggling fit. Billy pressed his palm over the phone's mouth piece and hoped Houston wouldn't hear his giggles; if he did, Houston would think he was crazy for sure.

And you'd really like to believe I'm crazy, wouldn't you, Mike? Because if I was crazy and I decided to start babbling about the little bottle and the little ivory spoon, why, no one would believe me anyway, would they? Goodness, no.

And that did it; the giggles passed.

'You asked him –'

'For a few details concerning the death? After the horror story your wife told me, you're damned right I asked him.' Houston's voice grew momentarily prim. 'You just ought to be damned glad that when he asked me why I wanted to know, I hung tough.'

'What did he say?'

'That Hopley's complexion was a mess, but nothing like the horror show you described to Heidi. Grand's description leads me to believe that it was a nasty outbreak of the adult acne I'd treated Duncan for off and on ever since I first examined him back in 1974. The outbreaks depressed him quite badly, and that came as no surprise to me – I'd have to say that adult acne, when it's severe, is one of the most psychologically bruising nonlethal ailments I know of.'

'You think he got depressed over the way he looked and killed himself.'

'In essence, yes.'

'Let me get this straight,' Billy said. 'You believe this was a more or less ordinary outbreak of the adult acne he'd had for years ... but at the same time you believe he killed himself because of what he was seeing in the mirror. That's a *weird* diagnosis, Mike.'

'I never said it was the skin outbreak alone,' Houston said. He sounded annoyed. 'The worst thing about problems is the way they seem to come in pairs and trios and whole gangs, never one by one. Psychiatrists have the most suicides per ten thousand members of the profession, Billy, but cops aren't far behind. Probably there was a combination of factors – this latest outbreak could have just been the straw that broke the camel's back.'

'You should have seen him,' Billy said grimly. 'That wasn't a straw, that was the fucking World Trade Center.'

'He didn't leave a note, so I guess we'll never know, will we?'

'Christ,' Billy said, and ran a hand through his hair. 'Jesus Christ.'

'And the reasons for Duncan Hopley's suicide are almost beside the point, aren't they?'

'Not to me,' Billy said. 'Not at all.'

'It seems to me that the real point is that your mind played you a nasty trick, Billy. It guilt-tripped you. You had this ... this bee in your bonnet about Gypsy curses ... and when you went over to Duncan Hopley's that night, you simply saw something that wasn't there.' Now Houston's voice took on a cozy, you-can-tell-me tone. 'Did you happen to drop into Andy's Pub for a couple before you went over to Duncan's house? Just to, you know, get yourself up for the encounter a little?'

'No.'

'You sure? Heidi says you've been spending quite a bit of your time in Andy's.'

'If I had,' Billy said, 'your wife would have seen me there, don't you think?'

There was a long period of silence. Then Houston said colorlessly: 'That was a damned low blow, Billy. But it's also exactly the sort of comment I'd expect from a man who is under severe mental stress.'

'Severe mental stress. Psychological anorexia. You guys have got a name for everything, I guess. But you should have seen him. You should have . . .' Billy paused, thinking of the flaming pimples on Duncan Hopley's cheeks, the oozing whiteheads, the nose that had become almost insignificant in the gruesome, erupting landscape of that haunted face.

'Billy, can't you see that your mind is hunting a logical explanation for what's happening to you? It feels guilt about the Gypsy woman, and so –'

'The curse ended when he shot himself,' Billy heard himself saying. 'Maybe that's why it didn't look so bad. It's like in the werewolf movies we saw when we were kids, Mike. When the werewolf finally gets killed, it turns back into a man again!'

Excitement replaced the confusion he had felt at the news of Hopley's suicide and Hopley's more or less ordinary skin ailment. His mind began to race down this new path, exploring it quickly, ticking off the possibilities and probabilities.

Where does a curse go when the cursee finally kicks it? Shit, might as well ask where a dying man's last breath goes. Or his soul. Away. It goes away. Away, away, away. Is there maybe a way to drive it away?

Rossington – that was the first thing. Rossington, out there at the Mayo Clinic, clinging desperately to the idea that he had skin cancer, because the alternative was so much worse. When Rossington died, would he change back to . . . ?

He became aware that Houston had fallen silent. And there was a noise in the background, unpleasant but familiar . . . Sobbing? Was that Heidi, sobbing?

'Why's she crying?' Billy rasped.

'Billy –'

'Put her on!'

'Billy, if you could *hear* yourself –'

'Goddammit, put her on!'

'No. I won't. Not while you're like this.'

'Why, you cheap coke-sniffing little –'

'Billy, quit it!'

Houston's roar was loud enough to make Billy hold the phone away from his ear for a moment. When he put it back, the sobbing had stopped.

'Now, listen,' Houston said. 'There are no such things as werewolves and Gypsy curses. I feel foolish even telling you that.'

'Man, don't you see that's part of the *problem*?' Billy asked softly. 'Don't you understand that's how these guys have been able to get away with this stuff for the last twenty centuries or so?'

'Billy, if there's a curse on you, it's been laid by your own subconscious mind. Old Gypsies can't lay curses. *But your own mind, masquerading as an old Gypsy, can.*'

'Me, Hopley, and Rossington,' Halleck said dully, 'all at the same time. You're the one who's blind, Mike. Add it up.'

'It adds up to coincidence, and nothing more. How many times do we have to go around the mulberry bush, Billy? Go back to the Glassman. Let them help you. Stop driving your wife crazy.'

For a moment he was tempted to just give in and believe Houston – the sanity and rationality in his voice, no matter how exasperated, were comforting.

Then he thought of Hopley turning the Tensor lamp so that it shone savagely up onto his face. He thought of Hopley saying *I'd kill him very slowly — I will spare you the details.*

'No,' he said. 'They can't help me at the Glassman, Mike.'

Houston sighed heavily. 'Then who can? The old Gypsy?'

'If he can be found, maybe,' Halleck said. 'Just maybe. And there's another guy I know who might be of some help. A pragmatist, like you.'

Ginelli. The name had surfaced in his mind as he was speaking.

'But mostly, I think I've got to help myself.'

'That's what I've been *telling* you!'

'Oh — I was under the impression you'd just advised me to check back into the Glassman Clinic.'

Houston sighed. 'I think your brains must be losing weight, too. Have you thought about what you're doing to your wife and daughter? Have you thought about that at all?'

Did Heidi tell you what she was doing to me when the accident happened? Billy almost blurted out. *Did she tell you that yet, Mikey? No? Oh, you ought to ask her . . . My, yes.*

'Billy?'

'Heidi and I will talk about it,' Billy said quietly.

'But don't you —'

'I think you were right about at least one thing, Mike.'

'Oh? Good for me. And what was that?'

'We've gone around the mulberry bush enough,' Billy said, and hung up the telephone.

But they didn't talk about it.

Billy tried a couple of times, but Heidi only shook her head, her face white and set, her eyes accusing him. She only responded once.

It was three days after the telephone conversation with

Houston, the one in which Heidi had been sobbing accompaniment in the background. They were just finishing dinner. Halleck had put away his usual lumberjack's meal – three hamburgers (with buns and fixin's), four ears of corn (with butter), half a pint of french fries, and two helpings of peach cobbler with hard sauce. He still had little or no appetite, but he had discovered an alarming fact – if he didn't eat, he lost more weight. Heidi had arrived back home following Billy's conversation – argument – with Houston pale and silent, her face puffed from the tears she had cried in Houston's office. Upset and miserable himself, he had skipped lunch and dinner . . . and when he weighed himself the next morning he saw that he had plummeted five pounds to 167.

He stared at the figure, feeling a coldly fluttering swirl of moths in his gut. *Five pounds*, he thought. *Five pounds in one single day! Christ!*

He had skipped no more meals since then.

Now he indicated his empty plate – the clean corn cobs, the remains of the burgers, salad, french fries, dessert.

'Does that look like anorexia nervosa to you, Heidi?' he asked. 'Does it?'

'No,' she said unwillingly. 'No, but –'

'I've been eating like this for the last *month*,' Halleck said, 'and in the last month I've lost just about sixty pounds. Now, would you like to explain how my subconscious managed that trick? Losing two pounds a day on an intake of roughly six thousand calories per twenty-four hours?'

'I . . . I don't know . . . but Mike . . . Mike says –'

'You don't know and I don't know,' Billy said, tossing his napkin into his plate angrily – his stomach was groaning and rolling under the weight of food he had dumped into it. 'And Michael Houston doesn't know either.'

'Well, if it's a curse, why isn't anything happening to me?' she shrieked at him suddenly, and although her eyes blazed with

anger, he could see the tears that were starting up in them.

Stung, scared, and temporarily unable to control himself, Halleck shouted back: '*Because he didn't know, that's why! That's the only reason! Because he didn't know!*'

Sobbing, she pushed her chair back, almost fell over, and then fled from the table. Her hand was pressed to the side of her face as if she had just come down with a monstrous headache.

'Heidi!' he yelled, getting up so fast he knocked his chair over. 'Heidi, come back!'

Her footsteps didn't pause on the stairs. He heard a door slam shut – not their bedroom door. Too far down the upstairs hall. Linda's room, or the guestroom.

Halleck was betting on the guestroom. He was right. She didn't sleep with him again during the week before he left home.

That week – the last week – had the consistency of a confused nightmare in Billy's mind when he tried to think about it later. The weather turned hot and oppressive and surly, as if dog days had come early this year. Even crisp, cool, double-knit Lantern Drive seemed to wilt a bit. Billy Halleck ate and sweated, sweated and ate . . . and his weight settled slowly but surely through it all. At the end of the week, when he rented an Avis car and left, heading up Interstate 95 toward New Hampshire and Maine, he was down another eleven pounds, to 156.

During that week the doctors from Glassman Clinic called again and again. Michael Houston called again and again. Heidi looked at Billy from her white-ringed eyes, smoked, and said nothing. When he spoke of calling Linda, she only said in a dead, brittle voice: 'I'd prefer you didn't do that.'

On Friday, the day before he left, Houston called again.

'Michael,' Billy said, closing his eyes. 'I've already stopped taking calls from the Glassman doctors. I'm going to stop taking them from you, if you don't cut the shit.'

'I wouldn't do that, just yet,' Houston said. 'I want you to listen to me very carefully, Billy. This is important.'

Billy listened to Houston's new rap with no real surprise and only the deepest, dullest stirrings of anger and betrayal. Hadn't he seen it coming, after all?

Heidi had been in again. She and Houston had had a long consultation that had ended with more tears. Houston had then held a long consultation with the Three Stooges at the Glassman Clinic ('Not to worry, Billy, it's all covered by professional privilege'). Houston had seen Heidi again. They all thought that Billy would perhaps profit from a battery of psychiatric tests.

'I want to urge you most strongly to take these of your own free will,' Houston finished.

'I bet. And I *also* bet I know where you'd like me to take the tests. At the Glassman Clinic, right? Do I win a Kewpie doll?'

'Well, we thought that was the logical –'

'Oh, uh-huh, I see. And while they're testing my brains, I assume the barium enemas will continue?'

Houston was eloquently silent.

'If I say no?'

'Heidi has legal recourse,' Houston said carefully. 'You understand?'

'I understand,' Billy said. 'You're talking about you and Heidi and the Three Stooges there at the Glassman Clinic getting together and committing me to Sunnyvale Acres, Basket-Weaving Our Speciality.'

'That's pretty melodramatic, Billy. She's worried about Linda as well as about you.'

'We're both worried about Linda,' Billy said. 'And I'm

worried about Heidi, as well. I mean, I have my moments when I'm so angry with her that I feel sick to my stomach, but I mostly still love her. And so I worry. You see, she's misled you to a degree, Mike.'

'I don't know what you're talking about.'

'I know you don't. And I'm not going to tell you. She might, but my guess is that she won't – all she wants to do is forget that the whole thing ever happened, and filling you in about certain details she may have overlooked the first time around would get in the way of that. Let's just say that Heidi's got her own guilt trip to work out. Her cigarette consumption is up from a pack a day to two and a half.'

A long pause . . . and then Mike Houston returned to his original chorus: 'However that may be, Billy, you must see that these tests are in the best interests of everyone con –'

'Good-bye, Mike,' Halleck said, and hung up softly.

CHAPTER FIFTEEN
Two Phone Conversations

Billy spent the rest of the afternoon stewing his way back and forth through the air-conditioned house, catching glimpses of his new self in mirrors and polished surfaces.

How we see ourselves depends a lot more on our conception of our physical bulk than we usually think.

He found nothing comforting in this idea at all.

My sense of what I'm worth depends on how much of the world I displace as I walk around? Christ, that's a demeaning thought. That guy Mr T. could pick up an Einstein and lug him around all day under one arm like a . . . a schoolbook or something. So does that make Mr T. somehow better, more important?

A haunting echo of T. S. Eliot chimed in his head like a faraway bell on Sunday morning: *That is not what I meant, that is not what I meant at all.* And it wasn't. The idea of size as a function of grace, or intelligence, or as a proof of God's love, had gone out around the time that the obesely waddling William Howard Taft had turned the presidency over to the epicene – almost gaunt – Woodrow Wilson.

How we see reality *depends a lot more on our conception of our physical bulk than we usually think.*

Yes – reality. That was a lot closer to the heart of the matter. When you saw yourself being erased pound by pound, like a complicated equation being erased from a blackboard line by line and computation by computation, it did something to your sense of reality. Your own personal reality, reality in general.

He had been fat – not bulky, not a few pounds overweight, but downright pig-fat. Then he had been stout, then just about normal (if there really was such a thing – the Three Stooges from the Glassman Clinic seemed to think there was, anyway), then thin. But now thinness was beginning to slip into a new state: scrawniness. What came after that? Emaciation, he supposed. And after that, something that still lingered just beyond the bounds of his imagination.

He was not seriously worried about being hauled away to the funny farm; such procedures took time. But the final conversation with Houston showed him clearly just how far things had gone, and how impossible it was that anyone was going to believe him – then or ever. He wanted to call Kirk Penschley – the urge was nearly insurmountable, even though he knew Kirk would call him when and if any of the three investigative agencies the firm employed had turned up something.

He called a New York number instead, paging to the back of his address book to find it. Richard Ginelli's name had bobbed uneasily up and down in his mind since the very beginning of this thing – now it was time to call him.

Just in case.

'Three Brothers,' the voice on the other end said. 'Specials tonight include veal marsala and our own version of fettuccine Alfredo.'

'My name is William Halleck, and I would like to speak to Mr Ginelli, if he's available.'

After a moment of considering silence, the voice said: 'Halleck.'

'Yes.'

The phone clunked down. Faintly Billy could hear pots and pans crashing and bashing together. Someone was swearing in Italian. Someone else was laughing., Like everything else in his life these days, it all seemed very far away.

At last the phone was picked up.

'William!' It occurred to Billy again that Ginelli was the only person in the world who called him that. 'How are you doing, *paisan?*'

'I've lost some weight.'

'Well, that's good,' Ginelli said. 'You were too big, William, I gotta say that, too big. How much you lose?'

'Twenty pounds.'

'Hey! Congratulations! And your heart thanks you, too. Hard to lose weight, isn't it? Don't tell me, I know. Fucking calories stick right on there. Micks like you, they hang over the front of your belt. Dagos like me, you discover one day you're ripping out the seat of your pants every time you bend over to tie your shoes.'

'It actually wasn't hard at all.'

'Well, you come on in to the Brothers, William. I'm gonna fix you my own special. Chicken Neapolitan. It'll put all that weight back on in one meal.'

'I might just take you up on that,' Billy said, smiling a little. He could see himself in the mirror on his study wall, and there seemed to be too many teeth in his smile. Too many teeth, too close to the front of his mouth. He stopped smiling.

'Yeah, well, I really mean it. I miss you. It's been too long. And life's short, *paisan*. I mean, life is *short*, am I right?'

'Yeah, I guess it is.'

Ginelli's voice dropped a notch. 'I heard you had some trouble out there in Connecticut,' he said. He made Connecticut sound as if it was someplace in Greenland, Billy thought. 'I was sorry to hear it.'

'How did you hear that?' Billy said, frankly startled. There had been a squib about the accident in the Fairview *Reporter* – decorous, no names mentioned – and that was all. Nothing in the New York papers.

'I keep my ear to the ground,' Ginelli replied. *Because keeping your ear to the ground is* really *what it's all about*, Billy thought, and shivered.

'I have some problems with that,' Billy said now, picking his words carefully. 'They are of an . . . extralegal nature. The woman – you know about the woman?'

'Yeah. I heard she was a Gyp.'

'A Gypsy, yes. She had a husband. He has . . . made some trouble for me.'

'What's his name?'

'Lemke, I believe. I'm going to try to handle this myself, but I wondered . . . if I can't . . .'

'Sure, sure, sure. You give me a call. Maybe I can do something, maybe I can't. Maybe I'll decide I don't want to. I mean, friends are always friends and business is always business, do you know what I mean?'

'Yes, I do.'

'Sometimes friends and business mix, but sometimes they don't, am I right?'

'Yes.'

'Is this guy trying to hit on you?'

Billy hesitated. 'I'd just as soon not say too much right now, Richard. It's pretty peculiar. But, yeah, he's hitting on me. He's hitting on me pretty hard.'

'Well, shit, William, we ought to talk now!'

The concern in Ginelli's voice was clear and immediate. Billy felt tears prick warmly at his eyelids and pushed the heel of his hand roughly up one cheek.

'I appreciate that – I really do. But I want to try to handle it myself, first. I'm not even entirely sure what I'd want you to do.'

'If you want to call, William, I'm around. Okay?'

'Okay. And thanks.' He hesitated. 'Tell me something, Richard – are you superstitious?'

'Me? You ask an old wop like me if I'm superstitious? Growing up in a family where my mother and grandmother and all my aunts went around hail-Marying and praying to every saint you ever heard of and another bunch you didn't ever hear of and covering up the mirrors when someone died and poking the sign of the evil eye at crows and black cats that crossed their path? *Me?* You ask *me* a question like that?'

'Yeah,' Billy said, smiling a little in spite of himself. 'I ask you a question like that.'

Richard Ginelli's voice came back, flat, hard, and totally devoid of humor. 'I believe in only two things, William. Guns and money, that's what I believe in. And you can quote me. Superstitious? Not me, *paisan.* You are thinking of some other dago.'

'That's good,' Billy said, and his own smile widened. It was the first real smile to sit on his face in almost a month, and it felt good – it felt *damned* good.

That evening, just after Heidi had come in, Penschley called.

'Your Gypsies have led us a merry chase,' he said. 'You've piled up damn near ten thousand dollars in charges already, Bill. Time to drop it?'

'Tell me what you've got first,' Billy said. His hands were sweating.

Penschley began to speak in his dry elder-statesman voice.

The Gypsy band had first gone to Greeno, a Connecticut city about thirty miles north of Milford. A week after they had been rousted from Greeno, they turned up in Pawtucket, near Providence, Rhode Island. After Pawtucket, Attleboro, Massachusetts. In Attleboro, one of them had been arrested for disturbing the peace and then had jumped his piddling bail.

'What seems to have happened is this,' Penschley said. 'There was a town fellow, sort of a bully, who lost ten bucks playing quarters on the wheel of chance. Told the operator it was rigged and that he would get even. Two days later he spotted the Gypsy coming out of a Nite Owl store. There were words between them, and then there was a fight in the parking lot. There were a couple of witnesses from out of town who say the town fellow provoked the fight. There were a couple more from in town who claim the Gypsy started it. Anyway, it was the Gypsy who got arrested. When he jumped bail, the local cops were delighted. Saved them the cost of a court case and got the Gypsies out of town.'

'That's usually how it works, isn't it?' Billy asked. His face was suddenly hot and burning. He was somehow quite sure that the man who had been arrested in Attleboro was the same young man who had been juggling the bowling pins on the Fairview town common.

'Yes, pretty much,' Penschley agreed. 'The Gypsies know the scoop; once the fellow is gone, the local cops are happy. There's no APB, no manhunt. It's like getting a fleck of dirt in your eye. That fleck of dirt is all one can think about. Then the eye waters and washes it out. And once it's gone and the pain stops, one doesn't care where that fleck of dirt went, does one?'

'A fleck of dirt,' Billy said. 'Is that what he was?'

'To the Attleboro police, that's exactly what he was. Do you want the rest of this now, Bill, or shall we moralize on the plight of various minority groups for a bit first?'

'Give me the rest, please.'

'The Gypsies stopped again in Lincoln, Mass. They lasted just about three days before getting the boot.'

'The same group every time? You're sure?'

'Yes. Always the same vehicles. There's a list here, with

registrations – mostly Texas and Delaware tags. You want the list?'

'Eventually. Not now. Go on.'

There wasn't much more. The Gypsies had shown up in Revere, just north of Boston, had stayed ten days, and moved on of their own accord. Four days at Portsmouth, New Hampshire . . . and then they had simply dropped out of sight.

'We can pick up their scent again, if you want,' Penschley said. 'We're less than a week behind now. There are three first-class investigators from Barton Detective Services on this, and they think the Gypsies are almost certainly some-where in Maine by now. They've paralleled I-95 all the way up the coast from Connecticut – hell, all the way up the coast from at least the Carolinas, from what the Greeley men were able to find of their back-trail. It's almost like a circus tour. They'll probably work the southern Maine tourist areas like Ogunquit and Kennebunkport, work their way up to Boothbay Harbor, and finish in Bar Harbor. Then, when the tourist season starts to run out, they'll head back down to Florida or the Texas gulf coast for the winter.'

'Is there an old man with them?' Billy asked. He was gripping the phone very tightly. 'About eighty? With a hor-rible nose condition – sore, cancer, something like that?'

A sound of riffling papers that seemed to go on forever. Then:

'Taduz Lemke,' Penschley said calmly. 'The father of the woman you struck with your car. Yes, he's with them.'

'*Father?*' Halleck barked. 'That's impossible, Kirk! The woman was *old*, around seventy, seventy-five –'

'Taduz Lemke is a hundred and six.'

For several moments Billy found it impossible to speak at all. His lips moved, but that was all. He looked like a man kissing a ghost. Then he managed to repeat: 'That's impossible.'

'An age we all could certainly envy,' Kirk Penschley said, 'but not at all impossible. There are records on all of these people, you know – they're not wandering around eastern Europe in caravans anymore, although I imagine some of the older ones, like this fellow Lemke, wish they were. I've got pix for you . . . Social Security numbers . . . fingerprints, if you want them. Lemke has variously claimed his age to be a hundred and six, a hundred and eight, and a hundred and twenty. I choose to believe a hundred and six, because it jibes with the Social Security information that Barton operatives were able to obtain. Susanna Lemke was his daughter, all right, no doubt at all about that. And, for whatever it's worth, he's listed as "president of the Taduz Company" on the various gaming permits they've had to obtain . . . which means he's the head of the tribe, or the band, or whatever they call themselves.'

His *daughter*? Lemke's *daughter*? In Billy's mind it seemed to change everything. Suppose someone had struck Linda? Suppose it had been Linda run down in the street like a mongrel dog?

'. . . it down?'

'Huh?' He tried to bring his mind back to Kirk Penschley.

'I said, are you sure you don't want us to close this down? It's costing you, Bill.'

'Please ask them to push on a little further,' Billy said. 'I'll call you in four days – no, three – and find out if you've located them.'

'You don't need to do that,' Penschley said. 'If – *when* – the Barton people locate them, you'll be the first to know.'

'I won't be here,' Halleck said slowly.

'Oh?' Penschley's voice was carefully noncommittal. 'Where do you expect to be?'

THINNER

'Traveling,' Halleck said, and hung up shortly afterward. He sat perfectly still, his mind a confused whirl, his fingers – his very *thin* fingers – drumming uneasily on the edge of his desk.

CHAPTER SIXTEEN
Billy's Letter

Heidi went out the next day just after ten to do some shopping. She did not look in on Billy to tell him where she was going or when she would be back – that old and amiable habit was no more. Billy sat in his study watching the Olds back down the driveway to the street. For just a moment Heidi's head turned and their eyes seemed to meet, his confused and scared, hers dumbly accusing: *You made me send our daughter away, you won't get the professional help you need, our friends are starting to talk. You seem to want someone to copilot you over into ha-ha-land, and I'm elected . . . Well, fuck you, Billy Halleck. Leave me alone. Burn if you want to, but you've got no right to ask me to join you in the pot.*

Just an illusion, of course. She couldn't see him far back in the shadows.

Just an illusion, but it hurt.

After the Olds had disappeared down the street, Billy ran a piece of paper into his Olivetti and wrote: 'Dear Heidi' at the top. It was the only part of the letter that came easily. He wrote it one painful sentence at a time, always thinking in the back of his mind that she would come back in while he was pecking it out. But she did not. He finally pulled the note from the typewriter and read it over:

Dear Heidi,

By the time you read this, I'll be gone. I don't know exactly where, and I don't know exactly for how long, but I hope that when I come back, all of this will be over. This nightmare we've been living with.

Heidi, Michael Houston is wrong – wrong about everything. Leda Rossington really *did* tell me that the old Gypsy – his name is Taduz Lemke, by the way – touched Cary, and she really *did* tell me that Cary's skin was plating. And Duncan Hopley really *was* covered with pimples . . . It was more horrible than you can imagine.

Houston refuses to allow himself any serious examination of the chain of logic I've presented in defense of my belief, and he's *certainly* refused to combine that chain of logic with the inexplicability of what's happening to me (155 this morning; almost a hundred pounds now). He cannot do these things – it would knock him out entirely of his orbit if he did. He would rather see me committed for the rest of my life than to even seriously *entertain* the possibility that all of this is happening as a result of a Gypsy's curse. The idea that such off-the-wall-things as Gypsy curses exist at all – anywhere in the world, but especially in Fairview, Connecticut – is anathema to everything Michael Houston has ever believed in. His gods come out of bottles, not out of the air.

But I believe that somewhere deep inside of yourself, *you* may believe it's possible. I think part of your anger at me this last week has been my insistence on believing what *your own heart knows to be true*. Accuse me of playing amateur shrink if you want, but I've reasoned it like this: to believe in the curse is to believe that only one of us is being punished for something in which we both played a part. I'm talking about guilt avoidance on your part . . . and God knows, Heidi, in the craven and cowardly part of my soul, I feel that if I'm going through this hellish decline, you should be going through one also . . . misery loves company, and I guess we've all got a streak of one hundred percent gold-plated bastard in our natures, tangled up so tightly with the good part of us that we can never get free of it.

There's another side of me, though, and that other part loves you, Heidi, and would never wish the slightest harm to come to you. That better part of me also has an intellectual, logical side, and that's why I've left. I need to find that Gypsy, Heidi. I need to find Taduz Lemke and tell him what I've worked out over the last six weeks or so. It's easy to blame, easy to want revenge. But when you look at things closely, you start to see that every event is locked onto every other event; that sometimes things happen just because they happen. None of us like to think that's so, because then we can never strike out at someone to ease the pain; we have to find another way, and none of the other ways are so simple, or so satisfying. I want to tell him that there was no evil intent. I want to ask him if he'll reverse what he's done . . . always assuming it's in his power to do so. But what I want to do more than anything else, I find, is to simply apologize. For me . . . for you . . . for all of Fairview. I know a lot more about Gypsies than I used to, you see. I guess you could say that my eyes have been opened. And I think it's only fair to tell you one more thing, Heidi – if he can reverse it, if I find I have a future to look forward to after all – I will not spend that future in Fairview. I find I've had a bellyful of Andy's Pub, Lantern Drive, the country club, the whole dirty hypocritical town. If I do have that future, I hope you and Linda will come along to some other, cleaner place and share it with me. If you won't, or can't, I'll go anyway. If Lemke won't or can't do anything to help me, I will at least feel that I've done all that I could. Then I can come home, and will happily check into the Glassman Clinic, if that's what you still want.

I encourage you to show this letter to Mike Houston if you want to, or the Glassman doctors. I think they'll agree that what I'm doing may be very good therapy. After all, they'll reason, if he's doing this to himself as a punishment (they keep talking about psychological anorexia nervosa, apparently believing that if you feel guilty enough, you can speed up your metabolism until it's burning umpty-umpty calories a day), facing Lemke may provide exactly the sort of expiation he needs. Or, they'll reason, there are two other possibilities; one, that Lemke will laugh and say he never cast a curse in his life, thereby shattering the psychological fulcrum my obsession is balanced on; or it may occur to them that Lemke will recognize the possibility of profit, lie and agree that he cursed me, and then charge me for some trumpery 'cure'– but, they'll think, a trumpery cure for a trumpery curse might be totally effective!

I've engaged detectives through Kirk Penschley and have determined that the Gypsies have been heading steadily north up Interstate 95. I hope to track them down in Maine. If something definitive happens, I will let you know soonest; in the meantime, I'll try not to try you. But believe I love you with all my heart.

Yours.

Billy

He put the letter in an envelope with Heidi's name scrawled across the front and propped it against the lazy Susan on the kitchen table. Then he called a cab to take him to the Hertz office in Westport. He stood out on the steps waiting for the cab to come, still hoping inside that Heidi would come first and they could talk about the things in the note.

It wasn't until the cab had swung into the driveway and Billy was in the backseat that he admitted to himself that talking to Heidi at this point maybe wasn't such a good idea – being able to talk to Heidi was part of the past, part of the time when he had been living in Fat City . . . in more ways than one, and without even knowing it. That was the past. If there was any future, it was up the turnpike, somewhere in Maine, and he ought to get chasing after it before he melted away to nothing.

CHAPTER SEVENTEEN
137

He stopped that night in Providence. He called the office, got the answering service, and left a message for Kirk Penschley: would he please send all available photographs of the Gypsies and all available particulars on their vehicles, including license-plate numbers and VIN numbers to the Sheraton Hotel in South Portland, Maine?

The service read the message back correctly – a minor miracle, in Billy's opinion – and he turned in. The drive from Fairview to Providence was less than a hundred and fifty miles, but he found himself exhausted. He slept dreamlessly for the first time in weeks. He discovered the following morning that there were no scales in the motel bathroom. Thank God, Billy Halleck thought, for small favors.

He dressed quickly, stopping only once, as he was tying his shoes, perfectly amazed to hear himself whistling. He was headed up the Interstate again by eight-thirty, and was checked into a Sheraton across from a huge shopping mall by six-thirty. A message from Penschley was waiting for him: *Information on its way, but difficult. May take a day or two.*

Great, Billy thought. *Two pounds a day, Kirk, what the hell – three days and I can lose the equivalent of a six-pack of tallboys. Five days and I can lose a medium-size bag of flour. Take your time, fella, why not?*

The South Portland Sheraton was round, and Billy's room was shaped like a pie wedge. His overtaxed mind, which had so far dealt with everything, found it somehow almost impossible to deal with a bedroom that came to a point. He was road-tired and headachy. The restaurant, he thought, was more than he could face . . . especially if it came to a point. He ordered up from room service instead.

He had just stepped out of the shower when the waiter's knock came. He donned the robe which the management had thoughtfully provided (THOU SHALT NOT STEAL, said a little card sticking out of the robe's pocket) and crossed the room, calling out 'Just a second!'

Halleck opened the door . . . and was greeted for the first time with the unpleasant realization of how circus freaks must feel. The waiter was a boy of no more than nineteen, scruffy-haired and hollow-cheeked, as if in imitation of the British punk rockers. No prize himself. He glanced at Billy with the vacant disinterest of a fellow who sees hundreds of men in hotel robes each shift; the disinterest would clear a little when he looked down at the bill to see how much the tip was, but that was all. Then the waiter's eyes widened in a look of startlement which was almost horror. It was only for a moment; then the look of disinterest was back again. But Billy had seen it.

Horror. It was almost horror.

And the expression of startlement was still there – hidden, but still there. Billy thought he could see it now because another element had been added – fascination.

The two of them were frozen for a moment, locked together in the uncomfortable and unwanted partnership of gawker and gawkee. Billy thought dizzily of Duncan Hopley sitting in his pleasant home on Ribbonmaker Lane with all the lights off.

'Well, bring it in,' he said harshly, breaking the moment with too much force. 'You going to stand out there all night?'

'Oh, no, sir,' the room-service waiter said, 'I'm sorry.' Hot blood filled his face, and Billy felt pity for him. He wasn't a punk rocker, not some sinister juvenile delinquent who had come to the circus to see the living crocodiles – he was only a college kid with a summer job who had been surprised by a haggard man who might or might not have some sort of disease.

The old guy cursed me in more ways than one, Billy thought.

It wasn't this kid's fault that Billy Halleck, late of Fairview, Connecticut, had lost enough weight to almost qualify for freak status. He tipped him an extra dollar and got rid of him as quickly as possible. Then he went into the bathroom and looked at himself, slowly spreading his robe open, the archetypal flasher practicing in the privacy of his own room. He had belted the robe loosely to begin with, and it had left most of his chest and some of his belly exposed. It was easy enough to understand the waiter's shock just looking at that much. It became even easier with the robe open and his entire front reflected in the mirror.

Every rib stood out clearly. His collarbones were exquisitely defined ridges covered with skin. His cheekbones bulged. His sternum was a congested knot, his belly a hollow, his pelvis a gruesome hinged wishbone. His legs were much as he remembered them, long and still quite well muscled, the bones still buried – he had never put on much weight there anyway. But above the waist, he really *was* turning into a carny freak – the Human Skeleton

A hundred pounds, he thought. *That's all it takes to bring the hidden ivory man out of the closet. Now you know what a thin edge there is between what you always took for granted and somehow thought would always be and this utter madness. If you ever wondered, now you know. You still look normal – well, fairly normal – with your clothes on, but how long will it be before you start getting looks like the one the waiter gave you even when you're dressed? Next week? The week after?*

His headache was worse, and although he had been

ravenous earlier, he found he could only pick at his dinner. He slept badly and rose early. He did not whistle as he dressed.

He decided Kirk Penschley and the investigators from Barton were right – the Gypsies would stick to the seacoast. During the summer in Maine, that was where the action was because that was where the tourists were. They came to swim in water that was too cold, to sun themselves (many days remained foggy and drizzly, but the tourists never seemed to remember them), to eat lobsters and clams, to buy ashtrays with seagulls painted on them, to attend the summer theaters in Ogunquit and Brunswick, to photograph the lighthouses at Portland and Pemaquid, or just to hang out in trendy places like Rockport, Camden, and, of course, Bar Harbor.

The tourists were along the seacoast, and so were the dollars they were so anxious to roll out of their wallets. That's where the Gypsies would be – but where, exactly?

Billy listed better than fifty seacoast towns, and then went downstairs. The bartender was an import from New Jersey who knew from nothing but Asbury Park, but Billy found a waitress who had lived in Maine all her life, was familiar with the seacoast, and loved to talk about it.

'I'm looking for some people, and I'm fairly sure they'll be in a seacoast town – but not a really ritzy one. More of a . . . a . . .'

'Honk-tonk kind of town?' she asked.

Billy nodded.

She bent over his list. 'Old Orchard Beach,' she said. 'That's the honkiest honky-tonk of them all. The way things are down there until Labor Day, your friends wouldn't get noticed unless they had three heads each.'

'Other ones?'

'Well . . . most of the seacoast towns get a little honky-tonky in the summer,' she said. 'Take Bar Harbor, for instance. Everybody who's ever heard of it has an image of Bar Harbor as real ritzy . . . dignified . . . full of rich people who go around in Rolls-Royces.'

'It's not like that?'

'No. Frenchman's Bay, maybe, but not Bar Harbor. In the winter it's just this dead little town where the ten-twenty-five ferry is the most exciting thing to happen all day. In the summer, Bar Harbor's a crazy town. It's like Fort Lauderdale is during spring break – full of heads and freaks and superannuated hippies. You can stand over the town line in Northeast Harbor, take a deep breath, and get stoned from all the dope in Bar Harbor if the wind's right. And the main drag – until after Labor Day, it's a street carnival. Most of these towns you got on your list are like that, mister, but Bar Harbor is like, top end, you know?'

'I hear you,' Billy said, smiling.

'I used to go up there sometimes in July or August and hang out, but not anymore. I'm too old for that now.'

Billy's smile became wistful. The waitress looked all of twenty-three.

Billy gave her five dollars; she wished him a pleasant summer and good luck finding his friends. Billy nodded, but for the first time he did not feel sanguine about the possibility.

'You mind a little piece of advice, mister?'

'Not at all,' Billy answered, thinking she meant to give him her idea on the best place to start – and *that* much he had already decided for himself.

'You ought to fatten yourself up a little,' she said. 'Eat pasta. That's what my mom would tell you. Eat lots of pasta. Put on a few pounds.'

★

A manila envelope full of photographs and automobile information arrived for Halleck on his third day in South Portland. He shuffled through the photographs slowly, looking at each. Here was the young man who had been juggling the pins; his name was also Lemke, Samuel Lemke. He was looking at the camera with an uncompromising openness that looked as ready for pleasure and friendship as it did anger and sullenness. Here was the pretty young girl who had been setting up the slingshot target-shoot when the cops landed – and yes, she was every bit as lovely as Halleck had surmised from his side of the common. Her name was Angelina Lemke. He put her picture next to the picture of Samuel Lemke. Brother and sister. The grandchildren of Susanna Lemke? he wondered. The great-grandchildren of Taduz Lemke?

Here was the elderly man who had been handing out fliers – Richard Crosskill. Other Crosskills were named. Stanchfields. Starbirds. More Lemkes. And then . . . near the bottom . . .

It was him. The eyes, caught in twin nets of wrinkles, were dark and level and filled with clear intelligence. A kerchief was drawn over his head and knotted beside the left cheek. A cigarette was tucked into the deeply cracked lips. The nose was a wet and open horror, festering and terrible.

Billy stared at the picture as if hypnotized. There was something almost familiar about the old man, some connection his mind wasn't quite making. Then it came to him. Taduz Lemke reminded him of those old men in the Dannon yogurt commercials, the ones from Russian Georgia who smoked unfiltered cigarettes, drank popskull vodka, and lived to such staggering ages as a hundred and thirty, a hundred and fifty, a hundred and seventy. And then a line of a Jerry Jeff Walker song occurred to him, the one about Mr Bojangles: *He looked at me to be the eyes of age . . .*

Yes. That was what he saw in the face of Taduz Lemke

– he was the very eyes of age. In those eyes Billy saw a deep knowledge that made all the twentieth century a shadow, and he trembled.

That night when he stepped on the scales in the bathroom adjoining his wedge-shaped bedroom, he was down to 137.

CHAPTER EIGHTEEN
The Search

Old Orchard Beach, the waitress had said. *That's the honkiest honky-tonk of them all.* The desk clerk agreed.

So did the girl in the tourist-information booth four miles down the highway, although she refused to put it in such blatantly pejorative terms. Billy turned his rental car toward Old Orchard Beach, which was about eighteen miles south.

Traffic slowed to a bumper-to-bumper crawl still a mile from the beach. Most of the vehicles in this parade bore Canadian license plates. A lot of them were thyroidal rec-ves which looked big enough to transport entire football teams. Most of the people Billy saw, both in the crawling traffic and walking along the sides of the road, seemed dressed in the least the law would allow and sometimes less – there were a lot of string bikinis, a lot of ball-hugger swim trunks, a lot of oiled flesh on display.

Billy was dressed in blue jeans, an open-collared white shirt, and a sport coat. He sat behind the wheel of his car and sweltered even with the air conditioning on full. But he hadn't forgotten the way the room-service kid had looked at him. This was as undressed as he was going to get, even if he finished the day with his sneakers full of sweat puddles.

The crawling traffic crossed salt marshes, passed two dozen lobster-and-clam shacks, and then wound through an area of summer houses that were crammed together hip to hip and shoulder to shoulder. Similarly undressed people sat on lawn furniture before most of these houses, eating, reading paperback novels, or simply watching the endless flow of traffic.

Christ, Billy thought, *how do they stand the stink of the exhaust?* It occurred to him that perhaps they liked it, that perhaps that was why they were sitting here instead of on the beach, that it reminded them of home.

Houses gave way to motels with signs reading ON PARLE FRANÇAIS ICI and CANADIAN CURRENCY AT PAR AFTER $250 and WE FEATURE MIDNITE BLUE ON CABLE and 3 MINUTES TO OCEAN BONJOUR A NOS AMIS DE LA BELLE PROVINCE!

The motels gave way to a main drag which seemed to feature mostly cut-rate camera stores, souvenir shops, the dirty-book emporiums. Kids in cut-offs and tank tops idled up and down, some holding hands, some staring into dirty windows with a blank lack of interest, some riding on skateboards and weaving their way through knots of pedestrians with bored élan. To Billy Halleck's fascinated, dismayed eyes, everyone seemed overweight and everyone – even the skateboard kids – seemed to be eating something: a slice of pizza here, a Chipwich there, a bag of Doritos, a bag of popcorn, a cone of cotton candy. He saw a fat man in an untucked white shirt, baggy green Bermudas, and thong sandals gobbling a foot-long dog. A string of something that was either onion or sauerkraut hung from his chin. He held two more dogs between the pudgy fingers of his left hand, and to Billy he looked like a stage magician displaying red rubber balls before making them disappear.

The midway came next. A roller coaster loomed against the sky. A giant replica of a Viking boat swung back and forth in steepening semicircles while the riders strapped inside shrieked. Bells bonged and lights flashed in an arcade to Billy's left; to his right, teenagers in striped muscle shirts drove dodge-'em cars into each other. Just beyond the arcade, a young man and a young woman were kissing. Her arms were locked around his neck. One of his hands cupped her buttocks; the other held a can of Budweiser.

Yeah, Billy thought. *Yeah, this is the place. Got to be.*

He parked his car in a baking macadam lot, paid the attendant seventeen dollars for a half-day stub, transferred his wallet from his hip pocket to the inside pocket of his sport coat, and started hunting.

At first he thought that the weight loss had perhaps speeded up. Everyone was looking at him. The rational part of his mind quickly assured him that it was just because of his clothes, not the way he looked *inside* his clothes.

People would stare at you the same way if you showed up on this boardwalk wearing a swimsuit and a T-shirt in October, Billy. Take it easy. You're just something to look at, and down here there's plenty to look at.

And that was certainly true. Billy saw a fat woman in a black bikini, her deeply tanned skin gleaming with oil. Her gut was prodigal, the flex of the long muscles in her thighs nearly mythic, and strangely exciting. She moved toward the wide sweep of white beach like an ocean liner, her buttocks flexing in wavelike undulations. He saw a grotesquely fat poodle dog, its curls summer-sheared, its tongue – more gray than pink – hanging out listlessly, sitting in the shade of a pizza shack. He saw two fistfights. He saw a huge gull with mottled gray wings and dead black eyes swoop down and snatch a greasy doughboy from the hand of an infant in a stroller.

Beyond all this was the bone-white crescent of Old Orchard beach, its whiteness now almost completely obscured by reclining sunbathers at just past noon on an early-summer day. But both the beach and the Atlantic beyond it seemed somehow reduced and cheapened by the erotic pulses and pauses of the midway – its snarls of people with food drying on their hands and lips and cheeks, the cry of the hucksters ('Guess your weight!' Billy heard from somewhere to his left: 'If I miss by more than five pounds, you win the dollaya choice!'), the thin screeches from the rides, the raucous rock music spilling out of the bars.

Billy suddenly began to feel decidedly unreal – outside of himself, as if he were having one of those *Fate* magazine instances of astral projection. Names – Heidi, Penschley, Linda, Houston – seemed suddenly to ring false and tinny, like names made up on the spur of the moment for a bad story. He had a feeling that he could look behind things and see the lights, the cameras, the key grips, and some unimaginable 'real world.' The smell of the sea seemed overwhelmed by a smell of rotten food and salt. Sounds became distant, as if floating down a very long hallway.

Astral projection, my ass, a dim voice pronounced. *You're getting ready to have sunstroke, my friend.*

That's ridiculous. I never had a sunstroke in my life.

Well, I guess when you lose a hundred and twenty pounds, it really fucks up your thermostat. Now are you going to get out of the sun or are you going to wind up in an emergency room somewhere giving your Blue Cross and Blue Shield number?

'Okay, you talked me into it,' Billy mumbled, and a kid who was passing by and dumping a box of Reese's Pieces into his mouth turned and gave him a sharp look.

There was a bar up ahead called The Seven Seas. There were two signs taped to the door. ICY COOL, read one. TERMINAL HAPPY HOUR, read the other. Billy went in.

The Seven Seas was not only icy cool, it was blessedly quiet. A sign on the juke read *SOME ASSHOLE KICKED ME LAST NIGHT AND NOW I AM OUT OF ORDER.* Below this was a French translation of the same sentiment. But Billy thought from the aged look of the sign and the dust on the juke that the 'last night' in question might have been a good many years ago. There were a few patrons in the bar, mostly older men who were dressed much as Billy himself was dressed – as if for the street rather than the beach. Some were playing checkers and backgammon. Almost all were wearing hats.

'Help you?' the bartender asked, coming over.

'I'd like a Schooner, please.'

'Okay.'

The beer came. Billy drank it slowly, watching the board-walk ebb and flow outside the windows of the bar, listening to the murmur of the old men. He felt some of his strength – some of his sense of *reality* – begin to come back.

The bartender returned. 'Hit you again?'

'Please. And I'd like a word with you, if you have time.'

'About what?'

'Some people who might have been through here.'

'Where's here? The Seas?'

'Old Orchard.'

The bartender laughed. 'So far as I can see, everyone in Maine and half of Canada comes through here in the summer, old son.'

'These were Gypsies.'

The bartender grunted and brought Billy a fresh bottle of Schooner.

'You mean they were drift trade. Everyone who comes to Old Orchard in the summer is. The place here is a little different. Most of the guys who come in here live here year-round. The people out there . . .' He waved at the window, dismissing them with a flick of the wrist. 'Drift trade. Like you, mister.'

Billy poured the Schooner carefully down the side of his glass and then laid a ten-dollar bill on the bar. 'I'm not sure we understand each other. I'm talking about real, actual Gypsies, not tourists or summer people.'

'Real . . . Oh, you must mean those guys who were camped out by the Salt Shack.'

Billy's heart speeded in his chest. 'Can I show you some pictures?'

'Wouldn't do any good. I didn't see them.' He looked at the ten for a moment and then called: 'Lon! Lonnie! Come over here a minute!'

One of the old men who had been sitting by the window got up and shuffled over to the bar. He was wearing gray cotton pants, a white shirt that was too big for him, and a snap-brim straw hat. His face was weary. Only his eyes were alive. He reminded Billy of someone, and after a few moments it came to him. The old man looked like Lee Strasberg, the teacher and actor.

'This is Lon Enders,' the bartender said. 'He's got a little place just on the west of town. Same side the Salt Shack's on. Lon sees everything that goes on in Old Orchard.'

'I'm Bill Halleck.'

'Meet you,' Lon Enders said in a papery voice, and took the stool next to Billy's. He did not really seem to sit; rather, his knees appeared to buckle the moment his buttocks were poised over the cushion.

'Would you like a beer?' Billy asked.

'Can't,' the paper voice rustled, and Billy moved his head slightly to avoid the oversweet smell of Enders' breath. 'Already had my one for the day. Doctor says no more than that. Guts're screwed up. If I was a car, I'd be ready for the scrap heap.'

'Oh,' Billy said lamely.

The bartender turned away from them and began loading beer glasses into a dishwasher. Enders looked at the ten-dollar bill. Then he looked at Billy.

Halleck explained again while Enders' tired, too-shiny face looked dreamily off into the shadows of the Seven Seas and the arcade bells bonged faintly, like sounds overheard in a dream, next door.

'They was here,' he said when Billy had finished. 'They was here, all right. I hadn't seen any Gypsies in seven years or more. Hadn't seen this bunch in maybe twenty years.'

Billy's right hand squeezed the beer glass he was holding, and he had to consciously make himself relax his grip before he broke it. He set the glass down carefully on the bar.

'When? Are you sure? Do you have any idea where they might have been going? Can you –?'

Enders held up one hand – it was as white as the hand of a drowned man pulled from a well, and to Billy it seemed dimly transparent.

'Easy, my friend,' he said in his whispering voice. 'I'll tell you what I know.'

With the same conscious effort, Billy forced himself to say nothing. To just wait.

'I'll take the tenspot because you look like you can afford it, my friend,' Enders whispered. He tucked it into his shirt pocket and then pushed the thumb and forefinger of his left hand into his mouth, adjusting his upper plate. 'But I'd talk for free. Hell, when you get old you find out you'd pay someone to listen . . . ask Timmy there if I can have a glass of cold water, would you? Even the one beer's too much, I reckon – it's burning what's left of my stomach something fierce – but it's hard for a man to give up all his pleasures, even when they don't pleasure him no more.'

Billy called the bartender over, and he brought Enders his ice water.

'You okay, Lon?' he asked as he put it down.

'I been better and I been worse,' Lon whispered, and picked up the glass. For a moment Billy thought it was going to prove too heavy. But the old man got it to his mouth, although some spilled on the way there.

'You want to talk to this guy?' Timmy asked.

The cold water seemed to revive Enders. He put the glass down, looked at Billy, looked back at the bartender. 'I think somebody ought to,' he said. 'He don't look as bad as me yet . . . but he's getting there.'

Enders lived in a small retirees' colony on Cove Road. He said Cove Road was part of 'the real Old Orchard – the one the tips don't care about.'

'Tips?' Billy asked.

'The crowds, my friend, the crowds. Me and the wife come to this town in 1946, just after the war. Been here ever since. I learned how to turn a tip from a master – Lonesome Tommy McGhee, dead these many years now. Yelled my guts out, I did, and what you hear now is all that's left.'

The chuckle, almost as faint as a breath of predawn breeze, came again.

Enders had known everyone associated with the summer carnival that was Old Orchard, it seemed – the vendors, the pitchmen, the roustabouts, the glass-chuckers (souvenir salesmen), the dogsmen (ride mechanics), the bumpers, the carnies, the pumps and the pimps. Most of them were year-round people he had known for decades or people who returned each summer like migratory birds. They formed a stable, mostly loving community that the summer people never saw.

He also knew a large portion of what the bartender had called 'drift trade.' These were the true transients, people who showed up for a week or two weeks, did some business in the feverish party-town atmosphere of Old Orchard, and then moved on again.

'And you remember them *all*?' Billy asked doubtfully.

'Oh, I wouldn't if they was all different from year to year,' Enders whispered, 'but that's not how drift trade is. They ain't as regular as the dogsmen and the dough-thumpers, but they have a pattern too. You see this fellow who comes on the boardwalk in 1957, selling Hula Hoops off'n his arm. You see him again in 1960, selling expensive watches for three bucks apiece. His hair is maybe black instead of blond, and so he thinks people don't recognize him, and I guess the summer people don't, even if they was around in 1957, because they go right back and get rooked again. But we know him. We know the drift trade. Nothing changes but what they sell, and what they sell is always a few steps outside the law.

'The pushers, they're different. There's too many, and they are always going to jail or dying off. And the whores get old too fast to want to remember. But you wanted to talk about Gypsies. I guess they're the oldest drift trade of all, when you stop to think about it.'

Billy took his envelope of photographs from his sport-coat pocket and laid them out carefully like a pat poker hand: Gina Lemke. Samuel Lemke. Richard Crosskill. Maura Starbird.

Taduz Lemke.

'Ah!' The old man on the stool breathed in sharply when Billy put that last one down, and then he spoke directly to the photograph, cooling Billy's skin: 'Teddy, you old whoremaster!'

He looked up at Billy and smiled, but Billy Halleck was not fooled – the old man was afraid.

'I thought it was him,' he said. 'I didn't see nothing but a shape in the dark – this was three weeks ago. Nothing but a shape in the dark, but I thought . . . no, I *knew* . . .'

He fumbled the ice water to his mouth again, spilling more, this time down the front of his shirt. The cold made him gasp.

The bartender came over and favored Billy with a hostile glance. Enders held his hand up absently to show he was all right. Timmy retreated to the dishwasher again. Enders turned the photograph of Taduz Lemke over. Written on the back was Photo taken Attleboro, Mass., mid-May 1983.

'And he hasn't aged a day since I first seen him and his friends here in the summer of 1963,' Enders finished.

They had set up camp behind Herk's Salt Shack Lobster Barn on Route 27. They had stayed four days and four nights. On the fifth morning they were simply gone. Cove Road lay close by, and Enders said he had walked the half-mile the second evening the Gypsies were there (it was hard for Billy to imagine this ghostly man walking around the block, but he let it pass). He wanted to see them, he said, because they reminded him of the old days when a man could run his business if he had a business to run, and John Law stayed out of his way and let him do it.

'I stood there by the side of the road quiet awhile,' he said. 'It was the usual raree and Gypsy turnout – the more things change, the more they stay the same. It used to be all tents and now it's vans and campers and such, but what goes on inside is just the same. A woman telling fortunes. Two, three women selling powders to the ladies . . . two, three men selling powders to the men. I guess they would have stayed longer, but I heard they arranged a dogfight for some rich Canucks and the state cops got wind of it.'

'*Dog*fight!'

'People want to bet, my friend, and drift trade is always willing to arrange the things they want to bet on – that's one of the things drift trade is for. Dogs or roosters with steel spurs or maybe even two men with these itty-bitty sharp knives that look almost like spikes, and each of 'em bites the end of a scarf, and the one who drops his end first is the loser. What the Gypsies call "a fair one." '

Enders was staring at himself in the back bar mirror – at himself and through himself.

'It was like the old days, all right,' he said dreamily. 'I could smell their meat, the way they cure it, and green peppers, and that olive oil they like that smells rancid when it comes out of the can and then sweet when it's been cooked. I could hear them talking their funny language, and this *thud! thud! thud!* that was someone throwing knives at a board. Someone was cooking bread the old way, on hot stones.

'It was like old times, but I wasn't. I felt scared. Well, the Gypsies *always* scared me a little – difference was, back then I would have gone in anyway. Hell, I was a white man, wasn't I? In the old days I would have walked right up to their fire just as big as billy-be-damned and bought a drink or maybe a few joysticks – not just 'cause I wanted a drink or a toke but just in order to get a look around. But the old days made me an old man, my friend, and when an old man is scared, he don't just go on regardless, like he did when he was just learning to shave.

'So I just stood there in the dark with the Salt Shack over on my one side and all those vans and campers and station wagons pulled up over here on my other, watching them walk back and forth in front of their fire, listening to them talk and laugh, smelling their food. And then the back of this one camper opened – it had a picture of a woman on the side, and a white horse with a horn sticking out of its head, a what–do–you–call–it . . .'

'Unicorn,' Billy said, and his voice seemed to come from somewhere or someone else. He knew that camper very well;

he had first seen it on the day the Gypsies came to the Fairview town common.

'Then someone got out,' Enders went on. 'Just a shadow and a red cigarette tip, but I knew who it was.' He tapped the photograph of the man in the kerchief with one pale finger. 'Him. Your pal.'

'You're sure?'

'He took a big drag on his butt and I saw . . . that.' He pointed at what was left of Taduz Lemke's nose but did not quite touch the glossy surface of the photograph, as if touch might be to risk contamination.

'Did you speak to him?'

'No,' Enders said, 'but he spoke to me. I stood there in the dark and I swear to God he wasn't even looking in my *direction*. And he said, "You miss your wife some, Flash, eh? Ess be all right, you be wid her soon now." Then he flicked his cigarette off the end of his fingers and walked away toward the fire. I seen the hoop in his ear flash once in the firelight, and that was all.'

He wiped little beads of water from his chin with the cup of his hand and looked at Billy.

'Flash was what they used to call me when I worked the penny-pitch on the pier back in the fifties, my friend, but nobody has called me that for years. I was way back in the shadows, but he saw me and he called me by my old name – what the Gypsies would call my secret name, I guess. They set a hell of a store by knowing a man's secret name.'

'Do they?' Billy asked, almost to himself.

Timmy, the bartender, came over again. This time he spoke to Billy almost kindly . . . and as though Lon Enders was not there. 'He earned the ten, buddy. Leave 'im alone. He ain't well, and this here little discussion ain't making him no weller.'

'I'm okay, Timmy,' Enders said.

Timmy didn't look at him. He looked at Billy Halleck instead. 'I want you to get out of here,' he said to Billy in that same reasonable, almost kind voice. 'I don't like your looks. You look like bad luck waiting for a place to happen. The beers are free. Just go.'

Billy looked at the bartender, feeling frightened and somehow humbled. 'Okay,' he said. 'Just one more question and I'll go.' He turned to Enders. 'Where did they head for?'

'I don't know,' Enders said at once. 'Gypsies don't leave forwarding addresses, my friend.'

Billy's shoulders slumped.

'But I was up when they pulled out the next morning. I don't sleep worth a shit anymore, and most of their vans and cars didn't have much in the way of mufflers. I seen them go out Highway 27 and turn north onto Route 1. My guess would be . . . Rockland.' The old man fetched in a deep, shuddering sigh that made Billy lean toward him, concerned. 'Rockland or maybe Boothbay Harbor. Yes. And that's all I know, my friend, except that when he called me Flash, when he called me by my secret name, I pissed all the way down my leg into my left tennis shoe.' And Lon Enders abruptly began to cry.

'Mister, would you *leave*?' Timmy asked.

'I'm going,' Billy said, and did, pausing only to squeeze the old man's narrow, almost ethereal shoulder.

Outside, the sun hit him like a hammer. It was midafternoon now, the sun heeling over toward the west, and when he looked to his left he saw his own shadow, as scrawny as a child's stick figure, poured on the hot white sand like ink.

He dialed area code 203.

They set a hell of a store by knowing a man's secret name.

He dialed 555.

I want you to get out of here. I don't like your looks.

He dialed 9231, and listened to the phone begin to ring back home in Fat City.

You look like bad luck waiting –

'Hello?' The voice, expectant and a little breathless, was not Heidi's but Linda's. Lying on his bed in his wedge-shaped hotel room, Billy closed his eyes against the sudden sting of tears. He saw her as she had been on the night he had walked her up Lantern Drive and talked to her about the accident – her old shorts, her long coltish legs.

What are you going to say to her, Billy-boy? That you spent the day at the beach sweating out moisture, that lunch was two beers, and that in spite of a big supper which featured not one but two sirloin steaks, you lost three pounds today instead of the usual two?

'Hello?'

That you're bad luck waiting for a place to happen? That you're sorry you lied, but all parents do it?

'Hello, is anyone there? Is that you, Bobby?'

Eyes still closed, he said: 'It's Dad, Linda.'

'Daddy?'

'Honey, I can't talk,' he said. *Because I'm almost crying.* 'I'm still losing weight, but I think I've found Lemke's trail. Tell your mother that. I think I've found Lemke's trail, will you remember?'

'Daddy, *please* come home!' She was crying. Billy's hand whitened on the telephone. 'I miss you and I'm not going to let *her* send you away anymore.'

Dimly he could hear Heidi now: 'Lin? Is it Dad?'

'I love you, doll,' he said. 'And I love your mother.'

'Daddy –'

A confusion of small sounds. Then Heidi was on the phone. 'Billy? Billy, please stop this and come home to us.'

Billy gently hung the phone up and rolled over on the bed and put his face into his crossed arms.

He checked out of the South Portland Sheraton the next morning and headed north on US 1, the long coastal highway which begins in Fort Kent, Maine, and ends in Key West, Florida. Rockland or maybe Boothbay Harbor, the old man in the Seven Seas had said, but Billy took no chances. He stopped at every second or third gas station on the northbound side of the road; he stopped at general stores where old men sat out front in lawn chairs, chewing toothpicks or wooden matches. He showed his pictures to everyone who would look; he swapped two one-hundred-dollar traveler's checks for two-dollar bills and passed them out like a man promoting a radio show with dubious ratings. The four photographs he showed most frequently were the girl, Gina, with her clear olive skin and her dark, promising eyes; the converted Cadillac hearse; the VW microbus with the girl and the unicorn painted on the side; Taduz Lemke.

Like Lon Enders, people didn't want to handle that one, or even touch it.

But they were helpful, and Billy Halleck had no trouble at all following the Gypsies up the coast. It wasn't the out-of-state plates; there were lots of out-of-state plates to be seen in Maine during the summer. It was the way the cars and vans traveled together, almost bumper to bumper; the colorful pictures on the sides; the Gypsies themselves. Most of the people Billy talked to claimed that the women or children had stolen things, but all seemed vague on just what had been stolen, and no one, so far as Billy could ascertain, had called the cops because of these supposed thefts.

Mostly they remembered the old Gypsy with the rotting

nose – if they had seen him, they remembered him most of all.

Sitting in the Seven Seas with Lon Enders, he had been three weeks behind the Gypsies. The owner of Bob's Speedy-Serv station wasn't able to remember the day he had filled up their cars and trucks and vans, one after another, only that 'they stunk like Injuns.' Billy thought that Bob smelled pretty ripe himself but decided that saying so might be rather imprudent. The college kid working at the Falmouth Beverage Barn across the road from the Speedy-Serv was able to peg the day exactly – it had been June 2, his birthday, and he had been unhappy about working. The day Billy spoke to them was June 20, and he was eighteen days behind. The Gypsies had tried to find a camping place a little farther north in the Brunswick area and had been moved along. On June 4 they had camped in Boothbay Harbor. Not on the seacoast itself, of course, but they had found a farmer willing to rent them a hayfield in the Kenniston Hill area for twenty dollars a night.

They had stayed only three days in the area – the summer season was still only getting under way, and pickings had apparently been slim. The farmer's name was Washburn. When Billy showed him the picture of Taduz Lemke he nodded and blessed himself, quickly and (Billy was convinced of this) unconsciously.

'I never seen an old man move as fast as that one did, and I seen him luggin' more wood stacked up than my sons could carry.' Washburn hesitated and added, 'I didn't like him. It wasn't just his nose. Hell, my own gramps had skin cancer and before it carried him off it had rotted a hole in his cheek the size of an ashtray. You could look right in there and see him chewin' his food. Well, we didn't like *that*, but we still liked *Gramps*, if you see what I mean.' Billy nodded. 'But this guy . . . I didn't like him. I thought he looked like a bugger.'

Billy thought to ask for a translation of that particular New Englandism, and then decided he didn't need one. *Bugger, bugbear, bogeyman*. The translation was in Farmer Washburn's eyes.

'He *is* a bugger,' Billy said with great sincerity.

'I had made up my mind to send 'em down the road,' he told Billy. 'Twenty bucks a night just for cleaning up some litter is a good piece of wages, but the wife was scairt of them and I was a little bit scairt of them too. So I went out that morning to give that Lemke guy the news before I could lose m'nerve, and they was already on the roll. Relieved me quite a bit.'

'They headed north again.'

'Ayuh, they sure did. I stood right on top of the hill there' – he pointed – 'and watched 'em turn into US 1. I watched 'em until they was right out of sight, and I was some glad to see 'em go.'

'Yes. I'll bet you were.'

Washburn cast a critical, rather worried eye on Billy. 'You want to come up to the house and have a glass of cold buttermilk, mister? You look peaked.'

'Thank you, but I want to get up around the Owl's Head area before sundown if I can.'

'Looking for him?'

'Yes.'

'Well, if you find him, I hope he don't eat you up, mister, because he looked hungry to me.'

Billy spoke to Washburn on the twenty-first – the first day of official summer, although the roads were already choked with tourists and he had to go all the way inland to Sheepscot before he was able to find a motel with a vacancy sign – and the Gypsies had rolled out of Boothbay Harbor on the morning of the eighth.

Thirteen days behind now.

He had a bad two days then when it seemed the Gypsies had fallen off the edge of the world. They had not been seen in Owl's Head, nor in Rockland, although both of them were prime summer tourist towns. Gas-station attendants and waitresses looked at his pictures and shook their heads.

Grimly battling an urge to vomit precious calories over the rail – he had never been much of a sailor – Billy rode the inter-island ferry from Owl's Head to Vinalhaven, but the Gypsies had not been there either.

On the evening of the twenty-third he called Kirk Penschley, hoping for fresh information, and when Kirk came on the line there was a funny double click just at the moment Kirk asked: 'How are you, Billy-boy? And *where* are you?'

Billy hung up quickly, sweating. He had snagged the final unit in Rockland's Harborview Motel, he knew there probably wasn't another motel unit to be had between here and Bangor, but he suddenly decided he was going to move on even if it meant he ended up spending the night sleeping in the car on some pasture road. That double click. He hadn't cared for that double click at all. You sometimes heard that sound when the wire was being tapped, or when trace-back equipment was being used.

Heidi's signed the papers on you, Billy.

That's the stupidest goddamn thing I ever heard.

She signed them and Houston co-signed them.

Give me a fucking break!

Get out of here, Billy.

He left. Heidi, Houston, and possible trace-back equipment aside, it turned out to be the best thing that he could have done. As he was checking into the Bangor Ramada Inn that morning at two o'clock, he showed the desk clerk the pictures – it had become a habit by now – and the clerk nodded at once.

'Yeah, I took my girl over and got her fortune read,' he said. He picked up the photograph of Gina Lemke and rolled his eyes. 'She could really work it on out with that slingshot of hers. And she looked like she would work it on out in a few other ways, if you know what I mean.' He shook his hand as if flicking water from the tips of his fingers. 'My girl got one look at the way I was lookin' at her and she dragged me out of there fast.' He laughed.

A moment before, Billy had been so tired that bed was all he could think about. Now he was wide-awake again, his stomach cramping with adrenaline.

'Where? Where were they? Or are they still –?'

'Nah, they're not there anymore. Parsons' is where they were, but they're gone, all right. I was by there the other day.'

'Is it a farmers' place?'

'No – it's where Parsons' Bargain Barn used to be until it burned down last year.' He cast an uneasy eye at the way Billy's sweatshirt bagged on his body, at the blades of Billy's cheekbones and the skull-like contours of Billy's face, in which the eyes burned like candleflames. 'Uh . . . you want to check in?'

Billy found Parsons' Bargain Barn the following morning – it was a scorched cinder-block shell in the middle of what seemed to be nine acres of deserted parking lot. He walked slowly across the crumbling macadam, heels clicking. Here were beer cans and soda cans. Here was a rind of cheese with beetles crawling in it. Here was a single shiny ball bearing. ('Hoy, Gina!' a ghostly voice called in his head).

Here were the dead skins of popped balloons and here were the dead skins of two used Trojans, so similar to the balloons.

Yes, they had been here.

'I smell you, old man,' Billy whispered to the empty hull of the Bargain Barn, and the empty spaces that had been windows seemed to stare back at this scrawny scarecrow-man with sallow distaste. The place looked haunted, but Billy felt no fear. The anger was back on him – he wore it like a coat. Anger at Heidi, anger at Taduz Lemke, anger at so-called friends like Kirk Penschley who were supposed to be on his side but who had turned against him. Had, or would.

It didn't matter. Even on his own, even at a hundred and thirty pounds, there was enough of him left to catch up to the old Gypsy man.

And what would happen then?

Well, they would see, wouldn't they?

'I smell you, old man,' Billy said again, and walked up to the side of the building. There was a realtor's sign there. Billy took his notebook from his back pocket and jotted down the information on it.

The realtor's name was Frank Quigley, but he insisted that Billy call him Biff. There were framed pictures of a high-school-age Biff Quigley on the walls. In most of them Biff was wearing a football helmet. On Biff's desk was a pile of bronzed dog turds, FRENCHMAN'S DRIVER'S LICENSE, the little sign beneath read.

Yes, Biff said, he had rented the space to the old Gyp with Mr Parsons' approval. 'He figured it couldn't look any worse than it does right now,' Biff Quigley said, 'and I guess he was right, at that.'

He leaned back in his swivel chair, his eyes crawling ceaselessly over Billy's face, measuring the gap between Billy's collar and Billy's neck, the way the front of Billy's shirt hung in folds like a flag on a still day. He laced his hands behind his head, rocked back in his office chair, and put his feet up on his desk beside the bronzed turds.

'Not that it isn't priced to sell, you understand. That's prime industrial land out there, and sooner or later someone with some vision is going to make himself one *hell* of a deal. Yessir, one *hell* of a –'

'When did the Gypsies leave, Biff?'

Biff Quigley removed his hands from behind his head and sat forward. His chair made a noise like a mechanical pig – *Squoink!* 'Mind telling me why you want to know?'

Billy Halleck's lips – they were thinner too now, and higher, so that they never quite met – drew back in a grin of frightening intensity and unearthly boniness. 'Yes, Biff, I mind.'

Biff recoiled for a moment, and then he nodded and leaned back in his chair again. His Quoddy mocs came down on his desk again. One crossed over the other and tapped thoughtfully at the turds.

'That's fine, Bill. A man's business ought to be his own. A man's *reasons* ought to be his own.'

'Good,' Billy said. He felt the rage coming back and was grappling with it. Getting mad at this disgusting man with his Quoddy mocs and his crude ethnic slurs and his blow-dried Jay-Cees haircut wasn't going to do him any good. 'Then since we agree –'

'But it's still going to cost you two hundred bucks.'

'What?' Billy's mouth dropped open. For a moment his anger was so great he was simply unable to move at all or to say anything else. This was probably just as well for Biff Quigley, because if Billy could have moved, Billy would have leapt upon him. His self-control had also lost quite a bit of weight over the last two months.

'Not the information I give you,' Biff Quigley said. 'That's a freebie. The two hundred's for the information I *won't* give them.'

'Won't . . . give . . . who?' Billy managed.

'Your wife,' Biff said, 'and your doctor, and a man who says he works for an outfit called Barton Detective Services.'

Billy saw everything in a flash. Things weren't as bad as his paranoid mind had imagined; they were even worse. Heidi and Mike Houston had gone to Kirk Penschley and had convinced him that Billy Halleck was mad. Penschley was still using the Barton agency to track the Gypsies, but now they were all like astronomers looking for Saturn only so they could study Titan – or bring Titan back to the Glassman Clinic.

He could also see the Barton operative who had sat in this chair a few days ago, talking to Biff Quigley, telling him that a very skinny man named Bill Halleck was going to show up soon, and when he did, this was the number to call.

This was followed by an even clearer vision: he saw himself leaping across Biff Quigley's desk, seizing the bronzed pile of dog turds in mid-leap, and then bashing Biff Quigley's head in with them. He saw this in utter, savage clarity: the skin breaking, the blood flying up in a fine spray of droplets (some of them splashing on the framed pictures), the white glimmer of bone shattering to reveal the physical texture of the man's creepy mind; then he saw himself slamming the dog turds back where they belonged – where, in a manner of speaking, they had come from.

Quigley must have seen this – or some of it – on Billy's haggard face, for an expression of alarm appeared on his own face. He hurriedly removed his feet from his desk and his hands from behind his neck. The chair emitted its mechanical pig squeal again.

'Now, we could talk this over . . .' he began, and Billy saw one manicured hand straying toward the intercom.

Billy's anger abruptly deflated, leaving him shaken and cold. He had just visualized beating the man's brains out, not in any vague way but in the mental equivalent of Technicolor and Dolby sound. And good old Biff had known he was doing it, too.

Whatever happened to the old Bill Halleck who used to give to the United Fund and make wassail on Christmas Eve?

His mind returned: *Yeah, that was the Billy Halleck that lived in Fat City. He moved. Gone, no forwarding.*

'No need for that,' Billy said, nodding at the intercom.

The hand jerked, then diverted to a desk drawer, as if that had been its objective all the time. Biff brought out a pack of cigarettes.

'Wasn't even thinking of it, ha-ha. Smoke, Mr Halleck?'

Billy took one, looked at it, and then leaned forward to get a light. One drag and he was light-headed. 'Thanks.'

'About the two hundred, maybe I was wrong.'

'No – you were right,' Billy said. He had cashed three hundred dollars' worth of traveler's checks on his way over here, thinking it might be necessary to grease the skids a little – but it had never occurred to him that he might have to grease them for such a reason as this. He took out his wallet, removed four fifties, and tossed them onto Biff's desk beside the dog turds. 'You'll keep your mouth shut when Penschley calls you?'

'Oh, yes, sir!' Biff took the money and put it into the drawer with the cigarettes. 'You know it!'

'I hope I do,' Billy said. 'Now, tell me about the Gypsies.'

It was short and easy to follow; the only really complicated part had been the preliminaries. The Gypsies had arrived in Bangor on June 10. Samuel Lemke, the young juggler, and a man who answered the description of Richard Crosskill

had come to Biff's office. After a call to Mr Parsons and one
to the Bangor chief of police, Richard Crosskill had signed
a standard short-term-renewable lease form – the short term
in this case was specified to be twenty-four hours. Crosskill
signed as secretary of the Taduz Corporation while young
Lemke stood by the door of Biff's office with his muscular
arms crossed.

'And just how much silver did they cross your palm with?'
Billy asked.

Biff raised his eyebrows. 'Beg your pardon?'

'You got two hundred from me, probably a hundred from
my concerned wife and friends via the Barton op who visited
you – I just wondered how much the Gypsies coughed up.
You've done pretty well out of this any way you cut it,
haven't you, Biff?'

Biff said nothing for a moment. Then, without answering
Billy's question, he finished his story.

Crosskill had come back on the two following days to
resign the lease agreement. On the thirteenth he arrived
again, but by then Biff had had a call from the chief of police
and from Parsons. The complaints from the local citizenry
had begun. The chief thought it was time for the Gypsies to
move on. Parsons thought the same, but he would be willing
to let them stay another day or so if they wanted to up the
ante a bit – say, from thirty bucks a night to fifty.

Crosskill listened to this and shook his head. He left without speaking. On a whim, Biff had driven out to the burned-
out shell of the Bargain Barn that noon. He was in time to
see the Gypsy caravan pulling out.

'They headed for the Chamberlain Bridge,' he said, 'and
that's all I know. Why don't you get out of here now, Bill?
To be honest, you look like an advertisement for a vacation
in Biafra. Looking at you sort of gives me the creeps.'

Billy was still holding the cigarette, although he hadn't

taken a puff since the first drag. Now he leaned forward and butted it on the bronze dog turds. It fell smoldering to Biff's desk. 'To be honest,' he said to Biff, 'I feel exactly the same way about you.'

The rage was back on him. He walked quickly out of Biff Quigley's office before it could move him in the wrong direction or make his hands speak in some terrible language they seemed to know.

It was the twenty-fourth of June. The Gypsies had left Bangor via the Chamberlain Bridge on the thirteenth. Now he was only eleven days behind. Closer . . . closer, but still too far.

He discovered that Route 15, which began on the Brewer side of the bridge, was known as the Bar Harbor Road. It looked as if he might be going there after all. But along the way he would speak to no more realtors and stay at no more first-class motels. If the Barton people were still ahead of him, Kirk might well have put more people on the lookout for him.

The Gypsies had driven the forty-four miles to Ellsworth on the thirteenth, and had been granted a permit to camp on the fairgrounds for three days. Then they had crossed the Penobscot River to Bucksport, where they had stayed another three days before moving on toward the coast again.

Billy discovered all of this on the twenty-fifth; the Gypsies had left Bucksport late on the afternoon of June 19.

Now he was only a week behind them.

Bar Harbor was as crazily booming as the waitress had told him it would be, and Billy thought she had also at least suggested some of the resort town's essential wrongness. *The main drag . . . until after Labor Day, it's a street carnival. Most of these towns are like that, but Bar Harbor is like, top end, you know? . . . I used to go up there sometimes in July or August and hang out, but not anymore. I'm too old for that now.*

Me too, Billy thought, sitting on a park bench in cotton pants, a T-shirt which read BANGOR'S GOT SOUL, and a sport coat that hung straight down from the bony rack of his shoulders. He was eating an ice-cream cone and drawing too many glances.

He was tired – he was alarmed to find that he was *always* tired now, unless he was in the grip of one of his rages. When he parked the car and got out this morning to begin flashing the pictures, he had experienced a moment of nightmarish *déjà vu* as his pants began to slide down his hips – *excusez-moi,* he thought, *as they slid down my non-hips.* The pants were corduroys he had bought in the Rockland army-navy store. They had a twenty-eight-inch waist. The clerk had told him (a little nervously) that he was going to run into trouble buying off-the-rack pants pretty soon, because he was almost into the boy waist sizes now. His leg size, however, was still thirty-two, and there just weren't that many thirteen-year-olds who stood six feet, two inches tall.

Now he sat eating a pistachio ice-cream cone, waiting for some of his strength to come back and trying to decide what was so distressing about this beautiful little town where you couldn't park your car and where you could barely walk on the sidewalks.

Old Orchard had been vulgar, but its vulgarity had been straightforward and somehow exhilarating; you knew the prizes to be won in the Pitch-Til-U-Win booths were junk that would fall apart immediately, that the souvenirs were junk that would fall apart at almost the exact moment you got too far away to turn around and go back and bitch until they gave you your money back. In Old Orchard many of the women were old, and almost all of them were fat. Some wore obscenely small bikinis but most wore tank suits that seemed relics of the 1950's – you felt, passing these jiggling women on the boardwalk, that those suits were under the same terrible pressures as a submarine cruising far below her rated depth. If any of that iridescent miracle fabric gave way, fat would fly.

The smells in the air had been pizza, ice cream, frying onions, every now and then the nervous vomit of some little kid who had stayed on the Tilt-A-Whirl too long. Most of the cars which cruised slowly up and down in the bumper-to-bumper Old Orchard traffic had been old, rusty around the bottoms of the doors, and usually too big. Many of them had been blowing oil.

Old Orchard had been vulgar, but it had also had a certain peeling innocence that seemed missing in Bar Harbor.

Here so many things were the exact reverse of Old Orchard that Billy felt a little as if he had stepped through the looking glass – there were few old women and apparently no fat women; hardly any women wearing bathing suits. The Bar Harbor uniform seemed to be tennis dress and white sneakers or faded jeans, rugby shirts, and boatniks. Billy saw few old cars and even fewer American cars. Most were Saabs, Volvos, Datsuns, BMW's, Hondas. All of them had bumper stickers saying things like SPLIT WOOD, NOT ATOMS and U.S. OUT OF EL SALVADOR and LEGALIZE THE WEED. The bike people were here too – they wove in and out of the slowly moving downtown throngs on expensive tenspeeds, wearing polarized sunglasses and sun visors, flashing their orthodontically perfect smiles and listening to Sony Walkmen. Below town, in the harbor itself, a forest of masts grew – not the thick, dull-colored masts of working boats, but the slim white ones of sailboats that would be drydocked after Labor Day.

The people hanging out in Bar Harbor were young,

brainy, fashionably liberal, and rich. They also partied all night long, apparently. Billy had phoned ahead to make a reservation at the Frenchman's Bay Motel and had lain awake until the small hours of the morning listening to conflicting rock music pouring from six or eight different bars. The tally of wrecked cars and traffic violations – mostly DWI's – in the local paper was impressive and a little disheartening.

Billy watched a Frisbee flying over the crowds in their preppy clothes and thought: *You want to know why this place and these people depress you? I'll tell you. They are studying to live in places like Fairview, that's why. They'll finish school, get married to women who will conclude their first affairs and rounds of analysis at roughly the same time, and settle down on the Lantern Drives of America. There they will wear red pants when they play golf, and each and every New Year's Eve will be the occasion of much tit-grabbing.*

'Yeah, that's depressing, all right,' he muttered, and a couple passing by looked at him strangely.

They're still here.

Yes. They were still here. The thought was so natural, so positive, that it was neither surprising nor particularly exciting. He had been a week behind them – they could be up in the Maritimes by now or halfway down the coast again; their previous pattern suggested they would be gone by now, and certainly Bar Harbor, where even the souvenir shops looked like expensive East Side auction rooms, was a little too tony to put up with a raggle-taggle band of Gypsies for long. All very true. Except they were still here, and he knew it.

'Old man, I smell you,' he whispered.

Of course you smell him. You are supposed *to.*

That thought caused a moment's unease. Then he got up, tossed the remainder of his cone into a trash barrel, and walked back to the ice-cream vendor. The vendor did not seem particularly pleased to see Billy returning.

'I wonder if you could help me,' Billy said.

'No, man, I really don't think so,' the vendor said, and Billy saw the revulsion in his eyes.

'You might be surprised.' Billy felt a sense of deep calm and predestination – not *déjà vu* but real predestination. The ice-cream vendor wanted to turn away, but Billy held him with his own eyes – he found he was capable of that now, as if he himself had become some sort of supernatural creature. He took out the packet of photographs – it was now rumpled and sweat-stained. He dealt out the familiar tarot hand of images, lining them up along the counter of the man's booth.

The vendor looked at them, and Billy felt no surprise at the recognition in the man's eyes, no pleasure – only that faint fear, like pain waiting to happen when the local anesthetic wears off. There was a clear salt tang in the air, and gulls were crying over the harbor.

'*This* guy,' the ice-cream vendor said, staring fascinated at the photograph of Taduz Lemke. '*This* guy – what a spook!'

'Are they still around?'

'Yeah,' the ice-cream vendor said. 'Yeah, I think they are. The cops kicked 'em out of town the second day, but they were able to rent a field from a farmer in Tecknor – that's one town inland from here. I've seen them around. The cops have gotten to the point where they're writing 'em up for broken taillights and stuff like that. You'd think they'd take the hint.'

'Thank you.' He began to collect his pictures again.

'You want another ice cream?'

'No, thank you.' The fear was stronger now – but the

anger was there too, a buzzing, pulsing tone under everything else.

'Then would you mind just sort of rambling on, mister? You're not particularly good for business.'

'No,' Billy said. 'I suppose I'm not.'

He headed back toward his car. The tiredness had left him.

That night at a quarter past nine, Billy parked his rental car on the soft shoulder of Route 37-A, which leaves Bar Harbor to the northwest. He was on top of a hill, and a sea breeze blew around him, ruffling his hair and making his loose clothes flap on his body. From behind him, carried on that breeze, came the sound of tonight's rock-'n-roll party starting to crank up in Bar Harbor.

Below him, to the right, he could see a large campfire surrounded by cars and trucks and vans. Closer in were the people – every now and then one of them strolled in front of the fire, a black cardboard cutout. He could hear conversation, occasional laughter.

He had caught up.

The old man is down there waiting for you, Billy – he knows you're here.

Yes. Yes, of course. The old man could have pulled his little band right off the edge of the world – at least, as far as Billy Halleck would have been able to tell – if he had wanted. But that hadn't been his pleasure. Instead he had taken Billy over the jumps from Old Orchard to here. *That* had been what he wanted.

The fear again, drifting like smoke through his hollow places – there were so many hollow places in him now, it seemed. But the rage was still there too.

It's what I wanted too – and I may just surprise him. The fear

204

I'm sure he expects. The anger . . . that may be a surprise.

Billy looked back at the car for a moment, then shook his head. He started down the grassy side of the hill toward the fire.

CHAPTER NINETEEN
In the Camp of the Gypsies

He paused in back of the camper with the unicorn and the maiden on the side, a narrow shadow among other shadows, but more constant than those thrown by the shifting flames. He stood there listening to their quiet conversation, the occasional burst of laughter, the pop of an exploding knot in the fire.

I can't go out there, his mind insisted with utter certainty. There was fear in this certainty, but also intertwined in it were inarticulate feelings of shame and propriety – he no more wanted to break into the concentric circles of their campfire and their talk and their privacy than he had wanted to have his pants fall down in Hilmer Boynton's courtroom. He, after all, was the offender. He was . . .

Then Linda's face rose up in his mind; he heard her asking him to come home, and beginning to cry as she did.

He was the offender, yes, but he was not the only one.

The rage began to come up in him again. He clamped down on it, tried to compress it, to turn it into something a little more useful – simple sternness would be enough, he thought. Then he walked between the camper and the station wagon parked next to it, his Gucci loafers whispering in the dry timothy grass, and into their midst.

There really were concentric circles: first the rough circle of vehicles, and inside that, a circle of men and women sitting around the fire, which burned in a dug hollow surrounded by a circle of stones. Nearby, a cut branch about six feet tall had been stuck into the earth. A yellow sheet of paper – a campfire permit, Billy supposed – was impaled on its tip.

The younger men and women sat on the flattened grass or on air mattresses. Many of the older people were sitting on lawn chairs made of tubular aluminum and woven plastic strips. Billy saw one old woman sitting propped up on pillows in a lounger, a blanket tucked around her. She was smoking a home-rolled cigarette and sticking S&H Green Stamps in a trading-stamp book.

Three dogs on the far side of the fire began to bark half-heartedly. One of the younger men looked up sharply and drew back one side of his vest, revealing a nickel-plated revolver in a shoulder holster.

'Enkelt!' one of the older men said sharply, putting his hand on the young man's hand.

'Bodde har?'

'Just det – han och Taduz!'

The young man looked toward Billy Halleck, who now stood in the midst of them, totally out of place in his baggy sport coat and city shoes. There was a look not of fear but momentary surprise and – Billy would have sworn it – compassion on his face. Then he was gone, pausing only long enough to administer a kick to one of the hounds and growl, *'Enkelt!'* The hound yipped once and then they all shut up.

Gone to get the old man, Billy thought.

He looked around at them. All conversation had ceased. They regarded him with their dark Gypsy eyes and no one said a word. *This is how it feels when your pants really do fall down in court,* he thought, but that wasn't a bit true. Now that he was actually in front of them, the complexity of his emotions had disappeared. The fear was there, and the anger, but both idled quietly, somewhere deep inside.

And there's something else. They're not surprised to see you . . . and they're not surprised at how you look, either.

Then it was true; all true. No psychological anorexia; no exotic form of cancer. Billy thought that even Michael Houston would have been convinced by those dark eyes. They knew what had happened to him. They knew why it was happening. And they knew how it would end.

They stared at each other, the Gypsies and the thin man from Fairview, Connecticut. And suddenly, for no reason at all, Billy began to grin.

The old woman with the trading stamps moaned and forked the sign of the evil eye at him.

Approaching footsteps and a young woman's voice, speaking rapidly and angrily: '*Vad sa han! Och plotsligt brast han dybbuk, Papa! Alskling, grat inte! Snalla dybbuk! Ta mig Mamma!*'

Taduz Lemke, dressed in a nightshirt which fell to his bony knees, stepped barefoot into the light of the campfire. Next to him, wearing a cotton nightgown that rounded sweetly against her hips as she walked, was Gina Lemke.

'*Ta mig Mamma! Ta mig —*' She caught sight of Billy standing in the center of the circle, his sport coat hanging, the seat of his pants bagging to almost below the coat's hem. She flung a hand up in his direction and then turned back to the old man as if to attack him. The others watched in silent impassivity. Another knot exploded in the fire. Sparks spiraled up in a tiny cyclone.

'*Ta mig Mamma! Va dybbuk! Ta mig inte till mormor! Ordo! Vu'derlak!*'

'*Sa hon lagt, Gina,*' the old man replied. His face and voice were both serene. One of his twisted hands stroked the smooth black flood of her hair, which fell to her waist.

So far Taduz Lemke had not looked at Billy at all. '*Vi ska stanna.*'

For a moment she sagged, and in spite of the lush curves she seemed very young to Billy. Then she wheeled toward him again, her face rekindling. It was as if someone had thrown a shot of gasoline onto a dying fire.

'*You don't understand our lingo, mister?*' she screamed at him. 'I say to my old-papa that you killed my old-mamma! I say you are a demon and we should kill you!'

The old man put a hand on her arm. She shook it free and rushed at Billy, barely skirting the campfire on flying bare feet. Her hair streamed out behind her.

'*Gina, verkligen glad!*' someone cried, alarmed, but no one else spoke. The old man's serene expression did not change; he watched Gina approach Billy as an indulgent parent watches a wayward child.

She spat on him – an enormous amount of warm white spittle, as if her mouth had been full of it. Billy could taste some of it on his lips. It tasted like tears. She looked up at him with her enormous dark eyes, and in spite of all that had happened, in spite of how much he had lost of himself, he was aware that he still wanted her. And she knew it too, he realized – the darkness in her eyes was mostly contempt.

'If it would bring her back, you could spit on me until I drowned in it,' he said. His voice was surprisingly clear and strong. 'But I'm not a *dybbuk*. Not a *dybbuk*, not a demon, not a monster. What you see . . .' He raised his arms and for a moment the firelight shone through his coat, making him look like a large but very malnourished white bat. He slowly lowered his hands to his sides again, '. . . is all that I am.'

For a moment she looked uncertain, almost fearful. Although her spittle was still trickling down his face, the contempt had left her eyes and Billy was wearily grateful for that.

'Gina!' It was Samuel Lemke, the juggler. He had appeared beside the old man and was still buckling his pants. He wore a T-shirt with a picture of Bruce Springsteen on it. '*Enkelt men tillrackligt!*'

'You are a murdering bastard,' she said to Billy, and walked back the way she had come. Her brother attempted to put an arm around her, but she shook him off and disappeared into the shadows. The old man turned to watch her go, and then at last he turned his gaze on Billy Halleck.

For a moment Billy stared at the festering hole in the middle of Lemke's face, and then his eyes were drawn to the man's eyes. The eyes of age, had he thought? They were something more than that ... and something less. It was emptiness he saw in them; it was emptiness which was their fundamental truth, not the surface awareness that gleamed on them like moonlight on dark water. Emptiness as deep and complete as the spaces which may lie between galaxies.

Lemke crooked a finger at Billy, and as if in a dream, Billy walked slowly around the campfire to where the old man stood in his dark gray nightshirt.

'Do you know Rom?' Lemke asked when Billy stood directly in front of him. His tone was almost intimate, but it carried clearly in the silent camp, where the only sound was the fire eating into dry wood.

Billy shook his head.

'In Rom we call you *skummade igenom*, which means "white man from town."'

He grinned, showing rotted tobacco-stained teeth. The dark hole where his nose had been stretched and writhed.

'But it also means how it sounds – *ignorant scum*.' Now his eyes finally let Billy's eyes go; Lemke seemed to lose all interest. 'Go on now, white man from town. You have no business with us, and we have no business with you. If we had business, it is done. Go back to your town.'

He began to turn away.

For a moment Billy only stood there with his mouth open, dimly realizing that the old man had hypnotized him – he had done it as easily as a farmer makes a chicken go to sleep by tucking its head under its wing.

That's IT? part of him suddenly screamed. *All of the driving, all of the walking, all of the questions, all of the bad dreams, all of the days and nights, and that's IT? You're just going to stand here without saying a word? Just let him call you ignorant scum and then go back to bed?*

'No, that is not *it*,' Billy said in a rough, loud voice.

Someone drew in a harsh, surprised breath. Samuel Lemke, who had been helping the old man toward the back of one of the campers, looked around, startled. After a moment Lemke himself turned around. His face was wearily amused, but Billy thought for just a moment, just as the firelight touched his face, he had seen surprise there as well.

Nearby, the young man who had first seen Billy reached under his vest again to where his revolver hung.

'She's very beautiful,' Billy said. 'Gina.'

'Shut up, white man from town,' Samuel Lemke said. 'I don't want to hear my sister's name come oud your mout.'

Billy ignored him. He looked at Lemke instead. 'Is she your granddaughter? Great-granddaughter?'

The old man studied him as if trying to decide whether or not something might be here after all – some sound other than the wind in a hollow ground. Then he began to turn away again.

'Perhaps you'd wait just a minute while I write down my own daughter's address,' Billy said, raising his voice. He did not raise it much; he did not need to in order to bring out its imperative edge, an edge he had honed in a good many courtrooms. 'She's not as lovely as your Gina, but we think she's very pretty. Perhaps they could correspond on the subject of injustice. What do you think, Lemke? Will they be able to talk about that after I'm as dead as your daughter? Who is able to finally sort out where an injustice really lay? Children? Grandchildren? Just a minute, I'll write down the address. It'll only take a second; I'll put it on the back of a photograph I have of you. If they can't figure this mess out, maybe they can get together someday and shoot each other and then *their* kids can give it a try. What do you think, old man . . . does that make any more sense than this shit?'

Samuel put an arm on Lemke's shoulder. Lemke shook it off and walked slowly back to where Billy stood. Now Lemke's eyes were filled with tears of fury. His knotted hands slowly opened and closed. All the others watched, silent and frightened.

'You run my daught' over in the road, white man,' he said. 'You run my daught' over in the road and then you have . . . you are *borjade rulla* enough to come here and speak out of your mout to my ear. Hey, I know who done what. I taken care of it. Mostly we turn and we drive out of town. Mostly, yeah, we do dat. But sometimes we get our justice.' The old man raised his gnarled hand in front of Billy's eyes. Suddenly it snapped into a closed fist. A moment later blood began to drip from it. From the others came a mutter not of fear or surprise but approval. '*Rom* justice, *skummade igenom*. The other two I take care of already. The judge, he jump out of a window two nights ago. He is . . .' Taduz Lemke snapped his fingers and then blew on the ball of his thumb as if it were a seedling dandelion.

'Did that bring your daughter back, Mr Lemke? Did she come back when Cary Rossington hit the ground out there in Minnesota?'

Lemke's lips twisted. 'I don't need her back. Justice ain't bringing the dead back, white man. Justice is justice. You want to get out of here before I fix you wit something else.

I know what you and your woman were up to. You think
I doan have the sight? I got the sight. You ask any of them.
I got the sight a hundred years.'

There was an assenting murmur from those around the
fire.

'I don't care how long you've had the sight,' Billy said. He
reached out deliberately and grasped the old man's shoulders.
From somewhere there was a growl of rage. Samuel Lemke
started forward. Taduz Lemke turned his head and spat a
single word in Romany. The younger man stopped, uncertain
and confused. There were similar expressions on many of
the faces around the campfire, but Billy did not see this; he
saw only Lemke. He leaned toward him, closer and closer,
until his nose almost touched the wrinkled, spongy mess that
was all that remained of Lemke's nose.

'Fuck your justice,' he said. 'You know about as much
about justice as I know about jet turbines. Take it off me.'

Lemke's eyes stared up into Billy's – that horrible emptiness just below the intelligence. 'Let go of me or I'll make
it worse,' he said calmly. 'So much worse you think I blessed
you the first time.'

The grin suddenly broke on Billy's face – the bony grin
which looked like a crescent moon that had been pushed
over on its back. 'Go ahead,' he said. 'Try. But you know,
I don't think you can.'

The old man stared at him wordlessly.

'Because I helped do it to myself,' Billy said. 'They were
right about that much, anyway – it's a partnership, isn't it?
The cursed and the one who does the cursing. We were all
in it with you together. Hopley, Rossington, and me. But I
am opting out, old man. My wife was jerking me off in my
big old expensive car, right, and your daughter came out
between two parked cars in the middle of the block like any
ordinary jaywalker, and that's right, too. If she had crossed

at the corner she would be alive now. There was fault on both sides, but she's dead and I can never go back to what my life was before. It balances. Not the best balance in the history of the world, maybe, but it balances. They've got a way of saying it in Las Vegas – they call it a push. This is a push, old man. Let it end here.'

A strange and almost alien fear had arisen in Lemke's eyes when Billy began to smile, but now his anger, stony and obdurate, replaced it. 'I *never* take it off, white man from town,' Taduz Lemke said. 'I die widdit in my mout.'

Billy slowly brought his face down on Lemke's until their foreheads touched and he could smell the old man's odor – it was the smell of cobwebs and tobacco and dim urine. 'Then make it worse. Go ahead. Make it – how did you say? – like you blessed me the first time.'

Lemke looked at him for a moment longer, and now Billy sensed it was Lemke who was the one caught. Then suddenly Lemke turned his head to Samuel.

'Enkelt av lakan och kanske alskade! Just det!'

Samuel Lemke and the young man with the pistol under his vest tore Billy away from Taduz Lemke. The old man's shallow chest rose and fell rapidly; his scant hair was disarrayed.

He's not used to being touched – not used to being spoken to in anger.

'It's a push,' Billy said as they pulled him away. 'Do you hear me?'

Lemke's face twisted. Suddenly, horribly, he was three hundred years old, a terrible living revenant.

'No poosh!' he cried at Billy, and shook his fist. *'No poosh, not never! You die thin, town man! You die like this!'* He brought his fists together, and Billy felt a sharp stabbing pain in his sides, as if he had been between those fists. For a moment

he could not get his breath and it felt as if all his guts were being squeezed together. *'You die thin!'*

'It's a push,' Billy said again, struggling not to gasp.

'No poosh!' the old man screamed. In his fury at this continued contradiction, thin red color had crisscrossed his cheeks in netlike patterns. 'Get him out of here!'

They began to drag him back across the circle. Taduz Lemke stood watching, his hands on his hips and his face a stone mask.

'Before they take me away, old man, you ought to know my own curse will fall on your family,' Billy called, and in spite of the dull pain in his sides his voice was strong, calm, almost cheerful. 'The curse of white men from town.'

Lemke's eyes widened slightly, he thought. From the corner of his eye Billy saw the old woman with the trading stamps in her blanketed lap fork the sign of the evil eye at him again.

The two young men stopped pulling him for a moment; Samuel Lemke uttered a short, bewildered laugh, perhaps at the idea of a white upper-middle-class lawyer from Fairview, Connecticut, cursing a man who was probably the oldest Gypsy in America. Billy himself would have laughed two months ago.

Taduz Lemke, however, was not laughing.

'You think men like me don't have the power to curse?' Billy asked. He held his hands – his thin, wasted hands – up on either side of his face and slowly splayed his fingers. He looked like a variety-show host asking an audience to end their applause. 'We have the power. We're good at cursing once we get started, old man. Don't make me start.'

There was movement behind the old man – a flash of white nightgown and black hair.

'Gina!' Samuel Lemke cried out.

Billy saw her step forward into the light. Saw her raise

the slingshot, draw the cradle back, and release it all in the same smooth gesture – like an artist drawing a line on a blank pad. He thought he saw a liquid, streaky gleam in the air as the steel ball flew across the circle, but that was almost certainly just imagination.

There was a hot, glassy spear of pain in his left hand. It was gone almost as soon as it came. He heard the steel ball bearing she had fired *thwang* off the steel side of a van. At the same moment he realized he could see the girl's drawn, furious face, not framed in his spread fingers, but through his palm, where there was a neat round hole.

She slingshotted me, he thought. *Holy Christ, she did!* Blood, black as tar in the firelight, ran down the pad of his palm and soaked the sleeve of his sport coat.

'*Enkelt!*' she shrieked. 'Get out of here, *eyelak!* Get out of here, killing *bastard!*'

She threw the slingshot. It landed at the edge of the fire, a wishbone shape with a rubber cup the size of an eyepatch caught in its fork. Then she fled, shrieking.

No one moved. Those around the fire, the two young men, the old man, and Billy himself – all of them stood in tableau. There was the slam of a door, and the girl's shrieks were muffled. And still there was no pain.

Suddenly, not even knowing he meant to do it, Billy held his bleeding hand out toward Lemke. The old man flinched back and forked the sign of the evil eye at Billy. Billy closed his hand as Lemke had done; blood ran from his closed fist as it had run from Lemke's closed fist.

'The curse of the white man is on you, Mr Lemke – they don't write about that one in books, but I'm telling you it's true – and *you* believe *that.*'

The old man screamed a flood of Romany. Billy felt himself hauled backward so suddenly that his head snapped on his neck. His feet left the ground.

They're going to throw me in the fire. Christ, they're going to roast me in it . . .

Instead he was carried back the way he had come, through the circle (people fell out of their chairs scrambling away from him) and between two pickups with camper caps. From one of them Billy heard a TV crackling out something with a laugh track.

The man in the vest grunted, Billy was swung like a sack of grain (a very underweight sack of grain), and then for a moment he was flying. He landed in the timothy grass beyond the parked vehicles with a thud. This hurt a good deal more than the hole in his hand; there were no padded places on him anymore, and he felt his bones rattle inside his body like loose stakes in an old truck. He tried to get up and at first could not. White lights danced in front of his eyes. He groaned.

Samuel Lemke came toward him. The boy's handsome face was smooth and deadly and expressionless. He reached into the pocket of his jeans and brought out something – Billy at first thought it was a stick and only recognized it for what it was when Lemke unfolded the blade.

He held his bleeding hand out, palm up, and Lemke hesitated. Now there was an expression on his face, one Billy recognized from his own bathroom mirror. It was fear.

His companion muttered something to him.

Lemke hesitated for a moment, looking down at Billy; then he refolded the blade into the knife's dark body. He spat in Billy's direction. A moment later the two of them were gone.

He lay there for a moment, trying to reconstruct everything, to make some sense of it . . . but that was a lawyer's trick, and it would not serve him here in this dark place. His hand was starting to talk very loudly about what had happened to it now, and he thought that very soon it would hurt a lot more. Unless, of course, they changed their minds and came back here for him. Then they might end all hurting in very short order, and forever.

That got him moving. He rolled over, slid his knees up to what was left of his stomach, then paused there a moment with his left cheek pressed against the beaten timothy and his ass in the air while a wave of faintness and nausea rode through him like a breaking wave. When it passed he was able to get to his feet and start up the hill to where his car was parked. He fell down twice on the way. The second time he believed it was going to be impossible to get to his feet again. Somehow – mostly by thinking about Linda, sleeping quietly and blamelessly in her bed – he was able to do it. Now his hand felt as if a dark red infection was pulsing in it and working its way up his forearm toward his elbow.

An endless time later he reached the rental Ford and scrabbled for the keys. He had put them in his left pocket, and so had to reach across his crotch with his right hand to get at them.

He started the car and paused for a moment, his screaming hand lying palm-up on his left thigh like a bird that has been shot. He looked down at the circle of vans and campers and the twinkle of the fire. A ghost of some old song came to him: *She danced around the fire to a Gypsy melody/Sweet young woman in motion, how she enchanted me . . .*

He lifted his left hand slowly in front of his face. Ghostly green light from the car's instrument panel spilled through the round dark hole in his palm.

She enchanted me, all right, Billy thought, and dropped the car in Drive. He wondered with almost clinical detachment if he would be able to make it back to the Frenchman's Bay Motel.

Somehow, he did.

CHAPTER TWENTY
118

'William? What's wrong?'

Ginelli's voice, which had been deeply blurred with sleep and ready to be angry, was now sharp with concern. Billy had found Ginelli's home number in his address book below the one for Three Brothers. He had dialed it without much hope at all, sure it would have been changed at some point during the intervening years.

His left hand, wrapped in a handkerchief, lay in his lap. It had turned into something like a radio station and was now broadcasting approximately fifty thousand watts of pain – the slightest movement sent it raving up his arm. Beads of sweat stood out on his forehead. Images of crucifixion kept occurring to him.

'I'm sorry to call you at home, Richard,' he said, 'and so late.'

'Fuck that, what's wrong?'

'Well, the immediate problem is that I've been shot through the hand with a . . .' He shifted slightly, his hand flared, and his lips peeled back over his teeth. '. . . with a ball bearing.'

Silence at the other end.

'I know how it sounds, but it's true. The woman used a slingshot.'

'Jesus! What –' A woman's voice in the background. Ginelli spoke briefly in Italian to her and then came back on the line. 'This is no joke, William? Some whore put a ball bearing through your hand with a slingshot?'

'I don't call people at . . .' He looked at his watch and another flare of pain raced up his arm. '. . . at three o'clock in the morning and tell jokes. I've been sitting here for the last three hours trying to wait until a more civilized hour. But the pain . . .' He laughed a little, a hurt, helpless, bewildered sound. 'The pain is very bad.'

'Does this have to do with what you called me about before?'

'Yes.'

'It was Gypsies?'

'Yes. Richard . . .'

'Yeah? Well, I promise you one thing. They don't fuck with you anymore after this.'

'Richard, I can't go to a doctor with this and I'm in . . . I really am in a lot of pain.' *Billy Halleck, Grandmaster of Understatement*, he thought. 'Can you send me something? Maybe by Federal Express? Some kind of painkiller?'

'Where are you?'

Billy hesitated for just a moment, then shook his head a little. Everyone he trusted had decided he was crazy; he thought it very likely that his wife and his boss had gone through or soon would be going through the motions necessary to effect an involuntary committal in the state of Connecticut. Now his choices were very simple, and marvelously ironic: either trust this dope-dealing hood he hadn't seen in nearly six years, or give up completely.

Closing his eyes, he said: 'I'm in Bar Harbor, Maine. The Frenchman's Bay Motel. Unit thirty-seven.'

'Just a second.'

Ginelli's voice moved away from the telephone again. Billy heard him speaking in a dim platter of Italian. He didn't open his eyes. At last Ginelli came back on the line again.

'My wife is making a couple of calls for me,' he said. 'You're wakin' up guys in Norwalk right now, *paisan*. I hope you're satisfied.'

'You're a gentleman, Richard,' Billy said. The words came out in a guttural slur and he had to clear his throat. He felt too cold. His lips were too dry and he tried to wet them, but his tongue was dry too.

'You be very still, my friend,' Ginelli said. The concern was back in his voice. 'You hear me? Very still. Wrap up in a blanket if you want, but that's all. You've been shot. You're in shock.'

'No shit,' Billy said, and laughed again. 'I've been in shock for about two months now.'

'What are you talking about?'

'Never mind.'

'All right. But we got to talk, William.'

'Yes.'

'I . . . Hold on a second.' Italian, soft and faint. Halleck closed his eyes again and listened to his hand broadcast pain. After a while Ginelli came back on the phone. 'A man is going to come by with some painkiller for you. He –'

'Oh, hey, Richard, that's not –'

'Don't tell me my business, William, just listen. His name is Fander. He's no doctor, this guy, at least not anymore, but he's going to look at you and decide if you ought to have some antibiotics as well as the dope. He'll be there before daylight.'

'Richard, I don't know how to thank you,' Billy said. Tears were running down his cheeks; he wiped at them absently with his right hand.

'I know you don't,' Ginelli said. 'You're not a wop. Remember, Richard: just sit still.'

★

Fander arrived shortly before six o'clock. He was a little man with prematurely white hair who carried a country doctor's bag. He gazed at Billy's scrawny, emaciated body for a long moment without speaking and then carefully unwound the handkerchief from Billy's left hand. Billy had to put his other hand over his mouth to stifle a scream.

'Raise it, please,' Fander said, and Billy did. The hand was badly swollen, the skin pulled taut and shiny. For a moment he and Fander gazed at each other through the hole in Billy's palm, which was ringed with dark blood. Fander took an odoscope from his bag and shone it through the wound. Then he turned it off.

'Clean and neat,' he said. 'If it was a ball bearing there's much less chance of infection than there would have been with a lead slug.'

He paused, considering.

'Unless, of course, the girl put something on it before she fired it.'

'What a comforting idea,' Billy croaked.

'I'm not paid to comfort people,' Fander said coolly, 'especially when I'm routed out of bed at three-thirty and have to change from my pajamas into my clothes in a light plane that is bouncing around at eleven thousand feet. You say it was a steel bearing?'

'Yes.'

'Then you're probably all right. You can't very well soak a steel ball bearing in poison the way the Jivaro Indians soaked their wooden arrowheads in *curare*, and it doesn't seem likely the woman could have painted it with anything if it was all as spur-of-the-moment as you say. This should heal well, with no complications.' He took out disinfectant, gauze, an elastic bandage. 'I'm going to pack the wound and then bandage it. The packing is going to hurt like hell, but believe me when I tell you that it's going to hurt a lot more in the long run if I leave it open.'

He cast another measuring eye on Billy – not so much the compassionate eye of a doctor, Billy thought, as the cold, appraising glance of an abortionist. 'This hand is going to be the least of your problems if you don't start eating again.'

Billy said nothing.

Fander looked at him a moment longer, then began packing the wound. At that point talk would have been impossible for Billy anyway; the pain-broadcasting station in his hand jumped from fifty thousand to two-hundred fifty thousand watts in one quick leap. He closed his eyes, clamped his teeth together, and waited for it to be over.

At last it *was* over. He sat with his throbbing bandaged hand in his lap and watched Fander root in his bag once more.

'All other considerations aside, your radical emaciation makes for problems when it comes to dealing with your pain. You're going to feel quite a bit more discomfort than you'd feel if your weight was normal, I'm afraid. I can't give you Darvon or Darvocet because they might put you in a coma or cause you to go into cardiac arrhythmia. How much *do* you weigh, Mr Halleck! A hundred and twenty-five?'

'About that,' Billy muttered. There was a scale in the bathroom, and he had stepped on it before going out to the camp of the Gypsies – it was his own bizarre form of pep rally, he supposed. The needle had centered on 118. All the running around in the hot summer sun had helped to speed things up considerably.

Fander nodded with a little moue of distaste. 'I'm going to give you some fairly strong Empirin. You take one single tablet. If you're not dozing off in half an hour, and if your hand is still very, very painful, you can take another half.

And you go on like that for the next three or four days.' He shook his head. 'I just flew six hundred miles to give a man a bottle of Empirin. I can't believe it. Life can be very perverse. But considering your weight, even Empirin's dangerous. It ought to be baby aspirin.'

Fander removed another small bottle from his bag, this one unmarked.

'Aureomycin,' he said. 'Take one by mouth every six hours. But – mark this well, Mr Halleck – if you start having diarrhea, *stop the antibiotic at once.* In your state, diarrhea is a lot more apt to kill you than an infection from this wound.'

He snapped the bag shut and stood up.

'One final piece of advice that has nothing to do with your adventures in the Maine countryside. Get some potassium tablets as soon as possible and begin taking two every day – one when you get up, one when you go to bed. You'll find them at the drugstore in the vitamin section.'

'Why?'

'If you continue to lose weight, you will very soon begin to experience instances of heart arrhythmia whether you take Darvon or any other drug. This sort of arrhythmia comes from radical potassium depletion in the body. It may have been what killed Karen Carpenter. Good day, Mr Halleck.'

Fander let himself out into the first mild light of dawn. For a moment he only stood there looking toward the sound of the ocean, which was very clear in the stillness.

'You really ought to get off whatever hunger strike you are on, Mr Halleck,' he said without turning around. 'In many ways the world is nothing but a pile of shit. But it can also be very beautiful.'

He walked toward a blue Chevrolet that was idling at the side of the building and got into the backseat. The car moved off.

'I'm trying to get off it,' Billy said to a disappearing car. 'I'm really trying.'

He closed the door and walked slowly back to the small table beside his chair. He looked at the medicine bottles and wondered how he was going to open them one-handed.

CHAPTER TWENTY-ONE
Ginelli

Billy ordered a large lunch sent in. He had never been less hungry in his life, but he ate all of it. When he was done he risked taking three of Fander's Empirin, reasoning that he was putting them on top of a turkey club sandwich, french fries, and a wedge of apple pie that had tasted quite a bit like stale asphalt.

The pills hit him hard. He was aware that the pain transmitter in his hand had suddenly been reduced to a mere five thousand watts, and then he was cavorting through a feverish series of dreams. Gina danced across one of them, naked except for gold hoop earrings. Then he was crawling through a long dark culvert toward a round circle of daylight that always, maddeningly, stayed the same distance away. Something was behind him. He had a terrible feeling it was a rat. A very *large* rat. Then he was out of the culvert. If he had believed that would mean escape, he had been wrong – he was back in that starving Fairview. Corpses lay heaped everywhere. Yard Stevens lay sprawled in the middle of the town common, his own barber's shears driven deep into what remained of his throat. Billy's daughter leaned against a lamppost, nothing but a bunch of jointed sticks in her purple-and-white cheerleader's outfit. It was impossible to tell if she were really dead like the others or only comatose. A vulture fluttered down and landed on her shoulder. Its talons flexed once and its head darted forward. It ripped out a great swatch of her hair with its rotting beak. Bloody strands of scalp still clung to the ends, as clumps of earth cling to the roots of a plant which has been roughly pulled out of the ground. And she was *not* dead; Billy heard her moan, saw her hands stir weakly in her lap. *No!* he shrieked in this dream. He found he had the girl's slingshot in his hand. The cradle was loaded not with a ball bearing but a glass paperweight that sat on a table in the hall of the Fairview house. There was something inside the paperweight – some flaw – that looked like a blue-black thunderhead. Linda had been fascinated with it as a child. Billy fired the paperweight at the bird. It missed, and suddenly the bird turned into Taduz Lemke. A heavy thudding sound started somewhere – Billy wondered if it was his heart going into a fatal spell of arrhythmia. *I never take it off, white man from town,* Lemke said, and suddenly Billy was somewhere else and the thudding sound was still going on.

He looked stupidly around the motel unit, at first thinking this was only another locale in his dreams.

'William!' someone called from the other side of the door. 'Are you in there? Open this up or I'm gonna break it in! William! William!'

Okay, he tried to say, and no sound came out of his mouth. His lips had dried and gummed shut. Nevertheless, he felt an overwhelming sense of relief. It was Ginelli.

'William? Will . . . Oh, fuck.' This last was in a lower I'm-talking-to-myself voice, and was followed by a thump as Ginelli threw his shoulder against the door.

Billy got to his feet and the whole world wavered in and out of focus for a moment. He got his mouth open at last, his lips parting with a soft rip that he felt rather than heard.

'That's okay,' he managed. 'That's okay, Richard. I'm here. I'm awake now.'

He went across the room and opened the door.

'Christ, William, I thought you were . . .'

Ginelli broke off and stared at him, his brown eyes widening and widening until Billy thought: *He's going to run. You can't look that way at anyone or anything and not take to your heels as soon as you get over the first shock of whatever it was.*

Then Ginelli kissed his right thumb, crossed himself, and said, 'Are you gonna let me in, William?'

Ginelli had brought better medicine than Fander's – Chivas. He took the bottle out of his calfskin briefcase and poured them each a stiff hooker. He touched the rim of his plastic motel tumbler to the rim of Billy's.

'Happier days than these,' he said. 'How's that?'

'That's just fine,' Billy said, and knocked the shot off in one big swallow. After the explosion of fire in his stomach had subsided to a glow, he excused himself and went into the bathroom. He didn't need to use the toilet, but he did not want Ginelli to see him cry.

'What did he do to you?' Ginelli asked. 'Did he poison your food?'

Billy began to laugh. It was the first good laugh in a long time. He sat down in his chair again and laughed until more tears rolled down his cheeks.

'I love you, Richard,' he said when the laughter had tapered off to chuckles and a few shrill giggles. 'Everyone else, including my wife, thinks I'm crazy. The last time you saw me I was forty pounds overweight and now I look like I'm trying out for the part of the scarecrow in the remake of *The Wizard of Oz* and the first thing out of your mouth is "Did he poison your food?"'

Ginelli waved away both Billy's half-hysterical laughter and the compliment with the same impatience. Billy thought,

Ike and Mike, they think alike, Lemke and Ginelli, too. When it comes to vengeance and countervengeance, they have no sense of humor.

'Well? Did he?'

'I suppose that he did. In a way, he did.'

'How much weight have you lost?'

Billy's eyes strayed to the wall-sized mirror across the room. He remembered reading – in a John D. MacDonald novel, he thought – that every modern motel room in America seems filled with mirrors, although most of those rooms are used by overweight businessmen who have no interest in looking at themselves in an undressed state. His state was very much the opposite of overweight, but he could understand the antimirror sentiment. He supposed it was his face – no, not just his face, his whole head – which had thrown such a fright into Richard. The size of his skull had remained the same, and the result was that his head perched atop his disappearing body like the hideously oversize head of a giant sunflower.

I never take it off you, white man from town, he heard Lemke say.

'How much weight, William?' Ginelli repeated. His voice was calm, gentle even, but his eyes sparkled in an odd, clear way. Billy had never seen a man's eyes sparkle in quite that way, and it made him a little nervous.

'When this began – when I came out of the courthouse and the old man touched me – I weighed two hundred and fifty pounds. This morning I weighed in at a hundred and sixteen just before lunch. That's what . . . a hundred and thirty-four pounds?'

'Jesus and Mary and Joseph the carpenter from Brooklyn Heights,' Ginelli whispered, and crossed himself again. 'He touched you?'

This is where he walks out – this is where they all walk out,

Billy thought, and for one wild second he thought of simply lying, of making up some mad story of systematic food poisoning. But if there had ever been a time for lying, it was gone now. And if Ginelli walked, Billy would walk with him, at least as far as Ginelli's car. He would open the door for him and thank him very much for coming. He would do it because Ginelli had listened when Billy called in the middle of the night, and sent his rather peculiar version of a doctor, and then come himself. But mostly he would perform those courtesies because Ginelli's eyes had widened like that when Billy opened the door, and he still hadn't run away.

So you tell him the truth. He says the only things he believes in are guns and money, and that's probably the truth, but you tell him the truth because that's the only way you can ever pay back a guy like him.

He touched you? Ginelli had asked, and although that was only a second ago it seemed much longer in Billy's scared, confused mind. Now he said what was the hardest thing for him to say. 'He didn't just touch me, Richard. He cursed me.'

He waited for that rather mad sparkle to die out of Ginelli's eyes. He waited for Ginelli to glance at his watch, hop to his feet, and grab his briefcase. *Time sure has a way of flying, doesn't it? I'd love to stay and talk over this curse business with you, William, but I've got a hot plate of veal marsala waiting for me back at the Brothers, and . . .*

The sparkle didn't die and Ginelli didn't get up. He crossed his legs, neated the crease, brought out a package of Camel cigarettes, and lit one.

'Tell me everything,' he said.

Billy Halleck told Ginelli everything. When he was done, there were four Camel butts in the ashtray. Ginelli was looking fixedly at Billy, as if hypnotized. A long silence spun out. It was uncomfortable, and Billy wanted to break it, but he didn't know how. He seemed to have used up all of his words.

'He did this to you,' Ginelli said at last. 'This . . .' He waved a hand at Billy.

'Yes. I don't expect you to believe it, but yes, he did.'

'I believe it,' Ginelli said almost absently.

'Yeah? What happened to the guy who only believed in guns and money?'

Ginelli smiled, then laughed. 'I told you that when you called that time, didn't I?'

'Yeah.'

The smile faded. 'Well, there's one more thing I believe in, William. I believe in what I see. That's why I'm a relatively rich man. That's also why I'm a *living* man. Most people, they don't believe what they see.'

'No?'

'No. Not unless it goes along with what they already believe. You know what I saw in this drugstore where I go? Just last week I saw this.'

'What?'

'They got a blood-pressure machine in there. I mean, they sometimes got them in shopping malls, too, but in the drugstore it's free. You put your arm through a loop and push a button. The loop closes. You sit there for a while and think serene thoughts and then it lets go. The reading flashes up in big red numbers. Then you look on the chart where it says "low," "normal," and "high" to figure out what the numbers mean. You get this picture?'

Billy nodded.

'Okay. So I am waiting for the guy to give me a bottle of this stomach medicine my mother has to take for her ulcers. And this fat guy comes in. I mean, he goes a good two-fifty and his ass looks like two dogs fightin' under a blanket. There's a drinker's road map on his nose and cheeks and I can see a pack of Marlboros in his pocket. He picks up some of those Dr Scholl's corn pads and he's taking them to the cash register when the high-blood-pressure machine catches his eye. So he sits down and the machine does its thing. Up comes the reading. Two-twenty over one-thirty, it says. Now, I don't know a whole fuck of a lot about the wonderful world of medicine, William, but I know two-twenty over one-thirty is in the creepy category. I mean, you might as well be walking around with the barrel of a loaded pistol stuck in your ear, am I right?'

'Yes.'

'So what does this dummocks do? He looks at me and says, "All this digital shit is fucked up." Then he pays for his corn pads and walks out. You know what the moral of that story is, William? Some guys – a *lot* of guys – don't believe what they are seeing, especially if it gets in the way of what they want to eat or drink or think or believe. Me, I don't believe in God. But if I saw him, I would. I wouldn't just go around saying, "Jesus, that was a great special effect." The definition of an asshole is a guy who doesn't believe what he's seeing. And you can quote me.'

Billy looked at him consideringly for a moment, and then burst out laughing. After a moment, Ginelli joined him.

'Well,' he said, 'you still sound like the old William when you laugh, anyway. The question is, William, what are we going to do about this geezer?'

'I don't know.' Billy laughed again, a shorter sound. 'But I guess I have to do something. After all, I cursed him.'

'So you told me. The curse of the white dude from town. Considering what all the white dudes from all the towns have done in the last couple hundred years, that could be a pretty heavy one.' Ginelli paused to light another cigarette and then said matter-of-factly through the smoke: 'I can hit him, you know.'

'No, that won't w –' Billy began, and then his mouth snapped closed. He'd had an image of Ginelli walking up to Lemke and punching him in the eye. Then suddenly he had realized that Ginelli was speaking of something much more final. 'No, you can't do that,' he finished.

Ginelli either didn't understand or affected not to. 'Sure I can. And I can't get anyone else to, that's for sure. At least, not anyone trustworthy. But I am as capable of doing it now as I was at twenty. It ain't business, but believe me, it *would* be a pleasure.'

'No, I don't want you to kill him or anyone else,' Billy said. 'That's what I meant.'

'Why not?' Ginelli asked, still reasonable – but his eyes, Billy saw, continued to whirl and twirl in that mad way. 'You worried about being an accessory to murder? It wouldn't be murder, it'd be self-defense. Because he is killing *you*, Billy. Another week of this and people will be able to read the signs you're standing in front of without asking you to move. Another two and you won't dare to go out in a high wind for fear of blowing away.'

'Your medical associate suggested that I might die of cardiac arrhythmia before it went that far. Presumably my heart is losing weight right along with the rest of me.' He swallowed. 'You know, I never had that particular thought until just now. I sort of wish I hadn't had it at all.'

'See? He's killing you . . . but never mind. You don't want me to hit him, I won't hit him. Probably not a good idea anyway. It might not end it.'

Billy nodded. This had occurred to him, as well. *Take it off me*, he had told Lemke – apparently even white men from town understood that was something that had to be done.

If Lemke was dead, the curse might simply have to run itself out.

'The trouble is,' Ginelli said reflectively, 'you can't take back a hit.'

'No.'

He rubbed out his cigarette and stood up. 'I gotta think about this, William. It's a lot to think about. And I got to get my mind in a serene state, you know? You can't get ideas about complicated shit like this when you're upset, and every time I look at you, *paisan*, I want to pull out this guy's pecker and stuff it in the hole where his nose used to be.'

Billy got up and almost fell. Ginelli grabbed him and Billy hugged him clumsily with his good arm. He didn't think he'd ever hugged a grown man in his life before this.

'Thank you for coming,' Billy said. 'And for believing me.'

'You're a good fellow,' Ginelli said, releasing him. 'You're in a bad mess, but maybe we can get you out of it. Either way, we're gonna put some stone blocks to this old dude. I'm gonna go out and walk around for a couple of hours, Billy. Get my mind serene. Think up some ideas. Also, I want to make some phone calls back to the city.'

'About what?'

'I'll tell you later. First I want to do some thinking. You be okay?'

'Yes.'

'Lie down. You have no color in your face at all.'

'All right.' He did feel sleepy again, sleepy and totally worn out.

'The girl who shot you,' Ginelli said. 'Pretty?'

'Very pretty.'

'Yeah?' That crazy light was back in Ginelli's eyes, brighter than ever. It troubled Billy.

'Yeah.'

'Lay down, Billy. Catch some Z's. Check you later. Okay to take your key?'

'Sure.'

Ginelli left. Billy lay down on the bed and put his bandaged hand carefully down beside him, knowing perfectly well that if he fell asleep he would probably just roll over on it and wake himself up again.

Probably just humoring me, Billy thought. *Probably on the phone to Heidi right now. And when I wake up, the men with the butterfly nets will be sitting on the foot of the bed. They . . .*

But there was no more. He drifted off and somehow managed to avoid rolling on his bad hand.

And this time there were no bad dreams.

There were no men with butterfly nets in the room when he woke up, either. Only Ginelli, sitting in the chair across the room. He was reading a book called *This Savage Rapture* and drinking a can of beer. It was dark outside.

There were four cans of a six-pack sitting on top of an ice bucket on the TV, and Billy licked his lips. 'Can I have one of those?' he croaked.

Ginelli looked up. 'It's Rip Van Winkle, back from the dead! Sure you can. Here, let me open you one.'

He brought it to Billy, and Billy drank half of it without stopping. The beer was fine and cold. He had heaped the contents of the Empirin bottle in one of the room's ashtrays (motel rooms did not have as many ashtrays as mirrors, he thought, but almost). Now he fished one out and washed it down with another swallow.

'How's the hand?' Ginelli asked.

'Better.' In a way it was a lie, because his hand hurt very badly indeed. But in a way it was the truth, too. Because Ginelli was here, and that did more to make the pain less than the Empirin or even the shot of Chivas. Things hurt more when you were alone, that was all. This caused him to think of Heidi, because she was the one who should have been with him, not this hood, and she wasn't. Heidi was back in Fairview, stubbornly ignoring all this, because to give it any mental house-room would mean she might have to explore the boundaries of her own culpability, and Heidi did not want to do that. Billy felt a dull, throbbing resentment. What had Ginelli said? *The definition of an asshole is a guy who doesn't believe what he's seeing.* He tried to push the resentment away — she was, after all, his wife. And she was doing what she believed was right and best for him . . . wasn't she? The resentment went, but not very far.

'What's in the shopping bag?' Billy asked. The bag was sitting on the floor.

'Goodies,' Ginelli said. He looked at the book he was reading, then tossed it into the wastebasket. 'That sucks like an Electrolux. I couldn't find a Louis Lamour.'

'What kind of goodies?'

'For later. When I go out and visit your Gypsy friends.'

'Don't be foolish,' Billy said sharply. 'You want to end up looking like me? Or maybe like a human umbrella stand?'

'Easy, easy,' Ginelli said. His voice was amused and soothing, but that light in his eyes whirled and twirled. Billy realized suddenly that it hadn't all been spur-of-the-moment bullshit; he really *had* cursed Taduz Lemke. The thing he had cursed him with was sitting across from him in a cheap leatherette motel chair and drinking a Miller Lite. And with equal parts amusement and horror, he realized something else as well: perhaps Lemke knew how to lift *his* curse, but Billy hadn't the slightest idea of how to lift the curse of the white man from town. Ginelli was having a good time. More fun, maybe, than he'd had in years. He was like a pro bowler coming eagerly out of retirement to take part in a charity event. They would talk, but their talk would change nothing. Ginelli was his friend. Ginelli was a courtly if not exactly grammatical man who called him William instead of Bill or Billy. He was also a very large, very proficient hunting dog which had just slipped its chain.

'Don't tell me to take it easy,' he said, 'just tell me what you plan to do.'

'No one gets hurt,' Ginelli said. 'Just hold that thought, William. I know that's important to you. I think you're holding on to some, you know, principles you can't exactly afford anymore, but I got to go along because that's what you want and you are the offended party. No one gets hurt in this at all. Okay?'

'Okay,' Billy said. He was a little relieved . . . but not much.

'At least, not unless you change your mind,' Ginelli said.

'I won't.'

'You might.'

'What's in the bag?'

'Steaks,' Ginelli said, and took one out. It was a porter-house wrapped in clear plastic and marked with a Sampson's label. 'Looks good, huh, I got four of 'em.'

'What are they for?'

'Let's keep things in order,' Ginelli said. 'I left here, I walked downtown. What a fucking horror show! You can't even walk on the sidewalk. Everyone's wearing Ferrari sunglasses and shirts with alligators on their tits. It looks like everyone in this town has had their teeth capped and most of 'em have had nose-jobs too.'

'I know.'

'Listen to this, William. I see this girl and guy walking along, right? And the guy has got his hand in the back pocket of her shorts. I mean, they are right out in public and he's got his hand in her back pocket, feeling her ass. Man, if that was my daughter she wouldn't sit down on what her boy-friend was feeling for about a week and a half.

'So I know I can't get my mind in a serene state there, and I gave it up. I found a telephone booth, made a few calls. Oh, I almost forgot. The phone was in front of a drugstore, so I went in and got these.' He took a bottle of pills from his pocket and tossed it to Billy, who caught it with his good hand. They were potassium capsules.

'Thank you, Richard,' he said, his voice a little uneven.

'Don't mention it, just take one. You don't need a fucking heart attack on top of everything else.'

Billy took one with a swallow of beer. His head was starting to buzz gently now.

'So I got some people sniffing around after a couple of things and then I went down by the harbor,' Ginelli resumed. 'I looked at the boats for a while. William, there must be twenty . . . thirty . . . maybe forty million dollars' worth of boats down there! Sloops, yawls, fucking frigates, for all I could tell. I don't know diddlyfuck about boats, but I love to look at them. They . . .'

He broke off and looked thoughtfully at Billy.

'You think some of those guys in the alligator shirts and the Ferrari sunglasses are running dope in those pussy-wagons?'

'Well, I read in the *Times* last winter that a lobsterman on one of the islands around here found about twenty bales of stuff floating around under the town dock, and it turned out to be some pretty good marijuana.'

'Yeah. Yeah, that's about what I thought. This whole place has that smell to it. Fucking amateurs. They ought to just sail their pretty boats and leave the work to people who understand it, you know? I mean, sometimes they get in the way and then measures have to be taken and some guy finds a few bodies floating around under a dock instead of a few bales of weed. It's too bad.'

Billy took another large swallow of beer and coughed on it.

'But that is neither here nor there. I took a walk, looked at all those boats, and got my mind serene. And then I figured out what to do . . . or at least, the start of it and the shape of how it should go afterward. I don't have all the details worked out yet, but that'll come.

'I walked back to the main drag and made a few more calls — follow-up calls. There is no warrant out for your arrest, William, but your wife and this nose-jockey doctor of yours sure did sign some papers on you. I wrote it down.' He took a piece of paper out of his breast pocket. '"Committal in absentia." That sound right?'

Billy Halleck's mouth dropped open and a wounded sound fell out of it. For a moment he was utterly stunned and then the fury which had become his intermittent companion swept through him again. He had *thought* it might happen, yes, had *thought* Houston would suggest it, and even *thought* Heidi might agree to it. But *thinking* about something and hearing it had actually happened — that your own wife had gone before a judge, had testified that you had gone loony, and had been granted a *res gestae* order of committal which she had then signed — that was very different.

'That cowardly *bitch*,' he muttered thickly, and then the world was blotted out by red agony. He had closed his hands into fists without thinking. He groaned and looked down at the bandage on his left hand. Flowers of red were blooming there.

I can't believe you just thought that about Heidi, a voice in his mind spoke up.

It's just because my mind is not serene, he answered the voice, and then the world grayed out for a while.

★

It wasn't quite a faint, and he came out of it quickly. Ginelli changed the bandage on his hand and repacked the wound, doing a job that was clumsy but fairly adequate. While he did it, he talked.

'My man says it don't mean a thing unless you go back to Connecticut, William.'

'No, that's true. But don't you see? My own *wife* – '

'Never mind that, William. It doesn't matter. If we can fix things up with this old Gypsy, you'll start to gain weight again and their case is out of the window. If that happens, you'll have plenty of time to decide what you want to do about your wife. Maybe she needs a slapping to sharpen her up a little, you know? Or maybe you just got to walk. You can decide that shit for yourself if we can fix things up with the Gyp – or you can write Dear Fucking Abby, if you want. And if we can't fix things up, you're gonna die. Either way, this thing is gonna get taken care of. So what's the big deal about them getting a paper on your head?'

Billy managed a white-lipped smile. 'You would have made a great lawyer, Richard. You have this unique way of putting things in perspective.'

'Yeah? You think so?'

'I do.'

'Well, thanks. Next I called Kirk Penschley.'

'*You* talked with Kirk Penschley?'

'Yes.'

'Jesus, Richard!'

'What, you think he wouldn't take a call from a cheap hood like me?' Ginelli managed to sound both wounded and amused at the same time. 'He took it, believe me. Of course, I called on my credit card – he wouldn't want my name on his phone bill, that much is true. But I've done a lot of business with your firm over the years, William.'

'That's news to me,' Billy said. 'I thought it was just that one time.'

'That time everything could be out in the open, and you were just right for it,' Ginelli said. 'Penschley and his big stud-lawyer partners would never have stuck you into something crooked. William – you were a comer. On the other hand, I suppose they knew you'd be meeting me sooner or later, if you hung around long enough in the firm, and that first piece of work would be a good introduction. Which it was – for me as well as for you, believe me. And if something went wrong – if our business that time had happened to turn the wrong corner or something – you could have been sacrificed. They wouldn't have liked to do it, but their view is better to sacrifice a comer than a genuine bull stud-lawyer. These guys all see the same – they are very predictable.'

'What other kind of business have you done with my firm?' Billy asked, frankly fascinated – this was a little like finding out your wife had been cheating on you long after you had divorced her for other reasons.

'Well, all kinds – and not exactly with your firm. Let's say they have brokered legal business for me and a number of my friends and leave it at that. Anyway, I know Kirk well enough to call him and ask for a favor. Which he granted.'

'What favor?'

'I asked him to call this Barton bunch and tell them to lay off for a week. Lay off you, and lay off the Gypsies. I'm actually more concerned about the Gypsies, you want to know the truth. We can do this, William, but it'll be easier if we don't have to chase them from hoot to holler and then back to fucking hoot again.'

'You called Kirk Penschley and told him to lay off,' Billy said, bemused.

'No, I called Kirk Penschley and told him to tell the Barton agency to lay off,' Ginelli corrected. 'And not exactly in those words, either. I can be a little bit political when I have to be, William. Give me *some* credit.'

'Man, I give you a lot of credit. More every minute.'

'Well, thank you. Thank you, William. I appreciate that.' He lit a cigarette. 'Anyway, your wife and her doctor friend will continue to get reports, but they'll be a little bit off. I mean, they'll be like the *National Enquirer* and *Reader's Digest* version of the truth – do you dig what I am saying?'

Billy laughed. 'Yeah, I see.'

'So, we got a week. And a week should be enough.'

'What are you going to do?'

'All you'll let me do, I guess. I am going to scare them, William. I'm going to scare *him*. I'm going to scare him so bad he's gonna need to put a fucking Delco tractor battery in his pacemaker. And I'm going to keep raising the level of the scares until one of two things happens. Either he is gonna cry uncle and take off what he put on you, or we decide he don't scare, that old man. If that happens, I come back to you and ask if you have changed your mind about hurting people. But maybe it won't go that far.'

'How are you going to scare him?'

Ginelli touched the shopping bag with the toe of one Bally boot and told him how he meant to start. Billy was appalled. Billy argued with Ginelli, as he had foreseen; then he talked with Ginelli, as he had also foreseen; and although Ginelli never raised his voice, his eyes continued to whirl and twirl with that mad light and Billy knew he might as well have been talking to the man in the moon.

And as the fresh pain in his hand slowly subsided to the former throbbing ache, he began to feel sleepy again.

'When are you going?' he asked, giving up.

Ginelli glanced at his watch. 'Ten past ten now. I'll give them another four or five hours. They been doing a good little business out there, from what I heard downtown.

Telling a lot of fortunes. And the dogs – those pit-bulls. Christ Almighty. The dogs you saw weren't pit-bulls, were they?'

'I never saw a pit-bull,' Billy said sleepily. 'The ones I saw all looked like hounds.'

'Pit-bulls look like a cross between terriers and bulldogs. They cost a lot of dough. If you want to see pit-bulls fight, you got to agree to pay for one dead dog before the wagers even get put down. It's one nasty business.

'They're into all the classy stuff in this town, ain't they, William – Ferrari sunglasses, dope boats, dogfights. Oh, sorry – and tarot and the *I Ching*.'

'Be careful,' Billy said.

'I'll be careful,' Ginelli said, 'don't worry.'

Billy fell asleep shortly after. When he woke up it was ten minutes until four and Ginelli was gone. He was seized with the certainty that Ginelli was dead. But Ginelli came in at a quarter to six, so fully alive that he seemed somehow too big for the place. His clothes, face, and hands were splattered with mud that reeked of sea salt. He was grinning. That crazy light danced in his eyes.

'William,' he said, 'we're going to pack your things and move you out of Bar Harbor. Just like a government witness going to a safe house.'

Alarmed, Billy asked, 'What did you do?'

'Take it easy, take it easy! Just what I said I was going to do – no more and no less. But when you stir up a hornet's nest with a stick, it's usually a good idea to flog your dogs on down the road afterward, William, don't you think so?'

'Yes, but –'

'No time now. I can talk and pack your stuff at the same time.'

'Where?' Billy almost wailed.

'Not far. I'll tell you on the way. Now, let's get going. And maybe you better start by changing your shirt. You're a good man, William, but you are starting to smell a little ripe.'

Billy had started up to the office with his key when Ginelli touched him on the shoulder and gently took it out of his hand.

'I'll just put this on the night table in your room. You checked in with a credit card, didn't you?'

'Yes, but –'

'Then we'll just make this sort of an informal check-out. No harm done, less attention attracted to us guys. Right?'

A woman jogging by on the berm of the highway looked casually at them, back at the road . . . and then her head snapped back in a wide-eyed double-take that Ginelli saw but Billy mercifully missed.

'I'll even leave ten bucks for the maid,' Ginelli said. 'We'll take your car. I'll drive.'

'Where's yours?' He knew Ginelli had rented one, and was now realizing belatedly that he hadn't heard an engine before Ginelli walked in. All of this was going too fast for Billy's mind – he couldn't keep up with it.

'It's okay. I left it on a back road about three miles from here and walked. Pulled the distributor cap and left a note on the windshield saying I was having engine trouble and would be back in a few hours, just in case anybody should get nosy. I don't think anyone will. There was grass growing up the middle of the road, you know?'

A car went by. The driver got a look at Billy Halleck and slowed down. Ginelli could see him leaning over and craning his neck.

'Come on, Billy. People looking at you. The next bunch could be the wrong people.'

An hour later Billy was sitting in front of the television in another motel room – this the living room of a seedy little suite in the Blue Moon Motor Court and Lodge in Northeast Harbor. They were less than fifteen miles from Bar Harbor, but Ginelli seemed satisfied. On the TV screen, Woody Woodpecker was trying to sell insurance to a talking bear.

'Okay,' Ginelli said. 'You rest up the hand, William. I'm gonna be gone all day.'

'You're going *back* there?'

'What, go back to the hornet's nest while the hornets are still flying? Not me, my friend. No, today I'm gonna play with cars. Tonight'll be time enough for Phase Two. Maybe I'll get time enough to look in on you, but don't count on it.'

Billy didn't see Richard Ginelli again until the following morning at nine, when he showed up driving a dark blue Chevy Nova that had certainly not come from Hertz or Avis. The paint was dull and spotted, there was a hairline crack in the passenger-side window, and a big dent in the trunk. But it was jacked in the back and there was a supercharger cowling on the hood.

This time Billy had given him up for dead a full six hours ago, and he greeted Ginelli shakily, trying not to weep with relief. He seemed to be losing all control of his emotions as he lost weight . . . and this morning, as the sun came up, he had felt the first unsteady racings of his heart. He had gasped for breath and pounded at his chest with one closed fist. The beat had finally smoothed out again, but that had been it: the first instance of arrhythmia.

'I thought you were dead,' he told Ginelli as he came in.

'You keep saying that and I keep turning up. I wish you would relax about me, William. I can take care of myself. I am a big boy. If you thought I was going to underestimate this old fuck, that would be one thing. But I'm not. He's smart, and he's dangerous.'

'What do you mean?'

'Nothing. I'll tell you later.'

'Now!'

'No.'

'Why not?'

'Two reasons,' Ginelli said patiently. 'First, because you might ask me to back off. Second, because I haven't been this tired in about twelve years. I'm gonna go in there to the bedroom and crash out for eight hours. Then I'm gonna get up and eat three pounds of the first food I can snag. Then I'm gonna go back out and shoot the moon.'

Ginelli did indeed look tired – almost haggard. *Except for his eyes*, Billy thought. *His eyes are still whirling and twirling like a couple of fluorescent carnival pinwheels.*

'Suppose I did ask you to back off?' Billy asked quietly. 'Would you do it, Richard?'

Richard looked at him for a long, considering moment and then gave Billy the answer he had known he would give ever since he had first seen that mad light in Ginelli's eyes.

'I couldn't now,' Ginelli said calmly. 'You're sick, William. It's through your whole body. You can't be trusted to know where your own best interest lies.'

In other words, you've taken out your own set of committal papers on me. Billy opened his mouth to speak this thought aloud and then closed his mouth again. Because Ginelli didn't mean what he said; he had only said what sounded sane.

'Also because it's personal, right?' Billy asked him.

'Yeah,' Ginelli replied. 'Now it's personal.'

He went into the bedroom, took off his shirt and pants, and lay down. He was asleep on top of the coverlet five minutes later.

Billy drew a glass of water, swallowed an Empirin, and then drank the rest of the water standing in the doorway. His eyes moved from Ginelli to the pants crumpled on the chair. Ginelli had arrived in a pair of impeccable cotton slacks, but somewhere in the last couple of days he had picked up a pair of blue jeans. The keys to the Nova parked out front would undoubtedly be in them. Billy could take them and drive away ... except he knew he wouldn't do that, and the fact that he would be signing his own death warrant by so doing now seemed actually secondary. The important thing now seemed to be how and where all of this would end.

At midday, while Ginelli was still sleeping deeply in the other room, Billy had another episode of arrhythmia. Shortly after, he dozed off himself and had a dream. It was short and totally mundane, but it filled him with a queer mixture of terror and hateful pleasure. In this dream he and Heidi were sitting in the breakfast nook of the Fairview house. Between them was a pie. She cut a large piece and gave it to Billy. It was an apple pie. 'This will fatten you up,' she said. 'I don't want to be fat,' he replied. 'I've decided I like being thin. You eat it.' He gave her the piece of pie, stretching an arm no thicker than a bone across the table. She took it. He sat watching as she ate every bite, and with every bite she took, his feelings of terror and dirty joy grew.

Another spell of light arrhythmia jolted him awake from his dream. He sat there for a moment, gasping, waiting for his heart to slow to its proper rhythm, and eventually it did. He was seized by the feeling that he had had more than a dream – that he had just experienced a prophetic vision of some kind. But such feelings often accompany vivid dreams, and as the dream itself fades, so does the feeling. This happened to Billy Halleck, although he had cause to remember this dream not long after.

Ginelli got up at six in the evening, showered, pulled on the jeans and a dark turtleneck sweater.

'Okay,' he said. 'I'll see you tomorrow morning, Billy. Then we'll know.'

Billy asked again what Ginelli meant to do, what had happened so far, and once again Ginelli refused to tell him.

'Tomorrow,' he said. 'Meantime, I'll give her your love.'

'Give who my love?'

Ginelli smiled. 'Lovely Gina. The whore who put the ball bearing through your hand.'

'Leave her alone,' Billy said. When he thought of those dark eyes, it seemed to be impossible to say anything else, no matter what she had done to him.

'No one gets hurt,' Ginelli reiterated, and then he was gone. Billy listened to the Nova start up, listened to the rough sound of its motor – that roughness would smooth out only when it got up to around sixty-five miles an hour – as Ginelli backed it out of the space, and reflected that *No one gets hurt* wasn't the same thing as agreeing to leave the girl alone. Not at all.

This time it was noon before Ginelli returned. There was a deep cut across his forehead and along his right arm – there the turtleneck sweater's sleeve hung in two flaps.

'You lost some more weight,' he said to Billy. 'You eating?'

'I'm trying,' Billy said, 'but anxiety isn't much good for the appetite. You look like you lost some blood.'

'A little. I'm okay.'

'Are you going to tell me now what the hell you've been doing?'

'Yes. I'm going to tell you everything just as soon as I get out of the shower and bandage myself. You're going to meet with him tonight, Billy. That's the important thing. That's what you want to psych yourself up for.'

A stab of mingled fear and excitement poked at his belly like a shard of glass. 'Him? Lemke?'

'Him,' Ginelli agreed. 'Now, let me get a shower, William. I must not be as young as I thought – all this excitement has got my ass dragging.' He called back over his shoulder, 'And order some coffee. Lots of coffee. Tell the guy to just leave it outside the door and slide the check underneath for you to sign.'

Billy watched him go, his mouth hanging open. Then, when he heard the shower start, he closed his mouth with a snap and went to the phone to order the coffee.

CHAPTER TWENTY-TWO
Ginelli's Story

He spoke at first in quick bursts, falling silent for a few moments after each to consider what came next. Ginelli's energy seemed really low for the first time since he had turned up at the Bar Harbor Motor Inn on Monday afternoon. He did not seem much hurt – his wounds were really only deep scratches – but Billy believed he was badly shaken.

All the same, that crazy glow eventually began to dawn in his eyes, at first stuttering on and off like a neon sign just after you turn the switch at dusk, then glowing steadily. He pulled a flask from the inside pocket of his jacket and dumped a capful of Chivas into his coffee. He offered Billy the flask. Billy declined – he didn't know what the booze might do to his heart.

Ginelli sat up straighter, brushed the hair off his forehead, and began to talk in a more normal rhythm.

At three o'clock on Tuesday morning, Ginelli had parked on a woods road which branched off from Route 37-A near the Gypsies camp. He fiddled with the steaks for a while and then walked back to the highway carrying the shopping bag. High clouds were sliding across the half-moon like shutters. He waited for them to clear off, and when they did for a moment he was able to spot the circle of vehicles. He crossed the road and set off cross-country in that direction.

'I'm a city boy, but my sense of direction ain't as bad as

it could be,' he said. 'I can trust it in a pinch. And I didn't want to go in the same way you did, William.'

He cut through a couple of fields and a thin copse of woods; splashed through one boggy place that smelled, he said, like twenty pounds of shit in a ten-pound bag. He also caught the seat of his pants in some very old barbed wire that had been all but invisible in the moonless dark.

'If all that is country living, William, the rubes can have it,' he said.

He had not expected any trouble from the camp hounds; Billy was a case in point. They hadn't bothered to make a sound until he actually stepped into the circle of the campfire, although they surely must have caught his scent before then.

'You'd expect Gypsies to have better watchdogs than that,' Billy commented. 'At least that's the image.'

'Nah,' Ginelli said. 'People can find all kinds of reasons to roust Gypsies without the Gyps themselves giving them more.'

'Like dogs that bark all night long?'

'Yeah, like that. You get much smarter, William, and people are gonna think you're Italian.'

Still, Ginelli had taken no chances – he moved slowly along the backs of the parked vehicles, skipping the vans and campers where people would be sleeping and only looking in the cars and station wagons. He saw what he wanted after checking only two or three vehicles: an old suit coat crumpled up on the seat of a Pontiac station wagon.

'Car wasn't locked,' he said. 'Jacket wasn't a bad fit, but it smelled like a weasel died in each pocket. I seen a pair of old sneakers on the floor in the back. *They* was a little tight, but I crammed 'em on just the same. Two cars later I found a hat that looked like something left over from a kidney transplant and put that on.'

He had wanted to smell like one of the Gypsies, Ginelli

explained, but not just as insurance against a bunch of worth-less mutts sleeping by the embers of the campfire – it was the *other* bunch of dogs that interested him. The valuable dogs. The pit-bulls.

Three-quarters of the way around the circle, he spotted a camper with a small rear window that had been covered with wire mesh instead of glass. He peered in and saw nothing at all – the back of the camper was completely bare.

'But it smelled of dog, William,' Ginelli said. 'Then I looked the other way and risked a quick poke on the penlight I brought. The hay-grass was all broken down in a path going away from the back of that camper. You didn't have to be Dan'l Boone to see it. They took the fucking dogs out of the rolling kennel and stashed them somewhere else so the local dog warden or humane-society babe wouldn't find them if someone blabbed. Only they left a path even a city boy could pick up with one quick poke of his flashlight. Stupid. *That's* when I really started to believe we could put some blocks to them.'

Ginelli followed the path over a knoll and to the edge of another small wooded area.

'I lost the path,' he said. 'I just stood there for a minute or two wondering what to do next. And then I heard it, William. I heard it loud and clear. Sometimes the gods give you a break.'

'What did you hear?'

'A dog farting,' Ginelli said. 'Good and loud. Sounded like someone blowing a trumpet with a mute on it.'

Less than twenty feet into the woods he had found a rough corral in a clearing. It was no more than a circle of thick branches driven into the ground and then laced up with barbed wire. Inside were seven pit-bulls. Five were fast asleep. The other two were looking dopily at Ginelli.

They looked dopy because they *were* dopy. 'I thought

they'd be stoned, although it wasn't safe to count on it. Once you train dogs to fight, they become a pain in the ass – they will fight with each other and wreck your investment unless you're careful. You either put them in separate cages or you dope them. Dope is cheaper and it's easy to hide. And if they had been straight, a rinky-dink piece of work like that dog corral wouldn't have held them. The ones getting their asses chewed would have busted out even if it meant leaving half their hides hanging on the wires behind them. They were only sobering them up when the betting line got heavy enough to justify the risk. First the dope, then the show, then more dope.' Ginelli laughed. 'See? Pit-bulls are just like fucking rock stars. It wears them out quick, but as long as you stay in the black, you can always find more pit-bulls. They didn't even have a guard.'

Ginelli opened his shopping bag and took out the steaks. After parking on the woods road, he had taken them out of their store shrink-wrap and injected a hypo of what he called Ginelli's Pit-Bull Cocktail into each: a mixture of Mexican brown heroin and strychnine. Now he waved them in the air and watched the sleeping dogs come slowly to life. One of them uttered a thick bark that sounded like the snore of a man with serious nasal problems.

'Shut up or no dinner,' Ginelli said mildly. The dog that had barked sat down. It immediately developed a fairly serious starboard list and began to go back to sleep.

Ginelli tossed one of the steaks into the enclosure. A second. A third. And the last. The dogs squabbled over them in listless fashion. There was some barking, but it had that same thick, snory quality, and Ginelli felt he could live with it. Besides, anyone coming from the camp to check on the makeshift kennel would be carrying a flashlight, and he would have plenty of time to fade back into the woods. But no one had come.

Billy listened with horrified fascination as Ginelli told him calmly how he had sat nearby, dry-smoking a Camel and watching the pit-bulls die. Most of them had gone very quietly, he reported (was there the faintest tinge of regret in his voice? Billy wondered uneasily) – probably because of the dope they had already been fed. Two of them had very mild convulsions. That was all. All in all, Ginelli felt, the dogs were not so badly off; the Gypsies had had worse things planned for them. It was over in a little less than an hour.

When he was sure they were all dead or at least deeply unconscious, he had taken a dollar bill from his wallet and a pen from his breast pocket. On the dollar bill he wrote: NEXT TIME IT COULD BE YOUR GRANDCHILDREN, OLD MAN. WILLIAM HALLECK SAYS TO TAKE IT OFF. The pit-bulls had worn twists of clothesrope for collars. Ginelli tucked the bill under one of them. He hung the foul-smelling coat on one of the corral posts and put the hat on top of it. He removed the sneakers and took his own shoes from his hip pockets. He put them on and left.

Coming back, he said, he *had* gotten lost for a while and had ended up taking a header in the bad-smelling boggy place. Finally, however, he had seen farmhouse lights and gotten himself oriented. He found the woods road, got into his car, and started back toward Bar Harbor.

He was halfway there, he said, when the car started to feel not right to him. He couldn't put it any better or make it any clearer – it just didn't seem right anymore. It wasn't that it looked different or smelled different; it just didn't seem right. He had had such feelings before, and on most occasions they had meant nothing at all. But on a couple . . .

'I decided I wanted to ditch it,' Ginelli said. 'I didn't want to take even a little chance that one of them might have had insomnia, been walking around, seen it. I didn't want them to know what I was driving, because then they could fan out, look for me, find me. Find you. See? I *do* take them serious. I look at you, William, and I got to.'

So he had parked the car on another deserted side road, pulling the distributor cap, and had walked the three miles back into town. When he got there, dawn was breaking.

After leaving Billy in his new Northeast Harbor quarters, Ginelli had cabbed back toward Bar Harbor, telling the driver to go slow because he was looking for something.

'What is it?' the driver asked. 'Maybe I know where it is.'

'That's all right,' Ginelli replied. 'I'll know it when I see it.'

And so he had – about two miles out of Northeast Harbor he had seen a Nova with a For Sale sign in the windshield sitting beside a small farmhouse. He checked to make sure the owner was home, paid off the cab, and made a cash deal on the spot. For an extra twenty the owner – a young fellow, Ginelli said, who looked like he might have more head lice than IQ points – had agreed to leave his Maine plates on the Nova, accepting Ginelli's promise to send them back in a week.

'I might even do it, too,' Ginelli said thoughtfully. 'If we're still alive, that is.'

Billy looked at him sharply, but Ginelli only resumed his story.

He had driven back toward Bar Harbor, skirting the town itself and heading out along 37-A toward the Gypsy camp. He had stopped long enough to call a person he would only identify to Billy as a 'business associate.' He told the 'business associate' to be at a certain pay-telephone kiosk in midtown New York at twelve-thirty P.M. – this was a kiosk Ginelli used often, and due to his influence it was one of the few in New York that was rarely out of order.

He drove by the encampment, saw signs of activity, turned

around about a mile up the road, and cruised back. A make-shift road had been carved through the hayfield from 37-A to the camp, and there was a car heading up it to 37-A.

'A Porsche turbo,' Ginelli said. 'Rich kid's toy. Decal in the back window that said Brown University. Two kids in the front, three more in the back. I pulled up and asked the kid driving if they were Gypsies down there, like I'd heard. He said they were, but if I'd been meaning to get my fortune read, I was out of luck. The kids had gone there to get theirs read, but all they got was a quick here's-your-hat, what's-your-hurry routine. They were moving out. After the pit-bulls, I wasn't surprised.

'I headed back toward Bar Harbor and pulled into a gas station – that Nova gobbles gas like you wouldn't believe, William, but it can walk and talk if you put the go to the mat. I also grabbed me a Coke and dropped a couple of bennies because by then I was starting to feel a little bit low.'

Ginelli had called his 'business associate' and had arranged to meet him at the Bar Harbor airport that evening at five o'clock. Then he had driven back to Bar Harbor. He parked the Nova in a public lot and walked around town for a while, looking for the man.

'What man?' Billy asked.

'The *man*,' Ginelli repeated patiently, as if speaking to an idiot. 'This guy, William, you always know him when you see him. He looks like all the other summer dudes, like he could take you for a ride on his daddy's sloop or drop ten grams of good cocaine on you or just decide to split the Bar Harbor scene and drive to Aspen for the Summerfest in his Trans Am. But he is not the same as they are, and there are two quick ways to find it out. You look at his shoes, that's one. This guy's shoes are bad shoes. They are shined, but they are bad shoes. They have no class, and you can tell by the way he walks that they hurt his feet. Then you look at his eyes. That's big number two. These guys, it seems like they never wear the Ferrari sunglasses and you can always see their eyes. It's like some guys got to advertise what they are just like some guys have got to pull jobs and then confess to the cops. Their eyes say, "Where's the next meal coming from? Where's the next joint coming from? Where's the guy I wanted to connect with when I came here?" Do you dig me?'

'Yes, I think I do.'

'Mostly what the eyes say is, "How do I score?" What did you say the old man in Old Orchard called the pushers and the quick-buck artists?'

'Drift trade,' Billy said.

'Yeah!' Ginelli kindled. The light in his eyes whirled. 'Drift trade, right good! The man I was looking for is high-class drift trade. These guys in resort towns float around like whores looking for steady customers. They rarely fall for big stuff, they move on all the time, and they are fairly smart . . . except for their shoes. They got J. Press shirts and Paul Stuart sport coats and designer jeans . . . but then you look at their feet and their fucking loafers say "Caldor's, nineteen-ninety-five." Their loafers say "I can be had, I'll do a job for you." With whores it's the blouses. Always rayon blouses. You have to train them out of it.

'But finally I saw the man, you know? So I, like, engaged him in conversation. We sat on a bench down by the public library – pretty place – and worked it all out. I had to pay a little more because I didn't have time to, you know, finesse him, but he was hungry enough and I thought he'd be trustworthy. Over the short haul, anyway. For these guys, the long haul doesn't fucking exist. They think the long haul is the place they used to walk through to get from American History to Algebra II.'

'How much did you pay him?'

Ginelli waved his hand.

'I am costing you money,' Billy said. Unconsciously he had fallen into Ginelli's rhythm of speech.

'You're a friend,' Ginelli said, a bit touchily. 'We can square it up later, but only if you want. I am having fun. This has been one *weird* detour, William. "How I Spent My Summer Vacation," if you can dig on that one time. Now can I tell you this? My mouth is getting dry and I got a long way to go and we got a lot to do later on.'

'Go ahead.'

The fellow Ginelli had picked out was Frank Spurton. He said he was an undergraduate at the University of Colorado on vacation, but to Ginelli he had looked to be about twenty-five – a pretty old undergrad. Not that it mattered. Ginelli wanted him to go out to the woods road where he had left the rental Ford and then follow the Gypsies when they took off. Spurton was to call the Bar Harbor Motor Inn when he was sure they had alighted for the night. Ginelli didn't think they would go too far. The name Spurton was to ask for when he called the motel was John Tree. Spurton wrote it down. Money changed hands – sixty percent of the total amount promised. The ignition keys and the distributor cap for the Ford also changed hands. Ginelli asked Spurton if he could put it on the distributor all right, and Spurton, with a car thief's smile, said he thought he could manage.

'Did you give him a ride out there?' Billy asked.

'For the money I was paying him, William, he could thumb.'

Ginelli drove back to the Bar Harbor Motor Inn instead and registered under the John Tree name. Although it was only two in the afternoon, he snagged the last room available for the night – the clerk handed him the key with the air of one conferring a great favor. The summer season was getting into high gear. Ginelli went to the room, set the alarm clock on the night table for four-thirty, and dozed until it went off. Then he got up and went to the airport.

At ten minutes past five, a small private plane – perhaps the same one that had ferried Fander up from Connecticut – landed. The 'business associate' deplaned, and packages, a large one and three small ones, were unloaded from the plane's cargo bay. Ginelli and the 'business associate' loaded the large package into the Nova's backseat and the small packages into the trunk. Then the 'business associate' went back to the plane. Ginelli didn't wait to see it take off, but returned to the motel, where he slept until eight o'clock, when the phone woke him.

It was Frank Spurton. He was calling from a Texaco station in the town of Bankerton, forty miles northwest of Bar Harbor. Around seven, Spurton said, the Gypsy caravan had turned into a field just outside of town – everything had been arranged in advance, it seemed.

'Probably Starbird,' Billy commented. 'He's their front man.'

Spurton had sounded uneasy . . . jumpy. 'He thought they had made him,' Ginelli said. 'He was loafing way back, and that was a mistake. Some of them turned off for gas or something. He didn't see them. He's doing about forty, just goofing along, and all of a sudden two old station wagons and a camper pass him, bang-boom-bang. That's the first he knows that he's all of a sudden in the middle of the fucking wagon train instead of behind it. He looks out his side window as the camper goes by, and he sees this old guy with no nose in the passenger seat, staring at him and waggling his fingers – not like he's waving but like he's throwing a spell. I'm not putting words in this guy's mouth, William; that's what he said to me on the phone. "Waggling his fingers like he was throwing a spell."'

'Jesus,' Billy muttered.

'You want a shot in your coffee?'

'No . . . yes.'

Ginelli dumped a capful of Chivas in Billy's cup and went on. He asked Spurton if the camper had had a picture on the side. It had. Girl and unicorn.

'Jesus,' Billy said again. 'You really think they recognized the car? That they looked around after they found the dogs and saw it on that road where you left it?'

'I know they did,' Ginelli said grimly. 'He gave me the name of the road they were on – Finson Road – and the number of the state road they turned off to get there. Then he asked me to leave the rest of his money in an envelope with his name on it in the motel safe. "I want to boogie" is what he said, and I didn't blame him much.'

Ginelli left the motel in the Nova at eight-fifteen. He passed the town-line marker between Bucksport and Bankerton at nine-thirty. Ten minutes later he passed a Texaco station that was closed for the night. There were a bunch of cars parked in a dirt lot to one side of it, some waiting for repair, some for sale. At the end of the row he saw the rental Ford. He drove on up the road, turned around, and drove back the other way.

'I did that twice more,' he said. 'I didn't get any of that feeling like before,' he said, 'so I went on up the road a little way and parked the heap on the shoulder. Then I walked back.'

'And?'

'Spurton was in the car,' Ginelli said. 'Behind the wheel. Dead. Hole in his forehead, just above the right eye. Not much blood. Might have been a forty-five, but I don't think so. No blood on the seat behind him. Whatever killed him didn't go all the way through. A forty-five slug would have gone through and left a hole in back the size of a Campbell's soup can. I think someone shot him with a ball bearing in a slingshot, just like the girl shot you. Maybe it was even her that did it.'

Ginelli paused, ruminating.

'There was a dead chicken in his lap. Cut open. One word written on Spurton's forehead, in blood. Chicken-blood is my guess, but I didn't exactly have time to give it the full crime-lab analysis, if you can dig that.'

'What word?' Billy asked, but he knew it before Ginelli said it.

' "NEVER." '

'Christ,' Billy said, and groped for the laced coffee. He got the cup to his mouth and then set it back down again. If he drank any of that, he was going to vomit. He couldn't afford to vomit. In his mind's eye he could see Spurton sitting behind the Ford's wheel, head tilted back, a dark hole over one eye, a ball of white feathers in his lap. This vision was clear enough so he could even see the bird's yellow beak, frozen half-open, its glazed black eyes . . .

The world swam in tones of gray . . . and then there was a flat hard smacking sound and dull heat in his cheek. He opened his eyes and saw Ginelli settling back into his seat.

'Sorry, William, but it's like that commercial for after-shave says – you needed that. I think you are getting the guilts over this fellow Spurton, and I want you to just quit it, you hear?' Ginelli's tone was mild, but his eyes were angry. 'You keep getting things all twisted around, like these bleeding-heart judges who want to blame everybody right up to the President of the United States for how some junkie knifed an old woman and stole her Social Security check – everyone, that is, but the junkie asshole who did it and is right now standing in front of him and waiting for a suspended sentence so he can go out and do it again.'

'That doesn't make any sense at all!' Billy began, but Ginelli cut him off.

'Fuck it doesn't,' he said. 'You didn't kill Spurton, William. Some Gypsy did, and whichever one it was, it was the old man at the bottom of it and we both know it. No one twisted Spurton's arm, either. He was doing a job for pay, that's all. A simple job. He got too far back and they boxed him. Now, tell me, William – do you want it taken off or not?'

Billy sighed heavily. His cheek still tingled warmly where Ginelli had slapped him. 'Yes,' he said. 'I still want it taken off.'

'All right, then, let's drop it.'

'Okay.' He let Ginelli speak on uninterrupted to the end of his tale. He was, in truth, too amazed by it to think much of interrupting.

Ginelli walked behind the gas station and sat down on a pile of old tires. He wanted to get his mind serene, he said, and so he sat there for the next twenty minutes or so, looking up at the night sky – the last glow of daylight had just faded out of the west – and thinking serene thoughts. When he felt he had his mind right, he went back to the Nova. He backed down to the Texaco station without turning on the lights. Then he dragged Spurton's body out of the rental Ford and put it into the Nova's trunk.

'They wanted to leave me a message, maybe, or maybe just hang me up by the heels when the guy who runs that station found a body in a car with my name on the rental papers in the glove compartment. But it was stupid, William, because if the guy *was* shot with a ball bearing instead of a bullet, the cops would take one quick sniff in my direction and then turn on them – the girl does a slingshot target-shooting act, for God's sake.

'Under other circumstances, I'd love to see the people I

was after paint themselves into a corner like that, but this is a funny situation – this is something we got to work out by ourselves. Also, I expected the cops to be out talking to the Gypsies the next day about something else entirely, if things went the way I expected, and Spurton would only complicate things. So I took the body. Thank God that station was just sitting there by its lonesome on a country road, or I couldn't have done it.'

With the body of Spurton in the trunk, curled around the smaller trio of boxes the 'business associate' had delivered that afternoon, Ginelli drove on. He found Finson Road less than half a mile farther up. On Route 37-A, a good secondary road leading west from Bar Harbor, the Gypsies had been clearly open for business. Finson Road – unpaved, potholed, and overgrown – was clearly a different proposition. They had gone to earth.

'It made things a little tougher, just like having to clean up after them down at the gas station, but in some ways I was absolutely delighted, William. I wanted to scare them, and they were behaving like people who *were* scared. Once people are scared, it gets easier and easier to keep them scared.'

Ginelli killed the Nova's headlights and drove a quarter of a mile down the Finson Road. He saw a turnout which led into an abandoned gravel pit. 'Couldn't have been more perfect if I'd ordered it,' he said.

He opened the trunk, removed Spurton's body, and pawed loose gravel over it. The body buried, he went back to the Nova, took two more bennies, and then unwrapped the big package which had been in the backseat. WORLD BOOK ENCYCLOPEDIA was stamped on the box. Inside was a Kalishnikov AK-47 assault rifle and four hundred rounds of ammunition, a spring-loaded knife, a lady's draw-string leather evening bag loaded with lead shot, a dispenser of Scotch strapping tape, and jar of lampblack.

Ginelli blacked his face and hands, then taped the knife to the fat part of his calf. He stuck the tape in his pocket and headed off.

'I left the sap,' he said. 'I already felt enough like a super-hero out of some fucking comic book.'

Spurton had said the Gypsies were camped in a field two miles up the road. Ginelli went into the woods and followed the road in that direction. He didn't dare lose sight of the road, he said, because he was afraid of getting lost.

'It was slow going,' he said. 'I kept stepping on sticks and running into branches. I hope I didn't walk through no fucking poison ivy. I'm very susceptible to poison ivy.'

After two hours spent struggling through the tangled second growth along the east side of Finson Road, Ginelli had seen a dark shape on the road's narrow shoulder. At first he thought it was a road sign or some sort of post. A moment later he realized it was a man.

'He was standing there just as cool as a butcher in a meat cooler, but I believed he had to be shitting me, William, I mean. I was *trying* to be quiet, but I hang out in New York City. Fucking Hiawatha I am not, if you can dig that. So I figured he was pretending not to hear me so he could get a fix on me. And when he had it he'd turn around and start chopping. I could have blown him out his socks where he stood, but it would have waked up everyone within a mile and a half, and besides, I promised you that I wouldn't hurt anyone.

'So I stood there and stood there. Fifteen minutes I stood there, thinking that if I move I'm gonna step on another stick and then the fun will begin. Then he moves from the side of the road into the ditch to take a piss, and I can't believe what I am seeing. I don't know where this guy took lessons in sentry duty, but it sure wasn't Fort Bragg. He's carrying the oldest shotgun I've seen in twenty years – what the Corsicans call a *loup*. And, William, he is wearing a pair of Walkman earphones! I could have walked up behind him, put my hands in my shirt, and armpit-farted out "Hail, Columbia" – he never would have moved.'

Ginelli laughed. 'I tell you one thing – I bet that old man didn't know the guy was rock and rolling while he was supposed to be watching for me.'

When the sentry moved back to his former place, Ginelli walked toward him on the sentry's blind side, no longer making much of an effort to be silent. He removed his belt as he walked. Something warned the sentry – something glimpsed out of the corner of his eye – at the last moment. The last moment is not always too late, but this time it was. Ginelli slipped the belt around his neck and pulled it tight. There was a short struggle. The young Gypsy dropped his shotgun and clawed at the belt. The earphones slid down his cheeks and Ginelli could hear the Rolling Stones, sounding lost between the stars, singing 'Under My Thumb.'

The young man began to make choked gargling noises. His struggles weakened, then stopped entirely. Ginelli kept the pressure on for another twenty seconds, then relaxed it ('I didn't want to make him foolish,' he explained seriously to Billy) and dragged him up the hill and into the underbush. He was a good-looking, well-muscled man of perhaps twenty-two, wearing jeans and Dingo boots. Ginelli guessed from Billy's description that it was Samuel Lemke, and Billy agreed. Ginelli found a good-sized tree and used strapping tape to bind him to it.

'It sounds stupid, saying you taped somebody to a tree, but only if you never had it done to you. Enough of that shit wound around you, and you might as well forget it. Strapping tape is *strong*. You're going to be where you are until someone comes along and cuts you loose. You can't break it and you sure as shit can't untie it.'

Ginelli cut off the bottom half of Lemke's T-shirt, stuffed it into his mouth, and taped it in place.

'Then I turned over the cassette in his machine and stuck the phones back on his head. I didn't want him to be too bored when he woke up.'

Ginelli now walked up the side of the road. He and Lemke were of similar height, and he was willing to take the risk that he would be able to stroll right up to another sentry before being challenged. Besides, it was getting late and he'd had no sleep but two short naps in the last forty-eight hours. 'Miss enough sleep and you goof up,' he said. 'If you're playing Monopoly, that's all right. But if you're dealing with fuckers that shoot people and then write discouraging words on their foreheads in chicken blood, you're apt to die. As it happens, I *did* make a mistake. I was just lucky enough to get away with it. Sometimes God forgives.'

This mistake was not seeing the second sentry until he was walking past him. It happened because the second man was well back in the shadows instead of standing at the edge of the road, as Lemke had been doing. Luckily for Ginelli, the reason was not concealment but comfort. 'This one wasn't just listening to a Walkman,' Ginelli said. 'This one was fast asleep. Lousy guards, but about what you expect from civilians. Also, they hadn't made up their minds that I was serious long-term trouble for them yet. If you think someone is seriously on the prod for your ass, that keeps you awake. Man, that keeps you awake even when you want to go to sleep.'

Ginelli walked over to the sleeping guard, picked his spot on the guard's skull, and then applied the butt of the Kalishnikov to that spot with a fair amount of force. There was a thud like the sound of a limp hand striking a mahogany table.

The guard, who had been propped comfortably against a tree, fell over in the grass. Ginelli bent and felt for a pulse. It was there, slow but not erratic. He pressed on.

Five minutes later he came to the top of a low hill. A sloping field opened out and down on the left. Ginelli could see the dark circle of vehicles parked about two hundred yards from the road. No campfire tonight. Dim, curtain-screened lights in a few of the campers, but that was all.

Ginelli worked his way halfway down the hill on his belly and his elbows, holding the assault rifle out in front of him. He found a rock outcropping that allowed him to both seat the stock firmly and to sight down the hill to the encampment.

'The moon was just coming up but I wasn't going to wait for it. Besides, I could see well enough for what I had to do – by then I was no more than seventy-five yards from them. And it wasn't as if I had to do any fine work. Kalishnikov's no good for that anyway. Might as well try to take out a guy's appendix with a chain saw. Kalishnikov's good to scare people with. I scared them, all right. I bet just about all of them made lemonade in the sheets. But not the old man. He's as tough as they come, William.'

With the automatic rifle firmly set, Ginelli pulled in a deep breath and sighted on the front tire of the unicorn camper. There was the sound of crickets and a small stream babbling somewhere close by. A whippoorwill cried out once across the dark field. Halfway through its second verse, Ginelli opened fire.

The Kalishnikov's thunder ripped the night in two. Fire hung around the end of the barrel in a corona as the clip – thirty .30-caliber bullets, each in a casing almost as long as a king-size cigarette, each powered with a hundred and forty grains of powder – ran out. The unicorn camper's front tire did not just blow; it exploded. Ginelli raked the bellowing gun the length of the camper – but low. 'Didn't put a single goddamn hole in the body,' he said. 'Tore the hell out of the ground beneath it. Didn't even cut it close, because of the gas tank. Ever see a camper blow? It's like what happens when you light a firecracker and put a can over it. I saw it happen once, on the New Jersey turnpike.'

The camper's back tire blew. Ginelli popped the first clip and slammed another one in. The uproar was beginning below. Voices yelled back and forth, some angry, most just scared. A woman screamed.

Some of them – how many of the total number, Ginelli had no way of telling – were spilling out of the backs of campers, most in pajamas and nightgowns, all looking confused and scared, all trying to stare in five different directions at the same time. And then Ginelli saw Taduz Lemke for the first time. The old man looked almost comic in his billowing nightshirt. Straggles of hair were escaping from beneath his tasseled nightcap. He came around the front of the unicorn van, took one look at the flattened, twisted tires, and then looked directly up toward where Ginelli was lying. He told Billy that there was nothing comic in that burning glance.

'I knew he couldn't see me,' he said. 'The moon wasn't up, I had lampblack on my face and hands, I was just another shadow in a whole field of them. But . . . I think he *did* see me, William, and it cooled off my heart.'

The old man turned toward his people, who were beginning to drift in his direction, still babbling and waving their hands. He shouted at them in Rom and swept an arm at the caravan. Ginelli didn't understand the language, but the gesture was clear enough: *Get under cover, you fools.*

'Too late, William,' Ginelli said smugly.

He had loosed the second burst directly into the air over their heads. Now a lot of people were screaming – men as well as women. Some hit the ground and began to crawl, most of them with their heads down and their butts waving in the air. The rest ran, breaking in all directions but the one from which the fire had come.

Lemke stood his ground, bellowing at them, bull-throated. His nightcap fell off. The runners went on running, the crawlers crawling. Lemke might ordinarily rule them with an iron hand, but Ginelli had panicked them.

The Pontiac station wagon from which he had taken the coat and sneakers the night before was parked next to the van, nose out. Ginelli slammed a third clip into the AK-47 and opened fire again.

'There wasn't anyone in it last night, and the way it smelled, I guessed no one would be in it tonight, either. I killed that station wagon – I mean, I *annihilated* that mother-fucker.

'An AK-47 is a very mean gun, William. People who have only seen war movies think that when you use a machine gun or an automatic rifle you end up with this neat little line of holes, but it ain't like that. It's messy, it's hard, and it happens *fast*. The windshield of that old Bonneville blew in. The hood popped up a little. Then the bullets caught it and tore it right off. The headlights blew. The tires blew. The grille fell off. I couldn't see the water spraying out of the radiator, it was too dark for that, but when the clip ran out I could sure hear it. When the clip ran out that son of a bitch looked like it had run into a brick wall. And during all of it, while the glass and chrome were flying, that old man never moved. Just looked for the muzzle flash so he could send the troops after me if I was stupid and waited for him to get his troops together. I decided to split before he could.'

Ginelli ran for the road, bent over low like a World War II soldier advancing under fire. Once there, he straightened up and sprinted. He passed the inner-perimeter sentry – the one he had used the gun butt on – with hardly a glance. But when he reached the spot where he had taken Mr Walkman, he stopped, catching his breath.

'Finding him wasn't hard, even in the dark,' Ginelli said. 'I could hear the underbush shaking and crackling. When I got a little closer I could hear him, too – *unth, unth, oooth, oooth, galump, galump.*'

Lemke had actually worked his way a quarter of the way around the tree he had been taped to – the net result being that he was more tightly bound than ever. The earphones had fallen off and were dangling around his neck by their wires. When he saw Ginelli he stopped struggling and just looked.

'I saw in his eyes that he thought I was going to kill him, and that he was good and fucking scared,' Ginelli said. 'That suited me just fine. The old dude wasn't scared, but I'll tell you, that *kid* wishes sincerely that they had never fucked with you, William. Unfortunately, I couldn't really make him sweat – there wasn't time.'

He knelt down by Lemke and held up the AK-47 so Lemke could see what it was. Lemke's eyes showed that he knew perfectly well.

'I don't have much time, asshole, so listen good,' Ginelli said. 'You tell the old man that next time I won't be shooting high or low or at empty cars. Tell him William Halleck says to take it off. You got that?'

Lemke nodded as much as the tape would allow. Ginelli tore it off his mouth and pulled the ball of shirting free.

'It's going to get busy around here,' Ginelli said. 'You yell, they'll find you. Remember the message.'

He turned to go.

'You don't understand,' Lemke said hoarsely. 'He'll *never* take it off. He's the last of the great Magyar chiefs – his heart is a brick. Please, mister, I'll remember, but he'll *never* take it off.'

On the road a pickup truck went bucketing by toward the Gypsy camp. Ginelli glanced in that direction and then back at Lemke.

'Bricks can be crushed,' he said. 'Tell him that, too.'

Ginelli broke out to the road again, crossed it, and jogged back toward the gravel pit. Another pickup truck passed him, then three cars in a line. These people, understandably curious about who had been firing an automatic weapon in their little town in the dead of night, presented no real problem for Ginelli. The glow of the approaching headlights allowed him plenty of time to fade back into the woods each time. He heard an approaching siren just as he ducked into the gravel pit.

He started the Nova up and rolled it dark to the end of the short access lane. A Chevrolet with a blue bubble on the dashboard roared by.

'After it was gone, I wiped the crap off my face and hands and followed it,' Ginelli said.

'*Followed* it?' Billy broke in.

'Safer. If there's shooting, innocent people break their legs getting to it so they can see some blood before the cops come and hose it off the sidewalk. People going in another direction are suspicious. Lots of times they are leaving because they've got guns in their pockets.'

By the time he reached the field again there were half a dozen cars parked along the shoulder of the road. Headlight beams crisscrossed each other. People were running back and forth and yelling. The constable's car was parked near the spot where Ginelli had sapped the second young man; the bubble light on the dash whipped flickers of blue across the trees. Ginelli unrolled the Nova's window. 'What's up, officer?'

'Nothing you need to worry about. Move along.' And just in case the fellow in the Nova might speak English but only understand Russian, the constable whipped his flashlight impatiently in the direction Finson Road was going.

Ginelli rolled slowly on up the road, threading his way between the parked vehicles – the ones that belonged to the local folks, he guessed. It was maybe harder for you to move along gawkers who were your neighbors, he told Billy. There were two distinct knots of people in front of the station wagon Ginelli had shot up. One comprised Gypsy men in pajamas and nightshirts. They were talking among themselves, some of them gesticulating extravagantly. The other comprised town men. They stood silently, hands in pockets, gazing at the wreck of the station wagon. Each group ignored the other.

Finson Road continued on for six miles, and Ginelli almost ditched the car not once but twice as people came barreling along what was little more than a dirt track at high speed.

'Just guys out in the middle of the night hoping to see a little blood before the cops hosed it off the sidewalk, William. Or off the grass, in this case.'

He connected with a feeder road that took him into Bucksport, and from there he turned north. He was back in the John Tree motel room by two in the morning. He set the alarm for seven-thirty and turned in.

Billy stared at him. 'You mean that all the time I was worrying that you were dead you were sleeping in the same motel we left?'

'Well, yeah.' Ginelli looked ashamed of himself for a moment, and then he grinned and shrugged at the same time. 'Put it down to inexperience, William. I am not used to people worrying about me. Except my momma, of course, and that is different.'

'You must have overslept – you didn't get here until nine or so.'

'No – I was up as soon as the alarm went off. I made a call and then walked downtown. Rented another car. From Avis this time. I don't have such good luck with Hertz.'

'You're going to be in trouble about that Hertz car, aren't you?' Billy asked.

'Nope. All's well. It could have been hairy, though. That's what the call was about – the Hertz car. I got that "business associate" of mine to fly back up from New York. There's a little airport in Ellsworth, and he came in there. Then the pilot hopped down to Bangor to wait for him. My associate thumbed over to Bankerton. He –'

'This thing is escalating,' Billy said. 'You know that? It's turning into Vietnam.'

'Fuck, no – don't be dumb, William.'

'Only the housekeeper flew up from New York.'

'Well, yeah. I don't know anyone in Maine, and the one connection I made here got his ass killed. Anyway, there was no problem. I got a full report last night. My associate got to Bankerton around noon yesterday, and the only guy at the station was this kid who looked like he was quite a few bricks short of a full load. Kid would pump gas when someone came, but mostly he was dicking around in one of the bays, lubing a car or something. While he was in there, my friend hot-wired the Ford and drove it away. Went right past the garage bay. Kid never even turned around. My associate drove to Bangor International Airport and parked the Ford car in one of the Hertz stalls. I told him to check for bloodstains, and when I talked to him on the phone he said he found some blood in the middle of the front seat – that was chicken blood, almost for sure – and cleaned it up with one of those Wet-Nap things. Then he filled in the information on the flap of the folder, dropped it into the Express Return box, and flew back to the Apple.'

'What about the keys? You said he hot-wired it.'

'Well,' Ginelli said, 'the keys were really the problem all along. That was another mistake. I chalk it up to short sleep, same as the other one, but maybe it really is old age creeping up. They were in Spurton's pocket and I forgot to get them when I laid him to rest. But now . . .' Ginelli took out a pair of keys on a bright yellow Hertz tab. He jingled them. '*Ta-da!*'

'You went back,' Billy said, his voice a little hoarse. 'Good Christ, you went back and dug him up to get the keys.'

'Well, sooner or later the woodchucks or the bears would have found him and dragged him around,' Ginelli said reasonably, 'or hunters would have found him. Probably in bird season, when they go out with their dogs. I mean, it's more than a minor annoyance to the Hertz people to get an express envelope without the keys – people are always forgetting to return keys to rental cars and hotel rooms. Sometimes they send them back, sometimes they don't bother. The service manager just dials an eight-hundred number, reads off the car's VIN, number, and the guy at the other end – from Ford or GM or Chrysler – gives him the key pattern. Presto! New keys. But if someone found a body in a gravel pit with a steel ball-bearing in his head and a set of car keys in his pocket that could be traced to me . . . bad. Very bad news. You get me?'

'Yes.'

'Besides, I had to go back out there anyway, you know,' Ginelli said mildly. 'And I couldn't go in the Nova.'

'Why not? They hadn't seen it.'

'I got to tell it in order, William. Then you'll see. Another shot?'

Billy shook his head. Ginelli helped himself.

'Okay. Early Tuesday morning, the dogs. Later Tuesday morning, the Nova. Tuesday night, the heavy firepower. Wednesday morning, early, the second rental car. You got all this?'

'I think so.'

'Now we're talking about a Buick sedan. The Avis guy wanted to give me an Aries K, said it was all he had left and I was lucky to get that, but an Aries K wasn't right. Had to be a sedan. Unobtrusive, but fairly big. Took twenty bucks to change his mind, but I finally got the car I wanted. I drove it back to the Bar Harbor Motor Inn, parked it, and made a couple more calls to make sure everything was happening the way I'd set it up. Then I drove over here in the Nova. I like that Nova, Billy – it looks like a mongrel and it smells like cowshit inside, but it's got *bones*.

'So I get here and *finally* set your mind at rest. By then I'm ready to crash again, and I'm too tired to even think about going back to Bar Harbor, and I spent the whole day in your bed.'

'You could have called me, you know, and saved at least one trip,' Billy said quietly.

Ginelli smiled at him. 'Yeah, I could have phoned, but fuck that. A phone call wouldn't have shown me how you were, William. You haven't been the only one worried.'

Billy lowered his head a little and swallowed with some difficulty. Almost crying again. Lately he was always almost crying, it seemed.

'So! Ginelli arises, refreshed and without too much of an amphetamine hangover. He showers, jumps into the Nova, which smells more like cowshit than ever after a day in the sun, and heads back to Bar Harbor. Once there, he takes the smaller packages out of the Nova's trunk and opens them in his room. There's a thirty-eight Colt Woodsman and a shoulder holster in one of them. The stuff in the other two packages fits into his sport-coat pockets. He then leaves the room and swaps the Nova for the Buick. He thinks for a minute that if there were two of him he wouldn't have had to spend half so much time shuffling cars like a parking-lot valet at a swanky Los Angeles restaurant. Then he heads out to scenic Bankerton for what he hopes will be the last fucking time. He makes just one stop along the way, at a supermarket. He goes in and buys two things: one of those Ball jars women put up preserves in and a sixteen-ounce bottle of Pepsi. He arrives in Bankerton just as twilight is starting to get really deep. He drives to the gravel pit and goes right in, knowing that being coy won't make a difference at this point – if the body has been found because of the excitement last night, he's going to be in the soup anyway. But no one is there, and there are no signs that anyone has *been* there. So he digs down to Spurton, feels around a little, and comes up with the prize. Just like in the Cracker Jack box.'

Ginelli's voice was perfectly expressionless, but Billy found this part of it unreeling in his mind like a movie – not a particularly pleasant one. Ginelli squatting down, pushing aside the gravel with his hands, finding Spurton's shirt . . . his belt . . . his pocket. Reaching in. Fumbling through sandy change that would never be spent. And underneath the pocket, chilly flesh that was stiffened into rigor mortis. At last, the keys, and the hasty reinterment.

'*Bruh,*' Billy said, and shivered.

'It is all a matter of perspective, William,' Ginelli said calmly. 'Believe me, it is.'

I think that's what scared me about it, Billy thought, and then listened with growing amazement as Ginelli finished the tale of his remarkable adventures.

★

Hertz keys in his pocket, Ginelli returned to the Avis Buick. He opened the Pepsi-Cola, poured it into the Ball jar, then closed the jar with a wire cap. That done, he drove up to the Gypsy camp.

'I knew they'd still be there,' he said. 'Not because they wanted to still be there, but because the State Bears would have damn well told them to stay put until the investigation was over. Here's a bunch of, well, nomads, you might as well call them, strangers in a hick town like Bakerton to be sure, and some other stranger or strangers come along in the middle of the night and shoot up the place. The cops tend to get interested in stuff like that.'

They were interested, all right. There was a Maine State Police cruiser and two unmarked Plymouths parked at the edge of the field. Ginelli parked between the Plymouths, got out of his car, and started down the hill to the camp. The dead station wagon had been hauled away, presumably to a place where the crime-lab people could go over it.

Halfway down the hill, Ginelli met a uniformed State Bear headed back up.

'You don't have any business here, sir,' the Bear said. 'You'll have to move along.'

'I convinced him that I did have a spot of business there,' Ginelli told Billy, grinning.

'How did you do that?'

'Showed him this.'

Ginelli reached into his back pocket and tossed Billy a leather folder. He opened it. He knew what he was looking at immediately; he had seen a couple of these in the course of his career as a lawyer. He supposed he would have seen a lot more of them if he had specialized in criminal cases. It was a laminated FBI identification card with Ginelli's picture on it. In the photo Ginelli looked five years younger. His hair was very short, almost brush-cut. The card identified him as Special Agent Ellis Stoner.

Everything suddenly clicked together in Billy's mind.

He looked up from the ID. 'You wanted the Buick because it looked more like –'

'Like a government car, sure. Big unobtrusive sedan. I didn't want to show up in the rolling tuna-fish can the Avis guy tried to give me, and I *surely* didn't want to show up in Farmer John's drive-in fuck-machine.'

'This – one of the things your associate brought up on his second trip?'

'Yes.'

Billy tossed it back. 'It looks almost real.'

Ginelli's smile faded. 'Except for the picture,' he said softly, 'it *is*.'

For a moment there was silence as Billy tried to grope his way around that one without thinking too much about what might have happened to Special Agent Stoner, and if he might have had kids.

Finally he said, 'You parked between two police cars and flipped that ID at a state cop five minutes after you finished digging a set of car keys out of a corpse's pocket in a gravel pit.'

'Nah,' Ginelli said, 'it was more like ten.'

As he made his way into the camp, he could see two guys, casually dressed but obviously cops, on their knees behind the unicorn camper. Each of them had a small garden trowel. A third stood, shining down a powerful flashlight while they dug through the earth.

'Wait, wait, here's another one,' one of them said. He picked a slug out of the dirt on his trowel and dropped it into a nearby bucket. *Blonk!* Two Gypsy children, obviously brothers, stood nearby watching this operation.

Ginelli was actually glad the cops were there. No one knew what he looked like here, and Samuel Lemke had seen only a dark smear of lampblack. Also, it was entirely plausible that an FBI agent would show up as a result of a shooting incident featuring a Russian automatic weapon. But he had developed a deep respect for Taduz Lemke. It was more than that word written on Spurton's forehead; it was the way Lemke had stood his ground in the face of those .30-caliber bullets coming at him out of the dark. And, of course, there was the thing that was happening to William. He felt it was just possible that the old man might know who he was. He might see it in Ginelli's eyes, or smell it on his skin, somehow.

Under no circumstances did he intend to let the old man with the rotten nose touch him.

It was the girl he wanted.

He crossed the inner circle and knocked on the door of one of the campers at random. He had to knock again before it was opened by a middle-aged woman with frightened, distrustful eyes.

'Whatever you want, we haven't got it for you,' she said. 'We've got troubles here. We're closed. Sorry.'

Ginelli flashed the folder. 'Special Agent Stoner, ma'am. FBI.'

Her eyes widened. She crossed herself rapidly and said something in Romany. Then she said, 'Oh, God, what next? Nothing is right anymore. Since Susanna died it's like we've been cursed. Or –'

She was pushed aside by her husband, who told her to shut up.

'Special Agent Stoner,' Ginelli began again.

'Yeah, I heard what you said.' He worked his way out. Ginelli guessed he was forty-five but he looked older, an extremely tall man who slumped so badly that he looked almost deformed. He wore a Disney World T-shirt and huge baggy Bermuda shorts. He smelled of Thunderbird wine and vomit waiting to happen. He looked like the sort of man to whom it happened fairly often. Like three and four times a week. Ginelli thought he recognized him from the night before – it had either been this guy or there was another Gypsy around here who went six-four or six-five. He had been one of those bounding away with all the grace of a blind epileptic having a heart attack, he told Billy.

'What do you want? We've had cops on our asses all day. We *always* got cops on our asses, but this is just . . . fucking . . . *ridiculous!*' He spoke in an ugly, hectoring tone, and his wife spoke to him agitatedly in Rom.

He turned his head toward her. '*Det krigiska jag-haller,*' he said, and added for good measure: 'Shut up, bitch.' The woman retreated. The man in the Disney shirt turned back to Ginelli. 'What do you want? Why don't you go talk to your buddies if you want something?' He nodded toward the crime-lab people.

'Could I have your name, please?' Ginelli asked with the same blank-faced politeness.

'Why don't you get it from them?' He crossed slabby, flabby arms truculently. Under his shirt his large breasts jiggled. 'We gave them our names, we gave them our statements. Someone took a few shots at us in the middle of the night, that's all any of us know. We just want to be let loose. We want to get out of Maine, out of New England, off the fucking East Coast.' In a slightly lower voice he added, 'And never come back.' The index and pinky fingers of his left hand popped out in a gesture Ginelli knew well from his mother and grandmother – it was the sign against the evil eye. He didn't believe this man was even aware he had done it.

'This can go one of two ways,' Ginelli said, still playing the ultrapolite FBI man to the hilt. 'You can give me a bit of information, sir, or you can end up in the State Detention Center pending a recommendation on whether or not to charge you with the obstruction of justice. If convicted of obstruction, you would face five years in jail and a fine of five thousand dollars.'

Another flood of Rom from the camper, this one nearly hysterical.

'*Enkelt!*' the man yelled hoarsely, but when he turned back to Ginelli again, his face had paled noticeably. 'You're nuts.'

'No, sir,' Ginelli said. 'It wasn't a matter of a few shots. It was at least three bursts fired from an automatic rifle. Private ownership of machine guns and rapid-fire automatic weapons is against the law in the United States. The FBI is involved in this case and I must sincerely advise you that you are currently waist-deep in shit, it's getting deeper, and I don't think you know how to swim.'

The man looked at him sullenly for a moment longer and then said, 'My name's Heilig. Trey Heilig. You coulda gotten it from those guys.' He nodded.

'They've got their jobs to do, I've got mine. Now, are you going to talk to me?' The big man nodded resignedly.

He put Trey Heilig through an account of what happened the night before. Halfway through it, one of the state detectives wandered over to see who he was. He glanced at Ginelli's ID and then left quickly, looking both impressed and a little worried.

Heilig claimed he had burst out of his camper at the sound of the first shots, had spotted the gun flashes, and had headed up the hill to the left, hoping to flank the shooter. But in the dark he had stumbled over a tree or something, hit his head on a rock, and blacked out for a while – otherwise he surely would have had the bastard. In support of his story he pointed to a fading bruise, at least three days old and probably incurred in a drunken stumble, and his left temple. *Uh-huh*, Ginelli thought, and turned to another page in his notebook. Enough of the hocus-pocus; it was time to get down to business.

'Thank you very much, Mr Heilig, you've been a great help.'

Telling the tale seemed to have mollified the man. 'Well . . . that's okay. I'm sorry I jumped on you like that. But if you were us . . .' He shrugged.

'Cops,' his wife said from behind him. She was looking out the door of the camper like a very old, very tired badger looking out of her hole to see how many dogs are around, and how vicious they look. 'Always cops, wherever we go. That's usual. But this is worse. People are scared.'

'Enkelt, Mamma,' Heilig said, but more gently now.

'I've got to talk to two more people, if you can direct me,' he said, and looked at a blank page in his notebook. 'Mr Taduz Lemke and a Mrs Angelina Lemke.'

'Taduz is asleep in there,' Heilig said, and pointed at the unicorn camper. Ginelli found this to be excellent news indeed, if it was true. 'He's very old and all of this has tired him out real bad. I think Gina's in her camper over there – she ain't a missus, though.'

He pointed a dirty finger at a small green Toyota with a neat wooden cap on the back.

'Thank you very much.' He closed the notebook and tucked it into his back pocket.

Heilig retreated to his camper (and his bottle, presumably), looking relieved. Ginelli walked across the inner circle again in the growing gloom, this time to the girl's camper. His heart, he told Billy, was beating high and hard and fast. He drew a deep breath and knocked on the door.

There was no immediate answer. He was raising his hand to knock again when it was opened. William had said she was lovely, but he was not prepared for the *depth* of her loveliness – the dark, direct eyes with corneas so white they were faintly bluish, the clean olive skin that glowed faintly pink deep down. He looked for a moment at her hands and saw that they were strong and corded. There was no polish in the nails, which were clean but clipped as bluntly close as the fingernails of a farmer. In one of those hands she held a book called *Statistical Sociology*.

'Yes?'

'Special Agent Ellis Stoner, Miss Lemke,' he said, and immediately that clear, lucent quality left her eyes – it was as if a shutter had fallen over them. 'FBI.'

'Yes?' she repeated, but with no more life than a tele-phone-answering machine.

'We're investigating the shooting incident that took place here last night.'

'You and half the world,' she said. 'Well, investigate away, but if I don't get my correspondence-course lessons in the mail by tomorrow morning I'm going to get grades taken off for lateness. So if you'll excuse me –'

'We've reason to believe that a man named William Halleck may have been behind it,' Ginelli said. 'Does that name mean anything to you?' Of course it did; for a moment her eyes opened wide and simply *blazed*. Ginelli had thought her lovely almost beyond believing. He still did, but he now also believed this girl really could have been the one who killed Frank Spurton.

'That *pig*!' she spat. '*Han satte sig pa en av stolarna! Han sneglade pa nytt mot hyllorna i vild! Vild!*'

'I have a number of pictures of a man we believe to be Halleck,' Ginelli said mildly. 'They were taken in Bar Harbor by an agent using a telephoto lens –'

'Of *course* it's Halleck!' she said. 'That pig killed my *tan-tenyjad* – my grandmother! But he won't bother us long. He . . .' She bit her full lower lip, bit it hard, and stopped the words. If Ginelli had been the man he was claiming to be she would already have assured herself of an extremely deep and detailed interrogation. Ginelli, however, affected not to notice.

'In one of the photographs, money appears to be passing between the two men. If one of the men is Halleck, then the other one is probably the shooter who visited your camp last night. I'd like you and your grandfather to identify Halleck positively if you can.'

'He's my great-grandfather,' she said absently. 'I think he's asleep. My brother is with him. I hate to wake him.' She paused. 'I hate to upset him with this. The last few days have been dreadfully hard on him.'

'Well, suppose we do this,' Ginelli said. 'You look through the photos, and if you can positively identify the man as Halleck, we won't need to bother the elder Mr Lemke.'

'That would be fine. If you catch this Halleck pig, you will arrest him?'

'Oh, yes. I have a federal John Doe warrant with me.'

That convinced her. As she swung out of the camper with a swirl of skirt and a heartbreaking flash of tanned leg, she said something that chilled Ginelli's heart: 'There won't be much of him to arrest, I don't think.'

They walked past the cops still sifting dirt in the deepening gloom. They passed several Gypsies, including the two brothers, now dressed for bed in identical pairs of camouflage pajamas. Gina nodded at several of them and they nodded back but steered clear – the tall Italian-looking man with Gina was FBI, and it was best not to meddle in such business.

They passed out of the circle and walked up the hill toward Ginelli's car, and the evening shadows swallowed them.

'It was just as easy as pie, William,' Ginelli said. 'Third night in a row, and it was still as easy as pie . . . why not? The place was crawling with cops. Was the guy who shot them up just going to come back and do something else while the cops were there? They didn't think so . . . but they were stupid, William. I expected it of the rest of them, but not of the old man – you don't spend your whole life learning how to hate and distrust the cops and then just suddenly decide they're gonna protect you from whoever has been biting on your ass. But the old man was sleeping. He's worn out. That's good. We may just take him, William. We may just.'

They walked back to the Buick. Ginelli opened the driver's-side door while the girl stood there. And as he leaned in, taking the .38 out of the shoulder holster with one hand and pushing the wire lid-holder off the Ball jar with the other, he felt the girl's mood abruptly change from bitter exultation to one of sudden wariness. Ginelli himself was pumped up, his emotions and intuitions turned outward and tuned to an almost exquisite degree. He seemed to sense her first awareness of the crickets, the surrounding darkness, the ease with which she had been split off from the others, by a man she had never seen before, at a time when she should have known better than to trust *any* man she'd never seen before. For the first time she was wondering why 'Ellis Stoner' hadn't brought the papers down to the camp with him if he was so hot to get an ID on Halleck. But it was all too late. He had mentioned the one name guaranteed to cause a knee-jerk spasm and hate and to blind her with eagerness.

'Here we are,' Ginelli said, and turned back to her with the gun in one hand and the glass Ball jar in the other.

Her eyes widened again. Her breasts heaved as she opened her mouth and drew in a breath.

'You can start to scream,' Ginelli said, 'but I guarantee it will be the last sound you ever hear yourself make, Gina.'

For a moment he thought she would do it anyway . . . and then she let the breath out in a long sigh.

'*You're* the one working for that pig,' she said. '*Hans satte sig pa –*'

'Talk English, whore,' he said almost casually, and she recoiled as if slapped.

'You don't call me a whore,' she whispered. 'No one is going to call me a whore.' Her hands – those strong hands – arched and hooked into claws.

'You call my friend William a pig, I call you a whore, your mother a whore, your father an asshole-licking toilet hound,' Ginelli said. He saw her lips draw back from her teeth in a snarl and he grinned. Something in that grin made her falter. She did not exactly look afraid – Ginelli told Billy later that he wasn't sure then if it was in her to look afraid – but some reason seemed to surface through her hot fury, some sense of who and what she was dealing with.

'What do you think this is, a game?' he asked her. 'You throw a curse onto someone with a wife and a kid, you think it is a game? You think he hit that woman, your gramma, on purpose? You think he had a contract on her? You think the Mafia had a contract put out on your old grandmother? Shit!'

The girl was now crying with rage and hate. 'He was getting a jerk-off job from his woman and he ran her down in the street! And then they . . . they *han tog in pojken* – whitewash him off – but we got him fixed. And you will be next, you friend of pigs. It don't matter what –'

He pushed the glass cap off the top of the wide-mouthed

jar with his thumb. Her eyes went to the jar for the first time. That was just where he wanted them.

'Acid, whore,' Ginelli said, and threw it in her face. 'See how many people you shoot with that slingshot of yours when you're blind.'

She made a high, windy screeching sound and clapped her hands over her eyes, too late. She fell to the ground. Ginelli put a foot on her neck.

'You scream and I'll kill you. You and the first three of your friends to make it up here.' He took the foot away. 'It was Pepsi-Cola.'

She got to her knees, staring at him through her spread fingers, and with those same exquisitely tuned, almost telepathic senses, Ginelli knew that she hadn't needed him to tell her it wasn't acid. She knew, had known almost at once in spite of the stinging. An instant later – barely in time – he knew she was going to go for his balls.

As she sprang at him, smooth as a cat, he sidestepped and kicked her in the side. The back of her head struck the chrome edging of the open driver's door with a loud crunch and she fell in a heap, blood flowing down one flawless cheek.

Ginelli bent toward her, sure she was unconscious, and she was at him, hissing. One hand tore across his forehead, opening a long cut there. The other ripped through the arm of his turtleneck and drew more blood.

Ginelli snarled and pushed her back down. He jammed the pistol against her nose. 'Come on, you want to go for it? You want to? Go for it, whore! Go on! You spoiled my face! I'd love for you to go for it!'

She lay still, staring at him with eyes now as dark as death.

'You'd do it,' he said. 'If it was just you, you'd come at me again. But it would just about kill him, wouldn't it? The old man?'

She said nothing, but a dim light seemed to flicker momentarily across the darkness of those eyes.

'Well, you think what it would do to him if that really *had* been acid I threw in your face. Think what it would do to him if instead of you I decided to throw it in the faces of those two kids in the GI Joe pajamas. I could do it, whore. I could do it and then go back home and eat a good dinner. You look into my face and you are gonna know I could.'

Now at last he saw confusion and a dawning of something that could have been fear – but not for herself.

'He cursed you,' he said. 'I was the curse.'

'Fuck his curse, that pig,' she whispered, and wiped blood from her face with a contemptuous flick of her fingers.

'He tells me not to hurt anyone,' Ginelli went on, as if she had not spoken. 'I haven't. But that ends tonight. I don't know how many times your old gramps has gotten away with this before, but he ain't going to get away with it this time. You tell him to take it off. You tell him it's the last time I ask. Here. Take this.'

He pressed a scrap of paper into her hand. On it he had written the telephone number of the 'safe kiosk' in New York.

'You gonna call this number by midnight tonight and tell me what that old man says. If you need to hear back from me, you call that number again two hours later. You can pick up your message . . . if there is one. And that's it. One way or another, the door is gonna be closed. No one at that number is gonna know what the fuck you are talking about after two o'clock tomorrow morning.'

'He'll never take it off.'

'Well, maybe he won't,' he said, 'because that is the same thing your brother said last night. But that's not your business. You just play square with him and let him make up his own mind what he's gonna do – make sure you explain to him that if he says no, that's when the boogie-woogie *really* starts. You go first, then the two kids, then anybody else I can get my hands on. Tell him that. Now, get in the car.'

'No.'

Ginelli rolled his eyes. 'Will you wise up? I just want to make sure I have time to get out of here without twelve cops on my tail. If I had wanted to kill you, I wouldn't have given you a message to deliver.'

The girl got up. She was a little wobbly, but she made it. She got in behind the wheel and then slid across the seat.

'Not far enough.' Ginelli wiped blood off his forehead and showed it to her on his fingers. 'After this, I want to see you crouched up against that door over there like a wallflower on her first date.'

She slid against the door. 'Good,' Ginelli said, getting in. 'Now, stay there.'

He backed out to Finson Road without turning on his lights – the Buick's wheels spun a little on the dry timothy grass. He shifted to drive with his gun hand, saw her twitch, and pointed the gun at her again.

'Wrong,' he said. 'Don't move. Don't move at *all*. You understand?'

'I understand.'

'Good.'

He drove back the way he had come, holding the gun on her.

'Always it's this way,' she said bitterly. 'For even a little justice we are asked to pay so much. He is your friend, this pig Halleck?'

'I told you, don't call him that. He's no pig.'

'He cursed us,' she said, and there was a kind of wondering contempt in her voice. 'Tell him for me, mister, that *God* cursed us long before him or any of his tribe ever were.'

'Save it for the social worker, babe.'

She fell silent.

A quarter of a mile before the gravel pit where Frank Spurton rested, Ginelli stopped the car.

'Okay, this is far enough. Get out.'

'Sure.' She looked at him steadily with those unfathomable eyes. 'But there is one thing you should know, mister – our paths will cross again. And when they do, I will kill you.'

'No,' he said. 'You won't. Because you owe me your life tonight. And if that ain't enough for you, you ungrateful bitch, you can add in your brother's life last night. You talk, but you still don't understand the way things are, or why you ain't home-free on this, or why you ain't *never* gonna be home-free on this until you quit. I got a friend you could fly like a kite if you hooked up some twine to his belt. What have *you* got? I'll tell you what you got. You got an old man with no nose who put a curse on my friend and then ran away in the night like a hyena.'

Now she was crying, and crying hard. The tears ran down her face in streams.

'Are you saying God is on your side?' she asked him, her voice so thick the words were almost unintelligible. 'Is that what I hear you saying? You should burn in hell for such blasphemy. Are we hyenas? If we are, it was people like your friend who made us so. My great-grandfather says there *are* no curses, only mirrors you hold up to the souls of men and women.'

'Get out,' he said. 'We can't talk. We can't even hear each other.'

'That's right.'

She opened the door and got out. As he pulled away she screamed: '*Your friend is a pig and he'll die thin!*'

★

'But I don't think you will,' Ginelli said.

'What do you mean?'

Ginelli looked at his watch. It was after three o'clock. 'Tell you in the car,' he said. 'You've got an appointment at seven o'clock.'

Billy felt that sharp, hollow needle of fear in his belly again. 'With him?'

'That's right. Let's go.'

As Billy got to his feet there was another arrhythmic episode – this the longest one yet. He closed his eyes and grasped at his chest. What remained of his chest. Ginelli grabbed him. 'William, are you okay?'

He looked in the mirror and saw Ginelli holding a grotesque sideshow freak in flapping clothes. The arrhythmia passed and was replaced by an even more familiar sensation – that milky, curdled rage that was directed at the old man . . . and at Heidi.

'I'm okay,' he said. 'Where are we going?'

'Bangor,' Ginelli said.

CHAPTER TWENTY-THREE
The Transcript

They took the Nova. Both things Ginelli had told him about it were true – it smelled quite strongly of cow manure, and it ate the road between Northeast Harbor and Bangor in great swallows. Ginelli stopped around four to pick up a huge basket of steamer clams. They parked at a roadside rest area and divided them, along with a six-pack of beer. The two or three family groups at the picnic tables got a look at Billy Halleck and moved as far away as possible.

While they ate, Ginelli finished his story. It didn't take long.

'I was back in the John Tree room by eleven o'clock last night,' he said. 'I could have gotten there quicker, maybe, but I did a few loops and figure-eights and turn-backs just to make sure no one was behind me.

'Once I was in the room, I called New York and sent a fellow out to the telephone I gave the girl the number for. I told him to take a tape deck and a steno plug with him – the kind of gadget reporters use to do phone interviews. I didn't want to have to rely on hearsay, William, if you can dig that. I told him to call me back with the tape as soon as she hung up.

'I disinfected the cuts she put in me while I waited for the call-back. I'm not gonna say she had hydrophobia or anything like that, William, but there was so much hate in her, you know . . .'

'I know,' Billy said, and thought grimly: *I really do know. Because I'm gaining. In that one way, I'm gaining.*

The call had come at a quarter past twelve. Closing his eyes and pressing the fingers of his left hand against his forehead, Ginelli was able to give Billy an almost exact recitation of how the playback had gone.

Ginelli's Man: Hello.

Gina Lemke: Do you work for the man I saw tonight?

Ginelli's Man: Yes, you could say that.

Gina: Tell him my great-grandfather says –

Ginelli's Man: I got a steno plug on this. I mean, you are being taped. I will play it back for the man you mentioned. So –

Gina: You can do that?

Ginelli's Man: Yes. So you are talking to him now, in a way of speaking.

Gina: All right. My great-grandfather says he will take it off. I tell him he is crazy, worse, that he is wrong, but he is firm. He says there can be no more hurting and no more fear for his people – he will take it off. But he needs to meet with Halleck. He can't take it off unless he does. At seven o'clock tomorrow evening my great-grandfather will be in Bangor. There is a park between two streets – Union and Hammond. He will be there sitting on a bench. He will be alone. So you win, big man – you win, *mi hela po klockan.* Have your pig friend in Fairmont Park, Bangor, tonight at seven.

Ginelli's Man: That's all?

Gina: Yes, except tell him I hope his cock turns black and falls off.

Ginelli's Man: You're telling him yourself, sister. But you wouldn't be if you knew who you was telling.

Gina: And fuck you, too.

Ginelli's Man: You should call back here at two, to see if there's an answer.

Gina: I'll call.

'She hung up,' Ginelli said. He dumped the empty clam shells in a litter basket, came back, and added with no pity at all: 'My guy said it sounded like she was crying all through it.'

'Christ Jesus,' Billy muttered.

'Anyway, I had my guy put the steno plug back on the phone and I recorded a message for him to play back to her when she called at two. It went like this. "Hello, Gina. This is Special Agent Stoner. I have your message. It sounds like a go. My friend William will come to the park at seven o'clock this evening. He will be alone, but I will be watching. Your people will be watching too, I imagine. That's fine. Let us both watch and let neither of us get in the way of what goes on between the two of them. If anything happens to my friend, you will pay a high price."'

'And that was it?'

'Yes. That was it.'

'The old man caved in.'

'I *think* he caved in. It could still be a trap, you know.' Ginelli looked at him soberly. 'They know I'll be watching. They may have decided to kill you where I can see it, as revenge on me, and then take their chances with what happens next.'

'They're killing me anyway,' Billy said.

'Or the girl could take it into her head to do it on her own. She's mad, William. People don't always do what they're told when they're mad.'

Billy looked at him reflectively. 'No, they don't. But either way, I don't have much choice, do I?'

'No . . . I don't think you do. You ready?'

Billy glanced toward the people staring at him and nodded. He'd been ready for a long time.

Halfway back to the car he said: 'Did you really do any of it for me, Richard?'

Ginelli stopped, looked at him, and smiled a little. The smile was almost vague . . . but that whirling, twirling light in his eyes was sharply focused – too sharply focused for Billy to look at. He had to shift his gaze.

'Does it matter, William?'

CHAPTER TWENTY-FOUR
Purpurfargade Ansiktet

They were in Bangor by late afternoon. Ginelli swung the Nova into a gas station, had it filled up, and got directions from the attendant. Billy sat exhaustedly in the passenger seat. Ginelli looked at him with sharp concern when he came back.

'William, are you all right?'

'I don't know,' he said, and then reconsidered. 'No.'

'Is it your ticker again?'

'Yeah.' He thought about what Ginelli's midnight doctor had said – potassium, electrolytes . . . something about how Karen Carpenter might have died. 'I ought to have something with potassium in it. Pineapple juice. Bananas. Or oranges.' His heart broke into a sudden disorganized gallop. Billy leaned back and shut his eyes and waited to see if he was going to die. At last the uproar quieted. 'A whole bag of oranges.'

There was a Shop and Save up ahead. Ginelli pulled in. 'I'll be right back, William. Hang in.'

'Sure,' Billy said vaguely, and fell into a light doze as soon as Ginelli left the car. He dreamed. In his dream he saw his house in Fairview. A vulture with a rotting beak flew down to the windowsill and peered in. From inside the house someone began to shriek.

Then someone else was shaking him roughly. Billy started awake. 'Huh!'

Ginelli leaned back and blew out breath. 'Jesus, William, don't scare me like that!'

'What are you talking about?'

'I thought you were dead, man. Here.' He put a net bag filled with navel oranges in Billy's lap. Billy plucked at the fastener with his thin fingers – fingers which now looked like white spider legs – and couldn't get it to give. Ginelli slit the bag open with his pocket knife, then cut an orange in quarters with it. Billy ate slowly at first, as one does a duty, then ravenously, seeming to rediscover his appetite for the first time in a week or more. And his disturbed heart seemed to calm down and rediscover something like its old steady beat . . . although that might have only been his mind playing games with itself.

He finished the first orange and borrowed Ginelli's knife to cut a second one into pieces.

'Better?' Ginelli asked.

'Yes. A lot. When do we get to the park?'

Ginelli pulled over to the curb, and Billy saw by the sign that they were on the corner of Union Street and West Broadway – summer trees, full of foliage, murmured in a mild breeze. Dapples and shadow moved lazily on the street.

'We're here,' Ginelli said simply, and Billy felt a finger touch his backbone and then slide coldly down it. 'As close as I want to get, anyway. I would have dropped you off downtown, only you would have attracted one hell of a lot of attention walking up here.'

'Yes,' Billy said. 'Like children fainting and pregnant women having miscarriages.'

'You couldn't have made it anyway,' Ginelli said kindly. 'Anyway, it don't matter. Park's right down at the foot of this hill. Quarter of a mile. Pick a bench in the shade and wait.'

'Where will you be?'

'I'll be around,' Ginelli said and smiled. 'Watching you and watching out for the girl. If she ever sees me again before

I see her, William, I ain't never going to have to change my shirt again. You understand?'

'Yes.'

'I'll be keeping my eye on you.'

'Thank you,' Billy said, and was not sure just how, or how much, he meant that. He *did* feel gratitude to Ginelli, but it was a strange, difficult emotion, like the hate he now bore for Houston and for his wife.

'*Por nada,*' Ginelli said, and shrugged. He leaned across the seat, hugged Billy, and kissed him firmly on both cheeks. 'Be tough with the old bastard, William.'

'I will,' Billy said, smiling, and got out of the car. The dented Nova pulled away. Billy stood watching until it had disappeared around the corner at the end of the block, and then he started down the hill, swinging the bag of oranges in one hand.

He barely noticed the little boy who, halfway up the block, abruptly turned off the sidewalk, scaled the Cowans' fence, and shot across their backyard. That night this little boy would awake screaming from a nightmare in which a shambling scarecrow with lifeless blowing hair on its skull-head bore down on him. Running down the hallway to his room, the boy's mother heard him screaming: '*It wants to make me eat oranges until I die! Eat oranges till I die! Eat till I die!*'

The park was wide and cool and green and deep. On one side, a gaggle of kids were variously climbing on the jungle gym, teeter-tottering, and whooshing down the slide. Far across the way a softball game was going on – the boys against the girls, it looked like. In between, people walked, flew kites, threw Frisbees, ate Twinkies, drank Cokes, slurped Slurpies. It was a cameo of American midsummer in the latter half of the twentieth century, and for a moment Billy warmed toward it – toward *them*.

All that's lacking is the Gypsies, a voice inside him whispered, and the chill came back – a chill real enough to bring goose bumps to his arms and cause him to abruptly cross his thin arms over his reed of a chest. *We ought to have the Gypsies, oughtn't we? The old station wagons with the NRA stickers on the rusty bumpers, the campers, the vans with the murals on the sides – then Samuel with his bowling pins and Gina with her slingshot. And they all came running. They always came running. To see the juggling, to try the slingshot, to hear the future, to get a potion or a lotion, to bed a girl – or at least to dream of it – to see the dogs tear at each other's guts. They always come running. Just for the strangeness of it. Sure, we need the Gypsies. We always have. Because if you don't have someone to run out of town once in a while, how are you going to know you yourself belong there? Well, they'll be along soon, right?*

'Right,' he croaked, and sat down on a bench that was almost in the shade. His legs were suddenly trembling, strengthless. He took an orange out of the bag and after some effort managed to tear it open. But now his appetite was gone again and he could only eat a little.

The bench was quite a distance apart from the others, and Billy attracted no undue attention, so far as he could tell – from a distance, he could have been a very thin old man taking in a little afternoon air.

He sat, and as the shade crept up first over his shoes, then his knees, and finally puddled in his lap, an almost fantastical sense of despair overtook him – a feeling of waste and futility much darker than these innocent afternoon shadows. Things had gone too far and nothing could be taken back. Not even Ginelli, with his psychotic energy, could change what had happened. He could only make things worse.

I should have never . . . Billy thought, but then whatever it was he should have never done broke up and faded out like a bad radio signal. He dozed again. He was in Fairview, a Fairview of the Living Dead. Corpses lay everywhere – starvelings. Something pecked sharply at his shoulder.

No.

Peck!

No!

But it came again, *peck*, and *peck* and *peck*, it was the vulture with the rotting nose, of course, and he didn't want to turn his head for fear it might peck his eyes out with the black remnants of its beak. But

(peck)

it insisted, and he

(!peck!peck!)

slowly turned his head, rising out of the dream at the same time and seeing –

—with no real surprise that it was Taduz Lemke beside him on the bench.

'Wake up, white man from town,' he said, and plucked sharply at Billy's sleeve again with his twisted, nicotine-stained fingers. *Peck!* 'Your dreams are bad. They have a stink I can smell on your breath.'

'I'm awake,' Billy said quickly.

'You sure?' Lemke asked, with some interest.

'Yes.'

The old man wore a gray serge suit, double-breasted. On his feet were high-topped black shoes. What little hair he had was parted in the middle and pulled sternly backward from his forehead, which was as lined as the leather of his shoes. A gold hoop sparked from one of his earlobes.

The rot, Billy saw, had spread – dark lines now radiated

out from the ruins of his nose and across most of his runneled
left cheek.

'Cancer,' Lemke said. His bright black eyes – the eyes of
a bird for sure – never left Billy's face. 'You like that? It
make you happy?' 'Happy' came out 'hoppy.'

'No,' Billy said. He was still trying to clean away the dregs
of the dream, to hook himself into this reality. 'No, of course
not.'

'Don't lie,' Lemke said. 'There is no need. It make you
happy, of course it make you happy.'

'None of it makes me happy,' he said. 'I'm sick about it
all. Believe me.'

'I don't believe nothing no white man from town ever
told me,' Lemke said. He spoke with a hideous sort of genial-
ity. 'But you sick, oh yeah. You think. You *nastan farsk* –
dying from being thin. So I brought you something. It's
gonna fatten you up, make you better.' His lips drew back
from the black stumps of his teeth in a hideous grin. 'But
only when somebody *else* eats it.'

Billy looked at what Lemke held on his lap and saw with
a floating kind of *déjà vu* that it was a pie in a disposable
aluminum pie plate. In his mind he heard his dream self
telling his dream wife: *I don't want to be fat. I've decided I like
being thin. You eat it.*

'You look scared,' Lemke said. 'It's too late to be scared,
white man from town.'

He took a pocketknife from his jacket and opened it,
performing the operation with an old man's grave and studied
slowness. The blade was shorter than the blade of Ginelli's
pocketknife, Billy saw, but it looked sharper.

The old man pushed the blade into the crust and then
drew it across, creating a slit about three inches long. He
withdrew the blade. Red droplets fell from it onto the crust.
The old man wiped the blade on the sleeve of his jacket,

leaving a dark red stain. Then he folded the blade and put the knife away. He hooked his misshapen thumbs over opposing sides of the pie plate and pulled gently. The slit gaped, showing a swimming viscous fluid in which dark things – strawberries, maybe – floated like clots. He relaxed his thumbs. The slit closed. He pulled the edges of the pie plate again. The slit opened. So he continued to pull and release as he spoke. Billy was unable to look away.

'So . . . you have convinced yourself that it is . . . What did you call it? A poosh. That what happened to my Susanna is no more your fault than my fault, or her fault, or God's fault. You tell yourself you can't be asked to pay for it – there is no blame, you say. It slides off you because your shoulders are broken. No blame, you say. You tell yourself and tell yourself and tell yourself. But there is no poosh, white man from town. Everybody pays, even for things they dint do. No poosh.'

Lemke fell reflectively silent for a moment. His thumbs tensed and relaxed, tensed and relaxed. The slit in the pie opened and closed.

'Because you won't take blame – not you, not your friends – I *make* you take it. I stick it on you like a sign. For my dear dead daughter that you killed I do this, and for her mother, and for her children. Then your friend comes. He poisons dogs, shoots guns in the night, uses his hands on a woman, threatens to throw acid into the faces of children. Take it off, he says – take it off and take it off and take it off. And finally I say okay as long as he will *podol enkelt* – get out of here! Not from what he did, but from what he *will* do – he is crazy, this friend of yours, and he will never stop. Even my 'Gelina says she sees from his eyes he will never stop. "But we'll never stop, either," she says, and I say, "Yes we will. Yes we will stop. Because if we don't, we are crazy like the town man's friend. If we don't stop, we must think what the white man says is right – God pays back, that it's a poosh." '

Tense and relax. Tense and relax. Open and close.

' "Take it off," he says, and at least he don't say "Make it disappear, make it not there anymore." Because a curse is in some way like a baby.'

His old dark thumbs pulled. The slit stretched open.

'No one understand these things. Not me, either, but I know a little. "Curse" is your word, but Rom is better. Listen: *Purpurfargade ansiktet.* You know that?'

Billy shook his head slowly, thinking the phrase had a richly dark texture.

'It mean something like "Child of the night-flowers." Is like to get a child who is *varsel* – changeling. Gypsies say *varsel* is always found under lilies or nightshade, which blooms at night. This way of saying is better because *curse* is a *thing.* What you have is not a *thing.* What you have is alive.'

'Yes,' Billy said. 'It's inside, isn't it! It's inside me, eating me.'

'Inside? Outside?' Lemke shrugged. 'Everywhere. This thing – *purpurfargade ansiktet* – you bring it into the world like a baby. Only it grows strong faster than a baby, and you can't kill it because you can't see it – only you can see what it *does.*'

The thumbs relaxed. The slit closed. A dark red rivulet trickled across the mild topography of the pie crust.

'This curse . . . you *dekent felt o gard da borg.* Be to it like a father. You still want to be rid of it?'

Billy nodded.

'You still believe in the *poosh?*'

'Yes.' It was only a croak.

The old Gypsy man with the rotting nose smiled. The black lines of rot under his left cheek dipped and wavered. The park was nearly empty now. The sun was nearing the horizon. The shadows covered them. Suddenly the knife was in Lemke's hand again, the blade out.

He's going to stab me, Billy thought dreamily. *Going to stab me in the heart and run away with his strawberry pie under his arm.*

'Unwrap your hand,' Lemke said.

Billy looked down.

'Yes – where she shot you.'

Billy pulled the clamps out of the elastic bandage and slowly unwrapped it. Underneath, his hand looked too white, fishlike. In contrast, the edges of the wound were dark, dark red – a liverish color. *The same color as those things inside his pie*, Billy thought. *The strawberries. Or whatever they are.* And the wound had lost its almost perfect circularity as the edges puffed together. Now it looked like . . .

Like a slit, Billy thought, his eyes drifting back to the pie.

Lemke handed Billy the knife.

How do I know you haven't coated this blade with curare or cyanide or D-Con Rat-Prufe? he thought about asking, and then didn't. Ginelli was the reason. Ginelli and the Curse of the White Man from Town.

The pocketknife's worn bone handle fitted comfortably into his hand.

'If you want to be rid of the *purpurfargade ansiktet*, first you give it to the pie . . . and then you give the pie with the curse-child inside it to someone else. But it has to be soon, or it come back on you double. You understand?'

'Yes,' Billy said.

'Then do it if you will,' Lemke said. His thumbs tightened again. The darkish slit in the pie crust spread open.

Billy hesitated, but only for a second – then his daughter's face rose in his mind. For a moment he saw her with all the clarity of a good photograph, looking back at him over her shoulder, laughing, her pom-poms held in her hands like big silly purple-and-white fruits.

You're wrong about the push, old man, he thought. *Heidi for Linda. My wife for my daughter. That's the push.*

He pushed the blade of Taduz Lemke's knife into the hole in his hand. The scab broke easily. Blood spattered into the slit in the pie. He was dimly aware that Lemke was speaking very rapidly in Rom, his black eyes never leaving Billy's white, gaunt face.

Billy turned the knife in the wound, watching as its puffy lips parted and it regained its former circularity. Now the blood came faster. He felt no pain.

'*Enkelt!* Enough.'

Lemke plucked the knife from his hand. Billy suddenly felt as if he had no strength at all. He collapsed back against the park bench, feeling wretchedly nauseated, wretchedly *empty* – the way a woman who has just given birth must feel, he imagined. Then he looked down at his hand and saw that the bleeding had already stopped.

No – that's impossible.

He looked at the pie in Lemke's lap and saw something else that was impossible – only this time the impossibility happened before his eyes. The old man's thumbs relaxed, the slit closed again . . . and then there was simply *no* slit. The crust was unbroken except for two small steam vents in the exact center. Where the slit had been was something like a zigzag wrinkle in the crust.

He looked back at his hand and saw no blood, no scab, no open flesh. The wound there had now healed completely, leaving only a short white scar – it also zigzagged, crossing life- and heartlines like a lightning bolt.

'This is yours, white man from town,' Lemke said, and he put the pie in Billy's lap. His first, almost ungovernable impulse was to dump it off, to get rid of it the way he would have gotten rid of a large spider someone had dropped in his lap. The pie was loathsomely warm, and it seemed to pulse inside its cheap aluminum plate like something alive.

Lemke stood up and looked down at him. 'You feel better?' he asked.

Billy realized that aside from the way he felt about the thing he was holding in his lap, he did. The weakness had passed. His heart was beating normally.

'A little,' he said cautiously.

Lemke nodded. 'You take weight now. But in a week, maybe two, you start to fall back. Only this time you fall back and there won't be no stopping it. Unless you find someone to eat that.'

'Yes.'

Lemke's eyes didn't waver. 'You sure?'

'Yes, yes!' Billy cried.

'I feel a little sorry for you,' Lemke said. 'Not much, but a little. Once you might have been *pokol* – strong. Now your shoulders are broken. Nothing is your fault . . . there are reasons . . . you have friends.' He smiled mirthlessly. 'Why not eat your own pie, white man from town? You die, but you die strong.'

'Get out of here,' Billy said. 'I don't have the slightest idea what you're talking about. Our business is done, that's all I know.'

'Yes. Our business is done.' His glance shifted briefly to the pie, then back to Billy's face. 'Be careful who eats the meal that was meant for you,' he said, and walked away. Halfway down one of the jogging paths, he turned back. It was the last time Billy ever saw his incredibly ancient, incredibly weary face. 'No poosh, white man from town,' Taduz Lemke said. 'Not *never*.' He turned and walked away.

Billy sat on the park bench and watched him until he was gone.

When Lemke had disappeared into the evening, Billy got up and started back the way he had come. He had walked twenty paces before he realized he had forgotten something. He went back to the bench, his face dazed and serious, eyes opaque, and got his pie. It was still warm and it still pulsed, but these things sickened him less now. He supposed a man could get used to anything, given sufficient incentive.

He started back toward Union Street.

Halfway up the hill to the place where Ginelli had let him off, he saw the blue Nova parked at the curb. And by then he knew the curse really was gone.

He was still terribly weak, and every now and then his heart skittered in his chest (like a man who has stepped in something greasy, he thought), but it was gone, just the same – and now that it was, he knew exactly what Lemke had meant when he said a curse was a living thing, something like a blind, irrational child that had been inside him, feeding him. *Purpurfargade ansiktet.* Gone now.

But he could feel the pie he carried throbbing very slowly in his hands, and when he looked down at it he could see the crust pulsing rhythmically. And the cheap aluminum pie plate held its dim heat. *It's sleeping*, he thought, and shuddered. He felt like a man carrying a sleeping devil.

The Nova stood at the curb on its jacked back wheels, its nose pointing down. The parking lights were on.

'It's over,' Billy said, opening the passenger door and getting in. 'It's ov . . .'

That was when he saw Ginelli wasn't in the car. At least, not very much of him. Because of the deepening shadows he didn't see that he had come within an inch of sitting on Ginelli's severed hand until a moment later. It was a disembodied fist trailing red gobbets of flesh onto the Nova's faded seat cover from the ragged wrist, a disembodied fist filled with ball bearings.

'Where are you?' Heidi's voice was angry, scared, tired. Billy was not particularly surprised to find he felt nothing at all for that voice anymore – not even curiosity.

'It doesn't matter,' he said. 'I'm coming home.'

'He sees the light! Thank God! He finally sees the light! Will you be flying into La Guardia or Kennedy? I'll pick you up.'

'I'll be driving,' Billy said. He paused. 'I want you to call Mike Houston, Heidi, and tell him you've changed your mind about the *res gestae*.'

'The what? Billy, what . . . ?' But he could tell by the sudden change in her tone that she knew exactly what he was talking about – it was the scared tone of a kid who has been caught filching candy, and he suddenly lost all patience with her.

'The involuntary committal order,' he said. 'In the trade it's sometimes known as the Loonybin Writ. I've taken care of the business I had and I'll be happy to check in wherever you two want me to – the Glassman Clinic, the New Jersey Goat Gland Center, the Midwestern College of Acupuncture. But if I get grabbed by the cops when I get to Connecticut and end up in the Norwalk state asylum, you're going to be a very sorry woman, Heidi.'

She was crying. 'We only did what we thought was best for you, Billy. Someday you'll see that.'

Inside his head Lemke spoke up. *Nothing is your fault . . .*

there are reasons . . . you have friends. He shook it off, but before he did, goose flesh had crawled up his arms and the sides of his neck to his face.

'Just . . .' He paused, hearing Ginelli in his head this time. *Just take it off. Take it off. William Halleck says take it off.*

The hand. The hand on the seat. Wide gold ring on the second finger, red stone – maybe ruby. Fine black hair growing between the second and third knuckles. Ginelli's hand.

Billy swallowed. There was an audible click in his throat.

'Just have that paper declared null and void,' he said.

'All right,' she said quickly, and then returned obsessively to the justification: 'We only . . . I only did what I thought . . . Billy, you were getting so *thin* – talking so crazy . . .'

'*Okay.*'

'You sound as if you hate me,' she said, and began crying again.

'Don't be silly,' he said – which was not precisely a denial. His voice was quieter now. 'Where's Linda? Is she there?'

'No, she's gone back to Rhoda's for a few days. She's . . . well, she's very upset by all of this.'

I bet, he thought. She had been at Rhoda's before, then had come home. He knew, because he had spoken to her on the phone. Now she was gone again, and something in Heidi's phrasing made him think that this time it had been Lin's idea to go. *Did she find out that you and good old Mike Houston were in the process of getting her father declared insane, Heidi? Is that what happened?* But it didn't really matter. Linda was gone, that was the important thing.

His eyes strayed to the pie, which he had placed on top of the TV in his Northeast Harbor motel room. The crust still pulsed slowly up and down, like a loathsome heart. It was important that his daughter got nowhere near that thing. It was dangerous.

'It would be best for her to stay there until we have our problems sorted out,' he said.

On the other end of the line, Heidi burst into loud sobs. Billy asked her what was wrong.

'*You're* wrong – you sound so cold.'

'I'll warm up,' he said. 'Don't worry.'

There was a moment when he could hear her swallowing back the sobs and trying to get herself under control. He waited for this to happen with neither patience nor impatience; he really felt nothing at all. The blast of horror which had swept through him when he realized the thing on the seat was Ginelli's hand – that was really the last strong emotion he had felt tonight. Except for the queer laughing fit that had come on him a bit later, of course.

'What kind of shape are you in?' she asked finally.

'There's been some improvement. I'm up to a hundred and twenty-two.'

She drew in her breath. 'That's six pounds less than you weighed when you left!'

'It's also six pounds more than when I weighed myself yesterday morning,' he said mildly.

'Billy . . . I want you to know that we can work all of this out. Really, we can. The most important thing is to get you well, and then we'll talk. If we have to talk with someone else . . . someone like a marriage counselor . . . well, I'm game if you are. It's just that we . . . we . . .'

Oh, Christ, she's going to start bawling again, he thought, and was shocked and amused – both in a very dim sort of way – at his own callousness. And then she said something that struck him as peculiarly touching, and for just a moment he regained a sense of the old Heidi . . . and with it, the old Billy Halleck.

'I'll give up smoking, if you want,' she said.

Billy looked at the pie on the TV. Its crust pulsed slowly.

Up and down, up and down. He thought about how dark it had been when the old Gypsy man slit it open. About the half-disclosed lumps that might have been all the physical woes of mankind or just strawberries. He thought about his blood, pouring out of the wound in his hand and into the pie. He thought about Ginelli. The moment of warmth passed.

'You better not,' he said. 'When you quit smoking, you get fat.'

Later, he lay on top of the made bed with his hands crossed behind his neck, looking up into the darkness. It was a quarter to one in the morning, but he had never felt less like sleeping. It was only now, in the dark, that some disjointed memory of the time between finding Ginelli's hand on the seat of the Nova and finding himself in this room and on the phone to his wife began to come back to him.

There was a sound in the darkened room.

No.

But there was. A sound like breathing.

No, it's your imagination:

But it wasn't imagination; that was Heidi's scripture, not William Halleck's. He knew better than to believe some things were just his imagination. If he hadn't before he did now. The crust moved, like a rind of white skin over living flesh; and even now, six hours after Lemke had given it to him, he knew that if he touched the aluminum plate, he would find it was warm.

'*Purpurfargade ansiktet,*' he murmured in the dark, and the sound was like an incantation.

When he saw the hand, he only saw it. When he realized half a second later what he was looking at, he screamed and lurched away from it. The movement caused the hand to rock first one way and then the other – it looked as if Billy had asked how it was and it was replying with a *comme ci, comme ça* gesture. Two of the ball bearings slipped out of it and rolled down to the crack between the bench and the back of the seat.

Billy screamed again, palms shoved against the shelf of jaw under his chin, fingernails pressed into his lower lip, eyes huge and wet. His heart set up a large weak clamor in his chest, and he realized that the pie was tipping to the right. It was within an ace of falling to the Nova's floorboards and shattering.

He grabbed it and righted it. The arrhythmia in his chest eased; he could breathe again. And that coldness Heidi would later hear in his voice began to steal over him. Ginelli was probably dead – no, on second thought, strike the probably. What had he said? *If she ever sees me again before I see her, William, I ain't never going to have to change my shirt again.*

Say it aloud, then.

No, he didn't want to do that. He didn't want to do that, and he didn't want to look at the hand. So he did both.

'Ginelli's dead,' he said. He paused, and then, because that seemed to make it a little better: 'Ginelli's dead and there's nothing I can do about it. Except get the fuck out of here before a cop . . .'

He looked at the steering wheel and saw that the key was in the ignition. The hick's keyring, which displayed a picture of Olivia Newton John in a sweatband, dangled from a piece of rawhide. He supposed the girl, Gina, might well have returned the key to the ignition when she delivered the hand – she had taken care of Ginelli, but would not presume to break whatever promises her great-grandfather might have made to Ginelli's friend, the fabled white man from town. The key was for him. It suddenly occurred to him that Ginelli had taken a car key from one dead man's pocket; now the girl had almost surely done the same thing. But the thought brought no chill.

His mind was very cold now. He welcomed the coldness.

He got out of the Nova, set the pie carefully on the floor, crossed to the driver's side, and got in. When he sat down, Ginelli's hand made that grisly seesawing gesture again. Billy opened the glove compartment and found a very old map of Maine inside. He unfolded it and put it over the hand. Then he started the Nova and drove down Union Street.

He had been driving almost five minutes when he realized he was going the wrong way – west instead of east. But by then he could see McDonald's golden arches up ahead in the deepening twilight. His stomach grumbled. Billy turned in and stopped at the drive-through intercom.

'Welcome to McDonald's,' the voice inside the speaker said. 'May I take your order?'

'Yes, please – I'd like three Big Macs, two large orders of french fries, and a coffee milkshake.'

Just like the old days, he thought, and smiled. *Gobble it all in the car, get rid of the trash, and don't tell Heidi when you get home.*

'Would you like any dessert with that?'

'Sure. A cherry pie.' He looked at the spread-out map beside him. He was pretty sure the small bulge just west of Augusta was Ginelli's ring. A wave of faintness washed through him. 'And a box of McDonaldland cookies for my friend,' he said, and laughed.

The voice read his order back to him and then finished. 'Your order comes to six-ninety, sir. Please drive through.'

'You bet,' Billy said. 'That's what it's all about, isn't it? Just driving through and trying to pick up your order.' He laughed again. He felt simultaneously very fine and like vomiting.

The girl handed him two warm white bags through the pickup window. Billy paid her, received his change, and drove on. He paused at the end of the building and picked up the old road map with the hand inside it. He folded the sides of the map under, reached out the open window, and deposited it in a trash barrel. On top of the barrel, a plastic Ronald McDonald danced with a plastic Grimace. Written on the swinging door of the trash barrel were the words PUT LITTER IN ITS PLACE.

'*That's* what it's all about, too,' Billy said. He was rubbing his hand on his leg and laughing. 'Just trying to put litter in its place . . . and keep it there.'

This time he turned east on Union Street, heading in the direction of Bar Harbor. He went on laughing. For a while he thought he would never be able to stop – that he would just go on laughing until the day he died.

Because someone might have noticed him giving the Nova what a lawyer colleague of Billy's had once called 'a finger-print massage' if he had done it in a relatively public place – the courtyard of the Bar Harbor Motor Inn, for instance – Billy pulled into a deserted roadside rest area about forty miles east of Bangor to do the job. He did not intend to be connected with this car in any way if he could help it. He go out, took off his sport coat, folded the buttons in, and then carefully wiped down every surface he could remember touching and every one he might have touched.

The No Vacancy light was on in front of the motor inn's office and there was only one empty parking space that Billy could see. It was in front of a dark unit, and he had little doubt that he was looking at Ginelli's John Tree room.

He slid the Nova into place, took out his handkerchief, and wiped the door and wiped off the inside handle. He got the pie. He opened the door and wiped off the inside handle. He put his handkerchief back in his pocket, got out of the car, and pushed the door with his butt to close it. Then he looked around. A tired-looking mother was squabbling with a child who looked even more tired than she; two old men stood outside the office, talking. He saw no one else, sensed no one looking at him. He heard TV's inside motel rooms and, from town, barroom rock 'n' roll cranking up as Bar Harbor's summer denizens prepared to party hearty.

Billy crossed the forecourt, walked downtown, and followed his ears to the sound of the loudest rock band. The bar was called the Salty Dog, and as Billy had hoped, there were cabs – three of them, waiting for the lame, the halt, and the drunk – parked outside. Billy spoke to one of the drivers, and for fifteen dollars the cabbie was delighted to run Billy over to Northeast Harbor.

'I see you got y'lunch,' the cabbie said as Billy got in.

'Or somebody's,' Billy replied, and laughed. 'Because *that*'s really what it's all about, isn't it? Just trying to make sure somebody gets their lunch.'

The cabbie looked dubiously at him in the rearview mirror for a moment, then shrugged. 'Whatever you say, my friend – you're paying the tab.'

A half-hour after that he had been on the phone to Heidi.

Now he lay here and listened to something breathe in the dark – something that looked like a pie but which was really a child he and that old man had created together.

Gina, he thought, almost randomly. *Where is she? 'Don't hurt her' – that's what I told Ginelli. But I think if I could lay my hands on her, I'd hurt her myself . . . hurt her plenty, for what she did to Richard. Her hand? I'd leave that old man her head . . . I'd stuff her mouth full of ball bearings and leave him the head.*

And that's why it's a good thing I don't know where to lay my hands on her, because no one knows exactly how things like this get started; they argue about that and they finally lose the truth altogether if it's inconvenient, but everybody knows how they keep on keeping on: they take one, we take one, then they take two, and we take three . . . they shoot up an airport so we blow a school . . . and blood runs in the gutters. Because that's what it's really all about, isn't it? Blood in the gutters. Blood . . .

Billy slept without knowing he slept; his thoughts simply merged into a series of ghastly, twisted dreams. In some of these he killed and in some he was killed, but in all of them something breathed and pulsed, and he could never see that something because it was inside himself.

CHAPTER TWENTY-SIX
127

MYSTERY DEATH MAY HAVE BEEN GANGLAND SLAYING

A man found shot to death last evening in the cellar of a
Union Street apartment building has been identified as a
New York City gangland figure. Richard Ginelli, known
as 'Richie the Hammer' in underworld circles, has been
indicted three times – for extortion, trafficking and sale
of illegal drugs, and murder – by New York State and
federal authorities. A combined state and federal investigation into Ginelli's affairs was dropped in 1981 following
the violent deaths of several prosecution witnesses.

A source close to the Maine state attorney general's
office said last night that the idea of a so-called 'gangland
hit' had come up even before the victim's identity was
learned, because of the peculiar circumstances of the murder. According to the source, one of Ginelli's hands had
been removed and the word 'pig' had been written on
his forehead in blood.

Ginelli was apparently shot with a large-caliber weapon,
but state-police ballistics officials have so far declined to
release their findings, which one state-police official
termed 'also a bit unusual.'

This story was on the front page of the Bangor *Daily News*
Billy Halleck had bought that morning. He now scanned
through it one final time, looked at the photograph of the

apartment building where his friend had been found, then rolled the paper up and pushed it into a trashbin with the state seal of Connecticut on the side and PUT LITTER IN ITS PLACE written on the swinging metal door.

'That *is* what it's all about,' he said.

'What, mister?' It was a little girl of about six with ribbons in her hair and a smear of dried chocolate on her chin. She was walking her dog.

'Nothing,' Billy said, and smiled at her.

'Marcy!' the little girl's mother called anxiously. 'Come over here!'

'Well, 'bye,' Marcy said.

''Bye, hon.' Billy watched her cross back to her mother, the small white poodle dog strutting ahead of her on its leash, toenails clicking. The girl had no more than reached her mother when the scolding began – Billy was sorry for the girl, who had reminded him of Linda when Lin was six or so, but he was also encouraged. It was one thing to have the scales tell him he had put back on eleven pounds; it was another – and better – thing to have someone treat him as a normal person again, even if someone happened to be a six-year-old girl walking the family dog in a turnpike rest area . . . a little girl who probably thought there were *lots* of people in the world who looked like walking gantry towers.

He had spent yesterday in Northeast Harbor, not so much resting as trying to recover a sense of sanity. He would feel it coming . . . and then he would look at the pie sitting atop the TV in its cheap aluminum plate and it would slip.

Near dusk he had put it in the trunk of his car, and that made it a little better.

After dark, when that sense of sanity and his own deep loneliness both seemed strongest, he had found his old battered address book and had called Rhoda Simonson in Westchester County. A moment or two later he had been talking to Linda, who was deliriously glad to hear from him. She had indeed found out about the *res gestae*. The chain of events leading to the discovery, as well as Billy could (or wanted to) follow it was as sordid as it was predictable. Mike Houston had told his wife. His wife had told their oldest daughter, probably while drunk. Linda and the Houston girl had had some sort of kids' falling-out the previous winter, and Samantha Houston had just about broken both legs getting to Linda to tell her that her dear old mom was trying to get her dear old dad committed to a basket-weaving factory.

'What did you say to her?' Billy asked.

'I told her to stick an umbrella up her ass,' Linda said, and Billy laughed until tears squirted out of his eyes . . . but part of him felt sad, too. He had been gone not quite three weeks, and his daughter sounded as if she had aged three years.

Linda had then gone directly home to ask Heidi if what Samantha Houston had said was true.

'What happened?' Billy asked.

'We had a really bad fight and then afterward I said I wanted to go back to Aunt Rhoda's and she said well, maybe that wasn't such a bad idea.'

Billy paused for a moment, and then said, 'I don't know if you need me to tell you this or not, Lin, but I'm not crazy.'

'Oh, Daddy, I know that,' she said, almost scoldingly.

'And I'm getting better. Putting on weight.'

She squealed so loudly he had to pull the telephone away from his ear. '*Are* you? Are you *really*?'

'I am, really.'

'Oh, Daddy, that's *great*! That's . . . Are you telling the truth? Are you *really*?'

'Scouts' honor,' he said, grinning.

'When are you going home?' she asked.

And Billy, who expected to leave Northeast Harbor

tomorrow morning and to walk in his own front door not much later than ten o'clock tomorrow night, answered: 'It'll still be a week or so, hon. I want to put on some more weight first. I still look pretty gross.'

'Oh,' Linda said, sounding deflated. 'Oh, okay.'

'But when I come I'll call you in time for you to get there at least six hours before me,' he said. 'You can make another lasagna, like when we came back from Mohonk, and fatten me up some more.'

'*Bitchin'!*' she said, laughing, and then, immediately: 'Whoops. Sorry, Daddy.'

'Forgiven,' he said. 'In the meantime, you stay right there at Rhoda's, kitten. I don't want any more yelling between you and Mom.'

'I don't want to go back until you're there anyway,' she said, and he heard bedrock in her voice. Had Heidi sensed that adult bedrock in Linda? He suspected she had – it accounted for some of her desperation on the phone last night.

He told Linda he loved her and rang off. Sleep came easier that second night, but the dreams were bad. In one of them he heard Ginelli in the trunk of his car, screaming to be let out. But when he opened the trunk it wasn't Ginelli but a bloody naked boy-child with the ageless eyes of Taduz Lemke and a gold hoop in one earlobe. The boy-child held gore-stained hands out to Billy. It grinned, and its teeth were silver needles.

'*Purpurfargade ansiktet,*' it said in a whining, inhuman voice, and Billy had awakened, trembling, in the cold gray Atlantic-seacoast dawn.

He checked out twenty minutes later and had headed south again. He stopped at a quarter of eight for a huge country breakfast and then could eat almost none of it when he opened the newspaper he had bought in the dispenser out front.

Didn't interfere with my lunch, though, he thought now as he walked back to the rental car. *Because putting on weight again is* also *what it's really all about.*

The pie sat on the seat beside him, pulsing, warm. He spared it a glance and then keyed the engine and backed out of the slanted parking slot. He realized that he would be home in less than an hour, and felt a strange, unpleasant emotion. He had gone twenty miles before he realized what it was: excitement.

CHAPTER TWENTY-SEVEN
Gypsy Pie

He parked the rental car in the driveway behind his own Buick, grabbed the Kluge bag which had been his only luggage, and started across the lawn. The white house with its bright green shutters, always a symbol of comfort and goodness and security to him, now looked strange – so strange it was really almost alien.

The white man from town lived there, he thought, *but I'm not sure he's come home, after all – this fellow crossing the lawn feels more like a Gypsy. A very thin Gypsy.*

The front door, flanked by two graceful flambeaux, opened, and Heidi came out on the front stoop. She was wearing a red skirt and a sleeveless white blouse Billy couldn't remember ever having seen before. She had also gotten her hair cut very short, and for one shocked moment he thought she wasn't Heidi at all but a stranger who looked a little like her.

She looked at him, face too white, eyes too dark, lips trembling. 'Billy?'

'I am,' he said, and stopped where he was.

They stood and looked at each other, Heidi with a species of wretched hope in her face, Billy with what felt like nothing at all in his – yet there must have been, because after a moment she burst out, 'For Christ's sake, Billy, don't look at me that way! I can't bear it!'

He felt a smile surface on his face – inside it felt like something dead floating to the top of a still lake, but it must have looked all right because Heidi answered it with a tentative, trembling smile of her own. Tears began to spill down her cheeks.

Oh, but you always did cry easy, Heidi, he thought.

She started down the steps. Billy dropped the Kluge bag and walked toward her, feeling the dead smile on his face.

'What's to eat?' he asked. 'I'm starved.'

She made him a giant meal — steak, salad, a baked potato almost as big as a torpedo, fresh green beans, blueberries in cream for dessert. Billy ate all of it. Although she never came right out and said it, every moment, every gesture, and every look she gave him conveyed the same message: *Give me a second chance, Billy — please give me a second chance.* In a way, he thought this was extremely funny — funny in a way the old Gypsy would have appreciated. She had swung from refusing to accept any culpability to accepting all of it.

And little by little, as midnight approached, he sensed something else in her gestures and movements: relief. She felt that she had been forgiven. That was very fine with Billy, because Heidi thinking she was forgiven was *also* what it was all about.

She sat across from him, watching him eat, occasionally touching his wasted face, and smoking one Vantage 100 after another as he talked. He told her about how he had chased the Gypsies up the coast; about getting the photographs from Kirk Penschley; and finally catching up to the Gypsies in Bar Harbor.

At that point the truth and Billy Halleck parted company.

The dramatic confrontation he had both hoped for and dreaded hadn't gone at all as he had expected, he told Heidi. To begin with, the old man had laughed at him. They had all laughed. 'If I could have cursed you, you would be under the earth now,' the old Gypsy told him. 'You think we are magic – all you white men from town think we are magic. If we were magic, would we be driving around in old cars and vans with mufflers held up with baling wire? If we were magic, would we be sleeping in fields? This is no magic show, white man from town – this is nothing but a traveling carny. We do business with rubes who have money burning holes in their pockets, and then we move on. Now, get out of here before I put some of these young men on you. *They* know a curse – it's called the Curse of the Brass Knuckles.'

'Is that what he really called you? White man from town?'

He smiled at her. 'Yes. That's really what he called me.'

He told Heidi that he had gone back to his motel room and simply stayed there for the next two days, too deeply depressed to do more than pick at his food. On the third day – three days ago – he got onto the bathroom scales and saw that he had gained three pounds in spite of how little he had eaten.

'But when I thought it over, I saw that that was no stranger than eating everything on the table and finding out I'd *lost* three pounds,' he said. 'And having *that* idea was what finally got me out of the mental rut I'd been in. I spent another day in that motel room doing some of the hardest thinking of my life. I started to realize they could have been right at the Glassman Clinic after all. Even Michael Houston could have been at least partly right, as much as I dislike the little prick.'

'Billy . . .' She touched his arm.

'Never mind,' he said. 'I'm not going to sock him when I see him.' *Might offer him a piece of pie, though,* Billy thought, and laughed.

'Share the joke?' She gave him a puzzled little smile.

'It's nothing,' he said. 'Anyway, the problem was that Houston, those guys at the Glassman Clinic – even you,

Heidi – were trying to ram it down my throat. Trying to force-feed me the truth. I just had to think it all out for myself. Simple guilt reaction, plus – I suppose – a combination of paranoid delusions and willful self-deception. But in the end, Heidi, I was partly right, too. Maybe for all the wrong reasons, but I *was* partly right – I said I had to see him again, and that was what turned the trick. Just not in the way I expected. He was smaller than I remembered, he was wearing a cheap Timex watch, and he had a Brooklyn accent. He said "coise" for "curse." It was that more than anything that broke through the delusion, I think – it was like hearing Tony Curtis say "Yonduh is da palace of my faddah" in that movie about the Arabian Empire. So I picked up the telephone and –'

In the parlor, the clock on the mantel began bonging musically.

'It's midnight,' he said. 'Let's go to bed. I'll help you stack the dishes in the sink.'

'No, I can do it,' she said, and then slipped her arms around him. 'I'm *glad* you came home, Billy. Go on upstairs. You must be exhausted.'

'I'm okay,' he said. 'I'll just . . .'

He suddenly snapped his fingers with the air of a man who has just remembered something.

'Almost forgot,' he said. 'I left something in the car.'

'What is it? Can it wait until the morning?'

'Yes, but I ought to bring it in.' He smiled at her. 'It's for you.'

He went out, his heart thudding heavily in his chest. He dropped the car keys on the driveway, then thumped his head on the side of the car in his haste to pick them up. His hands were trembling so badly that he could not at first stick the key into the trunk slot.

What if it's still pulsing up and down like that? his mind yammered. *Christ almighty, she'll run screaming when she sees it!*

He opened the trunk and when he saw nothing inside but the jack and the spare, he almost screamed himself. Then he remembered – it was on the passenger side of the front seat. He slammed the trunk down and went around in a hurry. The pie was there, and the crust was perfectly still – as he had known, really, that it would be.

His hands abruptly stopped trembling.

Heidi was standing on the porch again, watching him. He crossed back to her and put the pie into her hands. He was still smiling. *I'm delivering the goods,* he thought. And delivering the goods was yet another of the many things it was all about. His smile widened.

'*Voilà,*' he said.

'Wow!' She bent down close to the pie and sniffed. 'Strawberry pie . . . my favorite!'

'I know,' Billy said, smiling.

'And still warm! Thank you!'

'I pulled off the turnpike in Stratford to get gas and the Ladies' Aid or something was having a bake sale on the lawn of the church that was right there,' he said. 'And I thought . . . you know . . . if you came to the door with a rolling pin or something, I'd have a peace offering.'

'Oh, *Billy* . . .' She was starting to cry again. She gave him an impulsive one-armed hug, holding the pie balanced on the tented fingers of her other hand the way a waiter balances a tray. As she kissed him the pie tilted. Billy felt his heart tilt in his chest and fall crazily out of rhythm.

'Careful!' he gasped, and grabbed the pie just as it started to slide.

'God, I'm so clumsy,' she said, laughing and wiping her eyes with the corner of the apron she had put on. 'You bring me my favorite kind of pie and I almost drop it all over your sh-sh . . .' She broke down completely, leaning against his chest, sobbing. He stroked her new short hair with one hand, holding the pie on the palm of the other, prudently away from her body should she make any sudden moves.

'Billy, I'm so glad you're home,' she wept. 'And you promise you don't hate me for what I did? You promise?'

'I promise,' he said gently, stroking her hair. *She's right*, he thought. *It's still warm*. 'Let's go inside, huh?'

In the kitchen she put the pie on the counter and went back to the sink.

'Aren't you going to have a piece?' Billy asked.

'Maybe when I finish these,' she said. 'You have one if you like.'

'After the dinner I put away?' he asked, and laughed.

'You're going to need all the calories you can pack in for a while.'

'This is just a case of no room in the inn,' he said. 'Do you want me to dry those for you?'

'I want you to go up and get into bed,' she told him. 'I'll be right behind you.'

'All right.'

He went up without looking back, knowing she would be more likely to cut herself a slice of the pie if he wasn't there. But she probably wouldn't, not tonight. Tonight she would want to go to bed with him – might even want to make love with him. But he thought he knew how to discourage that. He would just go to bed naked. When she saw him . . .

And as far as the pie went . . .

' "Fiddle-de-dee," said Scarlett, "I'll eat my pie tomorrow. Tomorrow is another day." ' He laughed at the sound of his own dismal voice. He was in the bathroom by then, standing on the scales. He looked up into the mirror and in it he saw Ginelli's eyes.

The scales said he was now all the way up to 131 again, but he felt no happiness. He felt nothing at all – except tired. He was incredibly tired. He went down the hallway that now seemed so queer and unfamiliar and into the bedroom. He tripped over something in the dark and almost fell. She had changed some of the furniture around. Cut her hair, got a new blouse, rearranged the positions of the chair and the smaller of the two bedroom bureaus – but that was only the beginning of the strangeness that was now here. It had grown somehow while he was away, as if Heidi had been cursed after all, but in a much more subtle way. Was that really such a foolish idea? Billy didn't think so. Linda had sensed the strangeness and had fled from it.

Slowly he began to undress.

He lay in bed waiting for her to come up, and instead he heard noises which, although faint, were familiar enough to tell him a story. Squeak of an upper cupboard door – the one on the left, the one where they kept the dessert plates – opening. Rattle of a drawer; subtle clink of kitchen implements as she selected a knife.

Billy stared into the darkness, heart thumping.

Sound of her footsteps crossing the kitchen again – she was going to the counter where she had set the pie down. He heard the board in the middle of the kitchen floor creak when she passed over it, as it had been doing for years.

What will it do to her? Made me thin. Turned Cary into something like an animal that after it was dead you'd make a pair of shoes out of it. Turned Hopley in to a human pizza. What will it do to her?

The board in the middle of the floor creaked again as she

went back across the kitchen – he could see her, the plate held in her right hand, her cigarettes and matches in her left. He could see the wedge of pie. The strawberries, the pool of dark red juice.

He listened for the faint squeak of the hinges on the dining-room door, but it didn't come. That did not really surprise him. She was standing by the counter, looking out into the side yard and eating her pie in quick, economical Heidi-bites. An old habit. He could almost hear the fork scraping the plate.

He realized he was floating away.

Going to sleep? No – impossible. Impossible for anyone to fall asleep during the commission of murder.

But he was. He was listening for the floorboard in the middle of the kitchen floor again – he would hear it when she crossed to the sink. Running water as she rinsed her plate. The sound of her circling through all the rooms, setting thermostats and turning off lights and checking the burglar-alarm lights beside the doors – all the rituals of white folks from town.

He was lying in bed listening for the floorboard, and then he was sitting at his desk in his study in the town of Big Jubilee, Arizona, where he had been practicing law for the last six years. It was as simple as that. He was living there with his daughter, and practicing enough of the sort of law he called 'corporation shit' to keep food on the table; the rest of it was Legal Aid Society stuff. They lived simple lives. The old days – two-car garage, a groundsman three days a week, property taxes of twenty-five thousand dollars a year – were long gone. He didn't miss them, and he didn't believe Lin did either. He practiced what law he did practice in town, or sometimes in Yuma or Phoenix, but that was seldom enough and they lived far enough out of Jube to get a sense of the land around them. Linda would be going to college next year, and then he might move back in – but not, he had told her, unless the emptiness started getting to him, and he didn't think it would.

They had made a good life for themselves, and that was fine, that was just as fine as paint, because making a good life for you and yours was what it was all about.

There was a knock on his study door. He pushed back from his desk and turned around and Linda was standing there and Linda's nose was gone. No; not gone. It was in her right hand instead of on her face. Blood poured from the dark hole over her mouth.

'I don't understand, Daddy,' she said in a nasal, foghorning voice. *'It just fell off.'*

He awoke with a start, beating in the air with his arms, trying to beat this vision away. Beside him, Heidi grunted in her sleep, turned over on her left side, and pulled the covers up over her head.

Little by little reality flowed back into him. He was back in Fairview. Bright early-morning sunshine fell through the windows. He looked across the room and saw by the digital clock on the dresser that it was 6:25. There were six red roses in a vase beside the clock.

He got out of bed, crossed the room, pulled his robe off its hook, and went down to the bathroom. He turned on the shower and hung his robe up on the back of the door, noticing that Heidi had gotten a new robe as well as a new blouse and haircut – a pretty blue one.

He stepped on the scales. He had gained another pound. He got into the shower and washed off with a thoroughness that was almost compulsive, soaping every part of his body, rinsing, and then soaping again. *I'm going to watch my weight,* he promised himself. *After she's gone I'm really going to watch my weight. I'm never going to get fat the way I was again.*

He toweled himself off. He put on his robe and found himself standing by the closed door and looking fixedly at Heidi's new blue robe. He reached out one hand and caught a fold of nylon between his fingers. He rubbed its slickness. The robe looked new, but it also looked familiar.

She's just gone out and bought a robe that looks like one she owned sometime in the past, he thought. *Human creativity only goes so far, chumly — in the end, we all start to repeat ourselves. In the end, we're all obsessives.*

Houston spoke up in his mind: *It's the people who aren't scared who die young.*

Heidi: *For Christ's sake, Billy, don't look at me that way! I can't bear it!*

Leda: *He looks like an alligator now . . . like something that crawled out of a swamp and put on human clothes.*

Hopley: *You hang around thinking maybe this once, maybe just this once, there's going to be a little justice . . . an instant of justice to make up for a lifetime of crap.*

Billy fingered the blue nylon and a terrible idea began to slide up into his mind. He remembered his dream. Linda at his study door. The bleeding hole in her face. This robe . . . it didn't look familiar because Heidi had once owned one that looked like it. It looked familiar because Linda owned one that looked like it *right now.*

He turned around and opened a drawer to the right of the sink. Here was a brush with LINDA written along the red plastic handle.

Black hairs clung to the bristles.

Like a man in a dream he walked down the hall to her room.

Drift trade is always willing to arrange these things, my friend . . . that's one of the things drift trade is for.

An asshole, William, is a guy who doesn't believe what he's seeing.

Billy Halleck pushed open the door at the end of the hallway and saw his daughter, Linda, asleep in her bed, one arm across her face. Her old teddy bear, Amos, was in the crook of her other arm.

No. Oh, no. No, no.

He hung on to the sides of the door, swaying dreamily back and forth. Whatever else he was, he was no asshole, because he saw everything: her gray suede bomber jacket hung over the back of her chair, the one Samsonite suitcase, open, spilling out a collection of jeans and shorts and blouses and underthings. He saw the Greyhound tag on the handle. And he saw more. He saw the roses beside the clock in his and Heidi's bedroom. The roses hadn't been there when he went to bed last night. No . . . Linda had brought the roses. As a peace offering. She had come home early to make up with her mother before Billy came home.

The old Gypsy with the rotting nose: *No blame, you say. You tell yourself and tell yourself and tell yourself. But there is no poosh, white man from town. Everybody pays, even for things they didn't do. No poosh.*

He turned then and ran for the stairs. Terror had made him double-jointed and he shambled like a sailor at sea.

No, not Linda! his mind screamed. *Not Linda! God, please, not Linda!*

Everybody pays, white man from town – even for things they didn't do. Because that's what it's really all about.

What remained of the pie stood on the counter, neatly covered with Saran Wrap. Fully a quarter of it was gone. He looked at the kitchen table and saw Linda's purse there – a line of rockstar buttons had been pinned to the strap: Bruce Springsteen, John Cougar Mellancamp, Pat Benatar, Lionel Ritchie, Sting, Michael Jackson.

He went to the sink.

Two plates.

Two forks.

They sat here and ate pie and made up, he thought. *When? Right after I went to sleep? Must have been.*

He heard the old Gypsy laughing and his knees buckled. He had to clutch at the counter to keep from actually falling over.

When he had some strength, he turned and crossed the kitchen, hearing the board in the middle squeak under his feet as he crossed over it.

The pie was pulsing again – up and down, up and down. Its obscene, persistent warmth had fogged the Saran Wrap. He could hear a faint squelching sound.

He opened the overhead cupboard and got himself a dessert plate, opened the drawer beneath, and got out a knife and fork.

'Why not?' he whispered, and pulled the wrapping off the pie. Now it was still again. Now it was just a strawberry pie that looked extremely tempting in spite of the earliness of the hour.

And as Heidi herself had said, he still needed all the calories he could get.

'Eat hearty,' Billy Halleck whispered in the sunny silence of the kitchen, and cut himself a piece of Gypsy pie.

STEPHEN KING

WRITING AS
RICHARD BACHMAN

BLAZE

With a foreword by Stephen King

'Tightly written and compelling' – *Daily Express*

He's got a plan. But he hasn't got a clue . . .

Clayton Blaisdell's capers are strictly small time until he meets George Rackley. With Blaze's brawn and George's brains, they pull off a hundred successful cons. Then George plans the one big score every small timer dreams of: kidnapping the infant heir to a family fortune.

The trouble is that by the time the deal goes down, the brains of the operation has died. Or has he?

Now Blaze is running into the white hell of the Maine woods with a baby as hostage. The crime of the century just turned into a race against time . . .

'King's brilliance is in making his readers root for the kidnapper'
– *Daily Telegraph*

'An essential missing piece in King's oeuvre . . . compelling'
– *Independent on Sunday*

HODDER

STEPHEN KING

WRITING AS
RICHARD BACHMAN

THE REGULATORS

Wentworth, Ohio: a small friendly town where the Carver children bicker over sweets in the E-Z shop and writer Johnny Marinville is the only resident who minds his own business.

On Poplar Street, apart from the impending storm, it's just a normal summer's day – with Frisbees flying, lawn mowers humming and barbeques grilling. As the paperboy makes his round, he is unaware of the chrome red van idling up the hill.

Soon the residents will be caught up in a game of wills as the regulators arrive in force to face a child whose powers of expression are just awakening . . .

'Popular fiction's most prolific terror-monger' – *The Times*

'Slides slickly down an eager gullet' – *Daily Telegraph*

H

HODDER

STEPHEN KING

WRITING AS
RICHARD BACHMAN

THE BACHMAN BOOKS

For years, readers wrote asking if Richard Bachman was really world-bestselling author Stephen King writing under another name. Now the secret is out – and so, brought together in one volume, are these three spellbinding stories of future shock and suspense.

The Long Walk: A chilling look at the ultra-conservative America of the future where a gruelling 450-mile marathon is the ultimate sports competition.

Roadwork: An immovable man refuses to surrender to the irresistible forces of progress.

The Running Man: TV's future-favourite game show, where contestants are hunted to death in the attempt to win a $1 billion jackpot.

HODDER

**Don't miss the following titles from
Stephen King's 'dark half', Richard Bachman**

**To find out more about Stephen King's books,
including audio and electronic editions,
as well as news, Reading Group Notes,
competitions, videos and lots more please visit
www.hodder.co.uk and www.stephenking.co.uk**